Puzzled to Death

ALSO BY PARNELL HALL

A Clue for the Puzzle Lady
Last Puzzle and Testament

BANTAM BOOKS

New York   Toronto

London   Sydney

Auckland

PUZZLED TO DEATH

Parnell Hall

PUZZLED TO DEATH

A Bantam Book / November 2001

A FOOL SUCH AS I
Words and Music by Bill Trader
© Copyright 1968 Universal—MCA Music Publishing, a division of Universal
Studios, Inc. (ASCAP)
International Copyright Secured All Rights Reserved
I'M SORRY
Words and Music by Ronnie Self, Dub Allbritten
© Copyright 1968 Universal—Champion Music Corporation (BMI)
International Copyright Secured All Rights Reserved

SORRY (I RAN ALL THE WAY HOME), by Aristedes Giosasi and Artie Zwirn
© 1959 (Renewed) EMI Longitude Music
All Rights Reserved Used by Permission
WARNER BROS. PUBLICATIONS U.S. INC., Miami, FL. 33014

BOOK DESIGN BY GLEN M. EDELSTEIN.
Doodle design by Elizabeth DiPalma.
Puzzles edited by Ellen Ripstein.

Library of Congress Cataloging-in-Publication Data
Hall, Parnell.
Puzzled to death / Parnell Hall.
p. cm.
ISBN 0-553-80102-3
1. Crossword puzzle makers—Fiction. 2. Women detectives—Fiction.
3. Aged women—Fiction. I. Title.

PS3558.A37327 P8 2001
813'.54—dc21   2001025751

Published simultaneously in the United States and Canada

Bantam Books are published by Bantam Books, a division of Random House, Inc. Its
trademark, consisting of the words "Bantam Books" and the portrayal of a rooster, is
Registered in U.S. Patent and Trademark Office and in other countries. Marca
Registrada. Bantam Books, 1540 Broadway, New York, New York 10036.

PRINTED IN THE UNITED STATES OF AMERICA

BVG   10 9 8 7 6 5 4 3 2 1

For Kate,
who helped me
ditch the body

PUZZLE CLUE?

The Puzzle Lady will encounter the following cryptic clue in the course of this story. If you could help her decipher it, she'd be eternally grateful.

CORA FELTON PULLED THE HEAVY KNIT SWEATER AROUND HER shoulders, crinkled her nose, squinted her eyes against the sun, and declared: "I. Hate. Fall."

Her niece, Sherry Carter, smiled indulgently. "You don't hate fall, Cora. You're just not used to it."

"I'll say." Cora Felton kicked her foot absently at the dead oak and maple leaves that adorned the front lawn. "We don't have seasons in the city. It's warmer or colder, and that's it. Unless you go to the park, and why would I do that? There are no stores in the park."

"That's very true," Sherry agreed. She hiked up the sleeves on her green fleece pullover, stuck her hands in the pockets of her jeans, and tilted her chin up. "Just *breathe* that morning air."

"I can breathe it inside," Cora muttered. "That's why we have windows. What are we doing out here?"

In point of fact, Sherry Carter had lured Cora Felton out to the lawn of their tidy little Connecticut house in the hope that the brisk November air would take the edge off Cora's hangover. Sherry's aunt had been cranky at breakfast and seemed on the verge of mixing her second Bloody Mary, always a bad sign. Sherry loved her aunt dearly and looked out for Cora's welfare, usually against Cora's will.

Sherry smiled. "Cora, we're out here for just the reason you said. To notice the seasons. Something we don't do in Manhattan. I mean, isn't this a gorgeous day? And here we are, on a beautiful woodsy lot, on a deserted country road, no neighbors to speak of, the only sign of civilization the power line up the driveway. What's not to like?"

Cora Felton smiled, her patented trademark smile that lit up the picture that adorned the nationally syndicated crossword-puzzle column that ran under her name. "Sherry, sweetheart, it's nice. It's just not New York. I mean, take food, for instance. In my apartment, I open the kitchen drawer, I got twenty or thirty menus from the best restaurants in town that can be there at the drop of a hat. Can you name me one restaurant in Bakerhaven that delivers?"

"You could take a cooking class," Sherry suggested.

"I'd rather get married again."

"Aunt Cora."

"At my age, a husband wouldn't be nearly as annoying as some teacher telling me what to do." Cora yawned and stretched. "Well, that's enough of nature. Time for a drink."

"Little early in the day to be drinking," Sherry ventured.

"It's fall," Cora replied. "There's a time change. We set our clocks back. I'm still on daylight savings time."

"It's ten in the morning."

"What's your point?"

"You remember why we came out here?" Sherry asked. "We were going to walk around the house. So far we've managed to get down the front steps. Not good enough, Aunt Cora. We're going to stroll the perimeter of the property." Sherry took Cora's arm, led her away as she talked. "At least the tree line. I like the sound of that, don't you? The tree line. Doesn't it sound like we have a couple of hundred acres, instead of only one?"

"You're awfully talkative this morning," Cora grumbled. "Without really mentioning anything. And you're in a awfully good mood. Was Aaron here last night?"

Sherry flushed slightly. Lately she'd been seeing quite a lot of the young *Bakerhaven Gazette* reporter. "Aaron stopped by after work. Why do you ask?"

"I have no sex life of my own at the moment, I have to live vicariously. I didn't see his car when I got home. I guess he didn't stay over."

"Aunt Cora."

"And you couldn't go home with him, since he lives with his parents. It must be tough being young." Cora stopped, looked around. "Okay, this is the backyard. I remember it from last summer. There's the picnic table, there's the grill. As I recall, on various occasions you made hamburgers, steak, and a couple of kinds of fish. How'm I doin' so far? And look at these leaves." Cora kicked her feet. "They're so deep back here you can hardly walk. Tell you what, if there's a rake down in the cellar, maybe I'll clean 'em up."

"There's no cellar. It's a prefab house built on a slab."

"There's no cellar?"

"You don't know we don't have a cellar?"

Cora smiled and patted Sherry on the cheek. Her cornflower blue eyes twinkled. "Then I guess I can't rake the leaves. Well, it's the thought that counts."

Cora took two steps, struck a pose, jerked her thumb. "Come on, pardner. Let's check out the north forty."

Sherry Carter smiled to herself. Her plan was working. Once around the house and her aunt was in a much better mood.

Cora rounded the corner of the house and stopped abruptly, looking toward the road. Sherry hurried to catch up with her.

A blue Nissan was coming up the drive, but with the sun glinting off the windshield, Sherry couldn't see its driver.

"That's not Aaron's car," Cora observed. "Who can that be?"

The Nissan pulled to a stop next to Cora Felton's red Toyota. The door opened, and a nebbishy little man in a herringbone tweed suit climbed out. He ran his hand over his bald head, pushed thick-lensed glasses up his nose, then turned and carefully and deliberately locked his car door in a decidedly fussy manner.

Cora Felton's face fell. "Prim, prissy, picayune, precise," she muttered. "It's what's-his-name. The walking thesaurus."

"Harvey Beerbaum," Sherry murmured.

It was indeed the noted cruciverbalist, whose crossword puzzles often graced the pages of *The New York Times.* He spotted Cora Felton, smiled, and waved.

"Oh, my God, look at his face," Cora muttered under her breath. "He wants to marry me. Sherry, promise you won't let me."

"Aunt Cora—" Sherry hissed.

"Promise me."

"He doesn't want to marry you."

"What, you think I'm too old?"

"Don't be silly."

"Sherry, you let me marry that man, I'll never speak to you again."

"You're not going to marry him."

"What if he asks me?"

"Just say no."

"What are you, Nancy Reagan? I have a problem with marriage proposals. You know how many times I've been married?"

"I lost count after Henry."

"So did I. Back me up, Sherry. Here he comes."

The puzzle-maker came bustling across the lawn on little cat feet, with a neatly tied bow tie around his chubby neck and a beatific smile on his baby face. All he needed was a fat bouquet of flowers or a jeweler's box with an engagement ring to pass as a hopeful suitor. Harvey Beerbaum was empty-handed, and yet he looked so animated that for a split second Sherry began to share her aunt's apprehensions—the man was going to ask for Cora's hand.

Fortunately, on reaching Cora Felton, Harvey Beerbaum did not fall on one knee. Instead, he grabbed both of her hands, clasped them joyously, and declared, "Miss Felton! Miss Felton! Have you heard the news?"

Cora's brain was not working at lightning speed, yet she was clearheaded enough to grasp the concept that a marriage proposal as yet unmade was unlikely to have been reported by the media. "No, I haven't," she replied. She extracted her hands from his, straightened her sweater. "What news?"

Harvey Beerbaum could scarcely contain himself. He grabbed Cora's hands again and positively beamed as he made his announcement.

"We're a team! You and I! We're cohosting a charity crossword-puzzle tournament!"

2

"I won't do it."

"Aunt Cora."

"I *hate* crossword puzzles."

"That's not the point."

"And I can't do them."

"You don't have to do them. You're not a contestant, you're the host."

"How can I be the host when I don't know squat about puzzles?"

"You don't have to. It'll be just like your TV commercials. You just smile in a knowing way and everyone thinks you're smart."

"It's *not* like my TV commercials. My commercials are for breakfast cereal. They're thirty seconds long, and I have a script. I don't have to ad-lib. I don't have to pretend to know anything I don't. You put me in a roomful of cruciverbalists who think I'm a crossword-puzzle whiz, we got major trouble."

"Drink your coffee."

Sherry and Cora were seated at the kitchen table. The large, eat-in country kitchen was the best feature of the modest ranch house. Sherry and Cora hung out in it more than they did in the living room, which was still cluttered with unpacked boxes from when they'd moved in the previous spring.

Cora took a sip of coffee, made a face. "This is bad, Sherry. Is it decaffeinated?"

"Cora, don't start."

"Sherry, I need the caffeine. You talked me out of the Bloody Mary, then you give me *decaffeinated* coffee? Have a heart."

Cora's enormous drawstring purse was on the table in front of her. She pulled it open, rummaged inside, came out with a pack of cigarettes.

"I thought you weren't going to smoke in the house," Sherry said.

"No, you lost that battle." Cora pulled out a yellow plastic lighter, fired up a cigarette, took a greedy drag. "In fact, it was in the prenuptial agreement." Cora ticked them off. "You don't tell me what to drink. You don't tell me I can't smoke. You don't criticize my choice of men." She waggled her finger. "Unless I ask you to. For future reference, if I say, 'Don't let me marry that man,' the correct response is not, 'He isn't going to ask you,' it's, 'Don't worry, I won't let you.' " Cora exhaled noisily. "I don't see why that's such a difficult concept to grasp."

"I stand corrected."

Cora blinked. "You mean I won the argument. Something's wrong here." Her eyes widened. "Of course there is. You got me off the subject. The crossword-puzzle tournament."

"It's not a big problem."

"Not for you. You're a whiz at crosswords."

"Yeah, but no one knows it," Sherry pointed out serenely. "Our problems are really the same. I have to hide my expertise. You have to hide your lack of it."

"What a load of bull," Cora shot back. "You don't have to stand in front of a roomful of people and say, 'Hi, I'm Sherry Carter. I'm a very famous person who knows *nada* about crossword puzzles.

I'm pleased to meet you. Now then, do any of you have any questions about crossword puzzles that I won't know the answers to? I'm eager for an opportunity to demonstrate my abysmal lack of knowledge on the subject.' "

"See, Cora, you have a way with words. You'll do just fine."

"That's sarcasm. I can do sarcasm just fine. But I can't use it as a host."

"Oh, no? If Harvey Beerbaum's cohost, I certainly could."

"And so could I," Cora agreed. "But would you want me to?"

"No, of course not. But you don't have to. It's a charity event. You smile, look pleased, and shake the winner's hand."

"Oh, yeah," Cora snorted. "Easy for you to say. How about working with Harvey Beerbaum? He's a nerd and a nudge and all he wants to do is talk shop. I mean, how long can I keep nodding and smiling before he realizes I haven't the faintest idea what he's gabbling about?"

"You're getting all worked up."

"It's the caffeine in the coffee."

"It's decaffeinated."

"I knew it! Sherry, I *need* the caffeine."

"Clearly you don't."

Cora had a horrible thought. "And what if that's the point? What if he *knows* I can't do crossword puzzles? What if asking me to be his cohost is just a ploy to prove I can't?"

"Boy, are you paranoid," Sherry scoffed. "Which is it? Are you afraid he wants to marry you or afraid he wants to expose you?"

"Sherry, please. Let me turn it down. When did he say it was—first weekend in December? We call up, we say we're sorry, we didn't realize we're going to Spain that weekend, then we book a flight and go."

"Spain?"

"Wherever. You name it. The point is, we're not *here*."

"You can't do that, Cora."

"Why not?"

"It's for charity. And it's your hometown. You do it, it's nothing. You back out, it's news. PUZZLE LADY THUMBS NOSE AT CHARITY, WON'T HOST LOCAL EVENT."

"They wouldn't print that."

"You know they would. PUZZLE LADY WON'T WORK UNLESS PAID. REFUSES TO DONATE SERVICES TO HELP THE HOMELESS."

"*Is* this for the homeless?"

"It's for charity. What charity is not really important. What's important is what's-his-name already said yes. Accepted in your behalf. Now, I agree, he had no right to do that, he's way out of line. But, unfortunately, in this case that doesn't matter. Harvey Beerbaum put you on the hook and there's no tactful way to get you off."

"But I didn't say yes. I told him I'd have to think about it."

"He took that as a yes."

"How do you know?"

"If he hadn't, he wouldn't have left. Right now he's downtown telling everybody you agreed to do it."

"Why didn't you stop him?"

"Because I couldn't. It's a no-win situation, Cora. It's just one of those things. As long as you're the Puzzle Lady, there will be situations we can't control."

Cora took another drag on her cigarette. "Maybe it's time to admit that I'm not the Puzzle Lady."

"I don't think so, Cora."

"Why not? The column's established. People love it. Who cares who writes it?"

"People don't like to be fooled. There'll be a backlash."

"Maybe initially. But once it dies down—"

"Your career will be over. Maybe the column will survive, but the column doesn't pay for this house. Aren't you filming another TV spot?"

"Yeah. Next month."

"As the Puzzle Lady?"

Cora frowned.

"See?" Sherry said. "You admit you're not the Puzzle Lady, and it's bye-bye TV ads. There goes our best source of income, and what would we do then?"

Cora stubbed her cigarette out in the saucer of her coffee cup. "I'd probably have to get married again." She took her glasses off, rubbed her eyes, groaned. "What a nightmare. Okay, so I *don't* admit I'm not the Puzzle Lady. So what *do* I do now?"

Sherry smiled and spread her arms.

"You cohost a crossword-puzzle tournament."

3

FIRST SELECTMAN IRIS COOPER WAS ALL SMILES. "THIS IS WONDER-ful," she gushed. "This will put Bakerhaven right on the map. Not that we're not on the map already, but you know what I mean. If there's two things a town can't have enough of it's publicity and goodwill. Not to mention the opportunity of aiding a worthwhile cause." Iris raised an eyebrow in Harvey Beerbaum's direction. "Just what cause are we aiding?"

"That is yet to be determined," Harvey answered. "But that's the least of our worries. There's always someone willing to take our money." He laughed at his own joke and turned to include Cora Felton, who favored him with a frozen smile.

Cora and Harvey were on display, sitting on folding chairs in the front of the town-hall auditorium, along with the five Bakerhaven selectmen. Iris Cooper had called a special town meeting to deal with Harvey Beerbaum's proposal, and the turnout had been good. Over a hundred people had jammed into the meeting room to find out what was up.

Or to put in their two cents' worth. "That's all well and good," a cranky voice said from the middle of the crowd. The speaker stood up, proved to be a man in a red-and-black plaid hunting jacket, with a blond mustache under a flattened nose that accentuated his quarrelsome quality. "Before I donate my services to anything I want to know exactly where my money is going."

Cora Felton, who recognized the man as a mechanic from the service station on the edge of town, wondered just what services he might be donating to a crossword-puzzle tournament, but she held her tongue.

Iris Cooper, at the lectern, nodded. "That's a good point, Mr. Haskel. One of the first things we want to pin down is what charity we are representing." Iris turned to Cora Felton. "And I think I'll let our celebrity cohost do that. Miss Felton, would you care to choose a charity for this event?"

Cora Felton, stunned at being called on, racked her brain for her last charitable contribution. The fact that her husbands had always taken care of the family finances didn't help. Cora was painfully aware that Sherry was in the crowd and would take her to task for the damage done to the Puzzle Lady image if she came out and admitted she couldn't think of a single charity. "Well, that's a problem," Cora said. "I'm familiar with New York City charities. But something like this should be national. Let me look into it and see which national charity would be best."

"Fine," Iris agreed, nodding again. "We appreciate that."

"I'd appreciate an answer more," Mr. Haskel grumbled. When it was clear none was forthcoming, he sat down.

"Well," Iris Cooper said. "I would imagine most of you have never seen a crossword-puzzle tournament before. I know I never have. So I'd like to turn the floor over to Harvey Beerbaum to tell you what it's all about. Mr. Beerbaum."

Harvey Beerbaum sprang from his chair, pranced to the lectern. "It's extremely exciting," he informed the crowd. "You start off with a roomful of contestants and wind up with only three. Standing onstage in front of everyone. Solving the same identical puzzle. On giant grids for all to see. Positively thrilling."

In the back of the hall, Aaron Grant grinned and leaned closer to Sherry Carter. "Your aunt doesn't look happy. You think she can survive this?"

"Relax," Sherry replied. "She has nothing to fear from a man who would use a redundancy like *same identical*."

"Even so, Beerbaum's formidable. I hear he's contributed to *The London Times*."

"He's British."

"That makes it easier?"

"No, just more likely. Yes, *The London Times* is a tougher puzzle of a different type than the Puzzle Lady's. And, no, I've never created one. But that doesn't mean I couldn't."

"You're rather touchy this evening."

Sherry opened her mouth to retort, then closed it. "You're right, I am. Teaming Cora up with that man is my worst nightmare. It's funny in one respect. But in another, one little slip and that's the ball game."

"Your aunt's pretty quick on her feet."

"Yeah, but she doesn't know the first thing about crossword puzzles."

"So what? With Harvey in charge, she'll be lucky to get a word in edgewise."

Sherry looked toward the lectern, where the little cruciverbalist was carrying on blissfully, totally oblivious to the fact someone in the room might not care.

"In order to draw attention to our tournament," he was saying, "I have invited some of the brightest luminaries in the crossword-puzzle community, and they are here today to lend their support to our little endeavor and to assure us that they intend to compete. Ladies and gentlemen, may I introduce Mr. Paul Thornhill, Ms. Zelda Zisk, and Mr. Craig Carmichael."

Heads swiveled as the three experts stood and waved.

Paul Thornhill was a handsome, personable young man in a stylish sport jacket who seemed perfectly at ease, but Zelda Zisk was an enormous woman in a pink print dress the size of a circus tent who appeared to be sweating profusely, and Craig Carmichael was a pinched little man in a tweed suit and red bow tie, who had a twitchy nose and shifty eyes and who gave the distinct impression he'd much rather have been somewhere else.

Mr. Haskel from the gas station was certainly not sold. He jerked a thumb in their direction and challenged Harvey Beerbaum. "Now, just a minute here. You say you've invited these people? How can you have invited these people when we haven't even set a date for this thing yet? When we haven't sanctioned a tournament yet? Don't you think it premature for you to take it on yourself to invite people? And just what have you invited them to?"

Harvey Beerbaum was clearly not used to having his good works flung back in his face. He tugged at the collar of his crisply starched shirt. "I inquired as to their availability as to a crossword-puzzle tournament I was organizing for the weekend of December fifth. I merely pointed out if such a tournament could be arranged we would be honored by the presence of such celebrities. In organizing an event of this nature it is requisite to make preliminary inquiries into the availability of the contestants in order to assess the feasibility of the venture."

Haskel digested this barrage silently, then countered sullenly, "Oh, yeah? Suppose I don't want these people here? Suppose I'd like to win the thing myself?"

"Oh, do you do crossword puzzles?" Harvey Beerbaum inquired. His tone implied he would be less surprised if Mr. Haskel ran shuttle buses to the moon.

"That's not the point," Haskel snapped. "The point is, if I wanted to do crossword puzzles, I should be allowed. I shouldn't have to compete against professionals. I mean, is this an amateur contest or what?"

Harvey Beerbaum's smile was superior. "The words don't apply. They are basically *all* amateur contests. The prizes aren't large enough or the contests frequent enough for anyone to do it professionally. But if you mean a *novice* contest, no, it is not. It's a *charity* contest, open to everyone, beginners and experts alike. However, your point is well taken. And in addition to the first-, second-, and third-place winners, I see no reason why we shouldn't have a trophy for the highest-ranking *novice* contestant."

"A consolation prize?" Marty Haskel snorted. "Gee, isn't that just great!"

A rather attractive young woman with glossy red hair and honey-colored freckles sprang to her feet. "I'm with Marty on this. I've been listening to what you're saying, Mr. Beerbaum, and I'm not sure I like it." She batted her eyes in Paul Thornhill's direction. "Not that I'm not delighted to see these professionals you've brought in, but are you planning on giving them the prize money?"

Harvey Beerbaum's smile became somewhat forced. "You must remember we're doing this for charity. The monetary awards are negligible."

The feisty young woman with the flame red hair was not so easily dissuaded. "Just how negligible are they?"

Harvey Beerbaum cleared his throat. "Two hundred to the winner, a hundred to the runner-up, and fifty to third. Just enough to defray expenses, really."

"I don't understand. If the prizes are so small, why are these celebrities willing to come?"

Harvey Beerbaum nodded. "That's an extremely good point. I'd been saving this as a surprise, but since you bring it up . . ." Harvey positively beamed. "In order to make our little event more attractive, I have arranged for the Channel 8 news team to film a documentary of the tournament, including of course an in-depth profile and interview with the winner."

If Harvey had hoped to appease the woman, he was sorely disappointed. "Oh, is that so," she said. "Well, isn't that wonderful. You mean the whole purpose of this tournament is to get your celebrities on TV? And we all get to be extras? Unpaid extras? That doesn't sound so good to me. Maybe we should call the whole thing off."

That pronouncement was greeted by a rather loud murmur and much nodding of heads.

Iris Cooper pushed forward, hands raised, to calm the roiling waters. "Now, now, let's not get carried away here. TV coverage is certainly a wonderful thing. But I would like to point out, we are *not* doing this to get on television, we are doing this to aid a charity. Even if we're not sure *which* charity."

Cora Felton, who had been surreptitiously rooting through her bulging drawstring purse, stood up. "With regard to that . . . I have recollected one of my favorite national charities, which I think would be most appropriate. It's always nice to do something for children. Sets the right tone, shows our heart's in the right place. Not to mention helping the kiddies. So I propose that we donate all charitable contributions raised through this tournament to the National Children's Placement Fund, an organization devoted to the welfare of underprivileged children."

Iris Cooper was instantly all smiles. "Well, I think that should settle the matter," she said firmly, elbowing Harvey Beerbaum away from the lectern. "We have a date set, we have a charity selected and celebrities invited. It remains for us to organize committees to get this under way. Now then, I'm going to ask for volunteers."

It was nearly an hour later when Cora Felton managed to sneak offstage and she and Sherry were able to steal away.

"Good Lord," Cora fumed, as she peeled out of the parking lot in the Toyota. "How could they be that stupid?"

"You mean to put Harvey Beerbaum in charge?"

"No, I mean in general. Did you hear them picking committees? Are communities always this selfish and dense?"

"Come on, Cora. Didn't your apartment house ever have a co-op meeting?"

"You think I ever went? When I had a perfectly good husband to go for me?"

"Which husband?"

"What's the difference? If I was married, he went."

"What about when you were divorced?"

"You couldn't expect a woman in marital turmoil to care about an apartment."

"You always managed to hang on to them."

"I had good lawyers. Not that they'd go to co-op meetings for me. Say, who were those dodos Harvey Beerbaum brought in?"

"Crossword-puzzle experts."

"No kidding. I mean, do you know them?"

Sherry frowned. "I've heard of Zelda Zisk. I don't know the men."

"Too bad," Cora said. "That one guy looked dreamy."

"You thinking of getting married again?"

"No, but you might."

"Cora."

"Right, you got Aaron. But, trust me, you can never have too many men."

"Oh, for goodness sakes!"

"Hey, until someone proposes, you're single. It pays to line up prospective suitors."

"What a charming philosophy."

"Anyway, if you haven't heard of the men, then they're not that famous, and I won't lose points for not knowing them. I'll have to know what's-her-name though."

"Zelda Zisk."

Cora grimaced. "What a name. No wonder you remember it." She shook her head. "This whole thing is a nightmare. I'm constantly improvising, and I never know where I stand."

"Where'd you come up with that charity?" Sherry asked. "The National Children's Placement Fund? I never heard of it. You didn't make it up, did you, Cora?"

"It was on a flyer in my purse."

"A flyer?"

"Yeah. From before we moved up here. I know it's been some time, but you don't expect a charity to just go away. If it has, big deal, we'll quietly substitute another."

"Don't tell me you don't even know what the National Children's Placement Fund is?"

"It's a charity for kids. A national one. And it shut the gas-station jerk up. That's good enough for me."

"Aunt Cora, before you endorse something, you ought to know what it is."

"Sherry, I know I got that brochure from an earnest-looking young girl outside D'Agostino's handing out leaflets. Clean, presentable, attractive. An all-American girl."

"Even so . . ."

"Sherry. Sweetheart. Relax. It's a charity for kiddies." Cora shifted gears, whizzed around a turn, smiled sideways at her niece. "What could possibly go wrong?"

4

THE PICKET SIGNS READ, NO MONEY FOR SEX!!!, DON'T ENDORSE PROMISCUITY!, UP WITH ROE V. WADE!, DEFEND OUR RIGHT TO CHOOSE!, DOWN WITH SMUT!, and JUST SAY NO TO PORN!!! The women who carried the signs marched back and forth in front of First Selectman Iris Cooper's office window with grim-faced energy.

Harvey Beerbaum was properly aggrieved. "I assure you, I had nothing to do with this."

"I'm sure you didn't," Iris Cooper answered. "That's not the point."

"It is to me. I have a reputation. I am thinking of posting a disclaimer on my Web site."

"A disclaimer?" Iris Cooper's shrewd eyes narrowed. "You're disclaiming the tournament?"

"No, just the charity. I mean, *really*." Harvey rolled his eyes, looked at Cora Felton. "There are *pickets* out there."

The National Children's Placement Fund had turned out to be an organization devoted to helping single mothers. While the goals of the organization seemed beyond reproach—providing relief for children born without fathers, helping the mothers get back on their feet again, and placing unwanted children in foster care—the aim of the organization was still aiding unwed mothers, and the virtuous citizens of Bakerhaven were up in arms. Enough of them, at least, to cause an embarrassment to First Selectman Iris Cooper, who had to wade through picket lines to get to her office.

The first day there had been only two protesters. The next day there were four. But today the sky had fallen. It had finally dawned on someone that the National Children's Placement Fund, if not out and out encouraging young women to go out and get pregnant, as some of the picket signs proclaimed, did provide funds for pregnant young women to complete their pregnancies and place the children up for adoption. It was therefore seen as a pro-life, antiabortion fund, with all the resultant controversy those powder-keg words engendered.

Today there were nearly twenty pickets.

And so, in one fell swoop, Cora Felton, in her one and only contribution to the Bakerhaven Charity Crossword-Puzzle Tournament, had managed to offend both the right- and left-wing factions in town, pleasing absolutely no one.

"And you want to know the worst part," Iris Cooper said, looking up from the two petitions that lay on her desk calling for the tournament to drop the charity, "the worst part is it's in print." Iris picked up a copy of the brochure that had been mailed out the previous week. "It's in our brochure. It's in our ads. It's in the letters that went out to the contestants. It's in the entrance forms they signed to participate. We're a laughingstock."

"I had no idea," Cora Felton said.

"Of course you didn't," Iris said. "You're from the city, where these things are a matter of course. You give to a charity, it's no big deal. And if it turns out later that charity is running guns from South America, that's hardly your fault."

"Guns?"

"Just an example. But you see what I mean?"

Cora didn't. Cora was beginning to get a headache, just as she had every time in the last few weeks that the Bakerhaven Charity Crossword-Puzzle Tournament was mentioned. Now that it was just days off, Cora treated it like a trip to the dentist. She just wanted to get it over with.

If she had to.

"You wanna cancel?" Cora ventured hopefully.

"Oh, sure," Iris Cooper scoffed. "That's all we need to make ourselves look like total jackasses. We put this thing together, publicize it, screw it up, and quit." She pointed out the window. "Leaving those lamebrains to glory over their victory. You want them giving interviews? I can see tomorrow's headlines: SELECTMEN CAVE IN, CANCEL X-RATED FUND-RAISER." Iris grimaced. "No, we ride it out, proud and strong. We're helping children, that's all we know, and all we wanna know."

"We're funding the mothers," Cora pointed out.

"Who could be immaculately conceived, for all we know." Iris Cooper made a horrible face. "Please, don't anyone blurt *that* out."

"I most certainly won't," Harvey Beerbaum said prissily. "The mothers aren't immaculately conceived, the children are."

The look Iris Cooper gave him could have killed a bull moose, but Harvey Beerbaum took no notice.

"So," Iris said tartly, "how are we doing with registration?"

Harvey Beerbaum snapped open his briefcase, took out a folder, cleared his throat. "So far we have eighty-seven contestants."

Iris Cooper looked stricken. "Eighty-seven? Did I hear you right?"

"So far."

"The tournament's this weekend."

"And we'll be accepting registrations through Friday night."

"Are you expecting a last-minute turnout? We have space for three hundred contestants."

"It's a small, regional convention. This kind of thing is not that well attended."

"You didn't tell me that when you proposed it!"

"The precise attendance is not important. What's important is goodwill."

Iris Cooper raised her eyebrows at the pickets out the window but said nothing.

"Actually," Harvey hastened to assure her, "the protesters will probably get us more press than we would have gotten on our own."

"Not exactly the kind of press we want."

"There's no such thing as bad press. With the right spin, we come off as a civic-minded town, doing good work, despite the impediment of a few misguided kooks."

"Uh-huh," Iris Cooper said.

If Iris believed that, Cora Felton wouldn't have known it. Still, Cora felt grateful to have such strong support for her charity from Harvey Beerbaum. At the same time, she resented Harvey Beerbaum for supporting her position, feeling it shouldn't be *her* position to begin with. After all, the whole tournament was never her idea, and choosing a charity was never her idea, and it was entirely Harvey Beerbaum's fault she'd been roped into the whole mess in the first place.

Cora Felton sighed.

"What about the big names?" Iris Cooper asked Harvey. "How many celebrities have you got lined up?"

"I have Paul Thornhill, Craig Carmichael, and Zelda Zisk."

Iris Cooper frowned. "That's the same list as before. I thought you were working on others."

"I also have Ned Doowacker lined up."

"Who?"

"Another well-known contestant."

"You never mentioned him before."

"No, I just snagged him."

Iris Cooper was losing her patience. "What about the others you were trying to get? The *very* famous ones. Just who were they again?"

"Jon Delfin, Ellen Ripstein, and Trip Payne."

"That's right. What about them?"

"They had conflicts."

"All of them?"

"It was unfortunate."

"Wait a minute," Iris protested. "You said December fifth was an open date. You picked it yourself. To test availability. If no one was available, the date could change."

"Yes, and it certainly would have changed if it had done us any good. The celebrities I lined up *were* available for December fifth."

"Are they as famous as the other ones?"

"They are certainly well-known in the crossword-puzzle community," Harvey replied placidly.

"Are they finalists from the national tournament?"

"I believe Craig has been a finalist."

"Then they're not superstar finalists, like the ones you *couldn't* get. I thought your TV coverage was going to attract the big names."

"Actually," Harvey admitted, "Ellen, Jon, and Trip were interviewed on *Nightline* at the national convention. Which is sort of where I got the idea."

"Oh, is that right?" Iris Cooper said scathingly. "I don't recall you mentioning that before."

Cora Felton put her hand over her mouth to hide her delight. Harvey Beerbaum was clearly getting the worst of it, and Cora was actually beginning to enjoy herself—before Chief Harper broke up the meeting by driving right through the picket line with his siren on to deliver a murder suspect to the county court.

5

"A MURDER?" SHERRY CARTER SHOWED MORE INTEREST IN HOMI-
cide than she normally would. Her aunt had been so depressed
about the tournament debacle she figured it would take a good
murder to cheer her up.

Apparently this wasn't a good one.

Cora Felton made a face. "I suppose you could call it that. It's
really a domestic tiff." Cora jerked the pitcher of tomato juice out
of the refrigerator.

"The crime is so ordinary it's driving you to drink?" Sherry observed.

"That's not far off." Cora gathered her spices, assembled them
on the butcher-block table. "Now where did I leave my glass? Oh,
yes, next to the vodka. And did I put the vodka in?"

"You put it in."

"It pays to be sure," Cora Felton declared, adding another jolt.
She carried the glass of tomato juice and vodka to the butcher
block, began adding spices.

"So who got killed?" Sherry asked.

"Some housewife."

"I see. And that's not glamorous enough for you?"

"Not in this case."

"Why not?"

"Her husband did it."

"And this disappoints you because . . ."

"There's no mystery. There's no suspense. There's no *drama*. The case is solved before it's begun. Just an ordinary husband–wife thing, you know the kind I mean, so routine in New York City it wouldn't even make the headlines. The only reason we're talking about it at all is we've moved to this hick town where it's big news if someone's cow breaks a butter churn."

"This is not a cow town."

"Whatever."

"And the phrase *hick town* is one I would like to see disappear from the Puzzle Lady's vocabulary."

"Of course, of course. I would never say that in public, Sherry. Just with you."

"When you slug away vodka at your current clip, you sometimes forget your good intentions."

Cora scowled. "Sherry. What are the rules?"

Sherry stood firm. "I'm not telling you what to drink. I'm pointing out that if you do, you're less careful about what you say. So it would be good if there were certain phrases you were not in the habit of using, as they might have a tendency to slip out."

"Fine," Cora rejoined. "I'll watch my tongue. This isn't a *hick* town, or a *cow* town. It's a *one-horse* town. I haven't actually seen the horse, but I'll assume they have one. If so, it's probably the one they have that statue of in the middle of the village green—you know, the horse and rider with the plaque so worn you can't tell who they are?"

"You have tomato juice on your lip."

Cora grabbed a paper towel, dabbed her face.

"So, you gonna tell me about the murder?"

"I was trying to when you went off on the prohibition lecture."

"Who got killed?"

"I told you. A housewife. Name of Judy Vale. Apparently she had a *reputation*."

"Oh?"

"Town tart. Always running around on her husband, and him always beating her up. Joey Vale, that's the husband, is a simpleminded lout, works a factory job in Danbury, isn't home enough to keep his wife in line, so when he's gone Judy plays around, and when Joey's back he beats Judy up. This time he went too far."

"He confessed?"

"I imagine. Last I saw he was weeping and moaning and tearing his hair."

"You didn't talk to Harper?"

"I had no chance. He was in with the prisoner getting him arraigned."

"So where'd you get your facts?"

"Aaron Grant. He's covering the story now. I'm hoping he'll call you later on."

"You planning on elbowing me away from the phone?"

"Don't be dumb. I'm sure you'll know what to ask. Like I say, it's no big deal." Cora took a pull on her Bloody Mary. "Not like this puzzle contest you got me roped into."

"*I* got you roped into?"

"If you'd admit writing the column—"

"We've been through all that."

"I remember the conversation. That was *before* I chose a charity. I remember you saying it didn't matter which charity I chose. Well, guess what? It matters a *lot*."

"It never occurred to me you'd pick a charity you didn't know."

"You don't think I should back the charity?"

"No, I think you should. I just think you should have known you did."

"Sherry, that's convoluted even for you."

"You're sitting here grousing that you didn't know what this charity was. Wrong. Your position is you knew perfectly well what the charity was, and what's wrong with that?"

"The Puzzle Lady takes a stand on abortion?"

Sherry frowned. "How is this about abortion?"

"Oh, you didn't hear that wrinkle?"

There came the sound of a car in the driveway.

"Ah," Sherry said. "Maybe that's Aaron." She was eager to rouse her aunt out of the our-life-is-hell-because-of-the-puzzle-contest-so-I'm-drinking-myself-into-oblivion mode.

Sherry went to the living-room window, peered out. A Honda Accord was coming up the drive.

"Yeah, that's him," Sherry said. "Good. We'll get the news."

The Honda pulled to a stop beside Cora's red Toyota and the driver got out.

Sherry's mouth fell open.

It was not Aaron Grant.

It was Aaron's high-school sweetheart, former girlfriend, and current admirer, if Sherry was any judge of character, for even Sherry had to admit her views on Becky Baldwin were somewhat biased. Becky was her rival, her goad, her nemesis. Sherry couldn't believe it. Becky Baldwin coming to see her? But there she was, tripping up the path with her exquisitely shod feet, her blond curls framing her perfectly plucked eyebrows, so perfectly plucked one couldn't tell they were, her trim and youthful figure only slightly encumbered by the stylish cut of the winter business suit that looked tailor-made, but that, Sherry realized with a pang of envy, Wonder Woman had most likely purchased off the rack.

Good Lord. In public Becky Baldwin and Sherry Carter were barely civil. There was no question as to how they felt toward each other. Why on earth would Becky Baldwin be calling on her now?

She wasn't.

When Sherry Carter opened the front door, Becky smiled, a frosty, reserved smile, and said, "Hello. Is your aunt in?"

Sherry Carter blinked. "Yes." After a moment she added, "Won't you come in." Sherry smiled when she said it. Still, there was no masking the impression the words had been painfully extracted from her. Sherry stepped aside, said, "Cora, Becky Baldwin's here to see you."

"Is that so?" Cora said, coming to Sherry's aid. "Well, in that case, let's bring her in the kitchen." Cora escorted Becky through the living room, talking as she went. "It's the only room in the house where you can really sit down. I mean, look at this mess. It's not like we just moved in, but we still haven't unpacked. I guess a part of me can't believe I really left New York. Now, this," Cora said, entering the kitchen, "on the other hand, is a bit of all right. It's the main reason we took the house. Not that I can cook, mind, but Sherry's a regular Julia Child. And it's a great place to hang out. Would you care for a drink? I'm having a Bloody Mary, but we also have coffee."

"Ah, thank you, no. This isn't a social visit. The fact is, I need your help."

"My help?"

"Exactly," Becky said. "I'm the attorney for Joey Vale. He's just been arrested for the murder of his wife."

"You're representing him?" Sherry said skeptically.

"Is that so surprising? I'm basically the only game in town."

"Yes, I know," Sherry said, and cursed the fact. Becky had been visiting her old home town several months earlier when circumstances had conspired to make her stay. She had wound up practicing law in Bakerhaven. "I just mean, what can you do? Isn't it an open-and-shut case?"

"No case is open-and-shut," Becky replied grimly. "Even if my client were guilty and the police had all the evidence in the world against him, there would still be room to maneuver. Not that that's the case. Personally, I believe my client's innocent, and I mean to get him off."

"That's the spirit," Cora applauded. "I don't believe it for a minute, but it's the proper attitude to take."

"Which is where you come in," Becky Baldwin said.

Cora frowned. "What do you mean, me?"

"I need help," Becky said. "There are no private investigators in town. I can't afford to hire someone out of Hartford or Danbury and pay the travel time. It isn't cost-effective. It makes no sense. You, on the other hand, are right here."

Cora's blue eyes had widened. "You wanna hire *me?*"

"I need a private eye. You're the closest thing Bakerhaven's got."

Cora shot a glance at Sherry, didn't like what she saw. "I got bad news, Becky," she said dutifully. "I'm not for hire."

"I never thought you were," Becky Baldwin said. "I just thought it would appeal to you. I mean, here's a man going to be tried for his wife's murder. You know the investigation's going to be inadequate. Not their fault—the police don't have the manpower, they can't do the job. The true facts may never come to light."

"What true facts?" Cora asked. "A guy pops his two-timing slut wife. It's hardly the crime of the century."

"What if he didn't do it?"

"Then I'm sure you'll get him off."

Becky shook her head. "Not as things stand. Which is every lawyer's nightmare. Your best isn't good enough, and an innocent man goes to prison." She shivered, and Sherry wondered how many hours she'd practiced *that* in front of a mirror.

"What's his story?" Cora asked, fascinated. At Sherry's look, she added, "Not that I can do anything. But if it helps to talk it through . . ."

Becky slid gracefully into a chair, said, "I think I will take that coffee."

Cora sat opposite her, leaving Sherry to get the coffee. She hesitated just a moment, then crossed to the automatic-drip coffeemaker, poured a cup, and stuck it in the microwave. She was aware of the fact that Becky was silently watching her and hadn't answered Cora's question. Sherry punched in twenty seconds on medium high. "Cream and sugar?" she asked.

"Black is fine."

"Uh-huh." Sherry jerked her thumb at the microwave. "You got twenty seconds. Will that give you time to think up a story?"

Becky looked pained. "I'm not thinking up a story. I was wait-ing to include you in the conversation."

"Oh, don't wait for me," Sherry said. "An innocent man's life is at stake."

"Oh, I doubt if they'll execute him this afternoon," Becky ob-served blithely.

"Due doubtless to your skillful representation," Sherry coun-tered.

The two women smiled at each other. Their looks could have frozen the coffee.

The microwave bleeped.

Sherry slid the cup out, set it on the table in front of Becky Baldwin. She didn't sit but stood leaning against the counter near the sink, eyes on Becky.

Cora leaned back in her chair and waited, eyes bright.

"So," Becky began. "Joey got home from work last night, ac-cused his wife of playing around. They had an argument, he stormed out, went to drink in a bar. The Rainbow Room, a low-class dump on Jackson Road, five miles out of town. Joey was there till after midnight drinking beer and shooting pool.

"Then he went home to his wife. According to Joey, Judy was asleep when he got home. Lights in the bedroom were out. Joey had no wish to continue the conversation, so he pulled off his clothes, fell into bed.

"This morning the alarm rang at seven A.M. Joey slipped out of bed without waking his wife, pulled on his clothes, and went to work at a tool-and-die plant in Danbury. He was simply aston-ished when the police pulled him off the assembly line to arrest him."

"That's his story?"

"Yes."

"What's theirs?"

"I beg your pardon?"

"What do the cops have on him?"

"Judy was supposed to play tennis this morning with a girlfriend. Cindy Fuller. At a racket club in Clarksonville. Cindy dropped by to pick her up, found her dead."

"Where?"

Becky nodded sagely, as if Cora's question confirmed her own judgment. "There you've put your finger on it. She was on the floor of the kitchen. And the lock on the kitchen door was broken."

Cora Felton's bright eyes narrowed. "Is that right?"

"Yes, it is."

"Then how come they busted the husband?"

"That's the problem," Becky Baldwin said. "Chief Harper is not communicative. Apparently, it's not the chief's fault. That prosecutor who looks like a rat—what's his name?"

"Henry Firth."

"That's the one. Don't quote me on the rat line. Firth's running around behind the scenes playing it all very hush-hush."

"Your client make a statement?"

Becky Baldwin made a face. "Before I got to him. Told the police what I told you."

"Now you've made him shut up?"

"Of course."

"And you wonder why the cops won't talk to you?"

Becky shook her head. "The defendant's not supposed to incriminate himself. That's the law. The police are supposed to clear crimes up and not play games."

"It must be extremely frustrating," Cora murmured.

"So can you help me?"

Cora sighed. "I told you I couldn't. Even if I had the time, which I don't. I couldn't afford to work for you. I have a public image that sells breakfast cereal. The headline KILLER HIRES PUZZLE LADY would be regarded as a bad career move."

"Joey's not a killer."

"So you say. That's not the point. Basically, you want to hire me to pump Chief Harper, and I don't like the work."

Becky's eyes narrowed. "Chief Harper's consulted you?"

"No, of course not." Cora frowned. "Why should he?"

"No reason." Becky swirled the coffee in her cup. Sherry noticed that she hadn't touched it. "You know, the doctor's not talking either."

"Who?"

"The M.E. The medical examiner. Barney Nathan. Won't give me the time of day. What do you make of that?"

"I wouldn't make too much of it. Barney's a cranky sort, that's his normal demeanor. Look, if no one's talking, how do you know about the woman who found the body?"

"That young cop—Dan Finley—spilled it before Harper slammed the lid." Becky Baldwin got to her feet. "Look, if you can't help me, I gotta move on. This is not going to be easy."

"No, I don't imagine it is."

Cora Felton ushered Becky Baldwin out. Cora and Sherry stood at the window, watching Becky drive off. The minute the Honda was out of sight, Cora said, "Okay, let's go!"

"Go?" Sherry echoed, bewildered. "Go where?"

"Are you kidding! It's a murder!"

Sherry looked at her aunt in exasperation. "You just got through telling Becky Baldwin you couldn't investigate it."

"I can't investigate it for *her,*" Cora Felton said. "But you think I don't wanna know?"

"I thought this was an open-and-shut case."

"So did I. But if Becky wants to hire me, something's up!"

"Aunt Cora—"

"Figure it out, goosey! Why would that woman want to hire me if Joey did it? What could I possibly find?"

"But—"

"Phooey!" Cora Felton exclaimed, flinging the front door open. "You don't wanna come, fine! I'm outta here!"

Cora bounded down the front steps, jumped into the car, gunned the motor, and took off.

Sherry watched her go with mixed emotions.

Her aunt was about to stick her nose in where she had no business.

But her Bloody Mary was untouched on the kitchen table.

6

JOEY AND JUDY VALE LIVED ON THE WRONG SIDE OF TOWN, IF A
town such as Bakerhaven could be said to have a wrong side. To
Cora's surprise, it did. Cora gunned the Toyota rashly over the railroad crossing—the wooden bed of the trestle had worn low—and
turned onto a street of decidedly less-desirable housing. The lots to
the right were all close together and bordered on the train tracks.
The lots to the left were similarly squished and abutted a power
line.

Cora drove by slowly, looking for 23 Barlow Street. According
to the guy at the general store, Barlow should have been the next
street on the left.

It was. Barlow was a short street, curving down to a dead end at
the fence around the power-line towers. Twenty-three was an ex-
aggeration—there were only four houses on the road, with street
numbers ranging from seven to forty-six.

Cora had no problem finding the Vale house. There was a crime-
scene ribbon across the front door, and two women in housecoats

were on the front lawn, jabbering at each other in an animated fashion.

Cora snorted in disgust. How stereotypical. The men go off to work, and the women stay home. The fact Cora hadn't worked a day in her life never crossed her mind.

Cora got out of the car in full Miss Marple mode and made her way across the street. "Well, ladies," she said, "what seems to be the trouble?"

The women stopped gabbling, looked at her. The larger of the two, a horsey-faced woman in fat curlers and a pink scarf, said, "Well, look who it is. Hey, Charlotte, you know who this is?"

Charlotte, a smaller woman with curly blond hair, peered at Cora, then smiled in recognition. "Sure I do. She's the one running the dirty game."

Cora frowned.

"Oh, behave," the woman in curlers said to her pal. "Really. Dirty game." She shook her head, then turned to Cora, slapped on her hundred-watt smile. "It's the Puzzle Lady, just like on TV. You here for the murder?"

"I sure am," Cora answered. "You happen to know anything about it?"

"Anything?" the big woman in curlers said. "We know everything. He killed her, just like that. Oh, I'm Betty Felson, that's Charlotte Drake."

"Pleased to meetcha," Cora said. "Now, what do you mean, he killed her? Who killed her?"

"Her husband, of course," Betty said, and Charlotte nodded agreement. Betty seemed to be the more dominant of the pair. Cora wondered vaguely if that was due to her size.

"Her husband. That would be Joey Vale?"

"That's right."

"What makes you think he killed her?"

Betty snorted. "Well, who else? Damn near killed her many times. Not that she didn't give him cause." Charlotte's chimed-in approval seemed slightly halfhearted to Cora. "Hey, I'm not saying

PUZZLED TO DEATH / 35

playing around justifies murder," Betty added. "If it did, we'd all be dead."

This time, Charlotte's protests were vehement. Betty ignored them. "All I'm saying is, Judy overdid it. Stuck it in his face, you know what I mean. Like she'd have a new boyfriend on the side, and like as not Joey'd find out about it. 'Cause she wasn't careful what she said, you know what I mean? She was indiscreet."

"She'd tell her husband?" Cora asked skeptically.

"No, she wouldn't," Charlotte replied, clearly pleased to have the information. "And she wouldn't tell us either. But I live right next door, and I could hear. When they'd fight, I mean. And he was coming to her with rumors. Something he heard somewhere else."

"In the bar," Betty contributed. "In the Rainbow Room."

"Sometimes the Rainbow Room," Charlotte conceded. "But sometimes somewhere else."

"Well, it wasn't me," Betty protested. "I never told him anything about his wife. Even if I know things, I always keep them to myself."

"What sort of things?" Cora asked sweetly.

Betty made a face. "That was just a for-instance. I don't know anything. I didn't even know they'd had a fight."

"Well, I did," Charlotte said. "I heard Joey storm out of here. Last night, right before supper. At least before *my* supper. *He* didn't get any supper. Pulled into the driveway, slammed the car door. I knew it was going to be bad just from how hard that door slammed. Then he was inside yelling at her. Who's it this time, does she think he's a fool, does she think he doesn't know?"

"Did he?" Cora inquired.

"What?"

"Know," Cora said. "Did Joey know who it was this time?"

"Well, he knew who he thought it was. That Billy Pickens from the paper mill. At least that's what he said."

"And was it true?"

"I wouldn't know," Charlotte said. "I mind my own business."

Cora managed to keep a straight face. "That's too bad, under the circumstances. Is there anyone around here *doesn't* mind their business?"

"Of course," Betty said. She leveled her stubby finger at the house across the street. "Old lady Roth. She's a widow, living on Social Security, sits with her nose glued to the window. Probably watching us now."

"Did the police talk to her?"

"Sure did."

"What'd she say?"

Charlotte snorted derisively. "As if she talks to *us*."

The widow Roth lived in a modest two-story house that had fallen on hard times. Cora could feel eyes on her from the front window as she came up the walk. Cora went up on the porch and rang the doorbell. It didn't work. At least she heard nothing inside—no chime, no buzz, no bell. Cora knocked on the door. After a few moments, she knocked again.

There was no sound of footsteps approaching, but the door was suddenly yanked open, and a hideous troll face peered out of the gloom inside.

"Who are you and what do you want?" snarled the troll.

Cora Felton favored the troll with her best breakfast-cereal-selling smile. "I'm Cora Felton. I'd like to talk to you about the murder across the street. That is, if you're Mrs. Roth."

"That's me. Are you a reporter?"

"Oh, no. I assure you, I'm not from the press."

Cora Felton had the impression Mrs. Roth scowled, but her face had been so forbidding from the start that it was hard to tell.

"That's annoying," Mrs. Roth said. "I've been expecting reporters."

Cora swiftly reversed fields. "I know a reporter, and I'd be glad to send him over. If I could just ask you a few questions first . . ."

"Very well." Mrs. Roth stepped aside and ushered her in to a living room that was neat as a pin and looked as if it hadn't been used since the nineteen fifties. The couch was vinyl. A black-and-white TV was on a metal stand and had rabbit ears on top.

The windows had roller shades, which were down. The shade to the left, Cora noted, was slightly curled and had fingerprint smudges at eye level for anyone sitting down. A straight-backed chair stood between the windows in easy reach.

The living room was dark. The overhead light was out. The only illumination came from a floor lamp in a corner.

Cora sized Mrs. Roth up. The troll wore a simple print dress and a knit shawl and seemed less ogrelike in the shadows of the room.

And she had wanted to talk to a reporter.

Cora pointed to the smudges on the shade. "You watch from the window?"

"Absolutely." Far from being offended, Mrs. Roth seemed proud. "I see everything that goes on."

"You see the police come this morning?"

Mrs. Roth jerked her thumb at the couch. "Sit down. I'll tell you what happened, then you tell the reporter, then he can come."

Cora sat on the couch. Mrs. Roth sat opposite in an easy chair. "So," Mrs. Roth said. "The woman came this morning to pick her up for tennis. How do I know? Because it's the same woman all the time, and Judy always carries a racket when she leaves. So I see the woman's car pull in the drive, routine, no big deal, I don't bother to watch. In fact, I went in the kitchen, made myself a cup of tea. I get back and the car's still there. Which makes no sense. How long does it take to pick someone up? Then I hear the siren, and the police car pulls up. It's the chief himself. He runs inside, is out minutes later with Cindy Fuller. That's the woman came to pick her up. Believe me, he is not happy. Now I know why. Cops don't like it when you run around a crime scene. Cindy Fuller goes in, finds Judy dead on the kitchen floor, and—get this—uses the kitchen phone to call the cops. No wonder the chief's upset."

"And what happened then?" Cora prompted, unnecessarily. Mrs. Roth was clearly primed to spill all she knew.

"Another police car pulls up with the young cop in it. Dan Finley. The chief passes Cindy Fuller off to Finley. Just in time to deal with the EMS guys. They all go in together. The doctor shows up last."

"And the police talked to you?"

"Sure did. The chief, himself, came over to take my statement."

"And what did you tell him?"

"Oh, I knew a thing or two. But I didn't let him off as easy as that. You think he got anything out of me without talking first?"

"You made him tell you what was going on?"

Mrs. Roth's eyes twinkled. "I merely inquired why he needed to know. He soon realized he wasn't going to get any information unless I felt it was relevant."

"What did he tell you?"

"What I already knew. Cindy Fuller'd come to pick up Judy Vale, rung the bell, got no answer, gone inside, found her dead on the kitchen floor."

"How'd Cindy get in?"

"The front door was unlocked."

"Was that usual?"

"I don't know, because Judy always came to the door before."

"Good point," Cora agreed. "So what did you tell the chief?"

"What I saw."

"Which was?"

"Joey and Judy had a fight last night."

"Was *that* usual?"

"Like the sun coming up."

"What did they fight about?"

"Another man."

"Who?"

"Couldn't tell you."

Cora frowned. "How come?"

Mrs. Roth pointed toward the window. "The light over her front door. Most nights it's on. But some nights it's off. Those were the nights. The nights he'd come."

"Her lover?"

"Well, what do you think? The TV repairman? Who comes at night when her husband's gone and the lights are all out?"

"How often did he come?"

"*He?* What makes you think it's one?"

"What makes you think it's more?"

"Even in the dark you can tell the difference. Light step. Heavy tread."

"But never during the day? Why not during the day when her husband works?"

"For all to see?" Mrs. Roth scoffed. "Trip up the path in broad daylight? I think not. And most men work too. Anyway, that's how she does it. At night, when her husband takes off, she turns out the light. And then someone sneaks over."

"From where?"

"No one's stupid enough to drive up the drive. If it's no one from around here, they must leave the car down the road and walk up. Anyway, that's what Joey's bawling her out about last night. Then he takes off in a huff, and, wouldn't you know it, after he's gone her light goes out again."

Cora's eyes widened. "Her lover came by last night!"

"That he did. And isn't that a fine state of affairs, the very same night her husband's bawling her out."

"You told this to the police?"

"Absolutely. The chief was very interested. He was disappointed I couldn't give him a name."

"But you heard the man call on her. Around what time was that?"

"Late. Around ten o'clock."

"What time did the man leave?"

"I don't know. I went to bed."

"You went to bed?"

"Well, why not? It's not like I could see anything. Or hear anything. Their bedroom's in the back. So I don't know, it's just how long he stays, why should I wait up for that?"

"What if her husband came home?"

"But he wouldn't. Joey's off drinking, he stays till the Rainbow Room closes, one o'clock. Which is what she counts on, why it's safe for men to come. As long as they're gone before one. Not that she ever cuts it that close. Gone before midnight, sure enough, every time I've waited up."

"Except last night you didn't."

Mrs. Roth seemed crestfallen. "No, I didn't. The one time it would have done some good. 'Course, I would have had to wait up till after one. When Joey came home. And finally went too far."

"That's your theory?" Cora said, sensing a kindred spirit. "That Joey killed her when he got home?"

The look that Mrs. Roth gave her implied that Cora must not have a brain in her head. "Of course he did. He got home, found the proof she'd been seeing another man. What, I don't know, but he did. Maybe it was footprints from the guy's boots. Or something he dropped—a handkerchief, a card, maybe even a condom wrapper. Whatever, Joey *knows* the guy's been there, and he blows up and strangles Judy."

"At one o'clock in the morning?"

"That's right."

"And then he sits up all night with the corpse and calmly leaves for work in the morning."

"Calmly, no, but leaves for work, yes, he does, 'cause as far as he's concerned he's gotta go on acting like nothing happened."

"You saw him leave for work?"

"Oh, yes, I did."

"And he was excited?"

"Excited doesn't cover it. It's too mild a word."

"Wait a minute," Cora objected. "You're saying when Joey Vale left for work this morning you *knew* something was wrong?"

"That I did."

"Then how come you didn't call the police?"

"I knew something was *wrong*. I didn't know Judy was *dead*."

"Couldn't what was wrong be the fact they fought and never

made up? And he got up and left for work still in a foul mood? And after he did, someone came and strangled his wife?"

"Couldn't have happened." Mrs. Roth was firm.

"Why not?"

"No one came near that house from the time Joey left for work until Cindy Fuller came to pick Judy up to play tennis. I'd have seen anyone."

"Okay," Cora said. "So what about the night before? You say you went to bed. What if the guy who came last night killed Judy *before* he left? Then Joey gets home around one, climbs into bed in the dark, climbs out of bed in the morning, and goes off to work with no idea anything was wrong?"

"He didn't."

"Oh?"

"I told you. I saw Joey leave for work."

"And?"

Mrs. Roth looked smug. "He *knew* something was wrong."

"How do you know?"

Mrs. Roth grimaced. "Here's where the police are giving me a hard time. They claim I should have notified them. Like you were saying before. But is that fair? I think not. After all, it's his house."

"What do you mean, it's his house?"

"Just like I say. Maybe he was acting funny, but he wasn't doing anything illegal. So why should I call the police?"

"About what?" Cora said, baffled. "What did you see Joey Vale do?"

Mrs. Roth pointed toward her window. "The road curves. From that window there you can see the front of their house. You can also see the side. The kitchen side. Where she was found."

"So? What did you see?"

"Joey Vale, breaking the lock on his own kitchen door."

7

"HE DID IT," CORA FELTON SAID BITTERLY, TWISTING THE TOP off the vodka bottle. Cora was making herself a Bloody Mary, and nothing Sherry could say was going to stop her. Cora simply wasn't in the mood. She raised the glass, tilted the bottle, poured in a generous slug.

"What makes you think he did it?" Sherry had been seated at the kitchen table making up clues for the Puzzle Lady column when Cora stomped in.

"I don't think, I know," Cora said. "He lied to the police, and he lied to his lawyer. Claimed he didn't even know she was dead. Well, guess what? He knew perfectly well."

"That's an assumption."

Cora snorted, fetched the tomato juice from the refrigerator. "They got a witness who saw him breaking the lock on the kitchen door. So he could claim later that someone broke in and strangled her."

"I admit that's not good."

"You needn't sound so pleased," Cora groused. "I know you're eager to see Becky Baldwin fail. Well, boy, did you luck out. Her client's a lying, killing creep."

"Is that all you've got?" Sherry asked mildly.

"Isn't that enough?" Cora was so angry she skipped the spices. She stirred the vodka and tomato juice with her finger.

"Maybe not," Sherry said. "Say Joey found Judy's body, panicked, figured he'd be the chief suspect, and tried to make it look like someone else did it."

"I like it," Cora said, taking a huge gulp. "Now you're thinking like me. I don't believe it for a minute, but I like it just fine."

"Aunt Cora, I don't know if it's my place to point this out, but might I remind you that you didn't *take* Becky Baldwin's offer. You're under no obligation to her whatsoever. Her or her client. And if the guy turns out to be guilty, it's no skin off your nose."

"Oh," Cora said. "Is that tough-guy talk? *Skin off your nose?* Next you'll be talking about *grilling suspects* and *casing joints*."

"*Skin off your nose* is a standard figure of speech," Sherry pointed out. "It may be trite, but it's perfectly ordinary and not related to crime."

"It's also wrong," Cora said. "You think it doesn't bother me this guy did it? You think I shouldn't be disappointed that instead of an interesting murder it's *dull*?"

"I'm just surprised to see you give up so easy. So the guy lied to his lawyer. Half the suspects on TV lie to their lawyers."

"That's *fiction*. And not very good fiction at that. They lie to the lawyers to stretch it out for sixty minutes 'cause otherwise there's no plot. And they turn out to be innocent because it's TV. In real life, people lie to their lawyer because they committed the crime."

"Okay," Sherry said. "What if this guy comes home drunk as a skunk, passes out, wakes up the next morning, and finds his wife dead. He doesn't remember killing her, but he was so drunk he doesn't remember *anything*, so he thinks he must have. So he lies to his lawyer."

"And takes a crowbar to the kitchen door?"

"Why not? He's gotta back up his lie."

"That's mighty thin."

"You don't think it's worth investigating?"

"You want me to investigate this murder?"

"Well, what's stopping you?"

The doorbell rang.

Sherry got up, went out through the living room, and opened the door.

Chief Harper stood on the front steps. He didn't look happy, but it occurred to Sherry she couldn't remember the last time he did.

"Your aunt in?" Harper grunted.

"She's in the kitchen. Why?"

"She's doing it again."

Harper pushed by Sherry and headed for the kitchen.

Cora Felton had taken advantage of the interruption to freshen up her Bloody Mary. She was tasting the result when the chief walked in.

"Oh, great," he said. "Drinking a toast to your murder investigation, no doubt."

"Well, whatever's gotten into you?" Cora asked. "Would a cup of coffee make you less grouchy?"

"Skip the coffee. Didn't you just come from Joey Vale's house?"

"No."

"No?"

"There's a crime-scene ribbon up, Chief. I couldn't possibly go in there."

Harper's scowl deepened. "Don't trade words with me. You were out there talking to the neighbors."

"What's wrong with that?"

"That's not your job. That's *my* job. And it's rather irritating when people interfere with my job."

"It was *almost* my job," Cora Felton said.

That derailed Chief Harper's train of thought. "It was what?"

"Becky Baldwin tried to hire me to do her legwork. I turned her down."

Harper's eyes narrowed. "Becky Baldwin tried to hire you?"

"There're no PIs in town. The boys from the city want travel time."

"Is that right?" He considered this. "So what did she tell you about the case?"

"That's funny."

"What?"

"She was asking the same about you."

"It's a laugh riot. So what did she tell you?"

"The same thing her client told you."

"Nothing else?"

"No. What could there be?"

Chief Harper didn't answer, rubbed his chin. "So you turned her down and went out snooping anyway."

"What's wrong with that?"

"You're not denying you were out there talking to the neighbors?"

"Chief, what could it possibly matter? You got the killer in jail, you got an open-and-shut case. What's the big deal?"

Chief Harper slumped into a chair and sighed. "Barney Nathan just completed his autopsy."

"Don't tell me . . ."

"That's right. According to the doc, Judy Vale was killed sometime last night between the hours of nine and eleven. By all accounts Joey Vale didn't leave the Rainbow Room until after one."

"Hot damn! You mean he's innocent?"

"I just got through getting the guy arraigned. Now Becky Baldwin will be hunting up the judge and getting the charges dropped. Henry Firth's madder than a wet hen. I'm sure the prosecutor will have some choice words in the course of the proceeding about the police department. As if it's our fault the guy's got an alibi. The point is, I'm back to square one, and when I start in questioning the neighbors I find out someone's beat me to it."

"Second time around."

"Cora," Sherry cautioned. "I don't think the chief wants to argue."

"Good guess." Chief Harper leveled a finger at Cora Felton.

"You listen to your niece. She's like the voice of reason, you know what I mean? So listen to her and understand. This murder is very bad news. We got the charity event this weekend to get through—which won't be easy with those dingbats protesting. On top of that we got this unsolved murder hanging over our heads. With people coming to town, that's not good. I need to solve this case, and I need to solve it fast. And I don't need someone messing it up."

"I've helped you in the past," Cora pointed out.

"That you have," Chief Harper agreed. "When the crime was crossword puzzle–related. This one isn't. It's a simple, straightforward crime. There's no reason for you to be involved. And there's no way I can justify your involvement. The prosecutor asks, what's that woman doing messing around, I don't have an answer. So I can't have you snooping around Joey Vale's house."

Cora took a sip of Bloody Mary. "Chief. Say no more. I understand perfectly. You made your point. And you have my word. I promise you. I won't go near your crime scene."

8

THE RAINBOW ROOM WAS A LONG, LOW, CINDER-BLOCK BUILDING with neon in the windows and a front-door sign that was higher than the roof. It was dark when Cora got there, and the sign was blinking. The parking lot was half full and seemed to have as many trucks as cars. Cora pulled in between a green pickup truck and a white minivan, locked her car, and went inside.

The Rainbow Room was pretty much what Cora expected: a horseshoe-shaped bar, booths along the walls, a pool table, a juke-box, and a noisy cluster of bowling and basketball machines. The clientele was mostly working-class men.

There was a space at the bar, and Cora squeezed in. The bartender wore his hair short in front and long in back and looked too young to drink. He rubbed his closely trimmed mustache, said, "What'llya have?"

"Gin and tonic," Cora ventured, wondering what she'd get. The glass the bartender grabbed was a bad omen—an eight-ounce tumbler that might have served for a scotch and soda but was a far cry from the tall, cool, frosted glass she was accustomed to. But Cora accepted it without comment, offered a ten-dollar bill. The bartender rang it up, slid her change across the bar. The modest price of the mixed drink underlined what a step down the Rainbow Room was from her usual haunts.

"Thanks," Cora told him. "Could you help me out?"

The bartender frowned. Other customers were waiting for his service. "Whaddya need?"

"Joey Vale."

His eyebrows raised momentarily, then his eyes flicked around the room. "Shooting pool," he grunted in reply, and moved on down the bar.

There were two men at the pool table. A large man in work boots, overalls, and a New York Knicks T-shirt, and a smaller, wiry man in blue jeans, a T-shirt, and a heavy red-and-black checkered shirt. The shirt was untucked and unbuttoned, even the sleeves, and as the man bent over the pool table to line up a ball it hung off him like a sail.

Cora turned to the man on the barstool next to her, a geezer wearing horn-rimmed glasses and nursing a beer. He looked at her and his eyes lit up behind the thick lenses. "You're the breakfast-cereal lady. You solved those murders. Is that why you want Joey?"

"I'd like to talk to him."

"He didn't do it. The cops thought he did, but he didn't. How do you like that?"

"And how do you know that?" Cora countered.

"Joey told us."

"What did he tell you?"

"Just that. The police thought he killed her, now they know he didn't. Something about time of death. Turns out we're all witnesses."

"To the fact he was here last night?"

"That's right."

"And was he?"

"Sure. Joey's here every night."

"Yes, but did you see him here last night?"

"Oh, sure."

"The whole time? Could he have left at some point, gone away, and come back?"

"Joey? Nah. He always sticks around."

"Last night in particular?"

"Every night in particular. He'd lose his place at the table."

"I beg your pardon?"

The geezer pointed. "You see on the side of the pool table there? Where the coin slot is? There's a row of quarters lined up on the edge of the table. Those are the people waiting to play. You sit around, you sip your beer, you watch your quarter move up. When it gets to the head of the line you better have three more quarters ready, 'cause it costs a buck a game."

"And Joey was shooting pool last night?"

"Played him myself." He frowned. "Either last night or the night before."

"Is that right? And which one did you say was Joey?"

"Don't believe I did, but it's the guy in the floppy shirt."

"Uh-huh," Cora said. She watched the man in the dangling shirt line up a shot on one of the striped balls. The shot caromed around the pocket and didn't go in.

"First time here?" the man on the barstool asked.

Cora Felton smiled. "I didn't even know they had a place like this in Bakerhaven."

"That's cause they don't."

"What?"

The man was smug. "This here's Clarksonville. Just over the town line. Bakerhaven zoning don't cut no ice with us."

"Tell me something," Cora said. "Don't you think it's a little strange, Joey here shooting pool and his wife's newly dead?"

He grinned. "Well, you gotta remember. Joey's a celebrity, with his wife getting killed. Earlier, when he's talking about it, just about everyone bought him a beer. 'Course, he had to drink 'em just to be polite. At any rate, he's pretty snockered now. I wouldn't hold play-ing pool against him."

Cora watched Joey line up another shot. After he missed, Joey grabbed his bottle of beer by the neck, took a swig.

"What'll he do when the game's over?" she asked.

"If he wins, he'll play the guy who put up the next quarter."

He didn't win. Joey scratched on the eight ball, threw his cue down in disgust, and headed for the men's room.

Cora was waiting when he came out. She followed him to a booth where four empty beer bottles and three full ones were waiting. Sliding into the seat opposite him, she said, "Hi, Joey."

Joey Vale looked at Cora Felton as if she were a creature from Mars. "Who the hell are you?"

"I'm Cora Felton. I'm here to help you."

"Help me? You're here to help me?"

"If you want to know who killed your wife."

Joey's eyes widened. They were very red, whether from crying or alcohol Cora couldn't tell. "You *know*?" he murmured incredulously.

Cora felt a pang of guilt. "No, I don't. But I intend to find out."

Joey bobbed his head. "Good, good. You find out." His interest wandered to the beer bottles on the table. He stared at them, probably trying to figure out which were full. Cora could practically see his mind working, trying to come up with a means of determining this.

"Who do you think killed her?" Cora asked.

Joey looked at her in alarm. "Didn't do it," he mumbled. "I didn't do it."

"I know you didn't. So who do you think did?"

"Kill him," Joey muttered. "Kill the son of a bitch."

"Who?" Cora prompted. "Who you gonna kill?"

Joey's face crumpled. "Poor Judy. Poor little Judy." This time his hand unerringly snagged a full bottle of beer. He took a huge swallow, held the bottle in both hands.

"You had a fight with Judy," Cora said. "You accused her of seeing someone."

"Billy Pickens."

"Yes. Billy Pickens. Is he here tonight?"

"Better not be."

"Do you think he did it?"

"Did what?"

"Killed your wife?"

Joey's face reddened murderously. "Son of a bitch? That son of a bitch killed my Judy?"

"No, no, Joey. I was asking if *you* thought so."

Joey looked bewildered again. "Why would he do that?" His face twisted. "Poor Judy . . ."

"Yes. Poor Judy."

Cora was not entirely unhappy with the conversation. Incoherent as Joey Vale was, he'd confirmed what his neighbors had said. That he suspected the man seeing his wife was Billy Pickens. And Judy Vale had had a visitor last night, because she'd turned out the front light. In all likelihood that visitor murdered her. Joey Vale might not be able to come up with a reason why Billy Pickens would have strangled his wife, but Cora Felton could come up with several. In Cora's estimation, Billy Pickens was rapidly moving to the top of her suspect list.

Right behind Joey Vale himself.

9

AARON GRANT PARKED HIS CAR IN THE DRIVEWAY, SKIPPED UP THE
front steps, and rang the bell.

Sherry Carter opened the door with a grin.

"You look happy," Aaron observed. "What's up?"

"Cora's snooping," Sherry said, ushering him in.

"Oh?"

"She's out pumping Joey Vale. Not that she thinks there's anything to it, but Chief Harper told her not to, and she took it as a personal challenge."

"You try to talk her out of it?"

"Heavens, no. The crossword-puzzle contest was driving her to
drink. I'm grateful for any distraction. You want some coffee?"

"I'd kill for coffee."

"That won't be necessary." Sherry washed out the automatic-
drip coffeemaker, filled it with water and ground coffee beans, and
switched it on. "Your column done?"

"If it wasn't, I wouldn't be here."

"That's not very flattering."

Aaron shrugged. "If my column wasn't done, you'd accuse me of rushing over here to pump you for information."

"So, what'd you write about?"

"The murder, of course."

"And Joey Vale's release?"

"That's part of it. Not a big part, mind you, but still a part."

"What do you mean, not a big part?"

Aaron Grant sat at the table. "Joey Vale had the misfortune to get released the same day he got picked up. Bad timing. In terms of publicity, I mean. Now, if he had been released tomorrow, that would be big news. 'Cause we'd have already reported his arrest. As it is, the headline is BAKERHAVEN HOUSEWIFE MURDERED. A sidelight is *Husband Detained and Released.*" He grimaced. "Very poor from a news standpoint. I mean, one day later you get the headline HUSBAND CLEARED. *The Bakerhaven police yesterday dropped all charges against Joey Vale, husband of murdered housewife Judith Vale, when an autopsy on the body determined beyond a shadow of a doubt that the victim was killed at a time her husband was not home.* That only plays if we've had a day to report the murder and his arrest."

Sherry watched the coffeemaker burble. "You make it sound personal, Aaron."

He shrugged. "It's not personal, it's just how it is."

"Oh, yeah?" Sherry leaned on the counter, looked at him. "What part of the story did you cover?"

"I covered Joey Vale's arrest."

"And subsequent release?"

"That's right."

"So it's personal. HUSBAND RELEASED was *your* headline."

"I suppose."

"Where'd you get your facts? I don't imagine you talked to Joey Vale."

"He wasn't talking."

"You talk to his attorney?"

"I interviewed her, yes."

"What did she have to say?"

Aaron grinned.

"Why are you smiling?"

He put up his hand. "No, no. Nothing personal, I assure you. It's just when Becky was explaining how her client had been proved innocent and released, I got the impression she was disappointed."

"Disappointed? Disappointed how?"

"That she didn't have a murder suspect to defend anymore."

"You wrote that?"

"I most certainly did not. I'm telling you that in strictest confidence, and I do not want to be quoted as having said it. And that's the extent of my dealings with Becky Baldwin," Aaron said. "Just enough to provide me with a story. Not *the* story. Just *a* story."

"You came over here hoping for something better so you can have *the* story tomorrow?"

"I came over here for coffee," Aaron said patiently. "It's not as close as the diner, but you make better coffee."

"Flattery will get you nowhere," Sherry told him.

Aaron got up from the table. "That's too bad. When did you say your aunt was getting home?"

"I don't know."

Aaron moved closer, put his hands on Sherry's waist. "But she's out investigating a murder. That could take some time."

Sherry reached up, touched his cheek. "I thought you came for coffee."

"Coffee's overrated." Aaron nuzzled her ear.

"I'm not sure you can use a word like *overrated* in terms of coffee—" Sherry began before Aaron cut her off with a kiss.

10

"YOU'RE GLOWING," CORA SAID.

Sherry flushed. "I'm not glowing."

"Trust me, I've seen glowing, and you're glowing."

"You must be drunk."

"Not with the size drinks they serve in the Rainbow Room." Cora pushed by Sherry into the kitchen. "Ah, coffeepot's full. Made a batch and didn't drink it. Wasteful. You know there are poor people going through the whole day with no caffeine at all, and here you are wasting a whole pot." Cora stopped, pinched Sherry's cheek. "But that's all right. You're glowing."

"Aunt Cora, please."

"Hey, nothing wrong with that. I've glowed enough in my day." Cora poured a cup of coffee, added milk, stuck it in the microwave. "So, did he have any news?"

"Who?"

"Aaron. Did he have anything on the murder?"

"Nothing new."

"So he *was* here. Boy, I'm good."

"Aunt Cora." Sherry decided it was time to change the subject. "Did *you* get anything on the murder?"

"I'll say."

The microwave bleeped. Sherry took out the coffee, handed it to Cora. "So what have you got?"

"A suspect."

"Yeah? Who?"

Cora took a sip of coffee. "Joey Vale."

"I thought he had an alibi."

"He does."

"So?"

"So," Cora said, "that's why I suspect him. He doesn't just have an alibi. He has a *perfect* alibi. By all accounts he was in the Rainbow Room during the only possible hours the crime could have been committed."

Sherry looked at her aunt in exasperation, tried to determine despite Cora's assurances just how many drinks she might have had. "Aunt Cora, if he couldn't have done it, he couldn't have done it."

"Yes and no."

"What do you mean by that?"

"I find a perfect alibi extremely suspicious. An innocent man rarely has a perfect alibi. Why? Because he doesn't *need* one. So he doesn't *plan* one. Ergo, he doesn't *have* one. On the other hand, a man who intends to commit a crime goes out of his *way* to provide himself with a perfect alibi."

"Yeah, but if committing the crime was a physical impossibility—"

"Who says so? That numbnuts coroner? How much faith do you put in what he says? He didn't see the body till twelve hours later, but he constructs a two-hour window when the crime must have happened? Give me a break."

"You dispute the autopsy report?"

"Well, I don't think it's gospel."

"No, Cora. But the guy went to med school. His finding is based on something. He didn't make up his autopsy report just to frustrate you."

"Maybe not, but I'd like to know what it's based on. Stomach contents and body temperature, most likely. Well, if he knows exactly when she ate, that's one thing. But I'll bet he doesn't. The husband had a fight with her after work and stormed out. Which left her home alone. She could have eaten at any time, because there's no one to say when she did.

"So that throws out stomach contents as an accurate barometer. Which leaves body temperature. As I recall, under normal circumstances the body cools one and a half degrees Fahrenheit per hour after death. The doc says she was killed between nine and eleven. Those would be the outside limits, so the median time would be ten. The doc saw her around ten o'clock the next morning. The body temperature of the corpse would indicate she was killed approximately twelve hours earlier. Twelve hours at one point five degrees per hour would be eighteen degrees. Normal body temperature is ninety-eight point six. Take away eighteen, the body temperature would have to be eighty point six degrees when the doctor saw her. I wonder if it was."

"Aunt Cora."

"I'd just *love* to get a look at that autopsy report, see what that quack's basing his time of death on. You suppose Aaron could get a look?"

"I doubt it."

"Even if you asked nice? I bet he'd do anything if you asked him nice."

"I think *I* need a coffee," Sherry declared. She prepared another cup, switched on the microwave. "Okay, Cora. You went off on a tangent. You were telling me why the time of death doesn't rule out Joey Vale. I have no doubt you could get the coroner quite rattled with a barrage of questions. But, assuming your math is correct, and assuming he figures like you, and assuming the body temperature was eighty point six and indicated Judy'd been strangled between nine o'clock and eleven—can you advance any theory about how Joey could have done it?"

"Are you kidding? Of course I can." Cora warmed instantly to the subject. "Joey Vale gets home two in the morning, croaks his wife. So he drags her corpse into the kitchen, pulls all the food out of his deep freeze, dumps the body in, and closes the lid. After a couple of hours he pulls the body out, replaces the food, leaves her on the kitchen floor. The body temperature's been altered enough the medic puts the time of death between nine and eleven instead of one and three A.M., like he would have if it hadn't been tampered with."

Sherry pulled the coffee out of the microwave. "Joey Vale has a deep freeze?"

"How should I know?" Cora said airily. "No one's let me see the crime scene. Say he doesn't have a deep freeze. So he takes out all the shelves and stands her upright in the refrigerator. Same result."

"Oh, for goodness sakes!"

"I should see the body. If she was cramped in an unnatural position, I bet I could tell. And I bet that doctor couldn't. Now, there's a thought. Rigor mortis sets in, *and* she's frozen solid. I wonder if you could mistake one for the other."

Sherry sipped her coffee, revised her estimate of how many drinks her aunt had had. "That's very interesting, Cora. Do you have any theories that *don't* involve sticking the corpse in the fridge?"

"Oh, sure. Illusion."

"Illusion?"

"Yeah. Joey Vale creates the illusion he's in the Rainbow Room when really he's not."

Sherry grimaced. "This sounds worse than the deep freeze."

"I don't mean he wasn't there at all. I mean he creates the *illusion* he never left."

"And just how does he do that?"

"This one I kind of like," Cora said. "Joey Vale's in the Rainbow

Room shooting pool. As a lot of the pool players will testify. I watched how it works. It's a coin-operated pool table. The winner wins a dollar and the right to play the next challenger. The guys who want to play—it's mostly guys—put up quarters on the edge of the table to mark their spot. There's usually a row of five or six quarters of people waiting to play."

"What has this got to do with the illusion of Joey Vale being in the Rainbow Room?"

"Joey's playing eight ball. He loses. He pays the winner a dollar. He puts a quarter on the table to hold his place for the next game. He's now the fifth or sixth quarter in line. When his quarter comes up, he plays again. But that's four or five games later. Say the games take ten minutes apiece. What's to stop Joey Vale from losing the game, paying off the winner, putting up his quarter, and heading for the men's room—but instead of going to the john, he slips out the door, drives home, knocks off his wife, drives back, and slips in the bar? In all likelihood, he's standing there watching them shoot pool a good two or three games before his quarter even comes up again. When it does, as far as anyone in the place is concerned, he's been there all the time."

Sherry Carter blinked. "Would that work?"

"I don't know. I would guess it's about a ten-minute drive from the bar to his house. Add in the time to kill his wife, it's cutting it close, but it could be done."

"It's cutting it *very* close," Sherry said, "and in that case how do you account for the visitor that she turned out the light to meet?"

"Her husband gets there first. The light is out, Joey comes up the path, Judy figures he's her visitor and opens the door. Which makes it easier for Joey. He strangles her, thank you very much, leaves the body on the linoleum, and goes back to the bar. Right after that the mystery guest arrives, gets no answer, finds the door locked, and finally gives up. Or finds the door open, walks in, finds Judy dead as a mackerel on the linoleum, panics, and splits. Either way, it works pretty nice for Joey Vale."

"I thought the neighbor saw the mystery guest arrive. So why didn't she see Joey Vale?"

"Oh, but she did. What she saw was Joey Vale *arriving*. She says she went to sleep right after that. Joey Vale arrived and killed his wife. The witness, Mrs. Roth, went to bed and missed seeing Joey Vale leave, and she missed seeing the mystery guest arrive and leave, either in frustration or in a panic, depending on whether the door was locked or open, take your pick."

"I don't like it," Sherry said.

"Why not?"

"It's a horrible timetable. You're assuming this guy's smart enough to kill his wife and give himself an alibi—well, look at the huge risks he takes. He could be seen driving away from the bar. He could be seen driving back. He could be seen driving along the road. And when he gets home and sees the light out—if he's any smart at all— he'll figure it's off because his wife's lover's coming. In fact, that would have to be part of his plan, because if the light was *on*, he should know he would be seen by Mrs. Roth going into his house. So he's gotta *plan* on the light being out. He knows the man's coming, but he can't know when, so here's someone who could catch him in the act of killing his wife. It's just a very bad bet."

"Yeah, but it's *possible*," Cora insisted. "And the police let Joey go on the grounds it wasn't possible."

"Uh-huh," Sherry said, unimpressed. "You got any theories that don't involve such strict timetables?"

"Sure. Joey comes home, has a brouhaha with his wife. Pastes her one, knocks her unconscious. While she's out cold, he trusses her up like a chicken, gags her, stuffs her in a sack, sticks her in the trunk of his car. Drives to the Rainbow Room and shoots pool. Sometime between nine and eleven he slips out to the parking lot, pops the trunk, croaks his wife, goes back inside, and shoots pool for the rest of the night."

"And no one saw him lug her body in and out?"

"Dark when he leaves, dark when he comes back. Works for me."

"I'm not sure it will work for Chief Harper," Sherry observed.

"Never fear. I wouldn't try to sell the chief on anything unless I had more to go on." Cora chugged down the rest of her coffee, put the cup on the table, exhaled happily. "Well, it's certainly been a productive night." She looked at Sherry and repeated smugly, "Glowing."

11

"I DON'T SEE WHY YOU DON'T WANT TO DEMONSTRATE," HARVEY Beerbaum said peevishly. Harvey had come up with the bright idea that during the Friday-night festivities to kick off the tournament, he and Cora would demonstrate the art of crossword-puzzle construction by creating a puzzle on the spot in front of everyone. "It would be such fun. And we'd take turns. You'd add a word, I'd add a word, you'd add a word. Of course we could try to trip each other up."

Cora Felton, who could no more construct a crossword puzzle than she could a suspension bridge, would have loved to trip Harvey Beerbaum up there and then—physically, forcefully, and right on his erudite rump. "Fun for us, maybe, but for the participants? Boring, boring, boring. They don't want a lecture, they want to *play*. I thought Friday night was going to be fun."

"It is, it is," Harvey said. "I merely thought we could take ten minutes out to construct an uncomplicated puzzle."

Cora avoided looking at Sherry Carter, who was among those in attendance at the town hall for the tournament committee meeting, played instead to Iris Cooper. "It's not that I don't want to. It's just that this convention shouldn't be to glorify *us*. Now, the celebrities are another matter. Some of them are constructors, aren't they? How about getting them to donate a puzzle?"

Harvey Beerbaum frowned, but Iris Cooper said, "That's not a bad idea. We introduce it as a fun puzzle from the pros to do as a warm-up."

"Are you sure this tournament is even happening?" a committee member put in dubiously. "I heard a rumor the police were going to close us down. On account of the killing, I mean."

"Well, they're not going to," Iris Cooper declared. "We've already taken in our entrance fees. We've got a nice chunk of money to give to charity." She cleared her throat. "And as far as the charity's concerned, I looked into the Children's Placement Fund. They're a dedicated group of concerned citizens, and they do good work. And we're damn proud to be giving money to them, and that is our official position. I note this morning the pickets are gone. I assume that is a side effect of yesterday's unfortunate tragèdy. Not that I want to profit from that poor woman's death, but I would hope the pickets are still gone tomorrow when everyone arrives. Now, let's see how our committees have worked out."

As Iris Cooper began to deal with the committee members, Cora Felton stole out into the audience and slipped into the chair next to Sherry.

"He's on to me!" Cora hissed it out of the side of her mouth like a gangster.

"What in the world are you talking about?" Sherry said.

"Beerbaum. Weren't you listening? His little demonstration? I told you so. He's trying to show me up."

"No, he's not. Didn't you see how fast he dropped the idea?"

"Only because I suggested the celebrities donate puzzles. Well, that's fine for now. What if I can't come up with a bright idea next time?"

"Cool it. We got company," Sherry warned.

Chief Harper slid into the seat next to Cora.

"What are you doing here?" Cora asked. "Don't tell me you've solved the crime?"

"No, I haven't. And just where were you last night?"

"Oh."

"Yeah. Oh," Chief Harper mimicked. "You can wipe that innocent smirk off your face. Did you think I wouldn't find out? Tell me, did you have a nice time at the Rainbow Room last night?"

"Their drinks are a little skimpy."

"Is that so? By any chance do you recall a conversation we had a little earlier in the day?"

"What conversation might that be?"

"The one where I told you to butt out of my case."

"Oh, I doubt if you phrased it like that, Chief. I've always found you to be a perfect gentleman."

"That assessment may change," Chief Harper said sourly. "Didn't I tell you in no uncertain terms to keep your nose out of the Judy Vale murder?"

"Not that I recall."

"Well, perhaps your niece will bear me out here. She happened to be party to the conversation. Miss Carter, would you care to refresh your aunt's recollection?"

Sherry smiled. "I would if I thought it would do any good. But I'm afraid you're about to take one on the chin, Chief."

Chief Harper frowned. "What's she talking about?" he demanded of Cora.

Cora shrugged. "You bawled me out for going to Joey Vale's house, so I promised to stay away from the crime scene. But that's *all* I promised."

"You knew very well what I meant."

"Intent is tough to prove. Even in a court of law. When it's your *own* intent—or what's worse, when it's someone's *perception* of your intent—"

"Spare me," Chief Harper snapped. "Anyway, I trust you got nowhere. Other than confirming Joey Vale's alibi."

"On the contrary," Cora said cheerfully. "I came up with several ways Joey Vale could have committed the crime."

"Aunt Cora . . ." Sherry warned, but Cora waved her away and proceeded to tell Chief Harper the theories she'd outlined for her niece the night before.

As he listened, Chief Harper's scowl became a glower. "Fantastic. Absolutely fantastic. Did you read that in some mystery book? That's the only place that kind of thing happens, in mystery books. No one runs around killing people like that in real life."

"Why not?"

Chief Harper snorted. "Because nobody *thinks* like that. You'd have to have the most twisted brain imaginable just to come up with such a convoluted scheme. *I think I'll kill my wife, stick her in the freezer, and go shoot pool.* Wonderful. Could we come back to planet earth?"

"How about strangling her in the trunk of the car?"

"How about it?" Chief Harper scoffed. "Do you have any idea who you're dealing with? This is not some suave murderer here. This is Joey Vale, used to popping his wife one when she gets out of line. And don't you dare quote me on that. The point is, is there any way Joey Vale comes up with one of these schemes? No, he kills her and tells some clumsy lie, doesn't stand up ten minutes when we start asking him questions."

"I thought his lawyer wouldn't let him answer any questions."

"Yeah, but we had him a while before he asked for a lawyer. And his story isn't the sophisticated alibi you lay out, it's a moronic fabrication that wouldn't stand up even if he *hadn't* been seen breaking the lock on his kitchen door. Which is bad for him in one way, and good in another. Where it's good is, when it turns out he has an alibi, it's because he *has* an alibi. Not because he contrived to make it *look* like he had an alibi through some cockamamie scheme. You see what I mean?"

"Your logic is a trifle convoluted. Still, I get the fundamental idea."

"Do you? Good. Then you see where I'm at. Joey Vale is innocent. Which means I'm back to square one without a clue who could have killed this woman."

"What did she look like?" Cora asked.

Chief Harper blinked. "What?"

"Well, this picture in the paper . . ." Cora dug into her purse, pulled out a copy of the *Bakerhaven Gazette,* and flipped it open. HOUSEWIFE MURDERED screamed from the front page. The photograph under the headline showed a young woman without a blemish, every hair in place, smiling for the camera. "Look at this picture of Judy Vale. She looks eighteen years old."

"She is," Chief Harper said. "It's a yearbook photo."

"Why?"

"Her husband's not cooperating, and the *Gazette* couldn't get anything else."

"How old was she? When she died, I mean?"

"Twenty-eight."

"You wouldn't know it from this. Maybe I should see the body—"

"No, you *shouldn't* see the body," Chief Harper snarled in exasperation. "I didn't come here to facilitate your investigation. I came here to *stop* your investigation. I got a murder case to solve. I got this stupid tournament starting tomorrow, which I don't like, but I don't wanna call it off and make waves. I just want it run smoothly." He stabbed a finger at Cora. "*That's* your job. Keep everybody distracted, play down the murder, bring this puzzle event off without a hitch."

Cora Felton looked like she'd been told to gargle gasoline. "And what will *you* be doing while I'm doing this?"

"I'll be working on the murder case."

"Got any leads?"

Chief Harper grimaced. "What I've been trying to impress on you is that's not your concern."

"Gotta like the husband. I just showed you why you shouldn't cross him off."

"I just told you why I should."

"He's still your chief suspect," Cora persisted. "Say he's *not* bright enough to manufacture an alibi. Say he just *lucks* into it."

"All your theories involved sticking her into a refrigerator, or tying her up in a car trunk. You mind telling me how he *lucks* into that?"

"He doesn't luck into that. He lucks into doctor what's-his-face blowing the autopsy. Which frankly wouldn't surprise me in the least."

"How could he blow the time of death as much as that?"

"Easy," Cora replied, "if he's basing it on body temperature. Your quack's assuming her body temperature at time of death was ninety-eight point six. Suppose it wasn't. Suppose she was running a fever. Say the body temperature at time of death was a hundred and *one* point six. Three degrees higher. Since the body cools at a rate of a degree and a half per hour, three degrees would throw the time of death off by two hours. So instead of between nine and eleven, the possible time of death would be between seven and nine. *While* her husband was still home. Joey throttles her, then goes off to the bar to shoot pool to give himself an alibi, because he's too stupid to know the doctor will be able to tell when she was actually whacked. He lucks into the fact she had a fever. So, lo and behold, the stupid alibi that shouldn't hold up suddenly turns out to be valid."

Cora smiled. "But, hey, don't let me sell you anything, Chief. You go right ahead and solve your murder. I've got a tournament to run."

12

EARLY FRIDAY MORNING THE TOURNAMENT PLANNING COMMITTEE volunteers, heavily armed with ladders, hammers, nails, thumb-tacks, and masking tape, descended on the Bakerhaven town hall like locusts. They festooned it from top to bottom with red, yellow, and blue balloons, red, white, and blue streamers, and a long blue and white banner proudly proclaiming *The Bakerhaven Charity Crossword-Puzzle Tournament,* in preparation for the contestants' registration, scheduled to begin at noon.

At approximately eleven fifty-five it began to rain, a steady, drenching downpour that released over half the balloons, popped most of the others, and uncurled the streamers before washing them away.

Regrettably, one end of the banner tore loose. More regrettably, the other end held, creating a gigantic, soggy whip that lashed at anyone attempting to get up the town-hall steps.

Luckily, Fun Night didn't start until eight o'clock that evening, so there was a chance the storm would blow over, and under ordi-nary circumstances the contestants would just have holed up in their bed-and-breakfasts, inns, and motels until then. However, the Bakerhaven Charity Crossword-Puzzle Tournament was being run by committee, and the tournament welcoming committee, a splinter group formed by a vicious difference of opinion within the tournament reception committee, had in their infinite wisdom decreed that tournament contestants must register at the town hall on Friday afternoon before five o'clock.

This was utter nonsense, of course. The tournament was for charity, the contestants were paying to enter, the town wanted as many contestants as possible, and no one was going to be turned away, whether they met some arbitrary registration deadline or not. However, as a result of a deluge of officious memos on the part of the welcoming committee, which had gone out with the mailings, the majority of the contestants complied with their wishes and showed up at town hall before five P.M. Most of them, however, did not look happy about it.

None was less pleased than Cora Felton, whom the committee had decreed should be on hand with Harvey Beerbaum to greet each entrant. She and Sherry arrived at noon, a good hour before the first contestants, who began drifting in around one-thirty and continued to trickle in as the wet afternoon wore on. Most of them were people Cora had never seen before—crossword-puzzle enthusiasts who had shown up just for the tournament—but a few were locals, some of whom Cora recognized but could not place. She greeted them all with the trademark Puzzle Lady smile plastered on her face, apologizing for the inclement weather as if it were something over which she had some control, even as she attempted to dodge their dripping raincoats and umbrellas.

Her choice of such a mundane topic of conversation as the weather was not entirely accidental. Alarmed by the influx of so many puzzle experts, Cora was eager to deflect any conversation from her column. To her relief, none of the experts seemed inclined to discuss it. It was midafternoon before Cora learned why.

A man came in with a blue raincoat and blue rain hat. The brim, which turned up, was full of water, although the man did not seem to be aware of it. He made his way to the front of the room, where the Bakerhaven welcoming committee had pushed three tables together to form the registration area. Hanging from the front of the tables were the signs: A–H, I–P, Q–Z. Each table was manned by a beaming, welcoming committeewoman. Happy or not, the women displayed all outward signs of good cheer, as decided in their committee meeting.

The man in the blue raincoat approached the middle table, manned by Mrs. Cushman, the genial proprietor of Cushman's Bake Shop, whose actual baking skills were suspect and whose pastries were rumored to be trucked in daily from New York City. The man leaned forward, sending a shower of water from his hat brim cascading down on the table. Mrs. Cushman yelped and immediately put her hands protectively around the name tags, which were in plastic pin-on holders and which she had painstakingly arranged alphabetically in rows. She was less concerned with the plastic bags containing giveaways—crossword-puzzle magazines, pencils, and flyers consisting largely of local advertising, the inclusion of which had been hotly debated by the committee.

"My, my," Mrs. Cushman said, struggling to keep her smiling face within committee guidelines. "You could use a towel, couldn't you?"

The man frowned. "Why?"

He wasn't joking. His view of the world was clearly rather narrowly defined.

"Because of the rain," Mrs. Cushman said politely. "Are you here to register?"

The man nodded yes, releasing a fresh stream of water, but Mrs. Cushman had already swept most of the name tags to safety. "Fine," she said. "What's your name?"

"Ned Doowacker."

That response pleased Mrs. Cushman immensely. "Then I'm afraid you're in the wrong line. This is the I–P line. You want the A–H line over there."

"That's silly," Ned Doowacker retorted. "It's not like there was anyone in line behind me. Why can't *you* help me?"

"Because I don't have your personal name badge." Mrs. Cushman pointed to Edith Potter, the librarian, who was manning the A–H table. "She does. That's why it's alphabetical."

"Oh." Ned Doowacker wheeled around, sending an icy spray of water in all directions, and stomped to the next table, where Edith had already moved the name tags out of the line of fire and immediately produced his.

"Here you are, Mr. Doowacker," Edith told him. "I've already checked you off the list. Here's your name tag and your complimentary gift bag. Say hello to our cohosts and you're all set."

Ned Doowacker approached Harvey Beerbaum. Fortunately, Ned had already shaken off most of the water, for he bobbed his head up and down animatedly while he proceeded to take Harvey Beerbaum to task, to the best Cora could determine, for a puzzle Harvey had created over three years ago and could hardly remember, though Doowacker remembered it well, feeling that one of the clues was misleading if not out and out improperly worded.

Cora couldn't help smiling, until Mr. Doowacker wheeled on her. She braced herself, but the man just said bluntly, and apparently without the slightest concept of being rude, "I don't do *your* puzzles. They're way too easy."

"How do you like that?" Cora grumbled to Sherry, after Ned Doowacker had banged out the front door—most likely, in Cora's opinion, to reload his hat brim. "The man doesn't *do* my puzzles. My puzzles are too *easy*."

"It is rather amusing," Sherry said.

"Amusing?" Cora grumbled. "It's downright insulting. Am I supposed to smile and be nice while someone tells me that?"

"I don't see why not."

"You don't? Well, guess what: He's the first contestant all day to even *mention* my column. I mean, here I am, standing up there like a boob, introducing myself and shaking their hands, and none of them wants to talk about my column."

"You don't *have* a column."

"That's not the point. They *think* I do."

"Cora, let me be sure I understand this. You're taking umbrage at the fact no one's showing you sufficient respect for a talent you do not in fact possess?"

"When you put it like that it sounds stupid."

"Well, would you like to put it so it sounds smart?"

"Sherry, this is *your* work that's being disparaged. Aren't you hurt?"

"Why should I be? We have a mass-market column with a broad appeal. It's syndicated to 256 newspapers. Unlike *The New York Times* crossword, which starts out easy on Monday and gets harder every day, our column is consistent. The level of difficulty does not change. Basically, anyone entered in this tournament will find our puzzles too easy. Otherwise they wouldn't be *in* the tournament."

Aaron Grant came in the door, snapped his bright red umbrella shut, shook the water off, and hurried over. "Hi, gang. How's it going?"

"Cora's doing great," Sherry replied. "She's charming the experts. But she's offended none of them takes the Puzzle Lady column seriously."

Aaron grinned. "Gee, that's tough, Cora. Why don't you dazzle them with your linguistic dexterity?"

"All right, that's it," Cora snapped. "It's bad enough I gotta put up with Beerbaum. I don't have to stand here and be insulted by you."

"No, you have to stand over there," Sherry said, pointing to the tables at the front of the room. Another entrant was signing in, this one a tall, slender woman with wire-rimmed glasses. "Go welcome her, and try not to be too disappointed when she doesn't read your column."

"If she doesn't, I'll punch her out," Cora declared. "I cannot believe the committee voted this a nonsmoking zone. I'm dying for a cigarette, and they won't let me smoke."

"Friendly *and* nice," Sherry cautioned.

Cora muttered something that could hardly have been construed as either friendly or nice and stomped back toward the front of the room.

"If she gets through this, it'll be a miracle," Sherry told Aaron.

"If the tournament comes off at all, it'll be a miracle," Aaron said. "The murder's still wide open. Chief Harper's got no leads, and I got no story. What's this Fun Night scheduled for tonight?"

"Just what it sounds like. It's not part of the tournament itself. Scores don't mean anything tonight, except to win silly prizes."

"Like what?"

"Puzzle books. T-shirts. A crossword-puzzle murder mystery some guy wrote. Stupid stuff like that."

"Doesn't sound like a story." Aaron sounded dejected.

"Trust me, it isn't. Uh-oh. Look who's here."

"Who?"

"Guy from the service station. What's-his-name. Marty Haskel."

It was indeed the cranky mechanic who had voiced his displeasure at the early planning meeting. He stomped in, flipped the hood off his rain slicker, unzipped it, and shook off the water. He then proceeded to the front of the room, where the only other entrant, the tall, thin woman, also happened to be at the A–H table and was asking Edith Potter, the librarian, several questions. Haskel stood behind her, folding his arms, tapping his foot, and occasionally turning and rolling his eyes for the benefit of anyone who might be watching.

"Would have made a great cabbie," Sherry observed.

"What?" Aaron said.

Sherry jerked her thumb in Mr. Haskel's direction. "In New York City. He's the type of cab driver leans on the horn the second the light turns green."

"Hey, lady, could I get my badge?" Marty Haskel demanded in a voice loud enough to be heard even in the back of town hall.

The tall, thin woman turned to see if he was some expert whose rudeness should be excused because he was higher on the cruciverbal ladder than she. Finding he was not, she impaled him with a look, then turned back to resume her chat with Edith Potter.

Cora Felton, waiting with Harvey Beerbaum to greet the tall, thin woman, watched with amusement. Crossword puzzles didn't interest her, but she would have been perfectly content to see a pair of crossword-puzzle people rip each other apart.

It was not to be.

The back door of the meeting room banged open, and Joey Vale strode in.

He was not wearing a raincoat. His navy blue pea coat was soaked, as were his sneakers and jeans. His wet hair was plastered to his head. Water trickled down his brow.

He took no notice. He stood, swaying, looked around the room. "So," he declared in a loud, slurred voice, which left no doubt as to the state of his inebriation. "So, this is where they're gonna do it. Crosswords. Judy's dead, and you're doing crosswords. Fine. Sign me up. I wanna do crosswords too."

Joey headed for the front of the room, didn't get there, crashed instead into one of the many tables that were set up for the contestants. He stumbled, fell to the floor. Moments later he pulled himself up by the side of the table, like a monster in a horror movie rising up after everyone figured it was dead. He staggered to his feet, stumbled toward the front of the room.

"Do something," Sherry told Aaron.

"I am," Aaron said. He had a cell phone out, was punching in a number. "Chief, it's Aaron. Better get over to town hall."

Joey Vale careened through the tables, crashing into some, missing others, and eventually reached the front of the room.

Mrs. Cushman had moved the name tags as far out of harm's way as possible to one end of the table and pushed the giveaway bags to the other end, leaving only the sign-in sheet exposed and vulnerable.

"What's this?" Joey Vale cried, snatching it from her before she could protest. He wheeled from the table, out of arm's reach, and peered at the list. "What do we have here? Ah, yes. Names. List of names. Is the name of the man who killed Judy on here? That would be worth knowing. But no one cares." His face twisted in an expression of grief. *"No one cares,"* he told the room weepily.

Mrs. Cushman's sign-in sheet consisted of two pages on a clipboard. Joey Vale flipped to the second page. He stared at it, or at least appeared to. Whether he could actually see it or not was impossible to tell. After a few moments he flipped the page back.

"Worthless," he declared loudly. "Absolutely worthless."

He pulled the pages from the clipboard, crumpled them, and threw them on the floor. He turned, hurled the clipboard against the wall.

By that point the committeewomen at the tables were backing away, which was probably wise. With his left arm Joey Vale swept the name badges on the middle table to the floor. With his right arm he swept off the giveaway bags. Then he put both hands under the edge of the table, lifted it up, and flipped it over.

Next he descended on Edith Potter's table. He snatched up her clipboard and went through the same ritual with the sheets of paper, pulling them off, crumpling them up, and hurling the clipboard aside. He emptied the tabletop before flipping the table. This time he managed to achieve a little elevation and wipe out a table in the next row.

Joey Vale was just descending on the third table when Chief Harper showed up to handcuff him and lead him away.

13

ALL OF BAKERHAVEN WENT TO FUN NIGHT. WHETHER IT WAS the novelty of the puzzle contest, or the fact they'd been through a tragedy with the murder of Judy Vale, or merely because the event was free, the turnout for Fun Night was way beyond expectations. Even women who had picketed the tournament showed up. Political idealism had rapidly eroded at the prospect of the heavily publicized complimentary dessert buffet.

"We should have charged," Iris Cooper said glumly, surveying the packed room.

Harvey Beerbaum favored her with a superior smirk. "If we had, they wouldn't have come. This way is clearly best. We get an enormous attendance, a few more get interested and register for the tournament, and we come out on top. Believe me, I know how these things work."

Iris Cooper, who was getting damn sick of Harvey Beerbaum and what he knew, was beginning to appreciate Cora Felton, who offered no opinions at all.

"So, where's the TV people?" Iris demanded irritably. "Why aren't they covering this?"

"I invited them," Harvey said, "but they're not coming."

"Why not?"

"The station decided since Fun Night wasn't part of the official competition, it wasn't worth paying the crew."

Iris rolled her eyes. "Well, isn't that just great. We're not getting any publicity, and we're not making a dime. And everyone in town is here."

"All but one," Cora Felton observed dryly.

Joey Vale, much to the tournament planning committee's relief, was spending the night in jail.

"The celebrities are certainly a draw," Harvey Beerbaum ventured, in an attempt to get back in Iris Cooper's good graces.

This was only moderately true. Zelda Zisk was enormously odd, to the point of putting people off, or at least making them hesitant to approach her. She had a rather attractive face but had gone way overboard with her makeup, perhaps in an attempt to distract attention from her immense girth. Her eyeliner was nearly a quarter inch wide, her bloodred lipstick might have been put on with a trowel, and her false eyelashes looked like she'd stuck caterpillars on her eyelids. Her dark brown hair was piled carelessly on the top of her head with wooden combs. Hoop earrings the size of hubcaps framed mobiles that jingled when she moved. Her smile was inviting, but her appearance was unsettling, at best. She also had an uncommonly loud voice and a laugh that rattled the rafters. As a result, Zelda had a table all to herself, a small island from which she beckoned to those who passed like a siren of the sea. Or a beached whale.

Craig Carmichael, shy to the point of paranoia, was giving a good impression of a dweeby bookkeeper on the lam from the mob. Although not alone at his table, he kept his hands over his face at most times, avoided eye contact, and answered questions out of the side of his mouth in words that were scarcely audible. His manner could not have been more furtive had he been pilfering nuclear secrets.

Even Paul Thornhill was a bit of a bust. The handsome, personable young man, whose stylish good looks were undoubtedly responsible for the attendance of many of the unattached women in town—and probably some of the attached women as well—had disappointed one and all by showing up with his spouse. Mrs. Thornhill was a perfectly nice, polite, attractive, vibrant young woman, who seemed quite attentive to her husband and whom half the town already loathed.

"Yeah, your celebrities are wonderful," Iris Cooper told Harvey tersely. "It's nearly eight. Are you ready to begin?"

Harvey Beerbaum checked his watch. "Three minutes till," he declared in a punctilious tone that made Iris cringe.

Cora covered her mouth and pretended to sneeze to avoid laughing out loud. She moved away from Harvey and Iris and looked out over the crowded room.

Sherry Carter stood in the back by the door, having declined several offers to join teams. Sherry, who could rip through the puzzles like lightning, did not dare to do so tonight. Of course she could have just pretended to do poorly, but that would have been excruciating. No, tonight Sherry was much happier not to play.

Standing next to Sherry was Aaron Grant, who would have played if Sherry had wanted to but otherwise couldn't care. Aaron was there to find a story for his paper and to keep Sherry company.

While Cora watched, Becky Baldwin came in. She looked around the room, then moved over to Sherry and Aaron. It killed Cora not to be able to listen in, but she couldn't leave the stage.

"Well," Becky said, "what's the matter? Aren't you playing?"

"Just watching," Aaron said.

"That's dull. You wanna form a team?"

"The teams are four," Sherry said, and instantly regretted the comment, which pointed up the fact Becky was alone on the one hand and underlined the idea of a romantic triangle on the other. "Anyway, I don't want to play. I'm just here to root for Cora."

"As if she needs it," Becky said primly. "I'm not here to play either. Just checking out the scene for my client."

Sherry frowned. "I beg your pardon?"

"Joey Vale, up in the hoosegow. Having a rough time of it. In a cell, sleeping it off. That's who I'm concerned with at the moment."

"You're sweating a drunk-and-disorderly charge?"

"No." Becky pointed toward the stage. "Thanks to your dear interfering aunt, I'm sweating *murder*. It seems Cora bent Chief Harper's ear about how Joey could have killed his wife after all, and suddenly he's a suspect again."

"Are you serious?" Aaron said, brightening.

"Not really. Cora's theories are so wacky, no one's gonna believe them anyway. It just burns me up to think she turned me down and threw in with the chief."

Harvey Beerbaum stepped to the microphone. "Ladies and gentlemen," he announced, grinning from ear to ear and oblivious to the fact that the mike was turned up so loud a dog outside town hall started to howl, "welcome to our first annual Bakerhaven Charity Crossword-Puzzle Tournament."

Iris Cooper and Cora Felton looked at each other. This was the first indication Harvey Beerbaum had given either of them this was to be more than a onetime event.

"Tonight is your free introduction to crossword-puzzle tournaments," Harvey Beerbaum went on blithely. "Tonight's Fun Night, and we *do* intend to have *fun*. So let's get going. As you know, tonight you are going to attempt to solve some extremely interesting puzzles. The first has been contributed by Mr. Craig Carmichael, one of our famed contestants. Stand up and take a bow, Craig."

Harvey Beerbaum couldn't have chosen a worse way to kick off his Fun Night. Craig Carmichael shambled to his feet with all the enthusiasm of a man on his way to the gallows. He managed a feeble little wave and instantly sat back down.

"You will work on Craig's puzzle in teams of four. You will each have a copy of the puzzle. At a signal from me, you will all begin working. You will work only on your own copy of the puzzle, and on no one else's. And you may not help anyone else on your team.

"And why is that?" Harvey Beerbaum beamed paternally down at the crowd. "At a signal from me—I will say the word *switch*—you must pass your puzzle around the table according to my explicit directions. For instance, I may say, *pass left, pass right,* or *pass across.* You must then begin working on the copy of the puzzle you receive."

Harvey Beerbaum's eyes sparkled. "See where the fun comes in?" He paused expectantly but did not receive the appreciative chuckles he seemed to anticipate from the audience, so he went on. "The puzzle you get won't have all the same answers filled in that your previous puzzle did. So you'll have to fill those in again. And just when you get a good train of thought going, I'll yell *switch!*

"Volunteers are passing out the puzzles now. If you are competing, leave the puzzles facedown on your table until you hear the command *go* from me."

Volunteers from the tournament planning committee circulated through the room, passing out puzzles.

"They're all women," Becky Baldwin said.

"What's your point?" Aaron asked.

Becky slapped at him playfully. "Sexist pig. Real work is for men, volunteer work is only for women?"

"I notice you didn't volunteer," Aaron observed.

"I have a job. Not that it's paying well just now. If it were, I might have time to volunteer."

A woman came by with puzzles. Sherry recognized her as the wife of Mr. Gelman, the town banker. Mrs. Gelman offered her a puzzle.

"I'm not playing," Sherry told her.

Mrs. Gelman smiled. "It doesn't matter, dear. Everyone gets a puzzle, whether they're playing or not." She handed puzzles to Sherry, Aaron, and Becky and continued on around the room.

Sherry looked at her puzzle.

CURIOUS CANINES
by Craig Carmichael

ACROSS

1 Ways
6 Leers at
11 B–F connection
14 Eliot's cruelest month
15 "Arthur" star
16 Possessed
17 Sparring dog?
19 Bullfight cheer
20 Work record
21 German field marshal Rommel

DOWN

1 Fake jewelry
2 Genus of plant lice
3 Chaplin persona
4 Robbers' roost
5 Congressman and Union army
   officer Henry Warner
6 17th century card game
7 Not bad
8 Bagels and _____
9 Before (Arch.)

23 Marry
24 Shore of TV fame
26 Arbiter
27 Shoeless
30 Fancy dude
33 Handwoven wall hanging
34 Tiny Tim's instrument
35 Fuss
36 Most kempt
38 Gun club
39 Sass
40 Desert people
41 Cheese
42 Work obstruction
44 Clothing chain
46 "Goodnight, _____"
47 Most comfy (Var.)
51 Dames
53 Memento
54 Oil paintings
55 Fashionable dog?
58 Expire
59 Hindu princess
60 Detective's finds (Var.)
61 Corn unit
62 Affirmatives
63 Present, for instance

10 Most peaceful
11 Hungry dog?
12 Surrealist Salvador
13 Paradise
18 Stinging insect
22 English flyboys
24 Risks
25 Retirement funds
27 Payoff
28 Edible pod
29 Mets or Yankees
30 Fellas cohorts
31 Change text
32 Scoreless dog?
33 Saying
36 Carole King album
37 Persia, now
41 Letter
43 Before, in prefixes
44 Leaves
45 Feature
47 Gives up
48 Consumed
49 Angles
50 Curt
51 Green gemstone
52 Operatic solo
53 Leg joint
56 Actress _____ Dawn Chong
57 Printers' measures

A swift glance showed the puzzle was simple enough for Sherry to finish in a matter of minutes. She folded it up, stuck it in her purse.

At the microphone, Harvey Beerbaum bellowed, "Are you ready? Then, ready, set, go!"

The dog howled.

At the tables, the papers were turned over. In some cases, pencils began flashing. In others, puzzles were stared at.

"Care to have a go at it?" Harvey Beerbaum smirked, sidling up behind Cora and holding up two puzzle sheets.

"I don't think so," Cora told him.

"Come on," Harvey persisted. "A little friendly competition. Just you and me."

"Don't you have to keep time and say 'Switch'?" Cora pointed out.

Harvey was not so easily dissuaded. "I could do that in my sleep. I bet I can still beat you, even with one eye on the clock. What do you say?"

"No, thank you."

"Oh, but I insist."

"What's the matter?" Cora said irritably. "You think I can't do it?"

The moment the words were out of her mouth, Cora wanted to call them back.

Harvey looked at her sharply.

Cora was suddenly seized with icy dread. She felt hollow. Exposed. In the grip of an anxiety attack.

"Some other time," Cora mumbled. She fled from Harvey Beerbaum, caught Sherry's attention, and beckoned her over.

"What is it?" Sherry whispered when she had reached her aunt.

"Sherry, I think I blew it."

"What do you mean?"

"With Harvey Beerbaum. I think he *knows*."

"Cora—"

"You don't understand. He keeps asking me to do crossword puzzles."

"Cora," Sherry said in exasperation. "It's a *crossword-puzzle* tournament. You expect him to ask you to *dance* ?"

"No, but—"

"Cora, I just left Aaron Grant with Becky Baldwin to come over here. I have no time for this nonsense."

Sherry turned and stalked back.

Cora snorted indignantly. Well, if that didn't beat all. Just whose idea was it to keep up the Puzzle Lady pretense, anyway? If Sherry didn't care, why should she?

Of course, Cora *did* care. She immediately looked to see if Harvey Beerbaum was watching her, but he wasn't. Fine, she told herself. She was just imagining it, like Sherry said. She just had to calm down, get her mind on something else.

Like the murder. That was the ticket. That was just what the doctor ordered. What she needed to do was case the room for likely suspects.

Cora looked around. At the table in front of her was Marty Haskel, the cranky service-station man from the first planning meeting. Mr. Haskel was seated with three other men and was attacking his puzzle with a grim determination that made Cora's blood run cold.

At the table next to Marty were the two women Cora had met at the crime scene. Charlotte, whose fake-fur coat hung over the seat in back of her, was working on the puzzle. Opposite her sat her large friend Betty, whose hair was a true testament to the curlers she had been wearing when Cora met her. Her brown hair hung down the sides of her long face in tight rings, making her look like a horse in a wig.

Charlotte's husband was small like her, wore glasses, and looked like a graduate student. Betty's husband was something else, however. Cora Felton sucked in her breath. This was a *player.* The man was big, like Betty, only more so. His face was hard as a slab of rock. It was solid, square, and there was a fierce scar on his chin. He looked as if he had been an enforcer for the mob until the mob had decided he was just too scary and let him go.

Then he muttered something in a high-pitched nerdy voice, and the whole image evaporated in an instant.

"Switch!" Harvey Beerbaum announced gleefully from the microphone. "Pass your papers to the *left.*"

There was a flurry and rustle as papers changed places.

From the snort of disgust nearby, Cora noticed that Marty Haskel from the filling station was less than thrilled with the puzzle he had just received.

He looked even unhappier three switches later when someone screeched, "Done!"

Cora looked, saw a young woman jumping out of her seat and clapping her hands. Cora scowled.

The young woman's face was lit up, sparkling with exuberance. Even had she not been good-looking, there would have been something attractive in her ear-to-ear smile, her wide eyes, her look of boundless joy. The fact that she had blond hair, rosy cheeks, and a pert ski-jump nose was just the icing on the cake. She was the perfect blue-ribbon winner, a veritable poster girl for the tournament.

Except for one thing.

She was Paul Thornhill's wife.

She was sitting next to him at the table.

She had won because her celebrity-contestant husband was on her team.

Instead of applause at her victory, there was considerable grumbling.

None more than from Marty Haskel. "Come on, come on, keep working," Marty griped. "They still gotta check her paper. What if she got one wrong?"

Such hope was short-lived, however. Mrs. Thornhill's puzzle, quickly checked, proved correct, and the game was over, much to Marty Haskel's displeasure. The fact that the first-place prize turned out to be merely crossword-puzzle books did not appease him in the least. The man was obviously *miffed*.

Cora wasn't too pleased herself. As far as she was concerned, the much ballyhooed Fun Night was a huge bust. Fun, hell. Cora couldn't think of anything *less* fun than crossword puzzles.

Crossword puzzles and Harvey Beerbaum. What a deadly combination.

Cora clutched her drawstring purse to her chest and headed for the ladies' room. There was a faint smile on her lips as she went in the door.

Cora had expected to find Fun Night utterly boring: She had prepared for that eventuality by sticking a silver flask of vodka in her purse.

14

BLITHELY OBLIVIOUS TO ANY SIMMERING DISCONTENT IN THE CROWD, Harvey Beerbaum was once again at the microphone. "Now, ladies and gentlemen, for something entirely different—and something that's enormous fun—instead of sitting at your tables, we're going to let you get up and move around. Before you do, however, our volunteers are passing among you once again to hand out the next puzzle. You're probably wondering, if you're getting another puzzle, why are you going to move around? Well, what you're being handed is merely the *answer sheet*. So where's the puzzle, you might very well query? The puzzle, created by celebrity contestant Zelda Zisk—"

With a clatter of jewelry, Zelda surged to her feet and waved both meaty hands over her head to acknowledge a rather tepid applause that started only because her action seemed to demand it. She also laughed raucously, as if this were the funniest thing imaginable.

Harvey Beerbaum, to whom Zelda was a known quantity, patiently waited for her to subside. "As I was saying, this quite unique puzzle can be found taped to the walls of the meeting room. It consists of fifty-two separate drawings, cartoons, sketches, or what have you, drawn by Miss Zelda Zisk herself, representing fifty-two famous people whose names are in common crossword-puzzle use. Your task, of course, is to identify these celebrities. Which is what makes this such an interesting challenge. Because cruciverbalists usually know words, not faces. Except for a few like Zelda Zisk, who is of course not playing, having contributed the puzzle."

"I bet Pretty Boy's playing," Marty Haskel commented, loudly enough to be heard everywhere in the room.

A volunteer shushed him as she gave him the paper. Marty glared up at her.

"For this puzzle," Harvey Beerbaum persisted, "you may work singly or in groups of two, three, or four."

"Figures!" Marty Haskel snorted. "Might as well just hand little Miss Sunshine the prize."

"And we have a time limit of fifteen minutes. Due to the nature of the puzzle, it is considered most unlikely that anyone will finish in that time. So the winner will be whoever accumulates the most correct answers at the end of fifteen minutes. Are the answer sheets all handed out? All right, then, ready, set, *go!*"

People shot to their feet and began milling around the town hall meeting room, inspecting the cartoon drawings on the walls.

In the back of the room, Aaron nudged Sherry. "You know, this is something you could do."

Hearing him, Becky Baldwin frowned. "What do you mean by that?"

Sherry dug her elbow into Aaron's ribs. "He's kidding me. We play word games occasionally. He's always trying to one-up me."

"Yes, that's Aaron," Becky said, nodding complacently. "Whaddya think, Aaron? You think Sherry and I would have a chance against you with pictures?"

If the thought of Sherry teamed with Becky threw Aaron, he

didn't reveal it. "I'm not sure anyone would do well with these pictures," he replied smoothly, "but let's see what the *three* of us can do."

So they joined the stream of people eagerly wending their way around the edges of the room.

"Okay, here's a baseball player," Becky Baldwin said, stopping in front of one sketch. "But he doesn't look like anyone I know."

"Mel Ott," Sherry said.

Becky looked at her in surprise. "How do you know that?"

"Trust me. I've seen enough Puzzle Lady puzzles to know. *O-t-t* is an extremely useful three-letter word."

"So we got one," Becky said. "Number twenty-seven is *Ott*."

"Not so loud," Aaron cautioned. "We're not really playing, but let's not help anybody else."

Number twenty-eight was a bearded man with glasses.

"Well, who's that?" Becky Baldwin demanded.

"I have no idea," Sherry said happily. The drawing was unrecognizable. It was a pleasure to be playing a game where she didn't have to hide her expertise.

Sherry smiled at Aaron Grant and was actually feeling quite content until Becky Baldwin murmured, "Well, look who's here. . . ."

Even then Sherry had no premonition of doom. Not until she saw the naked embarrassment on Aaron's face. The poor man looked positively discombobulated. Not to mention discomposed and disconcerted.

If Becky Baldwin noticed his discomfiture she didn't show it; in fact, she looked pleased. She put on her sunniest smile, turned back in the direction she had been looking.

Sherry followed her gaze.

Striding across the floor was a youngish-looking middle-age couple—a robust man with a full head of curly hair that had just begun to turn gray, and a slender, attractive woman with a slightly homely face. The man wore a blue suit, the woman a print dress with a pink knit pullover. He had his arm around her shoulder in a totally comfortable way. Both smiled as they came walking up.

Becky Baldwin beamed as she took their hands in hers. "Mr. Grant. Mrs. Grant. How marvelous to see you. I didn't know you were puzzle people."

"We're not, of course." Mr. Grant chuckled. "I can't do puzzles, and Debbie can't either. We're just here to offer our support."

Mrs. Grant put her hand on her husband's arm. "Now, John, that's not true. I can do crossword puzzles. I'm just very slow." Her hazel eyes studied Aaron. "And what are you doing here? Writing it up for the paper?"

Aaron Grant seemed to have recovered his wits, but his face was still rather red. "Hardly. I'm just here like you to offer my support." He turned stiffly to Sherry. "Mom. Dad. This is Sherry Carter." After a moment's hesitation he added, "Sherry's Cora Felton's niece."

Aaron Grant's mother clasped Sherry's hands. "Is that right?" she said. "You know, I've seen you around town, dear, I just didn't know who you were. It must be exciting being involved with the Puzzle Lady. Please don't take anything John and I said to heart. Just because we can't do puzzles doesn't mean we have anything against them."

"Of course not," Sherry Carter said.

There was an awkward silence.

Mr. and Mrs. Grant stood there, smiling at her.

Sherry Carter felt suddenly self-conscious. She had been perfectly happy to go to Fun Night in a sweater and slacks. Now she was acutely aware of Becky Baldwin's impeccably tailored wool suit.

It didn't help when Becky Baldwin casually addressed Mr. Grant by his first name, as if to point out her familiarity with Aaron's family. "How's business, John?"

"Can't complain," John Grant replied. "Still seem to be scraping by."

"Oh, listen to him talk," Mrs. Grant said, smiling affectionately. "A hard worker all his life."

"Not at all," John Grant said with a grin. "I'm just there. Sooner or later people figure out they need insurance. Not my doing at all."

"And they just happen to come to John instead of the larger firms," Mrs. Grant informed them. "Not his doing at all."

"Anyway," Mr. Grant said, "Becky, I hear you're the attorney for Joey Vale."

"Where'd you hear that?"

"From Joey."

"You spoke to Joey?"

"I sure did. He had a big policy on his wife."

Becky groaned. "Don't tell me."

Mr. Grant smiled ruefully. "That's right. Double indemnity. Pays off double for accidental death. Murder counts as accidental, so there you are."

"I'm sorry," Becky Baldwin said. "I knew he had the policy. I didn't know it was with you."

"You knew he had the policy?"

"Of course I did. I'm his lawyer. There was the question of fees."

"Then you understand my interest in the case."

"Of course I do. Murder is considered an accident, but *not* if the policy holder commits the murder. If Joey Vale's found guilty of murder, you don't have to pay."

John Grant's smile became warmer. "It's not like we're rooting against you, Becky, but that is a fact."

"Yes, I know. I'm afraid he's got a pretty good alibi."

"Too bad," John Grant said.

The three of them chuckled over that. Then Mrs. Grant said, "We won't impose on you kids any longer. Nice meeting you, Sherry. I hope this tournament's a big success."

With that the Grants moved away in the direction of the coffee and dessert table.

"Well," Becky Baldwin said cheerily, "shall we ID some more pictures?"

It was a moment before either Sherry or Aaron responded. Aaron still looked embarrassed and ill at ease.

"Well, come on, Aaron," Sherry said. "It's not like you're a teenager. Once you're grown up, it's okay to have parents."

"Particularly when they're as nice as that," Becky Baldwin said.

"Are *your* parents here?" Sherry asked. There was an edge to her voice.

Becky merely smiled. "No, they're in Fort Lauderdale. My dad's retired. They winter down south. I have the run of the house."

It seemed to Sherry that Becky was looking at Aaron when she said that. But she couldn't tell if he blushed, because he was still blushing from the encounter with his parents.

"Well, shall we try our luck again?" Becky Baldwin suggested. It was an ambiguously vague suggestion.

Sherry turned grimly toward the next picture. It was of a woman with curly hair. It might have been Mia Farrow, Edith Piaf, or Clara Bow.

Sherry didn't recognize the woman and couldn't care less. To Sherry Carter, all the fun had just gone out of Fun Night.

She had finally met Aaron Grant's parents, and it couldn't have gone worse.

15

CORA FELTON CAME OUT OF THE BATHROOM IN A MUCH BETTER mood. She stopped in the doorway and surveyed the room.

For some reason people seemed to be walking around looking at the wall. That didn't make a lot of sense. Ah, yes. Cora vaguely remembered something about some atrocious drawings by Zelda Zisk. If only she had paid more attention in any of the planning meetings. But Cora's mind had a tendency to wander the moment Harvey Beerbaum began to pontificate. What was it about drawings . . .

As Cora watched, Sherry, Aaron, and Becky Baldwin went by and stopped to look at a picture on the wall. Sherry didn't seem particularly pleased. Probably due to the presence of Becky Baldwin. And the ugliness of the pictures. Good God, had someone really drawn that?

Cora's mind was going in circles, and not very productive ones. Now then, why was she here?

Cora's eyes widened. Ah, yes. Phooey on Fun Night. She was

here to trap a killer. To check out the crowd for suspects in the murder of Judy Vale.

Cora looked around.

Judy Vale's four neighbors had broken up into husband-and-wife teams and were attempting to identify Zelda's pictures. From what Cora could see, neither of the teams was doing a very good job. There seemed to be more bickering going on than identifying.

Next to Judy's neighbors, a guy was looking at a picture of what might have been a young girl. He seemed familiar, but with his back to Cora, it was impossible to tell. Fortunately, he turned away, grabbed a cup of coffee, and went and sat on a tabletop, which gave Cora a better look at him.

It was the man she'd seen shooting pool with Joey Vale in the Rainbow Room. He was even wearing the same Knicks T-shirt. He was a rather tall man, with a thin face and a beaky nose. He sipped his coffee as if he would have much preferred a beer.

Cora pushed her way over to his table. "Giving up so soon?"

He looked at her, frowned. "That's not allowed?"

"What do you mean, allowed?"

"Aren't you the Puzzle Lady?"

"Yeah. So?"

"Well, you're in charge, right? You here to tell me I can't quit?"

"Of course you can quit. This is just a stupid game. It's not like shooting pool."

His thin face altered. He pointed at her. "You were in the Rainbow Room the other night. Talking to Joey. I didn't put it together. I thought you were his mother, come to console him." At Cora's offended look he added, "Sorry. Didn't mean to be rude. I just didn't put it together then. You're the woman who figures out crime."

"Right, I'm Bakerhaven's *Murder, She Wrote* broad. I ask a few questions and zero in on the suspect."

"I'm a suspect?"

"I dunno. Did you strangle Judy Vale?"

"No."

Cora shrugged. "Then I guess you're not. What's your name?"

"Sy. Sy Fishman."

"I'm Cora Felton, and I'm damn glad you didn't kill Judy Vale." Cora scrunched up her nose. "There was something I wanted to ask you."

"About Joey Vale?"

"Yes," Cora said. "No," she amended. "Sort of," she decided. "The guy Joey Vale thought was fooling around with his wife . . ."

"Billy Pickens."

Cora's face brightened slyly. "Yes. Billy. Very good. So you knew about Billy Pickens?"

"Everybody knew about Billy. Joey'd get in the bag, he'd start whining about it."

"You happen to know Billy Pickens?"

" 'Course I do. He's a regular."

"At the Rainbow Room?"

"Sure."

"Was he there the other night?"

"No, but he's there a lot."

"So what's he look like?"

"I don't know," Sy said. Apparently descriptions weren't his forte. He raised his head, looked around the room.

Cora frowned at him, then got the idea. "You mean Billy's here?"

"Unless he left. I saw him earlier. Yeah, there he is. In the corner, looking at the cartoon of the old lady."

Cora followed Sy's gaze.

In the corner of the room stood a broad-shouldered, muscular, athletic-looking young man in gray slacks, tweed jacket, light blue dress shirt, and patterned tie. His curly brown hair was neatly trimmed, and his face was almost boyish.

The woman with him looked older but probably wasn't. It was just the fact her hair was up and she was wearing earrings, tiny, understated, tasteful.

They were studying a drawing of either an extremely flat-chested woman or a very long-haired man.

"That's Billy Pickens from the paper mill?" Cora asked Sy.

"That's right. Billy's the bookkeeper down there. Looks too young, don't you think?"

Cora didn't know about that, but Billy Pickens from the paper mill suddenly seemed a much better prospect on her suspect list. Particularly in light of the young woman at his side. "Is that his wife?"

"Probably. I think he's married, but I've never met her."

"Uh-huh," Cora Felton said. It occurred to her she had some questions for Billy Pickens, if she could just separate him from his date. Cora scratched her head, wondered how to go about it.

As Cora stood there pondering her next move, a young woman flitted by, peered at the androgynous picture the Pickenses were contemplating, scrawled a notation on her answer sheet, and scampered on.

Aha, Cora thought. Paul Thornhill's wife. Attacking the game with undisguised zeal. But without her celebrity husband.

Cora glanced over at the Thornhills' table. Paul Thornhill was seated facing Cora, partly obscured by the back of a woman who was bent over the table, talking to him. Cora was not surprised. With Mrs. Thornhill out of the way, her handsome husband would surely be besieged by female admirers.

This female admirer, however, seemed somewhat older than Cora would have expected. And there was something familiar about her. Cora looked more closely. The woman moved, and Cora saw her face.

"Now, isn't that odd," Cora murmured.

The woman talking to Paul Thornhill, giving a superb impression of a crossword-puzzle groupie, was none other than Judy Vale's reclusive neighbor.

Mrs. Roth.

The troll.

What, Cora wondered, could possibly have lured the old woman from her shadowy lair? From Cora's conversation with Mrs. Roth, it certainly wasn't a passion for crossword puzzles. And, despite appearances, Cora couldn't really imagine her making a play for Paul Thornhill.

Cora watched with growing interest.

"*Stop!*" Harvey Beerbaum commanded. There was a collective groan of disappointment, which seemed to delight him. "*Stop* where you are. Do not move on to the next picture. Stay right where you are standing, and volunteers will be around to collect your answer sheets. Be certain your name is printed legibly on the top. If we cannot read your name, you cannot win. As soon as your paper is collected, return to your table so we may begin the next exciting event."

A volunteer collected Mrs. Thornhill's paper, and she trotted back to the table and her husband.

Marty Haskel was right on her heels. He strode up to the table, jabbed his finger in Paul Thornhill's direction. Cora Felton was too far away to hear what he said, but his subtext was plain. If Mrs. Thornhill happened to come in first on this puzzle too, there'd be hell to pay.

For her part, Mrs. Thornhill looked surprised and aggrieved. Why should anyone be raining on her parade? Just when things were going so well. Why was this happening? Why wasn't someone rescuing her from this loathsome man?

To Cora's surprise, the troll saved the day.

Graceful as a girl, Mrs. Roth stepped smoothly between the Thornhills and Mr. Haskel, murmured something to the garage attendant, and swept him away.

At the microphone, Harvey Beerbaum prattled on, blissfully unaware of any percolating controversy. "Volunteers are passing out the next puzzle now. Please keep it facedown on your table. This puzzle you will work on in teams of two. Please sit across from each other and be prepared to pass the puzzle back and forth." He beamed. "And this puzzle, I am pleased to announce, comes from celebrity contestant Paul Thornhill."

Harvey gestured to Paul Thornhill, who stood and took a bow to some applause, although not nearly as much as there would have been had his wife not won the first event.

A volunteer handed a paper to Cora. She glanced at it, saw it was a puzzle. Her lip curled up, and she had to curb the strong urge to hurl it on the floor. She looked again, saw the name *Paul Thornhill* featured prominently.

APOLOGIES
by Paul Thornhill

ACROSS

1 "Maybe _____" (Buddy Holly hit)
5 Juniors' juniors (Abbr.)
10 Alack's partner

DOWN

1 Confederate general
2 Video's partner
3 "I was too _____" (Brenda Lee's apology)

14 Regulation
15 Coffee additive
16 Country bumpkin
17 Mine entrance
18 Greeting
19 Grad
20 Type of rummy
21 Beginning of Elvis's apology
23 Divinity
25 Mai _____
26 Tint
27 Uto-Aztecan languages
32 Packs away
34 Was able
35 "At the _____" (Danny and the Juniors hit)
36 British bottom
37 "I'm _____" (theme of this puzzle)
38 Cub's dad
39 Misery
40 _____ cum laude
41 Amusingly risque
42 Climbing plant
44 Wife of Zeus
45 Street guide
46 Tot's farewells
49 End of Elvis's apology
54 Head cover
55 Arab prince
56 Movie segment
57 Bear or Berra
58 Vocalize
59 "Exorcist" actress Burstyn
60 Prayer ending
61 Eye problem (Var.)
62 Burrito condiment
63 Brew

4 So far
5 Stupid bore (Var.)
6 Greek mountain nymph
7 Booty
8 Angel's wear
9 With finesse
10 Ali Baba's land
11 "To Sir With Love" singer
12 Border on
13 Trucking rig
21 Charged particles
22 Praise
24 British Revolutionary War general
27 "_____ Rae" (Sally Field Oscar winner)
28 Distinctive atmosphere
29 "I ran all _____" (Impalas' apology)
30 Heavy burden
31 Nimble
32 Sayings
33 Believe (archaic)
34 Arrive
37 Assumes
38 Pointed remark
40 Remain
41 Suds
43 Come out
44 Nocturnal scavenger (Var.)
46 Cofounder of Czechoslovakia
47 Champing at the bit
48 Reek
49 Not so much
50 Leave out
51 Ivy-covered
52 Bruins' school
53 "Farmer in the _____"
57 Bark shrilly

"Are we all ready now?" Harvey Beerbaum said, with all the warmth of a prissy schoolteacher about to administer a final exam. "In that case, ready, set, go!"

Cora looked from the puzzle to the man who had created it. At the table the Thornhills were having what could charitably be called an earnest discussion. Paul Thornhill looked defensive. Mrs. Thornhill looked thoroughly upset. The reason was obvious. As a result of Marty Haskel's objection, there was no way Paul Thornhill could let his wife solve his own puzzle. Mrs. Thornhill, not one to suffer long in silence, was clearly not happy to be barred from victory.

Cora snorted. Phooey on it. What about Billy Pickens?

Looking around, Cora was pleased to discover that the young man and his wife were not playing the third game but had moved to the table at the far side of the room where coffee and desserts were available. Now, if Cora could just figure out some way to separate Billy from the young woman . . .

A crackling of paper alerted Cora to the fact she was still holding the crossword puzzle. That would never do. If she wasn't careful, Harvey Beerbaum would materialize out of nowhere and ask her to solve it.

Unobtrusively, Cora managed to sidle up to a trash receptacle and drop the puzzle in. That task accomplished, Cora looked back over at the refreshment table: Billy Pickens and his wife were no longer there.

Wrong again. The woman with her back to Cora filling a cup with coffee from the big silver urn was indeed the young woman she had seen earlier with Billy Pickens.

Excellent. Billy Pickens must be alone. Now was her chance. She had only to find him. . . .

Cora's quest for Billy Pickens led her by the rest rooms again. This time, however, she managed to resist temptation and felt duly virtuous.

So where was the man? If Cora was going to give up a drink to find him, she damn well better find him. If he'd had any consideration and been easy to find, she'd have talked to him already and been back in the john. The fact she wasn't was entirely Billy Pickens's fault, and what did he have to say for himself?

Cora noticed Harvey Beerbaum peering in her direction. Drat the man. Officious, intrusive dweeb. Why wasn't he supervising the stupid game? It was all his idea. He should be keeping his eye on it. Not spying on her.

Unless *that* was his idea.

Damn.

Cora had just about decided to sneak back to the rest room when she spotted Billy Pickens.

Cora frowned. Her chances of talking to him alone had not improved.

For Billy Pickens seemed deeply involved in an earnest conversation with Judy Vale's nosy neighbor, Mrs. Roth.

16

CORA DREAMED SHE WAS ON TV. BUT NOT IN A BREAKFAST-CEREAL commercial. She was a cartoon character, an animated two-dimensional drawing, scooting across the TV screen like the Road Runner trying to get away from . . .

Harvey Beerbaum, with a double-barreled shotgun, all dressed up like Elmer Fudd.

Of course. She wasn't the Road Runner. She was Bugs Bunny. That wascally wabbit. Gnawing on a carrot and hoodwinking Harvey before her real identity dawned on him. Good thing he was so gullible, or he would have figured it out.

Because she didn't *look* like a rabbit. And she couldn't *do* cross-word puzzles. And surely even Elmer Fuddy-Duddy Beerbaum was going to see through her tricks if she gave him enough time.

Oh, why had she ever agreed to be in this cartoon? Cartoons weren't good for her. She couldn't be herself in cartoons. She had no *feel* for them. Why had she let Sherry talk her into it? It was all Sherry's fault. If Sherry would just leave her alone—

But Sherry wouldn't. Sherry kept pulling her into things. Pulling her, even as Cora tried to bat her away. Pulling and yelling, or at least talking way too loud. And—

Cora opened her eyes to find herself sitting upright in bed. Her niece had a hold of her arm. Now she gripped her shoulders to keep her from burrowing back under the tangled sheets.

Cora blinked at her in bewilderment. "You're not Elmer Fudd."

Sherry ignored that epiphany. "Good. You're awake. Now, do we have to go in the shower?"

Cora's brow furrowed. "Shower? What shower? Baby shower? Are you and Aaron having a baby?"

"No," Sherry said tersely.

That penetrated Cora's subconsciousness. She frowned. "Oh? Not so glowing?"

Sherry shook her. "Aunt Cora. *Focus.* It's Saturday morning. The crossword-puzzle tournament's in twenty minutes, and you gotta be there."

Cora's face fell. She groaned. "Oh, no . . ."

"Oh, yes."

Sherry grabbed her aunt's ankles, swung her legs over the side of the bed.

"Sherry," Cora babbled, as her niece wrenched her to her feet. "Last night. At Fun Night. What happened?"

"Nothing much, except you had a little too much to drink and forgot why you were there. When Aaron and I brought you home you were babbling about pickles. Dill pickles, as I recall."

"Dill pickles. Can't remember. God, my head hurts. Dill pickles." Cora's eyes widened. "Oh. No, no, no. Not dill pickles. Billy Pickens! Did I talk to him?"

Sherry piloted her aunt into the kitchen, flopped her in a chair. "Who's Billy Pickens?"

"Sherry, don't you know anything?" Cora wailed. "Billy Pickens is the murder suspect."

Sherry shoved a cup of coffee in front of Cora. When Cora made no move to take it, Sherry picked it up, put it in her hand. "Here, drink this. It should wake you up enough to get dressed."

104 / PARNELL HALL

"Dressed? Where are we going?"

"Aunt Cora, you gotta focus. The tournament's this morning. You gotta drink your coffee and get dressed."

"Sherry. I can't go. You go for me."

Sherry was sorely tempted, but if she left her aunt at home, Cora was very likely to get into further mischief. Which might lead to a most unfortunate surprise appearance at the tournament later on.

"You're going, Cora. And you're going to get right up there on the stage next to Harvey Beerbaum. And you're not going to screw up, and you're going to be fine. Now, drink that coffee, or I'll pour it on your head."

17

Aaron Grant met them in front of town hall. Any tension from the night before was lost in the immediate task of getting Cora inside. This was complicated by the fact that Cora did not take kindly to being assisted and kept batting their hands away as they helped her from the car.

"I'm fine," Cora muttered irritably.

"I'm sure you are," Aaron said pleasantly. He jerked his thumb in the direction of the Channel 8 van parked in the side lot. "The news crew's inside. Are you ready for your close-up?"

"No, but she will be." Sherry jerked a compact out of her purse and began to touch up Cora's face.

"Can do my own makeup," Cora protested.

"I know you can, but this morning you didn't, so just hold still."

Sherry whipped off Cora's glasses, touched up the bags under her eyes. "There. Ten times better."

Sherry stuck Cora's glasses back on, and she and Aaron marched her up the front steps.

"Remember," Sherry cautioned, "you're going to be on TV, so

when you stand next to Harvey Beerbaum, try not to look like you wish him dead."

Cora managed her most indignant version of *harrumph,* then wrenched herself free from Sherry and Aaron and sailed in the door.

The Channel 8 news team was waiting to pounce. Rick Reed, handsome, young, ambitious, and bright as the average fireplug, grabbed her by the shoulder and stuck a microphone in her face. "Miss Felton," he cried. "Any thoughts on the tournament? Which contestant do you pick to win?"

Cora's first instinct was to punch him in the nose; in the past the on-camera reporter had done his best to embarrass her every chance he got. She restrained herself and, with a twinkle in her eye, replied, "The one with the most points."

Cora smiled sweetly, patted Rick Reed on the cheek, and wove her way through the tables, reassuring herself that she *did* know how the scoring worked, and it actually *was* the most points that won, and she had not committed some gaffe that would be played gleefully on the six o'clock news.

Cora reached the stage and stepped up next to Harvey Beerbaum, who stood tapping his foot and looking at his watch just like a schoolteacher awaiting the arrival of a tardy child.

"Well, nice of you to join us, Miss Felton."

Cora frowned. The man even *sounded* like a schoolteacher. "Could have started without me," she muttered.

"Yes," Harvey said. "But we agreed that this morning you would make the opening remarks."

Cora blinked, thunderstruck. Somewhere in the deep recesses of her brain a vague memory of something to that effect chimed like a death knell. "We did?" she murmured.

"Yes, of course," Harvey said pedantically. "I did last night, you do today, and I do the finals tomorrow. You don't remember that? You *are* prepared, aren't you?"

Fortunately, nothing propelled Cora into action faster than the suggestion she was not capable of it. "Of course I'm prepared. Just give me a moment, and I'll be right with you."

Cora marched to a table at the side of the stage, shrugged off her coat, and made a show of fumbling in her purse as if looking for the paper on which she had written her carefully prepared welcoming speech. Of course, there was no speech to find—Cora was just stalling for time. As she dug in her purse, she glanced surreptitiously around the room, desperate for a clue as to what she was supposed to say.

The tables were pretty well filled. Most had only two people, though some had as many as four: two on the long side facing the stage, and one on each end. Sharpened pencils were lined up on the tables. Coats and scarves hung over the backs of the chairs.

As everyone would be doing the same puzzle, blue cardboard dividers stood on the tables between the contestants. Cora figured she could talk about that, though not much, since the dividers must have been explained when they were being set up.

All right, what about the contestants themselves?

At the table just in front of her sat the Thornhills. The divider between them indicated Paul's wife must be playing too. Or did just her presence indicate that? Cora couldn't remember if spectators were allowed at the tables at this juncture of the tournament. Another thing she could have commented on. Why on earth hadn't she been paying attention?

Most of the spectators were in the back of the room. Cora spotted Sherry and Aaron in the crowd. And the TV people, who were taking the camera off its tripod and bringing it up the aisle.

To film her opening remarks.

Cora was beginning to sweat.

And then she saw it.

Behind the stage, facing the tables, was the clock. A huge, old-fashioned wooden clock, with a circular dial. White, with black hands and black numbers. Only not the usual numbers. Where the twelve should have been was zero. Going round the dial, counter-clockwise, instead of eleven, ten, nine, eight . . . were the numbers five, ten, fifteen, twenty . . .

Yes.

She could do this.

Saved by the clock.

Cora pretended to find the lipstick she'd actually had in her hand for some time, pulled it out, and applied some lip gloss, much to Harvey Beerbaum's undisguised irritation. She ignored him, marched to the microphone. "Ladies and gentlemen," she purred. "I'd like to welcome you to the competitive part of the tournament." She had a rough moment with *competitive* but managed not to mangle it too badly. "Volunteers will be circulating among you, passing out the first puzzle. Keep it facedown in front of you on your table. Write your name on the back, otherwise we won't know it's you."

"And your contestant number," Harvey Beerbaum prompted.

"Yes, your contestant number." Cora forced a smile so as not to glare at Harvey for interrupting her. "Do you all *know* your contestant number?"

Everyone appeared to, since no one said anything and no hands went up.

"All right," Cora said. "As soon as the puzzles are passed out, we will be ready to begin. I call your attention to the clock in the front of the room. You will note that it is set for . . ." Cora had an instant of panic as she realized she didn't know what it was set for, then remembered there was nothing to figure out, it was what it said. "Fifteen minutes," she announced. "For those of you not familiar with the clock, it runs clockwise." This, unexpectedly, got a laugh. Cora smiled, as if she had actually been joking, then remembered the rest of the instructions that both Harvey Beerbaum and Sherry had drilled her on. "But you might not take fifteen minutes. In this competition, speed counts. So the second you are finished, raise your hand, and a volunteer will take your paper and note the time when you are done. Okay, if everyone is ready . . . Ready, set, GO!"

There was a great flutter of paper as all the puzzles were flipped over; the contestants began scribbling frantically.

Cora heaved a sigh of relief. Harvey Beerbaum came over, probably to comment on her speech, but she headed him off. "Be right back."

Cora grabbed her coat and purse, hopped down off the stage, and pushed by the camera crew. She threaded her way through the tables, fumbling for her cigarettes as she went, and banged out the door.

"Think she'll be back?" Aaron asked.

Sherry put up her finger, said, "Shhh."

Aaron snorted in exasperation. "Can I talk to you?"

"Not in here."

"Then come outside."

Sherry and Aaron slipped out the door. There they found Cora Felton smoking a cigarette on the front steps.

"Feeling better?" Sherry asked.

Cora glared at her. "I feel like garbage. How many more puzzles do I have to do?"

"Two more this morning, then they break for lunch. Relax, you're doing great."

"Easy for you to say. I'm up there without a script, ad-libbing. Harvey Beerbaum just looked at me like I told him the earth was flat."

"Well, now that you mention it . . ."

"Oh, hell!" Cora groaned. "What'd I get wrong?"

"Nothing much, because you didn't *say* much. You were supposed to mention the size of the puzzle. The one they're doing right now is a fifteen-by-fifteen. The next is a seventeen-by-seventeen."

"I knew that," Cora said. "I forgot to say it, but I knew it."

"You remember how the scoring works?"

"Oh, hell, was I supposed to announce that too?"

"It would have been nice."

"No wonder Harvey wasn't happy."

"He'll get over it," Sherry said. "But you should know the scoring."

"I know it, I know it," Cora grumbled. She ticked them off on her fingers. "You get a hundred and fifty points for a perfect puzzle. You get a bonus of twenty-five points for each full minute under the time limit."

"See how it works, Aaron?" Sherry said. "Say you finish eight minutes early. You get two hundred bonus points for that. If your puzzle's perfect, you get another hundred and fifty points. If you have an error, you don't. So a person who finished in slower time could be ahead."

Aaron looked pained. "Sherry—" he began, but before he could finish, the door banged open and Paul Thornhill came striding out.

As usual, Paul Thornhill looked like he'd just stepped out of a fashion magazine. He was dressed in slacks and a blue sweater. His tan topcoat was draped over his shoulders like a cape.

Cora looked at him in surprise. "Giving up so soon?"

Paul Thornhill smiled. Up close he had very white teeth. Even Cora was impressed. "I take it you don't go to crossword-puzzle tournaments very often?"

In spite of herself, Cora found herself actually melting under the warmth of that winning smile. Even with Aaron and Sherry looking on, Cora positively simpered. "Well, now, Mr. Thornhill, to tell you the truth, this is my first one."

Paul Thornhill nodded. "I thought so. Well, don't feel bad. I know a lot of constructors who've never been to a tournament. But if you had been, you'd know everybody leaves. They hand in their puzzle, get up, and walk out the door. It's a macho thing. Finish early, get up, walk away." He grinned. "I mean macho in a non-gender-specific way, of course. Men and women, they all do it. I imagine we'll have company pretty soon."

As he predicted, the door banged open and Craig Carmichael came out. If Craig was being macho, they wouldn't have known it, for he spoke to no one, avoided eye contact, and furtively wandered off to stand by himself on the far end of the steps.

Ned Doowacker emerged next. He sized up Sherry and Aaron, demanded, "You're not playing, are you?"

"No," Sherry told him.

"Well, that's a relief. Don't wanna start off fifth. Bad enough to be behind those two." He indicated Paul Thornhill and Craig Carmichael. "Don't need any local amateurs messing things up."

Ned Doowacker moved down to the edge of the steps to bully Craig Carmichael, who cringed visibly when he saw Ned coming.

After that, a steady stream of puzzle-solvers came banging out the door. They stood around in small clusters jabbering about the puzzle they had just solved.

"When will they go back?" Cora Felton asked.

Paul Thornhill looked at his watch. "A couple of minutes now. As soon as the first puzzle is over and the director announces time is up."

"Oh," Cora said. Her eyes widened as she realized *she* was the director. "Oh!"

Cora flipped the butt of her cigarette into the parking lot, turned, and hurried in the door.

"We should put that out," Aaron said.

"Go ahead," Sherry told him. "I'm not touching it."

Aaron skipped down the steps, ground the cigarette butt into the gravel. He stood in the parking lot, watched as the contestants went back inside.

Sherry stayed at the top of the steps. As the last few stragglers trickled in, Aaron went up to her. "Sherry. About last night."

"What about it?"

"About my parents."

"Nice people."

"Yes. Nice people." Aaron frowned. "Sherry—"

"What are you trying to say, Aaron?"

"I felt awkward introducing you to my parents. I shouldn't have."

"Well, you sure know how to make a girl feel good. Why did you feel awkward?"

"I don't know. I felt like a little boy. Maybe because I live at home."

"Uh-huh," Sherry said. "Well, thanks for explaining."

Aaron looked at her, couldn't think of what to say.

After a moment Sherry said, "Come on, let's go see the second puzzle."

But as Sherry opened the door and went inside, she couldn't help wondering how much Aaron's introducing her to his parents had actually been inhibited by the presence of Becky Baldwin.

18

Becky Baldwin showed up in a snit. She banged in the back door and stood, hands on hips, chin thrust out, looking around the room. The second puzzle had just begun, and everyone was working furiously. Or at least trying to. Becky was wearing a bright red topcoat and matching beret, which was only slightly less distracting than if she'd been wearing neon.

Sherry and Aaron, sensing trouble, moved in on her.

"What's the matter?" Aaron said.

Becky waved him away, continued to scan the room. "Just a minute, just a minute," she muttered. A moment later she snarled, "Damn it to hell!"

It was loud enough so that several heads turned.

Sherry put her finger to her lips, whispered, "Becky, not here. Come on outside."

Reluctantly, Becky allowed Sherry and Aaron to lead her onto the front steps.

"Okay," Sherry said. "What's the trouble?"

"What's the trouble?" Becky repeated. "I got a client in jail on a drunk-and-disorderly. Supposed to be released today. Shouldn't have been in jail in the first place. It's bad enough the guy's wife gets killed, then they go and blame him for getting drunk."

"You trying to bail out Joey Vale?" Sherry asked.

"Damn right I am! If there ever was a guy who shouldn't be in jail, it's him. I understand he tried to tear the place up. Fine. He was drunk, he was rowdy, he needed to sleep it off. So you clap him in a cell till he does. No problem. Well, he's not drunk anymore, just nursing a god-awful hangover. You don't keep a man like that in jail, you let him go."

"No argument here," Sherry said. "So what's the problem?"

"He was charged with drunk-and-disorderly, so the judge has to sign the release. I go to court to do that, and guess what? Judge Hobbs isn't there."

"Oh, no," Sherry said.

"Oh, yes. He's working on a crossword puzzle, just like every-body else in this damn town. And I can't interrupt him, because he's racing against a clock."

"Maybe he'll finish early," Aaron suggested mildly.

Becky glared at him.

"When contestants finish early they get up and come out here. It's a macho thing."

Becky crinkled her nose. "I beg your pardon?"

"According to Paul Pretty-boy Thornhill," Aaron explained. "People who finish early like to show off by getting up and walking out."

"Yeah, like Judge Hobbs is really going to be one of those," Becky scoffed. "Anyway, no one's out yet."

"They just got started. Give 'em time."

"How much time?"

"It's a twenty-five minute puzzle," Sherry said. "But some of them will finish in ten. They'll be coming out any minute now."

"And I'll bet you a nickel," Aaron said, "that the first one out the door is Paul Thornhill."

Aaron would have lost his nickel, because the first one out the door was Cora Felton. She winced at the sunlight as if it were the first time she'd been out in a month, moaned, and jerked her cigarettes from her purse.

It was then she noticed Becky Baldwin. "Not my fault," she said. "If Chief Harper likes Joey Vale, it's not because of me."

"You're a day late," Becky told her.

Cora blinked. "Huh?"

"That's yesterday's problem. Today's problem is Judge Hobbs is playing your stupid game, so I can't bail Joey out."

"Judge Hobbs is *here?*" Cora said. Her coy look was priceless. In the past, she had flirted with the judge.

"He's competing," Sherry said, "so he can't sign off on Joey Vale. Look, Becky, the bottom line is, I didn't see Judge Hobbs out early on the first puzzle, and I doubt if he'll be out early on this one. In all likelihood you won't get to see him till they break for lunch."

"When's that?"

"About an hour. There's one puzzle after this."

"Great," Becky snapped.

The door banged open. Paul Thornhill sized up their little group and noted the addition of Becky Baldwin. His eyes raised inquiringly as he flashed her a smile. "My dear young lady, I didn't see you leave. Are you finished already?"

Becky frowned. "Finished?"

"Yes. I finished in ten minutes flat. Did you really beat my time?"

"I'm not playing," Becky informed him.

"Well, I'm glad to hear it." Paul Thornhill smiled and ducked his head in an aw-shucks manner that made his hair fall in his eyes. "Not that I wouldn't want you in the game, I just wouldn't want you finishing first. And who might you be?"

"I'm Becky Baldwin. I'm the attorney for Joey Vale."

"And Joey Vale is . . ."

"Husband of Judy Vale, the woman who got strangled."

"Oh, yes. There was quite a buzz about that last night."

"Who was talking about it?" Cora said, perking up.

Paul Thornhill and Becky Baldwin's conversation had seemed more and more private. Both frowned at Cora's interruption.

Paul Thornhill shrugged. "I don't recall." He turned his attention back to Becky Baldwin. "Selective memory. I could tell you every word that was in the puzzle I just solved. But I couldn't tell you what person told me what particular thing."

Ned Doowacker came out the door. The tall, gawky contestant spotted Paul Thornhill and grimaced. "Beat me again. At least this time I beat Craig and Zelda. Just gotta get into the final, that's all. Anything can happen in the final."

"You sure you beat Zelda?" Paul Thornhill asked. "She never comes out."

"No, I looked. She's still working."

Craig Carmichael emerged from the building, furtively scanned the group of people for contestants, and retreated to his corner of the steps.

Paul Thornhill didn't notice. He only had eyes for one person. "So what's a nice girl like you doing representing a murderer?" he asked Becky Baldwin, flashing her the high-wattage smile.

"He's not a murderer. He's got an alibi for the time of the crime." With a glance at Cora Felton, Becky added, "He couldn't *possibly* have done it."

"And just when did he do it?" Paul Thornhill asked. "I'm sorry. I mean, just when *didn't* he do it?"

"She was killed Tuesday night. Half a dozen witnesses can place him in a local bar at the time."

"Well, that's convenient."

The door banged open and contestants began to stream out. It appeared as if some puzzle-solving plateau had been reached, because it swiftly became a mass exodus. In the space of the next two minutes, at least half of the people in the town hall emerged.

Judge Hobbs was not among them.

Neither was Paul Thornhill's wife. Further proof, if any was needed, that her winning the night before had been due largely to him. Indeed, Cora noted, Paul Thornhill continued to chat up

Becky Baldwin as if there were no possibility of his wife ever showing up.

She didn't, but Rick Reed did. He came out, stomped up to Cora
Felton, and demanded, "All right, what's the big idea?"

"I beg your pardon?" Cora said.

"You get me here for this big tournament, I got a camera crew
inside, and what's for me to film? *Dead silence.* A bunch of people
sitting at tables *writing*. Not only that, most of them leave. I got a
camera crew in there shooting an empty room."

"Well, it's not my idea. You got a problem, take it up with
Harvey Beerbaum."

"You're the cohost."

"Don't be dumb," Sherry butted in. "If I were you, I'd bring my
crew out here and interview the first ones out the door. That's who's
gonna win."

"That's an *excellent* idea," Rick Reed enthused. Sherry couldn't
tell if he was just trying to hit on her or if he was really too stupid
to have thought of it himself. "Who was out first?"

"He was," Becky Baldwin said. She stepped in front of Paul
Thornhill to introduce him to Rick Reed.

The two men shook hands, but they were both very aware of
Becky. Paul Thornhill bristled like a cat. Rick Reed, who had been
practically drooling over Sherry, might have forgotten she existed.
He seemed torn between whether to treat Paul Thornhill as a rival
or a prospective interview.

Becky Baldwin, who had unobtrusively managed to put herself
center stage, smiled demurely, as if unaware of any tension she
might be causing.

Cora Felton, with many marriages to her credit, recognized the
tactic and had to admit it was working. Even Aaron Grant was taking a keen interest in the scene. Sherry clearly wasn't pleased, but
Aaron didn't seem to notice.

Cora sighed at the stupidity of the world in general and men in
particular, and went back inside to check on the tournament.

Zelda Zisk was finished, as Paul Thornhill had predicted. The large woman sat at her table alone, drawing doodles on a piece of scrap paper. Without checking the time written on her puzzle, there was no way of knowing how long she'd been done.

At the table behind her, Mrs. Thornhill was working diligently. From a distance, Cora couldn't tell how much of her puzzle was finished, but it did not appear to be a lot.

Cora finally spotted Judge Hobbs sitting at a table way off to the side. The white-haired jurist was working diligently, if slowly, and was clearly no threat to win. Judge Hobbs, like many of the other prominent citizens in town, was competing for the purpose of paying the entry fee to donate to charity. In addition to the judge, Cora noted banker Marcus Gelman, county prosecutor Henry Firth, and Dr. Barney Nathan. All were bent over their papers with identical frowns, as if they'd accidentally been handed a puzzle in Japanese.

Marty Haskel, however, was no longer working on his puzzle. That caught Cora by surprise. The cranky service-station attendant sat slumped at his table, drumming his fingers impatiently. If finishing early pleased him, Cora wouldn't have known it. Mr. Haskel, as usual, looked peeved.

Cora got so caught up in watching him she almost missed the five-minute warning, and it took a cautionary *ahem* from Harvey Beerbaum to snap her out of it. Cora *had* missed the five-minute warning on the first puzzle, and while no contestants had complained, Harvey had acted as if it were the end of the world. Now Cora stepped to the microphone, watched the seconds tick down, said, "Five minutes please," and stepped back, reminding herself that Harvey Beerbaum was an officious prig.

Nonetheless, she was careful to keep her eye on the clock as it ticked down the last minute. "Time's up," she announced. "Please stop working. If you have a puzzle, raise your hand, and a volunteer will be around to collect it."

Within minutes the puzzles had been collected, the contestants outside had been herded back in, and the third puzzle had been passed out.

By now Cora was on top of her game, feeling pretty cocky. "All right," she announced, "puzzle number three is a nineteen-by-nineteen; you'll have thirty minutes to complete it. Does everyone have a puzzle? If so, then, ready, set, go!"

Cora pushed away from the microphone with a feeling of triumph. She had gotten through the morning. All she had to do was wait a half an hour, announce *time's up,* and everyone could go to lunch.

Cora wove her way through the tables, pushed by Rick Reed and his crew, who had just filmed her announcement, and went out the door onto the steps, where Sherry, Aaron, and Becky were waiting. Cora wasn't sure whether to be pleased Sherry had seen no need to monitor her performance or annoyed no one had bothered to watch her work. It occurred to her that Sherry hadn't wanted to leave Aaron and Becky alone. She fired up a cigarette, took a deep drag.

"So *that's* where you went," Iris Cooper said, coming out the door. "Do you *have* to smoke on the front steps?"

"I do if I can't smoke inside," Cora Felton informed her blithely, and blew a perfect ring. Having gotten through the morning, she was in too good a mood to let Iris Cooper upset her.

Cora had finished her cigarette, and was just wondering if there was any way she could get a Bloody Mary for lunch, when Chief Harper drove up with the news there'd been another murder.

19

"WHAT DO YOU MEAN I CAN'T GO IN THERE?" CHIEF HARPER scowled.

Iris Cooper held her ground. "I'm sorry, Chief, but that's a fact. The third puzzle's started, it's being timed. There'd be hell to pay if I stopped it now."

"There'll be hell to pay if you don't," Chief Harper told her. "I got my medical examiner in there, not to mention the county prosecutor. I could do without Henry Firth, but I need Barney Nathan, and I need him *now.*"

"He's right, Iris," Cora said. Her eyes gleamed at the prospect of calling off the tournament. "If there's a murder, it has to take precedence. It's a shame, but that's a fact."

"Hey, whose side are you on?" Iris exclaimed.

"I don't have time for an argument about this," Chief Harper snapped. "The fact is, I need the doc."

"I'll get him," Sherry Carter said. "I'll slip in quietly and send him out. But there's no reason to disturb anybody else."

"No reason except I might want to talk to 'em," Chief Harper grumbled, but Sherry Carter had already slipped inside.

"You mind telling us who?" Cora Felton asked the chief. "Or do you just enjoy keeping us in the dark? Who got killed?"

"Funny you should ask," Chief Harper said. "It just happens to be the witness you called on."

"The witness *I* called on? I called on a lot of witnesses." At the look on Chief Harper's face Cora said, "Scratch that, Chief. You're right. I only called on one witness. Mrs. Roth."

"Mrs. Roth!" Aaron Grant exclaimed. "You've gotta be kidding! I went out there especially at her request, and the woman knew next to nothing. It was all I could do to dredge up a quote."

"She knew enough to wind up dead," Chief Harper said dryly. "You mind telling me what it was she told you?"

"Yes, he would." Becky Baldwin stepped forward. As Chief Harper scowled, she added, "No, I'm not insisting you read Aaron his rights. And he's not my client. But Joey Vale is. If this new murder's connected in any way to the murder of his wife, I have a right to know. For starters, you mind telling us *how* Mrs. Roth was killed?"

Chief Harper frowned, considered, then said, "Well, that's one reason I'm gettin' Barney Nathan. So nothing's official yet. And this is not for publication. But it would appear that she was strangled."

"Like Judy Vale?" Cora was practically quivering with excitement.

"Yes."

"Interesting," Becky Baldwin murmured. "Just for the record, I would like to point out that I am here for the express purpose of getting Judge Hobbs to sign a release order for Joey Vale, who's been locked up in jail since yesterday afternoon. I don't suppose I need to point out the significance."

"Here, again, Barney Nathan should be a help," Chief Harper said.

As if on cue, Sherry Carter came out the door leading Barney Nathan. The doctor didn't look pleased.

"She tell you what's up?" Chief Harper asked him.

"She said it was an emergency. It better be important, because I was doing well."

"It's important, Barney. Another homicide. Judy Vale's neighbor. Dan and Sam are out at the crime scene. If you could take a run out there, I got some questions to ask here."

Whatever Barney Nathan had been prepared for, it wasn't that. He went from indignant to efficient at the drop of a hat. "On my way," he said, and hurried to his car.

Rick Reed came out the front door, followed by his camera crew. "Hey," he demanded. "What's going on?"

Aaron Grant flashed Chief Harper a pleading look.

"I'm not ready to make a statement," Harper said.

"You don't need it," Becky Baldwin said. "Judy Vale's neighbor got killed. The doctor's on his way out there now."

"Hot damn!" Rick Reed said. "Come on, guys. Let's go!"

The crew clomped down the stairs, headed for the van.

Becky Baldwin followed.

Aaron looked after them, said, "Sherry, I gotta go."

"Of course you do," Sherry said. "Cora, you don't need me anymore. I'm going with Aaron."

Cora Felton looked betrayed. "Hey, wait a minute. If anybody's going out there, it ought to be me."

"You got a tournament to run," Iris Cooper reminded her.

"Maybe, maybe not," Chief Harper said. "My gut feeling is to close this game down and start grilling everyone."

"You've gotta be kidding!" Iris Cooper was shocked.

"He's not," Cora Felton told her. "It's a murder, Iris. A double homicide. We've gotta cooperate. It's our civic responsibility." Cora was really enjoying this.

"She's right, Iris. I'm sorry, but this is murder."

"I know it is," Iris Cooper said. "You happen to have ten grand on you, Chief?"

Chief Harper blinked. "I beg your pardon?"

"This trivial little game has sold over a hundred tickets at a hundred bucks apiece. That's ten grand we'd have to refund if you close us down now. Ten grand we don't happen to have." Iris jerked her thumb at Cora. "Due to the controversy over the charity Cora picked, in order to show support and make it a moot point, the selectmen went ahead and sent the National Children's Placement Fund a check. Which means the refund money would have to be raised. And that's just the entry fees. Wait'll the out-of-towners start complaining about the money they spent on bed-and-breakfasts if the tournament doesn't happen."

"I got a homicide here," Chief Harper said unhappily.

"No, you got a homicide *there,*" Iris Cooper reminded him tartly. "Shouldn't you be out at the crime scene?"

"My boys can handle it. Right now it's my understanding Mrs. Roth was here for your so-called Fun Night."

"Where did you hear that, Chief?" Cora Felton asked it innocently.

Chief Harper grimaced. "Every now and then would you mind if *I* asked the questions? One of the neighbors saw her there. Was surprised to see her there, really, her being so reclusive and all. Now, if *I* might ask a question, did *you* happen to see Mrs. Roth at Fun Night?"

"As a matter of fact, I did."

"Did you happen to notice who she was talking to?"

"Yes, I did. First time I saw her she was talking to Paul Thornhill. You know. The boy-toy celebrity contestant. He'd be knee-deep in chicks if he hadn't shown up with his wife."

"Mrs. Roth was talking to him?"

"Yes, she was. And you'll get a chance to ask him about it, because he'll be out that door any minute." Cora Felton explained about Paul Thornhill's habit of finishing first.

"That'll be handy," Chief Harper said. "Did you see Mrs. Roth talking to anyone else?"

"Two people, actually. Though one of them isn't what you want."

"I'll be the judge of that. Why isn't it what I want?"

"You know the mechanic, Marty Haskel?"

"Of course I do. He services the cruisers."

"Oh, yeah? Well, I hope he's happy about that. All he's done since the tournament's begun is bitch, bitch, bitch."

"Marty was talking to Mrs. Roth?"

"In a manner of speaking. He was actually talking to Paul Thornhill. He came over to gripe about Thornhill's wife winning one of the games. Mrs. Thornhill won the first game because her husband helped her. Marty Haskel figured that was cheating."

"What's this got to do with Mrs. Roth?" The chief was no longer sounding quite so patient.

"She was talking to Thornhill when Marty Haskel came over. Haskel became abusive, Mrs. Roth intercepted him. She led him away."

"Abusive?"

"Verbally abusive. Anyway, that's when she talked to Marty Haskel, but it isn't what you want."

"And what is?" Chief Harper said through clenched teeth.

The door banged open and Paul Thornhill emerged. He frowned at the sight of the policeman, as if Chief Harper were a contestant who had somehow beaten him out the door.

"The police," Paul Thornhill said, taking in the chief's uniform. "Are you raiding the place?"

"Hardly," Chief Harper said. "And you would be . . ."

Paul Thornhill's sea-green eyes widened. He chuckled and shook his head, as if amused at not being recognized. "I'm Paul Thornhill. I'm one of the contestants." The phrase *one of the contestants* was also tossed off with a half chuckle, clearly quite a joke to those in the know.

"Yeah, well, you happen to be the one I want." Chief Harper sounded unimpressed. "I understand last night you were talking to Mrs. Roth."

"Who?"

"An elderly woman who showed up alone. Surely you remember her?"

Paul Thornhill shrugged helplessly. "I talk to so many people at these events. . . ."

"You remember the man who complained about you helping your wife?" Cora put in.

"Him I remember."

"Mrs. Roth was the woman who pulled him away."

"Oh, her. Yes, I remember her now." Thornhill looked inquiringly at the chief. "Why do you want to know?"

"She was found dead early this morning."

Paul Thornhill's mouth dropped open, but nothing emerged.

"The woman was murdered. It becomes necessary to trace her movements."

"But that's ridiculous."

"Yes, it is," Chief Harper said. "If I had to choose a word to sum up the situation, *ridiculous* would be a good choice. Unfortunately, that's what I'm stuck with. The woman was killed. I have to find out why. So I'd appreciate the answer to some ridiculous questions."

"A harmless old lady like that. Who would want to kill her?" Paul Thornhill seemed overwhelmed.

"Who, indeed? Can you recall what she was talking to you about?"

"Nothing much. I had been pointed out to her as a celebrity. She wanted to know what it was like playing in tournaments. At least, that was what she kept asking. I got the impression she didn't care about the questions, she just wanted to talk to someone famous. Not that I'm famous, but you know what I mean."

"She didn't mention the other murder?"

"The other murder? No, why should she?"

"She lived across the street from the victim."

Before Paul Thornhill could comment, Craig Carmichael came out the door. He took one look at the assembled gathering and slithered away to his corner of the steps.

"Who's he?" Chief Harper demanded.

"That's Craig Carmichael," Cora told him. "One of the contestants."

"Well, he acts guilty as hell."

"He isn't. That's how he always acts."

Ned Doowacker came out, looked around, announced glumly, "Still third." If he noted the presence of Bakerhaven's chief of police, he didn't acknowledge it. "That was a tough one. Even you took longer this time, Thornhill. No matter. I'm still third, and if I get in the finals, anything can happen."

More contestants came out the door. Chief Harper looked at them, scratched his head, and motioned Cora Felton off to the side. Iris Cooper came too.

"All right," Chief Harper said. "I got a hundred people in there, and I haven't a clue which ones are witnesses. You mentioned her talking to three people. This Thornhill guy. Marty the mechanic. And who would the third be?"

"Billy Pickens."

"Now, there's a name I've heard before. Is Pickens inside?"

"I'm a cohost, Chief, not a ticket taker."

"What about you, Iris?"

"I don't even know Billy Pickens."

"Well, can you find out?"

"As soon as the game's over."

Chief Harper shook his head grimly. "No. Find out now. Otherwise, I'm stoppin' your game."

Iris Cooper gave him a withering look but went inside. She was out a minute later with a clipboard. "Okay, I got a list of contestants here. It's not alphabetical, but Billy Pickens doesn't seem to be on it."

Chief Harper grabbed the list, scanned it quickly. He sighed. "Okay, Iris. You wanna keep your tournament going, we'll effect a compromise. Leave Harvey Beerbaum in charge." He jerked his thumb at Cora Felton. "But *she's* coming with me."

20

AARON AND SHERRY FOLLOWED BECKY BALDWIN'S CAR AS IT bumped over the tracks and turned onto the short street where Mrs. Roth's house stood. Two police cars, the doctor's car, an ambulance, and the Channel 8 van were parked out front. There was a crime-scene ribbon around the porch. Officer Sam Brogan sat on the front steps. The neighbors were gathered in the side yard.

Aaron pulled in behind Becky Baldwin, and he and Sherry got out.

The Channel 8 news team was preparing to shoot. The crew set up the camera, while Rick Reed combed his hair and made sure the crest of his Channel 8 blazer could be seen poking out from under his topcoat.

Rick Reed spotted Becky Baldwin, waved her over. "Ms. Baldwin," he said, thrusting the microphone in her face. "As attorney for Joey Vale, do you have any comment on this second murder, the murder of Judy Vale's friend and good neighbor—" He broke off and said, "Oh, hell! What's her name?"

"Felicity Roth," Becky Baldwin said. "Yes, I do. My client,

despondent over the tragic death of his wife, drank too much and was thrown in jail. He's been in jail since yesterday afternoon. He was behind bars when Ms. Roth was killed. This second murder, unfortunate as it is, completely exonerates my client from suspicion."

"Nice," Rick Reed said to Becky Baldwin. He turned to the camera crew. "Okay, on me. Medium close-up, crime-scene ribbon in the background. Are we focused? Good. *And there you have it. The violent murder of Mrs. Roth from the perspective of Joey Vale, whom just a day ago the police were touting as a suspect.*

"Now we have two murders, and according to Joey Vale's lawyer, we have two unsolved *murders. This is Rick Reed, Channel 8 News, in Bakerhaven, Connecticut.*

"Cut," Rick Reed said. To his sound man he added, "Remind me to loop a wild line of the name *Felicity Roth*." He swung back to Becky Baldwin. "Of course, we probably won't use that wrap-up. It's early in the day, who knows what we're gonna get. We always shoot a lot more than we use." He flashed a mouthful of capped teeth. "Of course, I'm *sure* we'll use *you*."

"Yeah," Becky said, but it was clear she wasn't listening. Having given her statement, she had no more use at the moment for Rick Reed. She strode over to Mrs. Roth's house, where Sam Brogan was riding herd over the crime-scene ribbon. If anyone was immune to Becky Baldwin's charm, it had to be the cranky Bakerhaven police officer. Brogan stroked his mustache, popped his gum, and declared, "Can't go in."

"I know that, Sam," Becky purred. "I'm just wondering what you can tell me."

"I can tell you you can't go in."

"Can you tell me anything about the crime?"

"Nope."

"Can you tell me who's in there now?"

Sam Brogan popped his gum.

"I know it's not Chief Harper," Becky persisted sweetly, " 'cause I just left him back at town hall. Is Dan Finley in there?"

"I ain't sayin'. You wanna count police cruisers, I can't stop you."

"I'm counting two, which means Dan's in there. You think I could talk to him?"

"Nope."

"Why not?"

"If he's not there, you can't talk to him. And if he is there, you can't go in."

"What if he came out?"

Sam Brogan said nothing.

"Thanks for your help," Becky said.

"Pleasure," Sam grunted.

Becky Baldwin looked at her watch, snorted in disgust. She walked back over to Rick Reed. "I'm out of here. This is a waste of time."

"Where are you going?"

"Back to town hall to hunt up the judge and bail out my client."

"Hold up a minute." Rick Reed seemed torn. "I should be here, the body's comin' out. But according to them"—he jerked his thumb at the neighbors—"old lady Roth was at your puzzle shindig last night, talking to your hotshot crossword-puzzle guy."

"Paul Thornhill?"

"Who else?" Rick Reed said. He was clearly not pleased. "Listen, guys," he told his crew. "Stay here and shoot the corpse. I'm running over to town hall to check out a lead. Soon as you're done, hurry over and meet me there."

Rick Reed and Becky Baldwin climbed into her car and took off.

Aaron Grant, watching them go, seemed as torn as Rick Reed had been. At least in Sherry's estimation.

"You wanna go too?" Sherry said to him.

"I gotta follow the story."

"That's the only reason?"

"What other reason would there be?"

"You tell me."

"No other reason."

"Fine."

Sherry turned her back, studied the crime scene.

Aaron grabbed her by the arm, turned her around. He held her by the shoulders, looked at her.

Sherry twisted away. "Don't do that."

"I just wanna talk."

"You wanna talk, talk. Lay off the physical."

"I thought we had a relationship."

"A relationship does not mean pushing someone around." Sherry exhaled, ran her hand over her face. "I'm sorry. My husband was an abusive schmuck. I won't be manhandled."

"That was not my intention."

"Maybe not. That doesn't make it any better." Sherry paused, then asked, "What did you want to say?"

"I was wrong. When I said there was no other reason. I hate that guy Reed. I don't want him getting a jump on me. It really burns me."

"I can see that it does," Sherry said.

Aaron looked at her sharply.

Sherry said, "You think the story's there or here? Because you thought the story was *here*. You were there, and we came here. Now you're here, and you wanna go there. Why the change of mind?"

"It would appear there's nothing here to get."

"In that case," Sherry said, "let's go."

"Where?"

"Back to town hall."

"You agree with me?"

"Agree? What's to agree? You're the reporter. I'm just along for the ride."

Sherry marched back to Aaron's car, opened the passenger door, and got in.

After a moment, Aaron followed.

21

CORA FELTON COULD HARDLY BELIEVE HER GOOD FORTUNE. BEING yanked out of the crossword-puzzle tournament to take part in a murder investigation. A *double* murder investigation. It was almost too good to be true. She sat in the front of Chief Harper's police cruiser, trying hard not to look like the cat who swallowed the cream *and* the canary.

"So, where are we going? To grill Billy Pickens?"

"No. To check out the crime scene."

"Haven't you already done that?"

"Yeah, but you haven't."

Cora blinked. "You want me to case the crime scene?"

"I value your opinion."

"Is that so? I thought you wanted me to finger Billy Pickens. As the guy seen talking to Mrs. Roth."

"I do, and you will. But I'd like you to see the crime scene first, before they move the body."

Cora shivered slightly, and her skin tingled. The words were strangely exciting. She'd seen a corpse before, but she'd never been *asked* to see one.

It was one of her finest moments.

"So, who found the body?" she asked.

"Ah," Chief Harper said. "I was wondering how long before you asked who found the body."

"I'd have got there sooner, except you kept giving me the I-ask-the-questions-here routine."

"That was in front of the others. Now it's just you and me."

"So who found it?"

"Cleaning lady."

"Oh?"

"Yeah. She had a cleaning lady once a week, two hours, Saturday morning, ten till twelve."

"Big spender."

"Yeah. Basically just to do the floors. Mrs. Roth didn't like mopping, couldn't get the vacuum up and down stairs."

"And this cleaning woman walked right in?"

"She had keys. That was the deal. Mrs. Roth didn't like her underfoot, always arranged to be shopping when she was around. The cleaning lady, one Selma Howe, arrived this morning, was a little surprised to see Mrs. Roth's car still in the driveway, walked in, and found her dead. Which is a bit of luck for Joey Vale. If it weren't for Selma, it could be days before Mrs. Roth was found. The way things are now, Joey's free and clear. He was arrested yesterday afternoon. Mrs. Roth was seen last night at Fun Night. *After* Joey Vale was arrested. She was alive when he went to jail, she's dead and he's still there." The chief was silent a moment, then he asked, "You have any theory involving iceboxes, trunks of cars, or what have you, any theory whatsoever how Joey Vale could have done it?"

"Two killers."

"Huh?"

"Joey Vale snuffed his wife. Someone else croaked Mrs. Roth."

Chief Harper grimaced. "Huge stretch. It was bad enough with your cockamamie theories that he killed his wife when all we were looking at was killing his wife. Now you wanna throw in a copycat killer who happens to kill the chief witness to the first murder. Only he's not the first murderer, he's just eliminating a witness who could have been real detrimental to Joey Vale, in the event one of your first stupid theories was true."

"Hey, did you bring me along just to beat me up?"

"Not at all. I brought you along to see the crime scene."

A car whizzed by them, going back the other way.

"Becky Baldwin," Chief Harper noted.

"Yeah. Joyriding with some guy," Cora observed. "She's sure in a hurry for someone whose client's just been cleared of murder. What's the speed limit here?"

"Forty-five. If I didn't have this murder, I'd nab her."

"I wish you would. Some people have no respect for the law." Cora punctuated her statement by nodding self-righteously just as Sherry and Aaron zoomed by, gaining on Becky Baldwin.

Chief Harper's eyes twinkled. "You were saying?"

Cora stuck out her chin, maintained a dignified silence.

Chief Harper bumped the cruiser over the railroad track and curved around toward Mrs. Roth's house. He pulled up behind the Emergency Medical Service vehicle and he and Cora climbed out. The camera crew lined him instantly in their sights, but to his surprise and relief, no one thrust a microphone in his face.

Sam Brogan, patrolling the crime-scene ribbon, said, "You bringin' *her* in?" His tone betrayed just what he thought of that.

Chief Harper gave Sam a look. He and Cora Felton ducked under the ribbon, went up on Mrs. Roth's porch. The front door was propped open with a bright orange traffic cone.

"Keep your hands at your sides, don't touch a thing," Harper warned Cora. "I'm gonna catch enough grief for letting you in here. And now those bozos got it on tape."

There were three emergency medical technicians in the tiny foyer, one of them holding up a folded gurney. Apparently they had been there for some time—despite the fact it was a murder, all looked bored.

From the living room came the distinctive, prissy whine of Dr. Barney Nathan—"Are you *about* done?"—then the voice of young Dan Finley: "Just a few more shots."

Chief Harper cautioned once again, "Don't touch."

Cora Felton tidily kept her hands glued to her sides, followed Chief Harper through the door.

And stepped into the living room where she had interviewed Mrs. Roth three days before. The fifties living room, with its vinyl couch and the rabbit ears on the TV.

Only now there was a dead woman on the floor.

Which made the whole thing rather surreal. It was as if a *Perry Mason* scene had gotten spliced into the middle of an episode of *Ozzie and Harriet*.

Officer Dan Finley bent over the corpse with his Polaroid, snapping another photo.

Barney Nathan stood nearby, arms folded, tapping his foot. His expression on seeing Chief Harper was priceless. It was *your-father's-here-little-boy-now-you're-really-going-to-get-whipped*.

"Dale," Barney Nathan said. "Wanna speed this up for me? If you want an accurate time of death, I gotta get her to the lab."

"You can't do that here?"

"Not unless you wanna risk contaminating your crime scene. I take the body temperature from the liver, and that means blood."

"You about finished, Dan?" Chief Harper asked his young officer patiently.

"Just one more shot."

Cora Felton got the impression that one more shot had more to do with Dan Finley not letting the doctor push him around than with any practical need for more photographs of the victim and the scene of the crime.

Dan moved to the side to fire off another shot, and Cora got her first good look at the body. It was unsettling at best. Cora had seen other bodies before, but none of them had been strangled. Mrs. Roth's eyes were bulged, and her tongue was bloated and lolling out of her mouth. Cora had to steel herself to keep from looking away.

She overcame her revulsion, said to Chief Harper, "This is exactly how she was found?"

"Yes, of course. Nothing's been disturbed."

"Well, it's about to be," Barney Nathan said, still tapping his foot. "Can I get her out of here now?"

"Yeah, take her," Chief Harper told him. "And get going on the time of death. It's gonna be important."

"I thought it would be," the doctor rejoined, shooting daggers at Dan Finley. He waved in the EMTs, who opened the gurney and lifted Mrs. Roth onto it. The EMTs, still looking bored, wheeled her out the door within minutes.

"Okay, Dan," Chief Harper said. "Start dusting for fingerprints."

"I'll get the kit," Dan Finley said, and went out the door after the medical team.

Cora Felton looked around the room. She walked over to the window. She rummaged in her purse, fished out a pen, used it to nudge aside the curtain.

"What are you doing?" Chief Harper asked.

"This is where she sat and watched. This is probably why she's dead. She was a busybody who spied on all her neighbors. From everything she told me and Aaron Grant, for all her spying she didn't really know a damn thing. Obviously that wasn't true." Cora indicated the chalk outline Dan Finley had drawn on the floor.

"Obviously," Chief Harper said humorlessly. "It would appear she tried to blackmail Judy's killer."

Cora Felton shook her head. "I don't think so."

Chief Harper frowned.

"I don't think money meant that much to her," Cora said.

"Then what did?"

Cora sighed. "I think she just wanted to be important. I can't imagine her blackmailing anyone. But I can see her bragging about what she knew. Gloating, almost. I think gloating's what got her killed."

"That's a theory," Chief Harper pointed out sourly, "based on your superficial impression of the woman. Not on any physical evidence. Against my better judgment, I let you in to see the crime scene. So what does it tell you?"

Cora Felton looked around the room in which Mrs. Roth had lived the final moments of her life. She shook her head.

"Not a damn thing."

22

BILLY PICKENS LIVED IN A TWO-STORY PALE YELLOW FRAME HOUSE
on a pleasant tree-lined street of similar structures three miles out
of town. Chief Harper pulled into the driveway and parked behind
a Ford station wagon. Cora and the chief got out, detoured around
a pair of girls' bicycles—one with training wheels—went up on the
front porch, and rang the bell.

The door was opened by the small woman Cora had seen the
night before with Billy Pickens. The woman was clearly not prepared for visitors. She wore a baggy sweatshirt and old blue jeans,
and her hair was tied up with a red kerchief. She looked exasper-
ated.

"Mrs. Pickens?" Chief Harper said.

"I'm Sara Pickens. What do you want?"

"Sorry to bother you, ma'am. It's a police matter. If I could talk
to you and your husband . . ."

"We're sort of busy. What's this about?"

"It's rather urgent. If you wouldn't mind getting your husband."

"Billy's cleaning out the basement. I'm painting a bookshelf for the girls."

When she said it, Cora noticed the flecks of pink on her cheek and could smell turpentine. "We're sorry to interrupt you," Cora said. "We'll try to be brief."

Sara Pickens frowned. "You're the puzzle woman."

"Yes, I am. I saw you at Fun Night."

"Fun for crossword-puzzle people, maybe. No offense, but frankly, it's not our thing."

"But you went."

"Yes, we did. And some of the desserts were quite nice. But once you pay the baby-sitter—"

"I understand," Chief Harper interposed. "If you wouldn't mind getting your husband . . ."

"What's this all about?"

"Someone got killed."

Mrs. Pickens clapped her hand to her mouth. A trace of pink paint adhered to her lip. She murmured, "Oh," then said, "Come in."

Sara Pickens led them into her kitchen, waved them in the general direction of the table, opened a door behind the refrigerator, and hollered down the stairs, "Billy, come up here!"

There came an indistinct rumble from the depths below. Sara tried one more *Billy!,* then gave up and clomped on down the stairs. She was back moments later, leading her husband, similarly dressed in sweatshirt and jeans. But while his wife sported paint, Billy Pickens was decked out in spiderwebs and grime. He was also sweating profusely. His face was flushed, and his dark hair was matted. Nonetheless, he looked young and handsome. Cora put his age at somewhere around thirty. But she was more intrigued by the fact that Billy Pickens appeared hostile. More hostile than the situation would seem to warrant. This young man definitely had a chip on his shoulder. He looked defiantly at Chief Harper and demanded, "What's this about a murder?"

"Hate to bother you," Chief Harper said, "but the fact is there's been another murder."

That instantly took the wind out of Billy's sails. He opened his mouth, snapped it shut. "Another murder?"

"Yes. I need to ask you and your wife a few questions. Relating to last night. At the Fun Night. This is Miss Cora Felton, who was in charge of the event. Perhaps if she could talk to your wife, you and I could talk together, and we could clear this up quickly."

Sara Pickens asserted herself. Though small of stature, she was not one to be pushed around. She thrust out her chin, pointed a paint-smeared finger at Chief Harper. "Now, just a minute. If you're asking questions about last night, I was there, and I want to hear. No offense, but I don't want to go off in the other room with her and talk about something else."

"I didn't say something else. I meant we could divide the task."

"That won't be necessary." Sara Pickens shot her cuff, looked at her watch. "Billy's taking the girls to the movies, that's at two o'clock. We've got plenty of time, even with picking up Lucy on the way. Isn't that right, Billy? No way you're leaving before one-fifteen. Even with time to take a shower and change, we've got time for this. So park yourself at the kitchen table, Chief, or stand up if you prefer, and fire away. Now, who got killed and what's the score?"

Before Chief Harper could answer, the door flew open and two little girls exploded into the room. The younger wore pigtails, the older, bright red barrettes.

"Daddy, Daddy," cried the younger. "Wendy stole my doll!"

"Did not," Wendy said. "Ellie's telling tales."

Ellie, cute as a button, folded her arms and stuck out her chin, looking uncannily like her mother as she did so. "Then where's my doll?"

Wendy played innocent. "How should I know?"

"Wendy, give Ellie back her doll," Sara Pickens said.

Wendy, who couldn't have been more than five, looked utterly betrayed. "How come you always take *her* side?" she wailed.

"How come you always take her doll?" Billy Pickens said.

Wendy gave him a *harrumph* look but couldn't help smiling as she stalked off. Ellie trailed along triumphantly, saying, "See? I *told* you."

Sara Pickens closed the door behind her daughters. Then she turned and said, "Now then. You were saying?"

Chief Harper weighed the possibilities of prying Billy Pickens away from his wife, didn't figure them as good. "Okay," he conceded. "The woman who got killed is a widow named Mrs. Roth."

"Mrs.?" Sara Pickens said. "No first name?"

"Actually, the murdered woman's name was Felicity Roth, though I can't find anyone who ever used it."

"That's sad," Sara said, though whether she referred to Mrs. Roth's demise or the fact that no one called her Felicity was unclear. "What's it got to do with us?"

"Probably nothing. It's probably connected to the other murder. See, Mrs. Roth happened to live across the street from Judy Vale."

Chief Harper was looking at Billy Pickens when he said this. So was Cora Felton. It seemed to her the young man winced.

If Sara Pickens noticed her husband's reaction, she didn't let on. "What's that got to do with us?" she demanded.

"Probably nothing," Chief Harper repeated. "The fact is, Mrs. Roth was at Fun Night. And you and your husband were at Fun Night."

"Half of Bakerhaven was at Fun Night."

"Yes, they were. Mrs. Pickens, may I ask you if you noticed Mrs. Roth?"

"I don't even know who you're talking about."

"An elderly woman at the event alone. You didn't notice anyone of that type?"

"No. I did not."

"How about you, Mr. Pickens? You notice anyone like that?"

Billy Pickens looked increasingly uncomfortable. "I don't see what this has to do with anything."

"Neither do I," Chief Harper agreed amiably. "But the woman

is dead, so we have to trace her movements. Did anyone of that description talk to you?"

"When you say *that description* . . ."

"I'm talking loosely," Chief Harper said. "But let there be no mistake. Did any woman identify herself to you, either by that name, or by describing herself as Judy Vale's neighbor?"

Billy Pickens squirmed.

"See here," Sara Pickens said. "This seems to me like an interrogation."

"It certainly shouldn't be," Chief Harper told her. "But Billy was observed talking to a woman of Mrs. Roth's description by several witnesses. Including Miss Felton here. So I'm fairly sure of my ground."

Sara's eyes narrowed. Then widened. "Billy. Is that the woman who was talking to you while I was getting a piece of cheesecake?"

"I suppose so," Billy mumbled. "Though what she wanted, I have no clue."

"What did she say?" Chief Harper asked.

"Just what you said. That she was a neighbor of the woman who got killed. Vale. That's what she was saying. That she was her neighbor. She was kinda boasting about it, like she was proud of the fact."

"Interesting," Chief Harper said. "And why was she telling this to you?"

"I have no idea." As if inspired, Billy Pickens added, "I got the impression she was telling everyone."

"What gave you that impression?"

"Her attitude. The fact she was bragging about it."

"And what else did she say? Aside from the fact that she was Judy Vale's neighbor? What other information did she claim to have?"

"She didn't claim anything. She just acted as if she knew something. As if she knew more than she was telling."

"Like what?"

"I have no idea."

"No hint that she knew the identity of Judy's murderer?"

"Good heavens, no," Billy Pickens said, shocked. "I'd have re-membered that!"

"Yes, I'd have thought you would," the chief agreed. "Was there anything else specific in what she told you?"

"Not at all. In fact, I gathered this was a recitation she'd been trying on several people." Having hit on that explanation, Billy Pickens clung to it.

"Interesting," Chief Harper repeated. "So, there was nothing specific involving you?"

"No. Of course not!"

"No suggestion of meeting her later to discuss this further?"

"There was nothing to discuss. Whether she made suggestions to others, I couldn't say. Obviously, since someone killed her, she struck pay dirt, so to speak. But whether she invited her killer or whether he showed up on his own, I certainly couldn't say. Perhaps others can be more helpful."

"Perhaps they can," Chief Harper agreed. "Did you notice her talking to anyone else at the town hall?"

"No, I didn't. I barely noticed her at all. If you hadn't reminded me, I wouldn't have remembered."

"And I can vouch for that," Sara Pickens interjected. "Because I just went to get some coffee and cheesecake. Which didn't take long. On my way back I saw Billy talking to this old woman. By the time I got to him, she was gone. It was a very brief conversation. And I didn't notice her after that either, if that's your next ques-tion."

"Actually, I was going to ask if you and your husband came home together after Fun Night."

"Of course we did," Billy Pickens said. "What kind of question is that?"

"And you were both home for the rest of the evening?"

Billy started to answer, then he hesitated.

"Yes? What is it?"

"Nothing, really," Sara Pickens interposed. "Except Billy drove the baby-sitter home."

"I see." Chief Harper nodded, as if this were the most natural thing in the world and he would have expected Billy to do no less. "And I assume he came right back?"

"Of course," Sara Pickens said, a little too hastily. She shot her husband a glance. "Now, if there's nothing else, we've got work to do—"

"Nothing else for the moment," Chief Harper answered. "Thank you both for your time."

Sara Pickens escorted them to her front door. Chief Harper leaned his ear in after it closed, but all he and Cora Felton could hear was the young housewife's footsteps fading away.

23

"ALL RIGHT, WHAT THE HECK'S GOING ON?"

Chief Harper swung the car out of the Pickenses' driveway. "On?"

Cora scowled. "Don't play coy with me, Chief. You didn't need me to grill Billy Pickens. You even tried to send me out of the room with his wife. I don't believe that's what you brought me along for. So why is it that you're so eager for my expertise that you yanked me out of the tournament—not that I wasn't happy to go—but why did you do it? Come on, what's up?"

"Now you're talking," Chief Harper said. "You were a little slow when I picked you up, but now you're right on the ball."

"Oh, is that so? Well, would you like to fill me in, because I'm really tired of playing games."

Chief Harper pulled the cruiser up on the shoulder of the country road, put the car in park. He reached in his pocket, pulled out a folded piece of paper, passed it over.

Cora unfolded it with mounting misgivings.

Sucked in her breath.

It was—

A crossword puzzle.

Her worst dread.

And yet . . .

The sudden rush of icy fear was replaced by a sudden surge of relief.

The heading read: *CURIOUS CANINES by Craig Carmichael.*

This was not some cryptic clue left by the killer. It was one of the games from Fun Night. The puzzle didn't have a thing to do with murder.

Better still, it had been filled in. So even if Chief Harper got the crazy idea it *might* mean something, Cora wouldn't have to solve it. As far as crossword puzzles went, it was the best of all possible worlds.

Cora looked it over with assurance.

"So," Cora said, looking at the chief. "It's a puzzle from Fun Night. What about it?"

"It was found on the body."

"Oh?"

"Under the body, actually. Mrs. Roth was lying on top of it, just a corner peeking out."

"It wasn't there when I saw her body."

"No, it wasn't. I'd removed it."

"And immediately bagged it for evidence?"

"Yes, that would have been better, wouldn't it?" the chief replied mildly. "But I didn't want anyone to see what it was."

"Why, Chief? It's just a stupid crossword puzzle from Fun Night. We know Mrs. Roth went to Fun Night. That fact was established by several witnesses, including me. We don't need a crossword puzzle to place her there."

"No, but we have to stop and figure. How does the puzzle wind up on her body?"

"Are you kidding? Half of the town got a puzzle. Volunteers were handing them to everybody there. They even gave one to me."

"What did you do with yours?"

P¹	A²	T³	H⁴	S⁵		O⁶	G⁷	L⁸	E⁹	S¹⁰		C¹¹	D¹²	E¹³
A¹⁴	P	R	I	L		M¹⁵	O	O	R	E		H¹⁶	A	D
S¹⁷	H	A	D	O	W¹⁸	B	O	X	E	R		O¹⁹	L	E
T²⁰	I	M	E	C	A	R	D		E²¹	R²²	W	I	N	
E²³	S	P	O	U	S	E		D²⁴	I²⁵	N	A	H		
		U²⁶	M	P		B²⁷	A	R	E	F	O	O²⁸	T²⁹	
G³⁰	E³¹	N³²	T		A³³	R	R	A	S		U³⁴	K	E	
A³⁵	D	O		T³⁶	I³⁷	D	I	E	S	T		N³⁸	R	A
L³⁹	I	P		A⁴⁰	R	A	B	S		E⁴¹	D	A	M	
S⁴²	T	O	P⁴³	P	A	G	E		G⁴⁴	A⁴⁵	P			
	I⁴⁶	R	E	N	E		C⁴⁷	O	S	I	E	S⁴⁸	T⁴⁹	T⁵⁰
J⁵¹	A⁵²	N	E	S		K⁵³	E	E	P	S	A	K	E	
A⁵⁴	R	T		T⁵⁵	R⁵⁶	E⁵⁷	N	D	S	E	T	T	E	R
D⁵⁸	I	E		R⁵⁹	A	N	E	E		C⁶⁰	L	E	W	S
E⁶¹	A	R		Y⁶²	E	S	E	S		T⁶³	E	N	S	E

CURIOUS CANINES
by Craig Carmichael

ACROSS

1 Ways
6 Leers at
11 B–F connection
14 Eliot's cruelest month
15 "Arthur" star
16 Possessed
17 Sparring dog?
19 Bullfight cheer
20 Work record
21 German field marshal Rommel

DOWN

1 Fake jewelry
2 Genus of plant lice
3 Chaplin persona
4 Robbers' roost
5 Congressman and Union army officer Henry Warner
6 17th century card game
7 Not bad
8 Bagels and _____
9 Before (Arch.)

23 Marry
24 Shore of TV fame
26 Arbiter
27 Shoeless
30 Fancy dude
33 Handwoven wall hanging
34 Tiny Tim's instrument
35 Fuss
36 Most kempt
38 Gun club
39 Sass
40 Desert people
41 Cheese
42 Work obstruction
44 Clothing chain
46 "Goodnight, ____"
47 Most comfy (Var.)
51 Dames
53 Memento
54 Oil paintings
55 Fashionable dog?
58 Expire
59 Hindu princess
60 Detective's finds (Var.)
61 Corn unit
62 Affirmatives
63 Present, for instance

10 Most peaceful
11 Hungry dog?
12 Surrealist Salvador
13 Paradise
18 Stinging insect
22 English flyboys
24 Risks
25 Retirement funds
27 Payoff
28 Edible pod
29 Mets or Yankees
30 Fellas cohorts
31 Change text
32 Scoreless dog?
33 Saying
36 Carole King album
37 Persia, now
41 Letter
43 Before, in prefixes
44 Leaves
45 Feature
47 Gives up
48 Consumed
49 Angles
50 Curt
51 Green gemstone
52 Operatic solo
53 Leg joint
56 Actress ____ Dawn Chong
57 Printers' measures

"Threw it away. What did I want with a puzzle?"

"Yeah, well, she took hers home. Assuming it's hers."

"Oh, come on, Chief. You think the killer deliberately left the puzzle on the body?"

"It's a theory."

"It's a *bad* theory. It makes no sense."

"Why?"

Cora exhaled in exasperation. "All right, this puzzle is folded. Did you fold it?"

"Yes and no."

"Could you be any more irritating?"

"Sorry. The puzzle was lying under the body. It was not folded, but it *had been* folded. Those crease marks were not made by me. I merely refolded it."

"Exactly," Cora said. "And do you know what that means?"

"I'd be happy to have you tell me."

"The woman was at Fun Night. Someone handed her a puzzle. She didn't know what to do with it. She wasn't near a garbage can, she wasn't going to just throw it on the floor. She folded it, stuck it in her pocket. Or her purse. Or whatever. And wound up taking it home."

"So who solved it?"

"She did."

"Oh, really? Did the woman ever express any interest in cross-word puzzles? Had she done one before?"

"Probably not. She probably never even tried. But this is different. She comes home, she's been given a puzzle, she finds it in her pocket or her purse, she checks it out. It's called *Curious Canines*. Who knows, maybe she likes dogs. She takes a pencil, starts to fiddle. Lo and behold, it's not that hard. So she keeps at it, and this is the result."

"Uh-huh."

"You don't buy that?"

"I can buy that. But *why* does she sit there doing the puzzle? Is that her normal routine?"

Cora considered. "No. That time of night she'd always be getting ready for bed. She isn't because she's expecting someone. So she's doing the puzzle to kill time."

"Exactly," Chief Harper said. "I'm going to have a handwriting expert check this out to see if she wrote it. Though what they can tell from just capital letters I have no idea. But it's certainly one explanation."

"You got another?"

"Sure. The killer left it on the body."

"Oh, come on."

"You got a problem with that?"

"I certainly do. The killer left the puzzle. For what purpose? It's a simple, ordinary puzzle, nothing special about it, everyone in town had one."

"That may be. But the clue may not be in the puzzle itself, but in the fact it was left."

Cora took a breath, exhaled. "It seems to me we're back where we started, Chief. You brought me out here to show me a crossword puzzle. On the one hand it has nothing to do with the crime, on the other it's already filled in. You can come up with as many theories as you like for how it got there, but most likely it's just like I say. The woman brought it home, did it herself. She was strangled and fell on the puzzle, and there you are, that's all there is to it. In which case I don't see why you need me."

Chief Harper looked at her for a moment, sighed, reached in his jacket pocket, pulled out another folded piece of paper. Handed it over without a word.

Cora unfolded it.

Her mouth fell open.

24

CORA FELTON STARED AT CHIEF HARPER IN DISBELIEF. "DON'T tell me. This was found on the body of Judy Vale?"

"It was on a notepad on the kitchen table. Her body was on the kitchen floor."

"And this was on the table in plain sight?"

"No, the pad was facedown."

"Uh-huh. When did you find this?"

"When I processed the crime scene."

"When you arrested Joey Vale?"

"Shortly thereafter."

"So when you came to see me—to tell me to butt out of the case—you already knew about this?"

"What's your point?"

"You told me the case was none of my business. You said I'd helped you in the past when the crimes were crossword-puzzle related, but this one wasn't."

The chief was silent.

"That was a lie."

"A pretty good one too," Chief Harper said complacently.

"Why did you lie to me?"

"I was trying to get a rise out of you. See if you'd contradict me. See if you knew any different."

"But how could I?"

"I thought Becky Baldwin tried to hire you."

"Oh, for goodness sakes."

"What's the matter?"

"Nothing, just kicking myself in the head. I bought her whole line of patter. *No PIs in town, travel time from Danbury.* She knew about this." Cora pointed to the paper. "She knew you'd ask me about it. She tried to sew me up so you couldn't."

Chief Harper nodded. "That's the way I see it. Which tells me something. Joey Vale must have known about this paper and told her about it. Because I certainly didn't."

"Then Joey knew it was there?"

"Only way it works."

"So why wouldn't he get rid of it?"

"That's what I'm asking you. How do you interpret this? What does this mean?"

Once again Cora felt an instinctive rush of dread at the thought of having to interpret words. She tried to tell herself it wasn't a crossword puzzle, it was just a clue. Even so, she found herself automatically prevaricating. "But why now, Chief? Why do you bring this to me now?"

He shrugged. "As long as Joey Vale was a suspect, I felt funny about it, what with Becky approaching you. As you so aptly pointed out, even his alibi didn't clear him. But this does. There's no way he killed Mrs. Roth. And not to pooh-pooh your two-killers theory, but not to give it any credence either, I would say I can safely cross Joey off my suspect list. So there's your clue. What do you think it means? And just a small hint—if you say it points to Joey Vale, I am not going to be pleased."

"Okay," Cora said, thinking hard. "To begin with, this is not a crossword puzzle, it's just a group of intersecting words. Doodled

on a piece of paper. Doodled. A person doodles when they're on the phone. Was there a phone near the kitchen table?"

"Absolutely."

"There's your theory. Judy Vale scribbled this while talking on the phone."

"If she did, what does it mean?"

Cora examined the page.

"It's perfectly obvious," Cora said. "She's thinking about her lover. She wrote the word *lover* and doodled a bunch of hearts. Then she's thinking Joey will be jealous of her lover. Which is what always happens and what she's afraid of. The *lights out* could mean a couple of things. She has to turn the lights out so Joey won't see her lover. Or, if Joey sees her lover, he'll punch his lights out."

"Oh, come on."

"What's wrong with that? The stars she doodles are what her lover sees after Joey hits him."

"Worse and worse. You got any ideas from the planet earth?"

Cora sniffed indignantly. "You want my opinion or not?"

"I'd like something I can work with."

"All right. Whatever else this may be, it's not a note to her lover."

"How do you figure?"

"If Judy's killed by a lover and a lover sees this, he's gonna get rid of it, figuring it points to him."

"Unless he figures it points to Joey Vale," Chief Harper argued.

"Yes. But would a person naturally think that?"

"Why not? I did. Not now, I mean when I arrested him. Why wouldn't I? His name's there, plus his motivation."

"Yeah, but you weren't Judy Vale's lover," Cora pointed out. "The lover sees this and all he's gonna see is the word *lover* screaming to high heaven. Assuming he killed her, I mean. In which case he'd get rid of it pronto."

"But Joey Vale wouldn't? Assuming he saw it and then told his lawyer about it?"

"I don't know, Chief, I gotta think about it. I've been trying to come up with ways Joey could have killed his wife. Now you want me to find ways he didn't."

"Can you do it?"

"If Joey's innocent, he comes home from the Rainbow Room absolutely blotto around one in the morning. His wife is dead on the kitchen floor. Joey doesn't see her. He staggers into the bedroom, pulls off his clothes, and falls into bed without even noticing his wife isn't there. In the morning he gets up, crashes around the house, and finds the body. He's thunderstruck. He can't remember strangling his wife, and while he's a little hazy on the night before, that sort of thing would be apt to stick in his mind."

"Don't be cute."

"Sorry. Anyway, Joey's not too out of it to realize he'll be the number-one suspect. So he takes a crowbar and breaks the lock on the kitchen door. I assume that wasn't hard?"

"The wood was old and rotten. All he had to do was stick the crowbar between the door and the jamb and pry. The screws popped off the metal covering and the bolt tore through the wood."

"What'd he do with the crowbar, by the way? Leave it by the door?"

Chief Harper shook his head. "Put it with his tools. Down in the cellar. Actually, not a bad move. It's his crowbar. He's gotta figure an intruder would bring his own crowbar, take it away with him."

"Okay, so that's what he does. Breaks the lock on his door to make it look like there'd been an intruder."

"And how does this intruder jibe with the lover mentioned on the pad? She can't be killed by an intruder *and* a lover. Unless they're one and the same. I mean, who breaks the lock on the kitchen door? Take it from Joey's point of view. *I'll break the lock on the kitchen door to make it look like someone broke in and then killed her. On the other hand, I'll leave the pad on the table so the police will think her lover did it.* You can't have it both ways."

"True."

"So how does that make sense?"

"Well, one possibility is we're all wet about the Becky Baldwin angle, and Joey never saw the pad."

"You buy that?"

"Nah. Becky's a little schemer, likes to play it real close to the vest. If you're withholding the clue, she's gonna withhold the fact she knows about it, until she can use it to her advantage. Plus the fact she tried to hire me, which is out of character." Cora shook her head. "No. Unless Becky found out some other way, Joey saw that pad."

"If she found out some other way, there's gonna be a major shake-up in the police department."

"Mmm. I say Joey saw the pad. He gets out of bed and he goes into the kitchen. Where's the kitchen phone?"

"On the wall just inside the door."

"So the table's next to that?"

"That's right."

"Where's the body?"

"On the other side of the room. Near the outside door. Which is probably what gave him the idea to break it in."

"Uh-huh. Is the outer kitchen door in a direct line with the inner kitchen door?"

"No, it's on the side wall. Why?"

"So Joey walks into the kitchen, doesn't see his wife, because her body is on the floor off to the side. But he sees this pad on the table. He picks it up, reads the cryptic message. The word *lover* is certainly clear. He slams the pad on the table, facedown. He goes to the refrigerator to get some milk or orange juice or maybe even a beer, and that's when he finds his wife's body on the floor. He panics, breaks the lock on the kitchen door, and goes off to work as if nothing happened. He doesn't take into account the pad of paper on the kitchen table. He doesn't even think of it until his lawyer cross-examines him on what he did."

Chief Harper nodded. "Works for me."

"In which case Becky Baldwin's never seen the pad, she just has Joey Vale's recollection of it."

"That's right."

"Crossed and double-crossed. No wonder she's so hot to hire me. She figures you'll bring me the clue. And I'll report it back to her. Maybe even give her a copy." Cora cocked her head. "Would I have had a copy to give?"

"Keep that one. Work on it in your spare time. See if you can come up with anything slightly more useful than what you just did."

"Don't be rude. Is it my fault your clue is an inexplicit jumble that implicates both Judy's husband *and* her lover?" Cora folded the doodle, stuck it in her purse. "So if Becky hasn't seen this and she knows you have it, why doesn't she just demand it?"

Chief Harper shrugged. "I'm sure she would have, if I hadn't dropped the charges against Joey. I think she sees the doodle as a bargaining chip. She knows I'm withholding it from the media. By not demanding I produce it, she's letting me know she'll cooperate as long as I lay off Joey Vale."

Cora rubbed her head. "Double-think. Don't you people ever play straight?"

"Don't blame me," Chief Harper said. "Joey Vale was in the middle of telling me his story when Becky Baldwin swooped down and made him clam up. He was cleared and released, and she *still* wouldn't let him talk. So I'm in no particular rush to show her all my evidence."

"No argument here. Just interested in your point of view."

"Okay, so tell me this," Chief Harper said. "Why does Judy Vale write a crossword-puzzle clue? Granted, it's not a crossword puzzle, it's a doodle, but why does she doodle in intersecting words? Why does her doodling take the form of a crossword puzzle? Riddle me that."

"Two reasons," Cora replied promptly.

Chief Harper groaned. "I should have known. I guess I'm lucky there aren't three."

"One, Judy Vale doodled on the phone while talking to her lover. Or talking to her girlfriend and thinking about her lover."

"And she doodled a crossword because . . ."

"Because of the tournament. It's the talk of the town. Has been for weeks. Everyone's been talking about it. Even people who aren't involved." Cora frowned. "She wasn't one of those picketing nuts, was she?"

"No, she wasn't. What's your other theory?"

Cora grimaced. "Well, you might not like it. But the clue strikes me as way too straightforward. In my humble opinion, it was planted."

"Planted?"

"Yeah. By the killer. To throw suspicion on someone else."

"Wait a minute," Chief Harper protested. "You're now suggesting the killer strangles Judy, then sits down at her kitchen table with her notepad and scribbles a cryptic message just to lead me off the track? In which case the killer isn't Joey Vale *or* Judy Vale's lover but someone *entirely* different, someone who decides that a crossword-puzzle message *alluding* to Joey Vale and Judy Vale's lover, without actually *implicating* either one of them, is *exactly* what the police need to draw suspicion away from her *real* killer. And instead of leaving this message on the *body,* where it might do the killer some good, *leaves it facedown on the kitchen table where there's no guarantee the police will even connect it to the crime at all!*" Chief Harper paused for breath. His face was very red. "Is *that* what you're suggesting?"

Cora smiled. "Don't pull your punches, Chief. If you don't like my theory, just say so."

25

JESSICA THORNHILL, AS A GRAPHIC PROCLAIMED PAUL THORNHILL'S wife to be, rolled soulful eyes at the camera and said, "I feel connected to this woman, because she protected me. A man was harrassing me about winning the first event, and she made him stop. Which was only right, because why shouldn't I have won the first event? My husband had nothing to do with that puzzle, so why should I be disqualified just because my husband happened to be on my team?"

"Why indeed?" Rick Reed soothed. "But with regard to the woman herself. Mrs. Felicity Roth. The woman who was violently slain. Just what exactly did she say to your husband?"

"I don't know. I was playing the picture game. You know, identifying the drawings on the wall. Paul wasn't helping me because of that *awful* man. And then I go back to our table, and there he is. Complaining again. And Paul's not even playing. And that's when the woman pulled him away."

"Very interesting," Rick Reed said, nodding sagely. One got the impression he had Jessica Thornhill on camera because she was pretty but couldn't care less what she had to say. "Mr. Thornhill. What was Mrs. Roth talking to you about?"

"She was confirming the fact that I was a local celebrity." Paul Thornhill made a self-deprecating gesture of false modesty. "I was afraid she was going to ask for an autograph."

"And did she mention the murder of Judy Vale?"

Paul Thornhill frowned. "I believe she said she was a neighbor. I got the impression she was trying to make herself seem important, but I really wasn't paying much attention."

"And why was that?"

"Frankly, I was watching my wife. I had noticed some resentment toward her during the first game." Paul Thornhill grinned and ducked his head boyishly. "And I *like* watching my wife."

As if on cue, the Thornhills beamed at each other, while still managing to keep their handsome faces turned to the camera.

"That's enough to make you puke," Cora Felton commented, waving her fork at the TV.

"I hope you're not referring to my pork medallions," Sherry said as she poured the wine. Sherry had whipped up a dinner of pork, egg noodles, and spinach. As usual, Sherry and Cora were eating in the living room in front of the TV.

"Dinner's great. Particularly since we didn't get lunch. But I've really had enough of glamour-puss Thornhill." Cora took a bite of pork and sipped her wine. "Even so . . . Oh, look, there's Iris." Cora pointed at the TV. "And what's-his-face."

On the screen, Iris Cooper stood next to Harvey Beerbaum on the marble steps of the Bakerhaven town hall. "These homicides are of course a genuine tragedy," Iris said with convincing sincerity, "and would be at any time. It's just doubly unfortunate that they should happen now, when the town is deeply involved in doing good work. I am referring, of course, to the Bakerhaven Crossword-Puzzle Tournament, which has raised over ten thousand dollars for charity. We just want to assure the public that in spite of these tragedies, the tournament will go on."

"That's right," Harvey Beerbaum piped up. "The last puzzle

will be given out at ten o'clock tomorrow morning, to be followed immediately by the final play-off between the top three finishers."

"*Among* the top three finishers," Sherry corrected automatically. As the TV went to commercial, she picked up the zapper, clicked it on mute. "What were you going to say?"

"I don't know. Was I going to say something?"

"About Paul Thornhill. Something about his interview."

Cora speared some noodles. "Oh, yes. He says Mrs. Roth bragged about being Judy's neighbor. Trying to make herself seem important."

"So? I'm sure that's what she did."

"Me too. Only thing is, when Chief Harper asked him about it this morning, Thornhill didn't remember that."

"Are you sure?"

"Positive. He said she didn't mention the murder and he seemed surprised to learn she lived across the street from the Vales."

"That's not what he just said."

"Exactly." Cora said it smugly. Or as smugly as you can say something with your mouth full of noodles.

"How do you account for it?"

"Well," Cora said, "either he was fibbing to cover up the fact he killed her, or he was lying because he didn't want to be involved, or he was dissembling to avoid adverse publicity, or he just plain didn't remember."

"That's helpful," Sherry said.

"Actually, it helps to state the problem," Cora said serenely. "These noodles are delicious. What's your secret?"

"Boiling water. It's a dish even you could make, Cora."

"Well, let's not be hasty. Just the thought of cooking gives me hives." Cora took another bite and gestured with her fork to the doodle, which was lying precariously close to her wineglass. "So, you give any thought to the puzzle?"

"Such as it is," Sherry said. She retrieved the paper, spread it out on the coffee table.

"I'm assuming Judy Vale doodled this. It's a woman's doodle.

Anyway, it concerns two people, her husband and her lover. Primarily her lover. Do you see why?"

"Sherry. I've had it up to here with puzzles."

"Sorry. The first word doodled was *lover*. It's in the middle of the pad, and it goes across. The way a person would normally write. Everything else grows from that. And the other words are all in pairs. For instance, *lights out* is a series. But it can't be the next series, because *out* intersects with *jealous*. So the next word would have to be *jealous*."

Cora, peering over Sherry's shoulder, said, "Why not *Joey*?"

"Because *Joey* doesn't connect with *lover*, it's parallel to it. It connects with the *j* in *jealous*. So *jealous* comes next. *Jealous* and then *Joey*. *Jealous* is written first, but the two words actually come together, making the phrase *jealous Joey* or *Joey jealous*.

"So what's next? Well, now you can do *lights out*. No problem. She doodles those next. Which fits just fine. Except, unluckily, she's got *or* left over from writing *Joey* over *lover*. So she scribbles an *else* onto *Joey*, creating the phrase *or else*. Which fits very nicely. *Joey jealous. Lights out or else.* Or even *Lights out or else Joey jealous.* But *lover*, that's who the note's about."

"I wish I could think like you," Cora said. "That's the sort of thing I need to do to get Harvey Beerbaum off my case. Explain a crossword puzzle. Convince him I have a nodding acquaintance with one."

"I'm afraid a simple analysis like that wouldn't impress him much."

"Maybe not," Cora said. "But it sure wouldn't hurt. Okay, never mind how the damn thing was doodled, what does it mean? All this stuff about Joey being jealous unless the lights are out."

"Or else."

"Huh?"

"It's not *unless*, it's *or else*."

"Whatever. What does it mean? Is it a message to her lover?"

"Not at all. It's what she scribbled while talking on the phone. She wasn't leaving a message, she was doodling her subconscious thoughts." Sherry sawed a piece of pork. "And that's what Aaron thinks too."

"You told Aaron?"

Sherry put up her hand. "Off the record, in strictest confidence. Not for publication."

"Chief Harper will kill me."

"Relax. He'd never write it. Anyway, Aaron agrees it's not a message, just a doodle."

"And the lover in the doodle?"

"The lover in the doodle is in serious trouble, what with Joey Vale cleared."

"I mean who is he?"

Sherry shrugged. "Mrs. Roth talked to three men: Paul Thornhill, Marty Haskel, Billy Pickens. Paul Thornhill's the type, but he wasn't in town. Marty Haskel was, but he's not the type. Billy Pickens qualifies on both counts."

"It wouldn't take a genius to figure that one out."

"So why does Harper need your help?"

"Maybe he figures the doodle's *too* straightforward, there must be something more to it."

"Yeah, well . . . Wasn't it Freud who said sometimes a cigar is just a cigar?"

"I think it was Bill Clinton."

"You're terrible."

The phone rang. Cora scooped up her plate and glass, headed for the kitchen. "I got it," she said. She plunked the dishes down on the counter, picked up the phone.

Sherry, following with her plate, saw her aunt stiffen.

"Hello, Harvey," Cora said.

"Hello, indeed!" Harvey Beerbaum had on his most peeved voice. "You ran out on me today. Left me to carry on alone."

"It was a murder, Harvey," Cora said defensively. "Chief Harper needed me."

This was only partly true. Chief Harper had actually brought

Cora back during lunch, but she had feigned police work and skipped out on the afternoon session.

"That may well be," Harvey said. "But we're supposed to be a team. So far, I've done almost everything. It's embarrassing. I feel like I'm showing off. I'd like to give you a chance to show off too."

A cold chill ran down Cora's spine. "What do you mean?" she asked. She reached up and hit speakerphone so Sherry could hear.

Harvey Beerbaum's voice filled the kitchen. "Tomorrow. During the finals. While the three finalists are solving the puzzle on-stage, *you're* going to do the commentary."

"The what?"

Harvey practically purred. "Just a little idea of mine. They do it at the national tournament, so there's no reason we can't do it here. The finalists wear headphones that play loud classical music. So they can't hear what you're saying. And you take the microphone and do a play-by-play commentary on how they're doing with their puzzles. Point out where they're making errors. Suggest lines of strategy they might take."

Cora could barely speak. "It's your idea, Harvey," she managed to croak. "I think you should do it."

"Not at all. It's your turn to shine. I want you to have a chance to show people what you can do." It seemed to Cora that Harvey's voice took on just a slight edge. "You can't hide your expertise forever."

The line clicked dead.

Cora hung up the phone with nerveless fingers. "Sherry. What the hell do I do?"

"I don't know."

"I can't do the commentary."

"That's for sure."

"How do I get out of it?"

"You could murder Harvey Beerbaum."

"Thank you for the gallows humor." Cora shrugged. "I suppose I could get drunk."

"Aunt *Cora* . . ."

"If I were drunk, no one could expect me to comment coherently on crossword puzzles."

"No. But videotape of you failing to do so would undoubtedly run on every nightly news show. It might even go national."

Cora muttered something any news show, local or national, would have to edit.

The doorbell rang. Sherry and Cora looked at each other.

"If that's Harvey Beerbaum I'm not here," Cora said decisively.

"Don't be silly. He just hung up."

"He could have been on a cell phone. If it's him, I'm gone."

"Aunt Cora."

"Phooey. You get the door. I'll be in here ready to bolt. And pick up that puzzle before you let anyone in."

Sherry detoured into the living room, folded up the doodle, and stuck it in her purse. Then she opened the front door to find a handsome curly-haired young man who looked familiar but whom she could not immediately place. "Yes?" she asked.

"Cora Felton. I've gotta see her. Is she here?"

Sherry frowned. "I'm afraid my aunt went out. And who are you?"

"Billy Pickens."

Cora popped out of the kitchen. "Mr. Pickens!"

Billy Pickens looked at her. "I thought you went out."

"I came back in. What are you doing here?"

"Miss Felton. I gotta talk to you. I'm going nuts."

This prospect made Cora's eyes light up. "What's the problem?"

"I'm married. I got a wife and two sweet girls."

"Then why were you running around with Judy Vale?"

"Miss Felton—"

"That's your problem, isn't it? That you were having a fling with Judy. At least, I hope that's your problem. Not that you killed someone."

"Of course I didn't kill anyone!"

"So what's the story?"

"I took the girls to the movies this afternoon. Two o'clock movie, like I said. I get home with the girls and guess who's waiting for me? A TV crew. Right in front of my house. Filming me as I get out of my car. Me and my sweet girls. So I said, 'No comment,' herded the girls into the house."

"What did you tell your wife?"

Billy Pickens looked at Sherry.

"That's my niece, Sherry Carter. Indispensable. Assists me with everything. Now, let's all three of us go into the kitchen, sit down, and work this out."

Cora herded Billy Pickens into the kitchen, plunked him at the table. "Can I get you a drink?"

"I could use a beer."

"Then you're out of luck. I got vodka, gin, and scotch."

"My wife will think something's wrong if I drink anything but beer."

"If your wife doesn't think something's wrong, she's a pretty dim bulb." Cora threw some ice cubes in a glass, poured a jolt of scotch, handed it to Billy. "Okay, you were telling me how you explained the TV crews to your wife."

"I said they wanted to ask about the old lady talking to me at Fun Night."

"And why'd you tell your wife you wouldn't talk to them?"

"I didn't want to talk in front of the girls."

"She buy that?"

Billy Pickens prickled. "Hey, I don't like your attitude."

"I'm sorry. Was I abrupt? Did your wife place any credence in this particular prevarication?"

Billy Pickens glared at her a moment, maybe translating her question, then seemed fascinated with stirring the ice in his drink with his finger. "My wife was suspicious, to say the least."

"She didn't suggest you go back out and see the TV people alone?"

"It came up. But by then they'd gone away by themselves."

"How come?"

Billy frowned, looked at her. "You watch the news?"

"Yeah."

"Was I on it?"

"No."

"I would imagine they're holding the shot of me saying 'No comment' until they can tie it in to the other story and lynch me."

"What other story?"

"You know what story. Me being involved with Judy Vale."

"Which you were?"

Billy set his jaw.

"If you want my help, you gotta tell me what's up. Let me make it easy for you. You and Judy Vale were a hot item, Mrs. Roth knew about it. That's what she chatted with you about at Fun Night. And that's why you're so upset now."

A huge sigh racked Billy Pickens's body. "That's not the half of it," he moaned.

Cora waited patiently.

"I was there," Billy said.

"At Mrs. Roth's house?"

Billy nodded.

"Last night?"

"That's right."

"What happened?"

"What you said. The old lady spotted me at Fun Night, came up, gloated about how she knew all about everything. Threatened to tell my wife."

"Right then and there?"

"Absolutely. Unless I'd come and see her."

"What for?"

Billy scowled. "What do you mean, what for?"

"Was it blackmail? Did she ask you for money?"

"No. At least not then. She just asked me to come."

"What time?"

"Ten-thirty."

"That's when she asked you to be there, or that's when you went?"

"Both. She said ten-thirty, and I was there on the dot. I didn't want to tick her off."

"So what happened?"

"I parked my car down the road and walked in. That's what the old lady told me to do. She said otherwise the nosy neighbors would see me drive up."

Cora made no comment about the nosiness of neighbors, although she was sorely tempted. "Did anyone see you?"

"I don't think so. It was dark. And Mrs. Roth's porch light was out."

"A trick she learned from Judy Vale," Cora commented dryly. "So what happened when you got there?"

"She opened the door and let me in."

"She was alive when you got there?"

"Yes, of course."

"No, not of course," Cora said patiently. "There were two possibilities: You found her alive, or you found her dead. Go on. What happened?"

"She led me into this creepy living room, made me sit down on the couch."

"The one with the plastic on it?"

"That's right. It sure felt funny."

"I'll bet it did. So your fingerprints are on it."

"No, I didn't touch it with my hands."

Cora raised her eyebrows. "Oh, you thought of that, did you?"

Billy grimaced. "No, it's not like that. Not like you mean. The whole thing just freaked me out. It was really creepy. I mean, here I am, scared to death, looking at my family falling apart. And here's this old witch, gloating, lording it over me, telling me what a fool I was. That was the main thing. What a fool I was for coming. Because she didn't really have anything on me. Just suspicions. But my coming confirmed them. The fact I was there meant it was all true.

And now she *really* had something to go to my wife with. And the cops too."

"And that's when Mrs. Roth asked you for money?"

"No, she didn't."

"If she didn't want money, what did she want?"

"I tell you, she didn't want anything. I ask her, point-blank, 'What do you want?' But she just laughs. 'I have everything I want,' she tells me."

"So what happened then?"

"I begged her to keep her mouth shut."

"What did she say?"

"Nothing. She laughs some more. I saw I was getting nowhere. I realized there was nowhere to get. So I left."

"You left her alive?"

"Of course!"

"What time was this?"

"I don't know. I was there ten, maybe fifteen minutes."

"You didn't look at your watch?"

"No, I didn't. I didn't know the time till I started my car and saw the clock on the dashboard."

"When was that?"

"About ten to eleven."

"Any cars drive up and park while you were there?"

"No."

"You pass anyone on your way home?"

"If I did I didn't notice. I was rather preoccupied."

"I can imagine." Cora turned to her niece, who had been sitting mute and attentive during the whole exchange. "What do you think, Sherry? How do you like his story?"

"It's fine as far as it goes. But I think it leaves a few things out."

"Yeah," Cora agreed.

"I find it hard to believe that Mrs. Roth merely hinted that he had a relationship with Judy and that was enough to make him run out of there."

"Good point." Cora nodded. "It would have to be something more specific."

"And related more directly to the first murder," Sherry added.

"Naturally," Cora said. "And what might that be?" Her eyes were bright.

"Considering the proximity of the woman's house and her predilection for peering out the window, there would seem to be only one answer."

"I agree." Cora turned back to Billy Pickens, who had been following their exchange with the doomed fascination of one mesmerized by a deadly cobra. "By and large, Billy, you doth protest a bit too much, playing up the family-values bit, saying your wife and kids must never find out. The problem is that from the word go you're acting like a man with more than that to conceal. The only thing that makes sense is that Mrs. Roth spotted you the night Judy Vale died."

"She didn't!"

"Are you sure?"

Billy Pickens glared at Cora Felton for a moment, then his face wilted. "Yes, I'm sure," he said in disgust. "She *said* she did, but she didn't. That was her bluff, that was what going to see her last night confirmed for her."

"So you were there. Tuesday night. At Judy Vale's. How did that happen?"

"I was in the Rainbow Room shooting pool. Don't look at me like that. It's not like I hang out there all the time. I play once a week, and I don't go straight from work, I go home and have dinner first. Then I go shoot pool with the boys from work. What's wrong with that?"

"Except you don't always shoot pool, do you?"

He grimaced. "I met Judy Vale," he confessed. "In the Rainbow Room. Her husband used to bring her, figure that. Jealous on the one hand, but proud as a peacock on the other. Struttin' around, showin' her off. Who wouldn't get interested?"

"And the night of her murder?"

"Was my night out. I was in the Rainbow Room. Joey was there, so I knew his wife was home alone. So after a couple of games I snuck out."

"And drove to her house."

"Well, not *to* her house. I left the car up the road as I always do. I walked in."

"What time was that?"

"A little after eleven. Say eleven-fifteen."

"What happened?"

"The light was out. The door was open. I let myself in. And I called out. Which I always do so as not to scare her to death. Only no one answered. Which was odd. Judy wouldn't be out that time of night. So I went inside, looked around, and there she was. Dead. On the kitchen floor."

Cora nodded, as he had just confirmed what she'd known all along. "So what did you do?"

"What was I gonna do? I suppose I should have called the cops. But then everything would come out—you know, about the affair and all, and my wife—Judy was dead. Nothing was gonna help her. It occurred to me I'd be a perfect suspect."

"That occurred to you?"

"Stupid, right?"

Cora shook her head. "No, Billy, that wasn't stupid at all. You're a very likely candidate. You're such a likely candidate you'll be lucky if the police even bother to look for another before they fry you for this. Your story stinks. You call on both murder victims just before they die. You claim one's alive and one's dead when you get there. The dead one you don't report. The alive one you deny killing but admit to visiting because she knew you visited the dead one. If I were a cop, you'd look awfully good to me."

"But I didn't do it."

"Maybe not, but your credibility's zero. If I were you, I would work very hard on building it up. I would talk to Chief Harper ASAP."

"I can't do that."

"Withholding evidence is a capital crime."

"But I didn't commit any crime."

"So you say. Fortunately, that's not my call."

"You're going to Harper? I spoke to you in confidence. I bared my soul." Billy had gone pale.

"Let's not talk about what you bared, Billy." Cora Felton looked him right in the eyes, said in her most stern voice, "I'm advising you to go to the police. You gonna do it?"

"I can't." Billy sighed heavily. "I know I made mistakes, but I didn't kill anybody. Why should my family pay for that? My little girls see their father on TV, arrested for murder? Please. You're very smart. You figure things out. Can't you help me?"

"You mean be an accessory to murder?" Cora demanded sarcastically. "You mean you want me to aid and abet you, withhold evidence, and conspire to conceal a crime?"

Billy looked at her pathetically, with pleading eyes.

Cora grinned.

"Thought you'd never ask."

26

SHERRY, SITTING BESIDE CORA FELTON ON THE PASSENGER SEAT of the red Toyota, said, "I like the way you included me in your decision."

"What do you mean?" Cora asked innocently.

"Well, here we are, not on our way to Chief Harper's with a bunch of vital information. Instead, we're out investigating on our own."

"Sherry, if we go to Chief Harper now he'll have no choice but to arrest Billy Pickens. Which would be a terrible mistake."

"At least it would be *his* mistake. And he couldn't go to jail for it."

"Sherry, give me a break. Do you really think Billy Pickens did it?"

"No, I don't. But that's not the point."

"How can that not be the point?"

"Billy may be innocent, but that's not why you're doing this. You're running around making your own investigation and holding out on Chief Harper—which is something you know you shouldn't do—just so you won't have to think about the tournament. Because you're so freaked out about this puzzle-commentary bit Harvey dreamed up."

"Well, you heard him," Cora said defensively. "Am I imagining it or not? Didn't he sound like he's looking to show me up?"

"Maybe. But it's sort of a self-fulfilling prophesy."

"A what?"

Sherry snorted in disgust. "For someone who's supposed to be a linguist, you might want to brush up on a few common phrases. I mean Harvey Beerbaum has no idea *at all* you might be a fake. But you *think* he does. So you *act* like he does. So he *notices* you acting like he does. He's *not* suspicious. But he *gets* suspicious. See what I mean?"

"Yeah," Cora said. "But what's the difference? If he's suspicious now, who cares how he got that way? Unless you just wanna load me up with guilt."

"Heaven forbid."

"So let's concentrate on the murders. If Billy Pickens didn't do it, then someone else did. It's up to us to find out who."

Cora pulled up in front of Olsens' Bed-and-Breakfast, a two-story colonial just three blocks from the center of town. She and Sherry got out, went up on the porch, and knocked on the door.

An elderly gentleman in a baggy herringbone sweater answered their knock. He was tall, thin, had gray hair, and carried a pipe. "Yes?" he inquired. His voice, Cora decided, sounded like rust.

"Mr. Olsen?"

"That's right."

"I'm Cora Felton. This is my niece, Sherry. We're looking for Paul Thornhill."

"I'm afraid I can't help you."

"Paul Thornhill's not staying here?"

"Yes, he is. But I believe he's gone out."

"With his wife?"

"No, I think he went out alone."

"So she's here," Cora said.

"She might be."

Cora blinked. This was like pulling teeth. "Why do you say she might be?"

"Well, I didn't see Mrs. Thornhill go out. But maybe she went out without me seein'."

Not likely, Cora figured. "We'd like to talk to her. Where might she be?"

"In her room."

"And where is that?"

"Second floor, to the right." The man chewed pensively on his pipe stem. "Only you can't go up there."

"Why not?"

"It wouldn't be right. A woman alone and all. You really wanna see her, I'll get my wife."

"We really wanna see her."

Mrs. Olsen proved to be a rather plump woman whom Cora recognized from Cushman's Bake Shop. From the number of mornings Cora had seen her there, it appeared that Olsens' Bed-and-Breakfast wasn't serving many breakfasts. Capturing the Thornhills during the crossword-puzzle tournament must have been a small windfall.

"Now, I don't want a commotion," Mrs. Olsen declared. "We do have other guests. If the Thornhills want, they can see you in the living room. We don't rent out rooms to entertain."

"I think he's out," Mr. Olsen put in.

He was. Mrs. Olsen came downstairs minutes later with only Paul Thornhill's wife.

Since her TV interview, Jessica Thornhill had changed into a soft cashmere sweater and velvet slacks. She was still wearing her jewelry—diamond-studded earrings and gold necklace and bracelet. Close up she had a perky face, vital, alert, interested. And highly competitive. She was, Cora concluded, just the type of woman to have won a game at Fun Night. Even if it took her husband's help.

"What's this about?" Jessica demanded.

"I'm awfully sorry to trouble you, Mrs. Thornhill. This is my niece, Sherry Carter. We'd like to ask you about your interview with the reporter from Channel 8."

"What about it?"

"Could you go in the TV room if you're gonna talk?" Mrs. Olsen told them. "I don't want the other guests disturbed."

"As if they could hear," Jessica Thornhill scoffed. Having registered her defiance, she conceded, "We might as well sit down. Come in the living room. I think they have a fire."

There was a fireplace with easy chairs nestled around it. A log crackled in the hearth.

"Paul went out for booze," Jessica Thornhill explained as they sat down. "They put a decanter of sherry in our bedroom, but I'd rather drink strychnine." She shuddered, then smiled. "What is it you want to know?"

"About the dead woman, of course," Cora said. "I understand she was talking to your husband while you were playing the game. The one about the pictures on the wall. As I recall, when you came back to the table that's when the mechanic followed you. The man who was so upset about you winning."

"He's a mechanic? That figures."

Cora ignored this class prejudice. "And that's when Mrs. Roth intervened and pulled him away, is that right?"

"Absolutely. And that is why her murder affects me so deeply. I owed a debt of gratitude to the woman, and before I could express it, she was gone."

"I understand," Cora said. "My point is, because of the incident you had particular reason to notice her. So I'm wondering if you happened to notice her talking to anyone else, aside from your husband."

"Yes, I did."

"And who would that be?"

"That terrible man. The one you say's a mechanic."

"I mean aside from him," Cora said patiently. "She only spoke to him because he interrupted her when she was talking to your husband. I mean did you see her talking to anyone else at another time?"

"Absolutely," Jessica Thornhill said, nodding emphatically.

"And who was that?"

Jessica spread her arms wide with the exasperation of someone who is being willfully misunderstood. "I told you. The mechanic. That horrid man."

Cora Felton frowned, feeling the beginning of a headache.

Sherry Carter leaned in. "You mean you saw her talking to him some other time?"

"Yes, of course."

Cora Felton could hardly hide her disappointment. "So you saw her talking to Mr. Haskel again. And when was that?"

"During the picture game."

Cora frowned. "The picture game?"

"Yes. He complained when I won the first game. Then he made a fuss when we started the second, the one with the pictures. That's why Paul wasn't playing with me. So I knew who he was, and I was giving him a wide berth. Then during the game I saw him talking to a woman near one of the drawings, so I skipped it and came back to it later. And the woman he was talking to turned out to be her."

"Wait a minute," Cora Felton said. "I don't understand. Are you telling me you saw Mrs. Roth talking to Marty Haskel *before* she spoke to your husband?"

Jessica Thornhill looked at Cora as if she were an idiot. "Yes, of course."

27

"NOW WE'RE GETTING SOMEWHERE," CORA SAID, AS THEY PULLED the Toyota away from the Olsens'.

Sherry groaned. "Getting somewhere? All you got is another lead to the mechanic, who we happen to know is a dead end."

"How do we know that?"

"How do we know anything? Aunt Cora, the town mechanic is *not* a serial killer."

"I never said he was."

"So what's your big lead?"

"He must know *something*. If he was talking to Mrs. Roth, he's a valuable witness. He knows what she said. So far we've had only Billy Pickens's version. Which is constantly changing and may or may not be the truth. And Paul Thornhill's version, which has also changed once. Granted only slightly, and perhaps just a sin of omission. But still, his accuracy is very much in question. Plus, everything he says appears to be totally egotistical. We've been looking for someone else to give us another angle on Mrs. Roth. Now we finally have it. Which is great. Give me an impartial witness with no ax to grind, and maybe we'll get a straight story."

"You'd describe Marty Haskel as having no ax to grind?"

"All right, rotten choice of words. But you know what I mean. The guy's not involved in Judy Vale's death. Not unless the whole world is topsy-turvy and nothing makes sense. So, from that point of view, he's an impartial witness."

As she said this, Cora pulled into the service station at the edge of town. A boy with sandy hair and a dirty ski jacket was manning the pumps. "Fill 'er up?"

"Yes, please," Cora told him. She pointed to the garage, which was dark. "Service and repair closed?"

"Yes, ma'am. You got a problem?"

"No. Just asking. Is there a phone book?"

"Pay phone on the corner had one last I looked."

Sherry followed Cora to the phone booth on the corner. Cora flipped the pages, looked up Marty Haskel's address. "Here we go—232 Arbor Drive."

"Where is that?"

"I have no idea. But the kid will."

They paid the young man for the gas and asked him if he knew where Arbor Drive was.

"Arbor Drive? Course I do. Marty Haskel lives there." He gave Cora the directions.

Marty Haskel's house was a modest affair about two miles outside of town. It was yellow with green shutters and had a breezeway and a garage. The garage door was open and the car was gone. The lights were out in the house.

"Looks like he's not home," Sherry said.

"That's a pretty safe deduction, but let's verify it."

Cora Felton hopped out of the car, went up on the porch, and pressed the doorbell. After several seconds she rang again.

Sherry watched impatiently from the car. The man was clearly gone and—

Cora tried the doorknob!

What was that woman doing?

In a flash Sherry was out of the car and on the porch. "Aunt Cora. You're not going in."

"No, I'm not," Cora assured her.

"Promise?"

"Absolutely. The door is locked, and the lock looks tough. I may have to try a window."

"Aunt Cora—"

"Get back in the car. If someone drives up, honk the horn. If it's *him,* honk twice."

"Cora. Be reasonable," Sherry pleaded. "This is insane. Even if you got in there, what would you be looking for?"

"A reason for Marty Haskel to murder those two women," Cora said promptly. "That or his dead body."

"Oh, for goodness sakes!"

"*We* think he's a witness," Cora pointed out. "Suppose the killer does too?"

"Aunt Cora," Sherry protested, but her aunt was already on her way around the house.

The side door was also locked, but the row of flowerpots next to it looked inviting. The key was in the third one. Cora fished it out, tried it in the door. The lock clicked open. Cora returned the key to the flowerpot, slipped inside, closing the door gently behind her.

Cora dug in her purse for her flashlight. She flicked it on. The batteries were almost dead. She shone the dim light, looked around.

She was in the kitchen. There were no bodies on the floor. That almost disappointed her. Judy Vale had been found in the kitchen.

On the other hand, Mrs. Roth had been found in the living room. Cora passed through the foyer, where a narrow staircase led to the second floor, and entered what clearly was a man's den. A TV, a couch, and a writing desk. And no doors off it. A small house with few rooms. This was the living room, no one was dead here, what else did she need to know?

Outside, a car horn honked. Cora Felton frowned, wondered if her niece would stoop to trickery to get her out of the house. She went to the window, pulled aside the blind.

A car had indeed driven up, but it was turning into the driveway across the street. Cora decided she'd give Sherry that one. The honk was unnecessary but arguably justified.

Cora let the blind fall back and continued her search.

Upstairs were a bathroom and two small bedrooms. One was storage, the other where the man slept. Marty Haskel was not dead in either of them.

Some papers on the bedside table looked familiar. Cora shone the light, saw that they were crossword puzzles. After an involuntary shudder of revulsion, she picked them up. They were the puzzles from Fun Night. Craig Carmichael's CURIOUS CANINES and Paul Thornhill's APOLOGIES. So these were the bones of contention—Marty Haskel's losing entries.

The Craig Carmichael puzzle, Cora noted, was nearly finished, while the Paul Thornhill one was completely blank.

Cora put the puzzles back and finished searching the bedroom. The most she learned was that Marty Haskel subscribed to *Playboy*.

Making sure she'd disturbed nothing, Cora went back downstairs and let herself out the side door. As expected, it locked behind her, and she didn't have to fish the key out of the flowerpot to secure it. Then she hurried down the driveway to where Sherry waited impatiently in the car.

"Crack the case?" Sherry asked as Cora climbed in.

"No."

"Where to now?"

"Check out the Olsens' B-and-B. See if Paul Thornhill's back."

He wasn't. There were no cars outside the house except those they'd seen before.

"Let's check out the Country Kitchen," Cora suggested.

"Why?"

"See if Marty Haskel's there."

"You ever see him in the Country Kitchen?"

"I never looked for him in the Country Kitchen. I never had reason to notice him in the Country Kitchen."

"Can you imagine him in the Country Kitchen?"

"Why, Sherry Carter. Was that really you making that class-prejudice remark?"

Cora Felton drove a little too fast for safety to the homey country restaurant where she often played bridge, swerved into the parking lot.

"Now, if he's not here we're not staying," Sherry Carter warned.

"Of course not," Cora agreed, getting out of the car. "You check out the dining room, I'll check out the bar."

"Aunt Cora."

"I can't smoke in the dining room."

"You could have smoked in the car."

"You hate it when I smoke in the car."

"That's never stopped you before."

"Are you telling me you *want* me to smoke in the car?"

Still squabbling, Sherry and Cora went inside. A young woman with menus hovered near the entrance to the dining room. "Two for dinner?"

"No," Cora said, and made a beeline for the bar.

Sherry sighed, debated whether to make a scene. "We're just looking for someone," she explained to the young woman, and slipped past her into the restaurant.

The Country Kitchen dining room, furnished with solid wood tables and chairs, had lantern-style lamps and a wagon-wheel chandelier. It boasted good old Yankee home cooking and featured a well-stocked salad bar.

Half the tables in the restaurant were filled, but a quick glance told Sherry that Marty Haskel wasn't there. A number of the diners were people Sherry had never seen before, most likely out-of-towners. It occurred to Sherry the Country Kitchen, too, was reaping the benefits of the tournament.

Scanning the tables one last time, Sherry Carter froze.

There, in a dimly lit corner at a table for two, sat Becky

Baldwin. Sherry's heart leaped, and she had a moment of icy dread. Becky's head was blocking Sherry's view of the young man at the table. Sherry took two steps sideways and collided with a waitress with a tray of entrees.

Becky Baldwin was sitting with . . .

Rick Reed.

The TV reporter.

Sherry didn't know whether to be relieved or embarrassed. She collected herself, hurried into the bar.

Her aunt was standing there with a cigarette in one hand and a drink in the other. Sherry snorted in disgust. "Have you even *looked* for Marty Haskel?" she hissed in Cora's ear.

"Of course I have," Cora replied blithely. "He doesn't seem to be here."

"Then we should be going."

"Not so fast," Cora told her. "Haskel's not the only fish in the sea."

"Just what do you mean by that?"

"Look who *is* here. It's fascinating, really."

"What are you talking about?"

"I'll show you. Just don't stare."

The Country Kitchen bar was jammed. All the barstools were taken, as were all the booths. Cora flicked her cigarette, took a drag, and blew out a stream of smoke as she maneuvered Sherry toward the middle of the room.

"Now then, if you'll look over my left shoulder at the booth on the far end . . . See who's sitting there?"

Sherry looked. Craig Carmichael was sitting alone, shoulders hunched, head bent, avoiding eye contact. His small hands cradled a glass of dark amber liquid. For all appearances he could have been at his favorite tournament table, working on a puzzle.

"Craig Carmichael stole your favorite booth," Sherry told Cora. "So?"

"Now look two booths down."

"Why?"

"Okay, don't," Cora said. She took a sip of scotch, smiled at her niece.

Sherry scowled at her aunt in exasperation, but her curiosity got the best of her. She craned her neck to peer around the side of Cora's head.

At a table two booths down from Craig Carmichael sat Zelda Zisk. She was drinking some sort of green liqueur in a tall thin glass. And she was not alone. Seated across the table from her was a round-faced woman with wing-tipped glasses. The woman was plump but appeared almost thin next to Zelda Zisk. The woman held a glass similar to Zelda's, though her liqueur had a bluish hue. The women were talking animatedly. Zelda Zisk's triple chins jiggled and her eyes were bright.

"What's your point?" Sherry asked Cora. "The contestants are swilling alcohol, so it's all right for you to do the same?"

"Not at all, but it's extremely interesting," Cora said meekly. "Craig Carmichael is a solitary drunk. Not a surprise, but interesting. And Zelda has a friend. A *girl*friend. Do you suppose she's gay?"

"What if she is?"

"Well, isn't that an intriguing item?"

"No, it isn't, Cora. Have you forgotten what we're supposed to be doing? We're supposed to be checking out leads to Mrs. Roth."

"Exactly," Cora said, and before Sherry could stop her she walked over and slid into the booth opposite Craig Carmichael. The little man glanced up, saw Cora, seemed astounded. He clearly didn't want to look at her, but with her sitting opposite him it was impossible to look away. Instead, he stared down at his drink.

"It's okay, sweetie," Cora said. "There's no reason to be alarmed. Yes, I'm the contest judge. But you have done nothing wrong, and I don't want to talk to you about that. A woman was killed last night. She was at Fun Night, she spoke to Paul Thornhill. I wonder if she talked to you too." When Craig Carmichael said nothing, Cora added, "Did she?"

Craig Carmichael stuck his tongue in his cheek, and his eyes probed the depths of his glass as if seeking the Loch Ness monster there. Cora Felton could practically see the wheels going, formulating a response. When he had it, he looked back at her.

"I've been asked that question by the authorities. I've given them my answer. They are satisfied with that answer. My attorney feels the matter is concluded. I have no further comment."

Cora Felton's mouth fell open. "You've consulted an attorney?"

"I have no further comment." After a moment Craig Carmichael added, "Was there anything else?"

"No," Cora replied. She slid from the booth, moved down the row.

"Hello," Cora told Zelda Zisk and her companion. "I'm sorry to disturb you ladies, but we're trying to trace the movements of that poor elderly woman who was murdered. She spoke to Paul Thornhill last night. I wonder if she spoke to either of you."

Zelda Zisk threw back her head and laughed, a loud, braying laugh that instantly turned every head in the bar. "See, Sue," she told the woman sitting across from her. "I told you she'd be over, and I knew just what she'd ask. That TV guy asked the same thing, but then he didn't use it."

"What was your answer?" Cora said, cocking her head.

"That I didn't notice her at all, and I'm not even sure what woman we're talking about."

"I see," Cora said. "You think the fact you didn't know anything might have had something to do with the TV guy's decision not to use your statement?"

Zelda Zisk laughed again. Luckily, no chandeliers shattered. "Good one. Got me there."

"So you never saw Mrs. Roth at all last night?"

Zelda grinned, an impressive hodgepodge of lipstick and teeth. "If I don't know her, how can I say?" She pointed her finger and laughed. "Got *you* there."

"That you did," Cora conceded cheerfully. "Well, thanks anyway. Sorry to have bothered you."

Cora joined Sherry at the door to the bar, said, "Okay, it's a washout, come on."

They went back out to the parking lot, got in the car.

"You ask Zelda if she's gay?" Sherry said ironically.

Cora gave her a dirty look, started the car.

"So what's the story?"

Cora backed up, guided the car out of the parking lot. "Zelda Triple Chins claims she never saw Mrs. Roth. Craig Carmichael's mum as a dead man. Isn't that interesting? And not only that, Carmichael's consulted a lawyer."

Sherry's eye faltered.

Cora pounced. "What's the matter?" she demanded.

"Nothing."

"What's the nothing?"

Sherry grimaced. "Becky Baldwin's in the dining room having dinner with Rick Reed."

"You're jealous of her and the TV idiot?"

"At first I thought it was Aaron."

"This time of night isn't he at the paper?"

"Yes, of course."

While they were talking, Cora breezed by the Olsens' bed-and-breakfast, where the parked-car situation remained unchanged, and Marty Haskel's driveway, still empty.

"Where we going now?" Sherry asked her.

"Check out the Rainbow Room. See if Marty Haskel's there."

He wasn't. Neither were Billy Pickens, Joey Vale, or anyone else Cora recognized. The bar was half full, the pool table was occupied, the row of quarters indicated it would be for some time.

"Spot anybody?" Sherry asked.

"No."

"Then you're not looking. Far wall, third booth from the door."

Cora looked, and her cornflower-blue eyes widened.

In the booth, Ned Doowacker was drinking with a young lady. For the occasion Mr. Doowacker had changed into a tweed jacket, white shirt, and pink bow tie. His face was scrubbed, and his hair was slicked back. He looked like a little boy whose mother had dressed him for Sunday school. But he was drinking a mixed drink, just like a big boy.

The woman sitting opposite him had also prettied herself up. She wore an unwise amount of makeup and jewelry. A fake-fur coat dangled from a hook on the side of the booth.

The makeup and hairstyle were distractions. If the truth be known, it was the fur coat Cora recognized, rather than the face. But at second glance there could be no doubt.

The woman having drinks with Ned Doowacker was none other than Judy Vale's gossipy next-door neighbor, Charlotte Drake.

28

"IT DOESN'T HAVE TO MEAN ANYTHING," SHERRY CARTER INSISTED as she and Cora Felton got ready for bed. As usual, they were crowded into the bathroom, fighting for mirror space.

"Everything means something," Cora Felton declared. She was dressed in her pink and white flannel nightgown and was taking off her makeup. Sherry, in terry-cloth robe and slippers, was attempting to do the same.

"I mean in terms of the murders."

"I know what you mean. And I totally agree. This particular sector of Bakerhaven seems to have a more active sex life than the norm, but that may be all there is to it." Cora sounded very insincere.

"I'm surprised you didn't break in on their date and question them."

"It would have been awkward. Charlotte knows me. Besides, I'd rather let this budding romance play out and see where it goes. Or where it's been."

"What do you mean by that?" Sherry asked, but Cora had turned the faucet on and was brushing her teeth.

Sherry leaned in and rubbed cold cream on her cheeks. "I mean, are you implying something here, Cora? Ned Doowacker, the Bakerhaven strangler, seducer and slayer of young women? He wasn't even around when Judy Vale was strangled."

Cora gurgled something unintelligible through her toothbrush.

"What did you say?"

Cora finished brushing, spat. "I'm not saying that Doowacker's our killer. I'm just saying isn't it interesting he's managed to pick up one of Judy's neighbors? One of her *married* neighbors, by the way. The lovely Mrs. Charlotte Drake. Whose husband happened to be with her at Fun Night."

"You think that's where Doowacker met her?"

"Unless he met her in the Rainbow Room just now."

"You think he did?"

"No way. Not in that outfit. The guy wasn't dressed to pick up girls, the guy was dressed for a date."

"So he met Charlotte Drake at Fun Night?"

"Mmm-hmm."

Sherry took a tissue, scrubbed the cold cream off a trifle too vigorously. "What could she possibly see in him?"

Cora shook her head. "What did you ever see in Dennis?"

Under the remaining smears of cold cream, Sherry's face hardened. "Hey. Watch it."

"No offense meant. I still don't know what I ever saw in George." Cora cupped her hands, splashed water on her face. She straightened, blinked at herself in the mirror. "Anyway, I'm much more interested in Marty Haskel."

Sherry groaned. "So the guy wasn't home. So he's got a girlfriend. Or he went to another bar. Or he's off somewhere playing poker with the boys."

"I'd like to get in on that," Cora said.

"I'm sure you would. At any rate, there could be lots of reasons why the guy isn't home."

"I don't like it."

"You want to sit outside his house all night? You got a tournament finals to run in the morning."

"No, I've got a tournament finals to *get out of* in the morning. I'm still not sure how I'm gonna do it." Cora grabbed a towel, rubbed her face. "I got a bad feeling."

"You'll be fine."

"Oh, yeah? You gonna stay up all night and teach me to do commentary?"

"No. You're gonna kid around and joke about the contestants and riff on whoever's ahead."

"Yeah. And Harvey Beerbaum's gonna notice I'm not talkin' shop, and he's gonna be more suspicious than ever. Assuming I don't out and out blow it and announce, 'All right, you got me, I'm a fraud,' right over the P.A. system."

Cora Felton tossed the towel on the floor, grabbed her glasses from the shelf over the sink, and put them on. "I need comfort food," she declared. "Sherry, didn't you make brownies yesterday? I'll bet there's a couple left."

"Aunt Cora. You just brushed your teeth."

"I never was good at sequencing. I didn't know I was hungry till now. Boy, would a brownie hit the spot."

Cora padded out of the bathroom and down the hall toward the kitchen.

Sherry followed to make sure her aunt chased the brownie with nothing stronger than milk. She got there in time to see Cora lift the aluminum foil off the square Pyrex baking pan.

"Look, Sherry. Four left. Two for you and two for me."

"I don't want any brownies," Sherry said.

"Good. More for me. These are great." Cora took a dessert plate down from the cabinet. "Where's the spatula?"

"In the sink."

"Right, we never did the dishes."

Cora padded over to the sink, fished the spatula out from among the dirty dishes, switched on the water, and proceeded to rinse it off.

In the kitchen window Cora could see her reflection, as well as the moonlit backyard. She tensed slightly, then went on washing the spatula.

"Sherry," she said casually, without looking around. "If you could do me a huge favor, just act natural and don't react to what I'm going to tell you."

"Aunt *Cora*!"

"Yeah, like that. Just try to avoid any sudden movements or expressions of alarm. We're being watched through the kitchen window."

"We're not!"

"Try not to look, you'll just tip him off. You can't see anything from there anyway. You have to be where I am, but don't come over or he'll know we've seen him."

"Aunt Cora, you're freaking me out."

"Sorry," Cora said, "but there's a man in the backyard crouched behind the picnic table watching us with a spyglass."

"A spyglass?"

"You know, like a single binoculars. A telescope. Don't you call that a spyglass?"

"Aunt Cora—"

"So here's the deal. I'll give you the spatula and walk out of his line of sight. As if I went to the refrigerator for milk or something. You're gonna stay here, make a show of cutting and serving the brownies. If you can talk to me as if I were still in the room, it couldn't hurt. If you can't, just concentrate on your task. But keep his interest. For a girl in her nightgown, that shouldn't be hard."

"Cora—"

But her aunt was already gone.

Cora came out the side door into the breezeway, crept around the garage. She shivered from the cold night air. Cora hadn't bothered to grab her coat, just her purse. She rummaged in it, came out with her snub-nosed revolver. She snapped the safety off. Crept into the backyard.

And there he was. Behind the picnic table. In the shadows, just out of the shaft of light from the kitchen window.

Cora still couldn't see his face, but she could see clearly enough to tell that her initial impression had been wrong. He was not crouched behind the picnic table but rather seated at it. He was scrunched down on the bench, which gave the impression of crouching. The hands and head were at table level. Only the outline of the spyglass could be seen sticking up.

The thought flashed on Cora, what if it's not a spyglass? What if it's a telescopic sight? What if it's a gun?

A cold chill ran down Cora's spine at the thought of Sherry in its sights. She had left Sherry as bait. Why hadn't she called the cops?

Cora gripped the pistol, crept forward. She circled the table, coming up from behind. Wondered what she would do if he ran. She didn't want to shoot him, but she might have no choice. She had to see his face.

The dry leaves rustled under Cora's slippers, sounded loud as thunder. Surely he must have heard. Any second his head would turn. If he brought the rifle—

Rifle? It's a spyglass. Get a grip.

Cora crept closer, and—

Headlights appeared in the driveway.

Cora's heart leaped. *Not now! Not now!*

Cora hunched over, slunk back into the shadows.

Tires rolled to a stop. A motor roared and died. A car door slammed.

Aaron Grant's voice called, "Hey, whaddya doin'?"

Cora nearly gagged. She stood, frozen, torn between shushing Aaron and keeping her gun on the man.

Who still hadn't moved. What's the matter? Was he deaf?

And was Aaron crazy? Here he came, walking right up to her in plain sight, with a killer in the backyard, and—

Cora's mouth fell open.

Realization dawned.

Cora straightened up, marched around the table. She kept the revolver leveled, but there was no need.

The man in shadows wasn't spying. His neck was twisted at an impossible angle, and his eyes bugged out of his head. And what had appeared to be a spyglass was a piece of paper that had been rolled up like a scroll and shoved in his mouth.

The man was Paul Thornhill.

The paper was a crossword puzzle.

29

CHIEF HARPER WAS FIT TO BE TIED. "YOU SAW HIM THROUGH THE window?"

"That's right."

"You thought he was alive?"

"Of course," Cora said. "If I thought he was dead, I'd have called the police at once."

"If he was only a stalker, you were going to take him on yourself?"

"I wasn't going to take him on. I just wanted to know who he was. If I'd called the police he'd have run, and we wouldn't have found out."

"He wouldn't have run."

Cora Felton stuck her nose in the air with all the dignity she could muster and tugged her coat about her shoulders. While waiting for the police, Cora had managed to attire herself in her finest Miss Marple wear, complete with tweed skirt, jacket, and frilly white blouse. She could probably not have chosen a less likely outfit to please the chief.

Chief Harper and Cora Felton were standing near the side of the garage watching Dr. Barney Nathan examine the body. An EMS crew with a gurney stood by waiting for him to finish.

Aaron Grant and Sherry Carter came walking up.

"Gotta move my car," Aaron said.

Chief Harper frowned at the interruption. "What?"

Aaron jerked his thumb toward the foot of the driveway. "Sam Brogan's stringing up a crime-scene ribbon. If I don't park on the road, I'll never get out."

"Technically, your car's part of the crime scene."

"Give me a break," Cora said. "He came ages later. He just drove up." Cora raised her eyebrow, shot Sherry a meaningful look. "Why don't you let him go?"

"Okay, move it," Chief Harper said.

Aaron and Sherry got in the car and backed down the drive. Sam Brogan, cranky as ever, grudgingly moved the ribbon to let them out.

Chief Harper, watching them go, noted that both Becky Baldwin and the Channel 8 news team had arrived. He turned back to Cora and scowled. "You have no idea how bad this is."

"Oh, really? *I* have no idea how bad this is? This happens to be my house." Cora pointed. "That's my picnic table. The murder happened here. Unless the killer drove up and dropped off the body. Those are the only possibilities, neither one of which I particularly like."

"Yes," Chief Harper said. "And how is it the killer was able to do that?"

"What do you mean?"

"How is it you happened to be out?"

"Oh."

"Yeah. Oh," Chief Harper said sarcastically. "Or perhaps I should say, how is it you happened to be out *looking for Paul Thornhill?*"

"And just how do you know that?"

"His wife called in a missing person's report. Said he went out for cognac and never came back. Said the reason she realized he was taking so long was the fact you came by looking for him. You mind telling me why?"

"Because Mrs. Roth talked to him at Fun Night."

"Yes. You were there when I asked him about it. I suppose you decided you could do better."

"Well, I didn't think it could do any harm."

"That's because you don't know who Jessica Thornhill is. I didn't either, but I sure do now. It turns out she's a Gattling-Finn."

"A what?"

"Of the Percival Gattling-Finns. Made so much money in cotton and sugar they could buy the state of Vermont. Her father, Percival Gattling-Finn the Fourth, alas, has no sons, and she's the eldest daughter. You do the math."

"Uh-oh."

"The woman made a missing person's report and I didn't act on it. Turned her down flat. Partly because she tried to bully me with how much money she had. So I did nothing, and this is the result."

"Doesn't a person have to be gone twenty-four hours before they're officially missing?"

"Yeah, great. I'm sorry your husband's dead, Mrs. Thornhill, but I'm technically right."

"I see your point."

"It's a real mess. The way I see it, the only way I'm off the hook is if she did it."

"Oh, for goodness sakes."

"Well, it would solve my problems. She'd have a hard time suing me then."

"That's your thought?" Cora said skeptically. "She found him here and strangled him?"

"You don't like that theory?"

"I haven't had time to think about it. But I don't need time. It's the stupidest thing I ever heard. I can poke a million holes in it."

"Be my guest."

"How does she know he's here? And how does she *get* here, if he's got the car? Does she have a car service bring her here and wait while she kills him? And why does she *want* to kill him? What does she gain? And *how* does she kill him, little woman like her? How does she strangle such a big man? I mean, he was strangled, wasn't he?"

"I won't know till Barney's done, but it sure looks like it."

"How could she have done it?"

"He was her husband. He wouldn't be suspecting anything. She could have got him in a position—"

"And strangled him? He could have snapped her like a stick." Cora lowered her voice. "And if it's her, how do you account for this?"

Chief Harper frowned. "What?"

Cora reached in her jacket pocket and surreptitiously handed him a folded up piece of paper. He stared at her in amazement, then turned and unfolded it, shielding it from the crowd. His eyes widened. He refolded the paper, turned back to Cora. The look on his face was not cordial. "Where the hell did you get this?" he demanded.

"It was stuck in Thornhill's mouth."

"You removed it from the body?" Chief Harper said incredulously.

"If I hadn't, people might have seen it. I thought you wanted the puzzles withheld."

"Not from *me*!" Harper hissed. A vein in his forehead was bulging. It occurred to Cora it was the first time she had ever noticed it.

"Relax, Chief," Cora said. "I gave you the puzzle at the first opportunity. It was rolled up and stuck in the guy's mouth. It's his own puzzle, it isn't filled in, and what it means is anyone's guess. But for what it's worth, you have it."

"Who knows about this?" Chief Harper said ominously.

"Just you, me, Sherry, and Aaron."

"Aaron *Grant*?"

Cora put up her hands. "Off the record. I promise, he won't write it."

Sam Brogan came walking up. "I found his car."

Chief Harper jammed the puzzle in his pocket, turned to the policeman. "Where?"

"Parked out on the road."

"You didn't see it when you drove in?" Chief Harper asked Cora.

"No," Cora said. "Where is it parked?"

"North of the driveway."

"That's why. We came in the other way."

"You secure the car?" Harper asked.

Sam Brogan nodded. "Locked the doors and took the keys. They were in the ignition."

"Put a crime-scene ribbon on it?"

Sam shook his head. "That'd just call attention to it. There's so many cars parked out there now, no one will notice."

Harper frowned, considered.

"And I reached his wife. She's on her way."

"How'd you find her?"

"Bed-and-breakfast had her cell-phone number. She's out driving around. I had to give her directions. She's damn near hysterical."

"You tell her he's dead?"

"Well, what was I gonna say? I found your husband, but he doesn't wanna come? I had to tell her."

"I suppose so," Chief Harper said. In the distance he could hear the roar of a motor, the squeal of tires.

The TV crew heard it too. They perked up, swung around, hoisted the camera.

Chief Harper began to feel a headache coming on. He turned to Cora Felton. "Tell me again why she couldn't have done it."

30

JESSICA THORNHILL BROUGHT HER CAR TO A SCREECHING STOP, erupted from the door, ducked under the crime-scene ribbon, and raced up the driveway. She was a fright. Her hair was mussed, her eyes were wide, tears caked her cheeks. She looked like a wild woman. "Where is he?" she cried. "Where is he?"

Unfortunately, her arrival coincided with the EMS unit bringing her husband out on a gurney. She raced to it, flung herself on the body, weeping and wailing, "No! No!"

The news crew filmed this gleefully. The ambulance was parked out on the road, so the cameraman got close-ups of the body being loaded, which took some time and maneuvering, including one of the technicians leaving the gurney teetering on the back of the van while he abandoned his position to pry Mrs. Thornhill free. Finally the doors were closed and the ambulance took off, leaving the poor woman standing staring like a lost soul.

Becky Baldwin seemed poised to offer comfort, but at that moment Chief Harper appeared.

Jessica Thornhill rushed to him. "Who did this?" she cried. "Do you know? Can you tell me? Who did this awful thing?"

"That's what I intend to find out," Chief Harper said.

It was an unfortunate choice of words.

"You mean you don't *know*?" she demanded. "You have no idea? How is that possible? Tell me it isn't true. Tell me you have a lead."

Cora Felton, watching closely, said, "We have leads. That's why I came to talk to you tonight."

"Yes," Jessica said. "Because that woman talked to my husband. Now she's dead, and so is he, and what does it mean? Nothing."

"Oh, it means something, all right," Chief Harper said. "And I intend to get to the bottom of it. Now then, you were worried about your husband."

"Of course I was. Of course I was."

"Because he went out for brandy and didn't come back."

"You're telling me stuff I know."

"I need to get it straight. How did you get here just now?"

"How did I get here?"

"Your husband had the car. What are you driving?"

"I rented a car."

"You rented a car and went looking for him?"

"That's right."

"There's no car rentals in town. Where'd you find one?"

"In Danbury."

Chief Harper frowned. "How'd you get to Danbury?"

"I didn't. I called them, had them deliver a car." Jessica snuffled. Her eyes were wide. "Why are you asking me this? What does it matter?"

"I'm just trying to get the picture, Mrs. Thornhill. So you were out this evening, driving around, looking for your husband—is that right?"

Rick Reed suddenly perked up.

So did Becky Baldwin. "Chief Harper. If you're suspecting Mrs.

Thornhill of a crime, may I point out you've not advised her of her rights."

Jessica Thornhill looked at her. "You're a lawyer?"

"That's right."

"Yes. You're the one Paul was talking to this afternoon when I came out. He said you were a lawyer. I said, 'Why would we ever need a lawyer?' And now I do. Can I hire you?"

"You don't have a lawyer?"

"I have New York lawyers. They're in New York. If I need advice now, let me hire you. What's one lawyer, more or less."

"Sorry," Becky said. "There's a conflict of interest. I'm representing Joey Vale."

"Who's that?"

"A suspect in the killings. At least he was. I doubt if he is now, but I still represent his interests."

"So you can't advise me?"

"No, just him," Becky said, pointing to Chief Harper. "I'm advising him to read you your rights."

"My rights," Jessica cried. "My rights. I didn't kill my husband, what's this talk of rights?"

"It's a formality," Chief Harper said. "I'm questioning you in your husband's death. You have the right to an attorney, you don't have to say anything if you don't want to."

"That's an awfully informal Miranda," Becky Baldwin pointed out.

Chief Harper glared at her.

Jessica Thornhill began to cry.

Rick Reed moved in, as if to console her, but she jerked away. "No," she said. "I have to be strong, I have to get through this. Whoever did this must pay." She wheeled on Chief Harper. "What do you want to know?"

"Can you think of anyone who would want to kill your husband?"

Her lip trembled. "Of course not. Everybody loved Paul. He was a wonderful man, so smart, so talented. Obviously it had nothing to do with him. It had to do with that old woman." Jessica added, as if by inspiration, "What about that awful man? The one she pulled away from my husband. There's someone connected to both of them. Why aren't you looking for him?"

"I will, Mrs. Thornhill. He'll be one of the first ones I question," Chief Harper assured her, but he couldn't for a moment imagine Marty Haskel killing anyone. "Can you think of anyone else?"

Jessica Thornhill studied him. It was as if in spite of the enormity of the tragedy, she could still recognize the stupidity of the question.

"No, I can't," she said. "We're from New York. We don't know anyone here. Just the other contestants and Harvey Beerbaum."

"What about the other contestants?" Chief Harper asked. "Is there anything there? Any he's known for some time who for some reason or other don't happen to like him?"

"Not at all. I tell you, everyone liked him. Oh, Ned Doowacker was jealous, but so what? Ned Doowacker was always jealous."

"And Ned Doowacker is . . ."

"One of the contestants."

"And you say he was jealous of your husband?"

"Yes, but so what? It's no big deal."

Chief Harper barely restrained himself from saying, *I'll be the judge of that.* "Even so," he said. "Tell me more. Was this just in terms of this tournament or was it an ongoing thing?"

"Just in general. It's a competitive thing among the top contestants. Ned often felt slighted. In this tournament, for instance. Paul, Craig, and Zelda were singled out as celebrity contestants while Ned wasn't."

"And this caused resentment?"

Jessica waved her arm angrily. "Chief, you're off on the wrong track. Ned didn't want to kill him, just beat him. He couldn't stand it that Paul was number one."

"You mean in general? Nationwide?"

204 / PARNELL HALL

Jessica Thornhill frowned. Said irritably, "No, of course not. There's lots of stars at the nationals. But Paul was always ahead of him, and in this tournament he was number one."

"Is that right?" Chief Harper asked Cora.

"Most likely."

"Not most likely," Jessica said. "He was number one so far."

"How do you know that?" Cora asked.

"Don't you even know your own tournament? They posted the standings right after dinner."

"That's interesting," Chief Harper said. "Where did they post them?"

"In the town-hall lobby. So anyone could come in and get their score."

"And your husband was number one?" Chief Harper said.

"Didn't I just say that? Of course he was. By a wide margin."

"Who was number two?" Cora asked.

"I don't remember."

"Was it this Ned Doowacker?" Chief Harper asked.

"I don't think Ned was that high. But he might have been. I really didn't pay that much attention."

"And you say this was posted after dinner? Where any of the contestants could have gone in and seen it?"

"Yes. But I tell you, this had nothing to do with it. Who would want to kill Paul over a lousy contest?"

"Who indeed?" Chief Harper said. He raised his voice, called, "Sam. Look out for Mrs. Thornhill, will you? I'm leaving you in charge. I have to run into town."

"Where you going, Chief?" Cora said as he headed for the car.

"Town hall. I wanna see that score."

"Oh, come on, Chief. You really think it means something?"

"I don't know. But at this point I'll take anything I can get."

"Can I come too?"

"It might look better if you drove your own car."

"It's blocked in."

"Okay, so get Aaron and Sherry to take you."

Cora Felton said nothing.

Looking around, Chief Harper said, "Say, where are they? I thought I just saw them."

"I was busy talking to you," Cora said.

"Well, they're not here now."

Cora Felton smiled slightly.

"Gee, I guess they aren't."

31

"WHAT DO YOU MEAN, I CAN'T WRITE IT?" AARON GRANT complained.

"Just what I said," Sherry Carter told him. "You're getting the inside track on a very interesting story, and you can't write it."

"How can you do that to me?"

"I didn't do that to you. Cora did that to you. When she slipped us the high sign and told us to leave."

"And you knew what that meant?"

"Yes, I did."

"And just how did you happen to know what that meant?"

"Speaking not for publication, I'd be happy to tell you."

"Give me a break," Aaron said. "At least tell me where we're going."

"We're driving along this road. We're following my directions. When we come to an understanding, I'll name our destination."

"Come on, Sherry. We just left a murder scene. I should be writing it up, not following some lead I can't write about."

"I thought the paper'd gone to bed."

"It has."

"So you've got all day to write up your murder scene, haven't you? Unless you're expecting an extra."

"The *Gazette* hasn't run an extra in twenty years."

"So what's your problem?"

"I'd like to know what we're doing."

"You will, as soon as we have a deal."

"How can I make a deal without knowing the facts?"

"It's called trust, Aaron," Sherry said pointedly. "You trust me not to do anything to hurt you."

Aaron didn't like her tone of voice, tried to make light of it. "Of course I do. I also trust you to always try to win."

"This isn't a game. This is a case of doing the right thing."

"The right thing being . . ."

"Do we have a deal?"

"Why did we sneak off? Is this something you're keeping from Chief Harper?"

"Of course."

"Deal," Aaron said firmly.

Sherry made a face. "You're making all the wrong moves lately, Aaron. You won't make a deal just to please me. But to spite Chief Harper, you can't wait."

"I'm doing this to please you. Spiting Chief Harper's just the icing on the cake."

"I thought you liked Chief Harper."

"I do. Hey, didn't I agree to withhold the minor detail about the crossword puzzle in the guy's mouth? I play ball with Harper. But he's a cop. It's always nice to put one over on a cop."

Aaron reached an intersection, turned left.

"I didn't tell you to turn," Sherry said.

"I know, but this is the way to Billy Pickens's."

"How do you know that's where we're going?"

"Isn't it?"

"Yeah, but how'd you know?"

"The way his name didn't come up in the conversation."

"Sure hope he has an alibi."

"Yeah, that would be nice, wouldn't it?"

Aaron pulled into Billy Pickens's driveway behind a Ford station wagon. Sara Pickens opened the door in her nightgown. "Yes?" she said. She didn't look pleased to see them.

Sherry Carter didn't waste time. "There was another murder tonight. Get your husband—we need to talk before the police get here."

Sara Pickens gaped at them, then said softly, "Come in." She left them in the kitchen, returned minutes later with her husband.

Billy Pickens was wearing blue pajamas and his bathrobe. At the sight of Aaron Grant he drew back in alarm. "You are not putting our family in the paper."

"That's right," Aaron said. "This is off the record. At least until the police take some action."

"What's that supposed to mean? And what's this about another murder? Who got killed?"

"Paul Thornhill, the big-deal celebrity contestant. Someone murdered him."

"When?" Sara Pickens asked.

Billy Pickens frowned.

"The police don't know yet," Aaron answered, "but it was apparently sometime this evening. According to his wife, he went out to the liquor store and never came back. So it's important to pin down where everybody was tonight. Was your husband home all evening, Mrs. Pickens?"

Sara Pickens stared at him. "How can you ask me that? Billy had absolutely nothing to do with that man."

"Maybe not," Aaron said, "but Mrs. Roth was seen talking to him, just as she was seen talking to Billy."

"This is insane," Billy said. "Absolutely insane. Are you telling me I'm in danger?"

"That may well be," Sherry Carter said before Aaron could reply. "But the immediate danger is that the police may suspect anyone with any connection to Mrs. Roth. She talked to both of you, and that's enough for them. You're gonna need an alibi, so if you had one it would be good. So were you here all evening?"

Billy glared at her. Sherry knew how he felt. It was a hell of a thing to be asking him in front of his wife, in light of the fact he'd snuck out to call on Cora.

"I went out earlier for pizza," he said. "For the girls."

"How much earlier?"

"I don't know. Say around seven."

"And after that?"

"I was home."

"Is that right, Mrs. Pickens?"

"You doubt his word?" Sara Pickens said.

"Don't be absurd," Sherry told her. "If the police want an alibi, they don't take anyone's word, they want corroboration. Can you vouch for your husband's whereabouts the rest of the evening?"

Sara Pickens grimaced. "Actually, I went out."

"At what time?"

"Eight-thirty, nine."

"Which was it, eight-thirty or nine?"

"Hey," Billy said. "Leave my wife alone."

"Get real," Sherry told him. "When the police ask these questions, they'll be very insistent. Let's try to pin it down now."

"It was probably closer to eight-thirty," Sara told her. "I went to the store. The supermarket. Out at the mall."

"When'd you get back?"

"I don't know. Somewhere around ten."

"You were gone an hour and a half?" Aaron said.

"Something like that. I walked around the mall awhile before I shopped."

"So," Sherry said. "You can't vouch for your husband's whereabouts. But if you were out at the mall, then you had the car. So Billy couldn't have gone anywhere."

"Actually, we have two cars," Sara said.

"Really? There's only one in the driveway."

"The other's in our garage."

"Oh? And what kind of car is that?"

"What difference does that make?"

"Just trying to get things straight," Sherry said. "You have a Ford station wagon in the driveway. What kind of car is in the garage?"

"A Nissan Sentra."

"Uh-huh," Sherry said. She turned to Billy Pickens. "When you went out for pizza, what car did you take?"

"Why?"

"Someone may have seen you there at the pizza place. Or recognized your car there, or seen you getting into it. All of which would be corroboration of the fact that that's where you were."

"How about the fact I brought a pizza home for my kids?"

"That's good too, but I'd like to try to keep your daughters out of this. What time did they go to bed?"

"Ellie at eight-thirty. Wendy at nine. You're not going to wake them up, are you?"

"No, I'm not. Do you still have the pizza box?"

"It's in the garbage."

"Good. Leave it there. If the police ask, you can show them."

"This is ridiculous," Sara Pickens said.

"Maybe," Sherry agreed. "You remember what car you took out for pizza, Billy?"

"I took the Nissan. And Jed Benson saw me get into it. Carrying the pizza box. Is that enough for you?"

"Not quite," Sherry said. "Sara, which car did you take to the mall?"

Sara Pickens hesitated.

Sherry grimaced. "See, there's your problem. If Billy took the Nissan for pizza, then the Nissan should be parked *behind* the station wagon. And you'd naturally take the Nissan to the mall. But then when you came back, you'd still be parked *behind* the station wagon. The station wagon might even be in the garage. But it isn't. The Nissan's in the garage, and the station wagon's parked behind it. That looks like you took the station wagon to the mall. But if you did, how did you get out of the garage with the Nissan parked behind it? See the problem? I'm sure you do, because that's why you hesitate to answer. You know neither answer works. And you know why. And it's the same reason you're not telling us to go to hell and throwing us out of here. It's because you're really upset, you haven't had time to talk and get your stories straight, but you're trying to test your theories and see what you could do." Sherry raised a finger. "Now, *I'll* tell *you* what really happened. Billy went out for pizza, like he said. He admits he drove the Nissan because he has to, since he was seen in it. He drove home with the pizza. After dinner, Sara, you took the Nissan and went shopping in the mall. You've got groceries to prove it, though an hour and a half is a long time for grocery shopping, but I won't get into that now. The point is, you got back and found the garage door open and the station wagon gone. You put the Nissan in the garage, unloaded your groceries, and proceeded to sweat. Billy drove up minutes later in the station wagon, and you proceeded to sweat *him*. Was he out of his mind, what was he thinking of, leaving your girls alone? He must have had a good enough story to satisfy you, otherwise you two wouldn't be ready for bed. You'd still be arguing about it."

Billy and Sara Pickens said nothing.

"You have anything you want to tell us?" Sherry asked.

They said nothing.

"Okay, that's it. I would imagine the police will be here rather soon. I'd advise you to be forthcoming, direct, and helpful. In particular, don't let them catch you in a lie."

"We're not lying," Billy protested.

"I'm glad to hear it. On the other hand, you don't have to volunteer everything unless specifically asked. That's not to say don't be cooperative, that's just to say don't be stupid. Sorry to bother you, we'll let ourselves out."

Sherry turned, guided a rather dazed Aaron Grant out the door.

"What was that all about?" Aaron demanded, as he followed Sherry back to the car.

"Nothing, I hope," Sherry said. She left Aaron standing there, got in the passenger seat. After a moment he walked around the car and climbed in.

"Okay," Aaron said, backing out of the driveway, "I know Billy is rumored to be linked to Judy. And you're tap-dancing all around the subject, talking to his wife. What's that got to do with tonight, and what's this bit about the cars?"

"I got a bad feeling," Sherry said. "Pull over and kill your lights and motor."

"What?"

"Please, pull over to the side."

They were about a block and a half from the Pickenses' house. Aaron Grant pulled the car over to the curb, killed the motor, and turned off the lights. "Now what?" he demanded.

"We wait and watch," Sherry told him. "Is your mirror angled toward their house?"

"More or less."

"Make it more, so we don't have to turn around."

"How long are we going to be?"

"Not long enough for what you're thinking," Sherry told him. "If anything's gonna happen, it should happen right now."

She was right. Within a minute there came the roar of a motor, then headlights came on, and the Ford station wagon backed out of the Pickenses' driveway and turned onto the road. It didn't drive off, however. It sat there idling, waiting. Moments later the Nissan Sentra backed out of the driveway and pulled up ahead. The minute it was out of the way, the station wagon pulled into the driveway and drove into the garage. The Nissan Sentra backed up, then pulled into the driveway behind it. The motor died and the headlights went out.

Sherry shook her head. "Too bad," she said grimly. "I was afraid that would happen."

32

"So what was Paul Thornhill doing at your house?" Chief Harper asked as he and Cora pulled out in the police car.

"I have no idea," Cora told him.

"Had he ever been there before?"

"No, he hadn't."

"Then how did he know where you lived?"

"You got me."

"Could he have followed you home?"

Cora shook her head. "Not then. Sherry and I came home, got ready for bed, and found the body. There just wasn't time for him to follow us, someone else to follow *him*, kill him, leave the body in our backyard, and get away. Even if there were, it simply makes no sense."

"So you figure he was killed while you were out?"

"Had to be."

"You were out looking for him. While you were, he came looking for you and got killed?"

Cora grimaced. "I admit, it sounds bad."

"How long was this window of opportunity? How long were you gone?"

"I don't know. Two and a half, three hours."

"You spent that long looking for Paul Thornhill?"

"No, of course not."

"So, what were you doing?"

"Well," Cora said reluctantly, "we were also looking for Marty Haskel."

"Oh, is that right?"

"Yes, it is."

"Drive by his house?"

"Yes, we did."

"Was he home?"

"No, he wasn't."

"What did you do then?"

"We kept looking for him." Cora felt virtuous that she hadn't actually lied.

"Where did you look?"

"Around. The Rainbow Room and the Country Kitchen."

"Did you find him?"

"No, we didn't."

"And just why were you looking for Marty Haskel?"

"Because Jessica Thornhill thought she remembered Mrs. Roth talking to him *before* the incident with her husband."

"Oh?"

"Which meant she had to be talking to him about something else."

"Of course," Chief Harper said. "And you were checking up on everyone Mrs. Roth talked to?"

"Something like that."

"Seems to me she talked to Billy Pickens."

"What's your point?"

"Did you call on Billy Pickens this evening?"

"No, I did not."

"That's interesting. A direct answer. I wonder why?"

"You don't like direct answers?"

"With you I'm suspicious of them. You happen to know where Sherry and Aaron are right now?"

"Chief. They're young. They're in love."

"And they've just seen a dead body. What an aphrodisiac. I wouldn't want to stay and find out what happened. I'd rush right off to bed."

"That's rather crude, Chief."

"You're the one who suggested it."

"Yes, but in much nicer language." Cora said it in her purest Puzzle Lady rectitude.

Chief Harper pulled up at an intersection, turned toward town. "I notice Mrs. Thornhill mentioned finding her husband talking to Becky Baldwin."

"I believe she did," Cora said, glad that Chief Harper had changed the subject. "What do you make of that?"

"It's an interesting point. You were saying Jessica had no motive to kill him. But if she found him with another woman . . ."

"Talking on the town-hall steps? How compromising. Guaranteed to drive a woman mad with jealousy. Come on, give me a break."

"There's talking and there's talking," Chief Harper told her. "You women are awfully good at reading body language."

"I'll give you that," Cora said. "With my husband Frank I could always tell. But I didn't strangle him. Not that I didn't want to."

Chief Harper ignored this tangent. "Especially when you consider the other woman's Becky Baldwin. There's something about that girl makes men silly."

"You noticed that?"

"I'm over forty, but I'm not blind. All I'm saying is, granted, it's not like catching your husband in bed. But if it wasn't the first time. And if he happened to be smitten with Becky. You didn't see the two of them together at all, did you?"

"Oh."

Chief Harper grimaced. "See, there is something to it."

"No, there's nothing to it," Cora said irritably. "But you notice how Paul Thornhill was always the first one to finish his puzzle? He came out on the front steps and Becky was there with us, and that's who he chose to talk to. Evidently he was doing it again this afternoon when his wife showed up. But it couldn't have been any big deal, 'cause that TV guy was hanging around Becky Baldwin too."

"Yeah, but if it's the wife, it solves one of my problems."

"What's that?"

"How did the killer know you wouldn't be home? If the killer's gonna lure Paul Thornhill out to your house and kill him, the killer's gotta be damn sure you're not there. Well, here's one person who knows you won't be home. Mrs. Thornhill. She knows you're out looking for her husband. Plus, she's sent you off on a wild-goose chase after Marty Haskel."

"What makes you think it's a wild-goose chase?"

Chief Harper sighed in exasperation. "Are you telling me you like *Marty Haskel* for this crime?"

"Don't be absurd, Chief. I don't like Marty Haskel at all. I wanted to talk to him about what Mrs. Roth said to him, but that's it. He has absolutely no motive. I don't for a second think he did it."

"Well, that's a relief," Chief Harper said. "The way this case is going, I thought you were going to try to sell me on some wacky theory."

Cora stuck her nose in the air, maintained a dignified silence.

"So what do you make of the puzzle?" the chief asked.

"You mean what's my wacky theory?"

"I'd be happy with *any* theory."

"I have two theories. One, the killer's mocking me. The crossword puzzle's left for the same reason the body's left at my house." Cora sighed. "The problem is, it's the third puzzle. If you wanna count the crossword puzzle found under Mrs. Roth and Judy Vale's squiggles. Which is completely wrong and makes no sense at all. If the killer were doing this to mock me, this puzzle would be the first

clue. In response to my investigation. It would be like the killer saying, 'You think you're gonna solve these crimes? Fat chance, lady.' "

"What's wrong with that?"

"The Judy Vale clue was left *before* I started investigating. And
there's no connection between me and Judy Vale at all."

"The killer could have known you'd investigate."

"And left the clue? It's a woman's handwriting, Chief."

"So what if the killer's a woman? Or a man trying to make his
handwriting *look* like a woman?"

"A man would have trouble. I'm not saying it couldn't be done."

"I'm glad to hear it," Chief Harper said. "Do I dare ask what
your other theory is?"

"The more obvious theory," Cora said, "is the killer leaves the
puzzle to mock Paul Thornhill. It's Thornhill's puzzle. The killer
rolls it up, shoves it in his mouth to spite him."

"I admit that seems more likely," Chief Harper said.

"Of course it does," Cora said serenely. Miss Marple couldn't
have sounded more sage. "In which case, our killer's not Billy
Pickens. Billy Pickens doesn't know from crossword puzzles. Billy
Pickens couldn't care less about crossword puzzles. No, the crossword puzzle makes it look like a contestant. Someone who was
jealous of Paul Thornhill's success and fame. Not to mention his
constructing expertise. It's the killer sayin', 'Hi, pretty boy, how do
you like that, you with your fancy puzzles.' "

"You do vindictive well," Chief Harper said approvingly.

"Oh, it's easy," Cora said. "When you've been married as often
as I have. The point is, the crossword puzzle is awfully suggestive,
particularly with Paul Thornhill being in first place in the tournament."

"No kidding."

Chief Harper drove down Main Street, pulled up in front of
town hall.

There was a large bulletin board in the lobby, where public notices were posted, most of them relating to potluck suppers or stray

cats. On the left of the bulletin board, clean, fresh, typewritten pages had been posted with pushpins.

The heading, in caps, read: 1ST ANNUAL BAKERHAVEN CROSS-WORD-PUZZLE TOURNAMENT STANDINGS *(Puzzles #1–#6)*

Underneath was an alphabetical list of the contestants. Each player's name was followed by their score on each puzzle, their cumulative score, and finally their current rank in the tournament.

"That's a pain," Chief Harper said. "Why couldn't they post them in numerical order?"

"Bet it's the damn computer's fault," Cora said. "But there's no problem. Look. Here's Thornhill. He's ranked number one."

"Who's number two?" Chief Harper asked.

Cora put her finger on the last column, began scanning down from the top. "Let's see. Here's number three. That's Craig Carmichael. Number four is Ned Doowacker. And number two—"

Cora's voice broke off.

Chief Harper frowned, looked over her shoulder.

Number two was Marty Haskel.

33

THE LIGHTS WERE OUT AT MARTY HASKEL'S HOUSE, BUT THERE was a pickup truck parked in his drive.

"That his truck?" Cora asked.

"Yes, it is." Chief Harper frowned, shook his head. "The lights are out. I just can't imagine, he kills somebody, then calmly goes home and goes to bed."

"Your theory is murderers never sleep, Chief?"

"You know what I mean. So you like Marty Haskel for the crime?"

"I haven't heard his story yet," Cora said.

"I'm sure you'll get your chance."

Chief Harper went up on the front porch, began ringing the bell. Long, insistent rings.

After a couple of minutes there came the sound of footsteps, and a voice on the other side of the door mumbled, "Who is it?"

"Police. Open up."

The lock clicked back and the door swung open.

Marty Haskel stood there, bleary-eyed, dressed in a sleeveless

T-shirt and pink boxer shorts. "What is it?" he growled at Harper. Then he saw Cora Felton. "Sheesh. You might have warned me you had a woman with you."

"It's okay, Marty. She doesn't mind."

"Well, I do. I'm gettin' my robe."

Marty Haskel darted up the stairs, was back minutes later in a silk robe that looked as if it had never been worn. "All right, what's this all about?" he demanded.

"Where were you this evening, Marty?" Chief Harper asked.

"What's that got to do with the price of salami? Come on, Dale, what gives? I ask you what happened and you start the third-degree?"

"Sorry," Chief Harper said. "You want to go in the living room and sit down? Would that make you feel better?"

"No. A straight answer would make me feel better. What's so all-fired important you had to roust me out of bed?"

"Paul Thornhill was murdered tonight."

Marty Haskel's mouth fell open. "Are you kidding me?"

"Be a hell of a bad joke," Chief Harper said dryly. "Thornhill's dead, I'm investigating his murder. Where were you tonight?"

"Here."

"No, you weren't," Chief Harper said patiently. "Miss Felton came by to see you and you were gone."

"You came by to see me?" Marty Haskel asked Cora.

"Yes, I did." Cora Felton felt somewhat funny saying it. She wondered if Marty Haskel had discovered anything that indicated she had broken into his home.

If so, he didn't let on. He looked at Cora Felton and Chief Harper for a minute, then said, "Okay. Come in, I guess."

Without another word he shuffled into the living room and flopped down on the couch. Chief Harper and Cora followed him in, sat in chairs.

Marty Haskel rubbed his head, appeared somewhat dazed. "This can't be happening."

"I assure you it is," Chief Harper told him. "Miss Felton and I have just come from the crime scene."

Marty Haskel scowled. "What's the idea? I'm supposed to slip up, say something like I know where the crime scene is? I'm sorry to disappoint you, but I didn't happen to kill him."

"But you admit the two of you had words?"

"Words? At a crossword-puzzle tournament? Very funny, Chief."

"It's not funny," Chief Harper said. "It's late, I'm tired, and I got my third murder in a week. But the fact is, at this Fun Night event you seemed pretty upset with Mr. Thornhill."

"Oh, for goodness sakes," Marty Haskel said. "I objected to him winning the games for his wife. I thought it was mighty poor form. You think I'd kill him over that?"

"I don't know what I think at this point," Chief Harper said. "I'm merely following up leads. The lead I'm following up now is that on Fun Night you talked to Mrs. Roth and Mr. Thornhill and now both are dead. Now, don't you find that a little suspicious?"

Marty Haskel set his jaw. "I most certainly do not. And if you had a brain in your head, you wouldn't either. I went to talk to him when the two of them were talking together. That puts the two of *them* together. It doesn't put them together with *me*. I would think that would be obvious."

"Except for one thing," Cora pointed out. "You were seen talking to Mrs. Roth *before* the incident with Paul Thornhill."

Marty Haskel frowned. "Seen by who?"

"That's not the point," Chief Harper said. "I'm asking if you spoke to Mrs. Roth before you had words with Paul Thornhill about his wife winning the first event."

"As a matter of fact, I did."

"Really? And what did you talk to her about?"

"Same thing. And I didn't talk to her, she talked to *me*. She talked to me at the end of the first puzzle, told me to calm down, not make a big deal. So I wasn't surprised when she intervened again."

"Why exactly were you making a big deal about the puzzle?"

"They call it Fun Night. What's fun about watching Paul Smarty-Pants win everything?"

"You didn't like Thornhill?"

"No, I didn't. Did you?"

"I didn't know him."

"You didn't have to know him. You just had to see him. Smug, arrogant, God's gift to women." At Chief Harper's look Marty snapped, "What, I shouldn't say that? I can't speak ill of the dead? It makes me guilty? Well, you asked me what I had against him, and that's what I had against him."

"Uh-huh," Chief Harper said noncommittally. "And just where were you this evening?"

"I was out."

"I gathered that, Marty, from the fact you weren't here. You care to elaborate on that?"

"Not particularly," Haskel snapped.

Chief Harper frowned and battled for patience. "Marty. I'm not sure I'm making myself clear. I'm investigating a murder. I'm asking you questions with regard to that investigation. If you choose not to answer them, that's going to be considered suspicious. Which is just too bad. Because I don't think you had anything to do with this, and I'd like to cross you off my list. You're making it very hard to do that. So I'll ask you one last time: Where were you tonight?"

Marty Haskel cupped his chin, ran his thumb and forefinger down over his mustache. His eyes flicked to Cora Felton. "I have to tell you in front of her?"

"Is it like that, Marty? You're saying you were with a woman?"

Marty snorted. "Sheesh. If I was, Chief, you think I wouldn't just say so? At least then I'd have an alibi witness, wouldn't I, which is what you're lookin' for here."

"I'm afraid I am. We happen to know you weren't home at the time Paul Thornhill was murdered. Doesn't mean you murdered him, but it means we'd like to know where you were."

"How come she's got to be here?" Marty Haskel persisted.

"She's helping me investigate the crime. She's helped me in the past, and this time the crime relates to the crossword-puzzle tournament."

"Why do you think it relates to the tournament?"

"Because one of the contestants was killed."

"That's dumb. It's your third killing and your first contestant. Clearly the tournament's got nothing to do with it."

"Is that how you figure?"

"Fact's a fact. You can't get away from it." Haskel put his hands on his knees, rocked forward on the couch. "What a nightmare. You'll pardon me if I'm not thinkin' as quick as you. You know the guy's dead. You come in here and spring it on me. I got to adjust. I didn't like him, but it's still quite a shock."

"I'm sure it is," Chief Harper said. "You happen to remember yet where you were tonight?"

"I know where I was. I don't think it's anybody's damn business."

"Well, Marty, tell us where."

Marty Haskel stroked his mustache again. "I was out by the lake."

"The lake?"

"Yeah. North Lake. I was at North Lake."

"It's December, Marty."

"I didn't say I was swimmin' in it," Marty Haskel snapped. "I drove out there, walked around some. I do that nights when I'm thinkin' through things."

"What were you thinking through tonight, Marty?"

Marty Haskel clamped his lips together, looked at Cora Felton. Then he exhaled, looked at the floor. "I was thinkin' about the tournament."

"What about the tournament?"

Marty Haskel muttered something under his breath.

"Couldn't hear you," Chief Harper said.

Marty Haskel inhaled, said angrily, "I was thinkin' I'd like to win. I know that sounds stupid, comin' from me. You work in a garage, you gotta be stupid. You work with your hands, you can't work with your head. Well, stupid or not, I wanted to win. To beat all the big shots. To have that TV profile be about me. I still do."

"You drop by the town hall this evening?" Chief Harper asked.

"To look at the standings? Of course I did."

"Found out you were in second place?"

"That's right."

"You realize now you're in first?" Chief Harper said it very casually.

Marty Haskel's face darkened. "Is that how you're thinkin'? Boy, is that dumb." He looked at Cora Felton. "Why didn't you straighten him out?"

Cora, who'd been left out of the conversation for some time, blinked at being addressed. "Straighten him out on what?"

"How the tournament works. Don't tell me you don't know."

"I know how the tournament works," Cora Felton said. "Precisely what aspect of the tournament are you referring to?"

"The finals, of course. I'm talking about the finals."

Cora Felton's head began to hurt at the prospect of having to explain how the finals worked.

Fortunately, Chief Harper rescued her. "I'm sure Miss Felton knows how it works, Marty. At the moment, I'm more concerned with how *you* think it works."

"I don't think, I *know,*" Marty Haskel said. "Three people make the finals. Doesn't matter who's first, second, or third, all three get in. And their score isn't carried over. It's a fresh start, one puzzle, winner-take-all. All your old score matters is, whoever has the highest score gets a few seconds' head start. Big deal. The last puzzle's so hard a few seconds won't matter." He peered at Chief Harper. "You get what I'm sayin'? I was second, now he's dead so I'm first. Big deal. Either way I get to play. Same thing with whoever's third. Now they're second, and so what? It's really no difference."

Marty stroked his mustache. "Now, I don't happen to know who it is, I wasn't payin' that much attention, 'cause what did I care? But if you wanna know who profits from Paul Thornhill's death, you gotta look and see who was *fourth.*"

34

NED DOOWACKER SEEMED NERVOUS. OF COURSE, HE WASN'T ACCUS-tomed to being rousted out of bed to answer questions for the chief of police.

It was late, because it had taken Chief Harper and Cora Felton a long time to run Ned down. As there was no record of where he was staying, it had taken trial and error to hit the right bed-and-breakfast. Elsie Dixon in her nightgown had let them in, pointed Chief Harper in the direction of Ned's door, and clumped back to bed without so much as asking what had brought the Bakerhaven police chief calling on one of her guests in the middle of the night. Chief Harper had clumped up after Elsie, returning minutes later with the aforementioned Ned Doowacker.

"But I didn't do anything," Mr. Doowacker protested. "I don't understand. What did I do?"

Cora Felton sized him up. Ned Doowacker was dressed in a white terry-cloth bathrobe and socks. His legs were bare, which made him appear tall and gawky, though he was actually no taller than Chief Harper. Cora took an instant dislike to him, wondered if it was because he had dismissed her puzzles as too easy when he'd signed up for the tournament.

"No one's accusing you of anything," Chief Harper said. "We just want to ask you a few questions."

"Questions about what?"

"Where were you tonight?"

Ned Doowacker blinked. He straightened himself up, pulled his robe around him, said with what dignity he could muster, "I fail to see how that's any of your business."

"I'm sorry," Chief Harper said. "I should have asked you to bring your shoes."

"Shoes?"

"Yes. If you're going down to the police station, you can hardly go in socks. Let's go back up to your room and get your shoes. You might pull on some pants while you're at it."

Ned Doowacker was alarmed. "Police station? What are you talking about? Why are we going to the police station?"

"Because you don't want to answer my questions. Which means I have to advise you of your rights, take you in, and give you a chance to consult an attorney. So come on, let's get your shoes."

Ned Doowacker fell all over himself trying to backtrack. He flailed his arms in front of his face, making him look like a tipsy stork. "Wait a minute, wait a minute. Did I say I wouldn't answer your questions? Not at all. I merely wondered why you're asking. Why *are* you asking, by the way?"

"Paul Thornhill was killed tonight."

Ned Doowacker's eyes bugged out of his head. He stuttered, "Pau—Pau—Pau—"

"That's right. Paul Thornhill. That's why we're asking everyone connected with him what they were doing tonight. So you needn't feel picked on. However, I must advise you you have the right to remain silent. Should you give up the right to remain silent—"

"Stop it! Stop it!" Ned Doowacker cried. He rubbed his face. "Oh, my God, this can't be happening."

"It's happened," Chief Harper said. "Now, let's try again. What were you doing tonight?"

"When?"

"After the tournament?"

"Oh? Well, I went out to eat, of course. At a restaurant near town hall. So I could go back and check on the standings. They were supposed to be posted at six, but they were late. They weren't put up till six-fifteen. Rather annoying, if you ask me. If you say six o'clock, you should do six o'clock." Ned frowned, remembering his irritation.

"So you hung out until six-fifteen just to get the scores?"

"That's right."

"And how did you do?"

"I was in fourth. Really annoying. I should have been third."

"You mean your score was wrong?"

"No, I don't mean that. I just mean I should have done better. I was ahead of Zelda Zisk, sure. But I was four points behind Craig Carmichael. *Four* points. What a pain."

"I can imagine," Chief Harper agreed. "Any particular reason you wanted to beat Craig Carmichael?"

"Of course I wanted to beat everybody," Ned Doowacker said. "But Craig in particular."

"How come?"

"Because he was a 'celebrity' contestant." Ned Doowacker held up two fingers on each hand to make quotation marks around the word. "Chosen by good old Harvey Beerbaum himself."

"You resented that?"

"Well, was it right? How's Craig Carmichael any better than I am, that's what I want to know? Four points is nothing. I can make that up like that." He snapped his fingers to indicate the speed. The gesture might have been more impressive had it been less awkward and actually managed to make a sound.

"You expect to beat Craig Carmichael tomorrow?"

"Of course I do."

"And move into third place?"

"Absolutely."

"You're in third now."

"Huh?"

"Paul Thornhill's dead. You don't have to beat Craig Carmichael. You're already in third."

Ned Doowacker tugged at his ear. "Oh. Oh," he said. "That's right, I am. But it doesn't matter. I'm going to beat him anyway."

Chief Harper frowned. His interrogation stalled. Unless Ned Doowacker was a hell of an actor, he didn't seem that concerned with moving from fourth place to third. Which killed his motivation for murder.

Sensing Chief Harper's distress, Cora Felton swooped in. "Mr. Doowacker, let me get something straight. You want to beat Craig Carmichael because he's a celebrity contestant—why is that so important?"

"I told you. Because Harvey chose him. Out of the people at the barbecue."

"Barbecue? What barbecue?"

"Harvey Beerbaum's barbecue." With a *how-could-you-be-so-stupid-not-to-know-this* look, Ned Doowacker said, as if explaining to a child, "You know, in his backyard. Here in Bakerhaven."

Cora Felton frowned. She had a vague memory of some invitation for which she'd had to invent an excuse. "A couple of months ago?"

"Sometime in September, I think. We were all there. Me, Craig, Paul, Zelda, Don, and Bev. We were all there when he pitched the idea. A big-deal puzzle tournament for charity. But when it goes forward, who does he choose? Just those three."

"Who are Don and Bev?"

"Don Hinkle and Beverly Platt." Ned Doowacker waved it away. "They're not here. When they weren't picked, they didn't come. I suppose I shouldn't have either, but it made me mad. Made me want to win."

"So you came here, determined to beat the people he picked?"

"Well, wouldn't that serve Harvey right?" Ned Doowacker said.

"It certainly would," Cora said. "So, when you finally got a look at the score tonight, you were ahead of Zelda Zisk. You were only four points away from Craig Carmichael. Unfortunately, Paul Thornhill's score was out of reach. No way to beat him."

"No need to beat him," Ned Doowacker pointed out. "I only had to get in the finals."

"Yeah, but could you beat him then? His scores were consistently better. He was top dog. You have to admit you had a motive for eliminating Paul Thornhill."

"Are you kidding me?" Ned Doowacker looked genuinely surprised. "There's been other murders. You suspect me of them as well?"

"We're still waiting to hear where you were tonight."

"Well, it's somewhat delicate."

"Delicate?" Cora twisted her tongue around the word. "Listen here, Mr. Scooby Dooby Doowacker. This is a murder case. We got no time for *delicate*. Let's go get those shoes."

Ned Doowacker gulped. "Can I trust you to be discreet?"

"Sure," Cora said. "You can trust us not to blab the fact you were out with Charlotte Drake, a married woman who was Judy Vale's next-door neighbor."

Ned Doowacker, sucker punched, deflated like a paper bag.

"Is that right?" Chief Harper said. "So what were you doing having drinks with her? Perhaps trying to find out how much she knew?"

"Of course not," Ned Doowacker said in a panicked whisper. "I swear. It never crossed my mind. I never knew she was the woman's next-door neighbor until I started talking to her."

"And then you pumped her for information," Cora said. "About whether she saw you call on Judy the night she was killed. When it turned out Charlotte hadn't seen you, you let her live."

Ned Doowacker's mouth fell open. He stared at Cora, unable to speak.

"And that's when you went to kill Thornhill instead."

Ned Doowacker struggled to recover. "Are you crazy? What are you talking about? Why in the world would I kill Judy Vale?"

"You seem to know her name well enough."

"Well, why wouldn't I after talking to her neighbor?"

"And just how did that come about?" Chief Harper countered. "That you had a rendezvous with this married woman? Do you want me to believe you just picked Charlotte Drake up in a bar?"

"Of course not," Ned fumbled. "I saw her last night. At Fun Night. At the dessert table, getting a cup of decaffeinated coffee. She asked me out for drinks."

"Charlotte Drake asked you out?"

"She asked me to meet her at the Rainbow Room. That's what I did."

"How long were you at the bar?"

"We were there from eight till nine."

"What did you do then?"

"Went for a drive, if it's any of your business."

"Anyone see you where you parked your car?"

"I didn't say I parked the car."

"No, you didn't. Anyone see you driving around, parked, or flying to the moon, for that matter? Anyone at all besides this married woman who can vouch for your whereabouts at the time?"

"Isn't she enough?"

"I don't know. I'll have to talk to her. Should I do that now? Her husband's probably home."

Ned Doowacker put up his hands. "Please, please. This is awful. I was with her from eight to eleven. She was with me the whole time. I couldn't possibly have killed Paul Thornhill. But there's no reason to go about it this way. Good God, don't get them out of bed. I'm cooperating, what more do you want?"

Chief Harper's face hardened. "I would like to know one thing, Mr. Doowacker. Not to knock your prowess as a ladies' man, but it strikes me as somewhat extraordinary that in the middle of a crowded event you walk up to a woman you never met before, whose husband happens to be there, and charm her into asking you out the next night. I can think of a lot of men in the world who would like to have your skill."

Ned frowned. "What do you mean, a woman I never met before? Did I say I never met her before?"

"Oh? When did you meet her?"

"Back in September, when Harvey had the barbecue."

"You mean Mrs. Drake was at the barbecue?"

"No, of course not. But I stayed over. It's a trek from Bakerhaven back to New York, and I don't like to drive at night, particularly after a few drinks. Anyway, I went out to this bar, the Rainbow Room, and that's where I met her."

"Her husband wasn't there?" Cora asked.

"No, of course not. That's how I got to know her. Because he wasn't there."

"Who was she there with?"

"I don't know. Some other women."

"Judy Vale?"

Ned Doowacker made a face. "I really don't know."

Chief Harper moved in, grabbed him by the bathrobe, pulled him up close. "Last chance. Think very carefully before you answer, or we're going downtown. You met Charlotte Drake with some of her friends. Was one of them Judy Vale?"

"I tell you, I don't know. It's a while ago; frankly I wasn't paying attention to anyone but her." Ned Doowacker grimaced, sucked air through his teeth. "Now, she'll tell you different. She'll tell you Judy Vale was there and I met her. Well, maybe so, but it made no impression at all. Only I can't tell Charlotte that, or she'll think I'm a noodge. So tonight I'm just nodding and saying, Yes, yes, Judy Vale, but I *don't know who she was.* I don't know if I actually met her, saw her, or even remember. Even though Charlotte says I do."

"So," Cora said, "Charlotte Drake will say you knew Judy Vale, despite the fact you claim you did not?"

"Sounds bad when you put it that way."

"Sounds bad no matter how you put it," Chief Harper said. "Tell me something. Were any of the others there in the Rainbow Room that night? Craig Carmichael? Paul Thornhill? Zelda Zisk?"

"Paul might have been. Craig and Zelda I don't remember."

"Uh-huh," Chief Harper said. "But Paul Thornhill might have been. So you're now putting yourself in this bar with *two* of the murder victims?"

"Hey, hey, hey," Ned Doowacker protested miserably. "I said he might have been. I'm not sure. And as for her, I don't know if I met her or not."

"But you might have?"

"I might have. I simply don't recall."

"If you saw her again, you think it might jog your memory?"

"Saw her again? What are you talking about? I thought she was dead."

Chief Harper nodded grimly.

"Good thinking."

35

"YOU LIKE HIM FOR THIS?" CORA FELTON ASKED CHIEF HARPER, as they headed for the funeral home out on Sunset Drive.

Cora Felton and Chief Harper were in the cruiser. Ned Doowacker was following along behind in his rental, in the hope of being allowed to go home after viewing the corpse.

"I don't like him at all," Chief Harper said. "Wrong type. I'd like Paul Thornhill for it a lot more if he wasn't dead."

"Being the victim does make him a less likely suspect," Cora agreed. "So what's wrong with Ned Doowacker?"

"Everything. The guy's too stupid to have done it." Chief Harper grimaced. "I don't mean stupid. I know the guy's a puzzle whiz. But socially, he's totally inept."

"And yet he picked up a woman," Cora pointed out.

"So what?" Chief Harper said. "Women are nuts when it comes to men. For no good reason at all they're apt to take up the least likely type and they won't even know why."

"You running for public office, Chief?"

"Of course not. Why?"

"Every now and then you come out with something, the publication of which would not be in your best interests."

Chief Harper snorted. "Every now and then you come out with a sentence, the phrasing of which would drive a normal person nuts. You wanna talk this out or not? We only got a few minutes before we get to the morgue."

"The morgue?"

"All right, so we don't have a morgue. I mean the funeral home. You wanna talk it out or not?"

"Sure. You were telling me why you don't like Ned Doowacker for the perp. And I see your point. The idea of him killing someone seems ludicrous. But say he could. Say he's wacko—not that big a stretch. I could see him killing the women, but I have a problem with Paul Thornhill."

"Me too," Chief Harper said. "You put Doowacker up against Thornhill, Thornhill wins. Doowacker doesn't wind up strangling him. It would take somebody young and athletic and strong."

"Is that how you see it?" Cora Felton said.

"I certainly do. Now, who in this case is young and athletic and strong?"

"Lots of people," Cora Felton said.

"No," Chief Harper said. "One person. Billy Pickens. The man with the motive, the man with the means, the man with the opportunity."

"Come on, Chief," Cora Felton said. "You don't suspect Billy Pickens anymore. Not with Paul Thornhill being killed. It sends the investigation off in a whole different direction."

"It did," Chief Harper said, "but it just made a U-turn. If Doowacker met Judy Vale back in September, there's a good possibility Paul Thornhill met her back then too. Say that was around the time Billy Pickens was involved with Judy. Say Billy Pickens strangled her. Say Paul Thornhill suspects this. Say *that's* what Thornhill was chatting about with Mrs. Roth."

"I'd say that's a big stretch, Chief."

"Yeah, but what isn't? We got new facts comin' in a mile a minute, and everything's a jumble. Some of this stuff's gotta play. Will you at least concede that it would take someone as strong as Billy Pickens to kill Paul Thornhill?"

"I'll accept it as a reasonable premise, Chief. But Billy's not the only strong man in town. It could be anyone who works with his hands. A mechanic, for instance."

"You're back to Marty Haskel?"

"Well, you're back to Billy Pickens."

"For good reason. Give me a reason for Marty Haskel to commit the murders."

"The reason to kill Paul Thornhill is obvious."

"And Mrs. Roth and Judy Vale?"

"I have no motive there," Cora admitted. "But I'm not ready to concede your strong-man theory. Suppose Paul Thornhill was drugged? Then Ned Doowacker could have strangled him just fine. So could Thornhill's wife. Or Billy Pickens's wife, for that matter."

"You pushing that?"

"I'm not pushing anything," Cora said. "I'm really irritated that nothing makes sense. Like you say, it's confusing to have these new facts thrown at us."

"Yeah, like that little barbecue. Remind me to give Beerbaum a piece of my mind."

"Why?" Cora Felton said. "Not that I like the guy, but how is that his fault? I mean, how could Harvey know the barbecue might be important until after Thornhill gets killed?"

"Even so," Chief Harper grumbled. He slowed the cruiser, hung a left into the driveway of the Mosely Funeral Home.

Chief Harper had called ahead, so the porch light was on, and the proprietor was actually in the doorway.

Sal Mosely, a gaunt man with sunken cheeks and a thick black hairpiece, could have passed for a cadaver himself. "This is extremely irregular," he said, as Chief Harper, Cora Felton, and Ned Doowacker came up on his porch.

"I know, Sal, but do us the favor," Chief Harper said. "I'm bringin' you business."

Sal Mosely frowned.

"We got another one," the chief told him. "Barney Nathan's cuttin' him up now. On second thought, you won't get him, though. They'll ship him home to New York."

"Another murder?" Sal Mosely said, twitching slightly.

Cora Felton couldn't tell if he was alarmed or if he regarded the prospect of a serial killer as a business opportunity.

"Right. And this guy," Chief Harper said, pointing at Ned Doowacker, "is a murder witness. That's why we need to see the body."

"Of course," Sal Mosely said. He stood aside and ushered them into a room with so many caskets in it that at first glance one would have thought the whole town of Bakerhaven had recently died. "Demonstration models," he explained. "The viewing rooms are back here."

He went to the door, switched on a light, and led them into a smaller room hung with red velvet drapes, containing a single casket. He stepped up to it, raised the lid. Ned Doowacker whimpered.

After a moment's hesitation, however, he stepped up, looked inside. "Never saw her before in my life," he said, turning away.

Cora Felton, at his shoulder, said, "Of course he hasn't. That's not Judy Vale. That's Mrs. Roth."

Sal Mosely fell all over himself apologizing. "Of course, of course. I'm extremely sorry. When you said *the body* I thought you meant the last one. Mrs. Vale's right through here. Come on."

Sal Mosely opened another door, switched on another light, led them into a more starkly furnished and much cooler room. Here a casket sat on a slab.

"Sorry about the temperature," Sal Mosely said, "but you understand, it's been a longer time than usual with this one, what with her husband . . . er, incapacitated and all. Anyway, she's all made up for a viewing, though whether that will happen remains to be seen. Extremely distressing, the way things turned out."

"Yes, it is," Chief Harper said. "If we could take a look . . ."

"Certainly," Sal Mosely said. He moved to the casket, raised the lid.

The effect was startling. Particularly after Mrs. Roth. Despite the mortician's best efforts, Mrs. Roth had seemed old, preserved, a wax figure, not really real.

But Judy Vale had died young. And she had been attractive. Alive, she had drawn men like moths to a flame.

Even in death, her beauty was evident. She had full lips and a turned-up nose. Curly red hair framed a freckled face. It was a face that in life had been saucy, impudent.

Ned Doowacker sucked in his breath. "Yes," he whispered. "I know her."

Cora Felton's mouth fell open. She was light-headed, and her stomach felt hollow.

"So do I," she said.

36

CHIEF HARPER DUMPED CREAM IN HIS COFFEE, STIRRED IT AROUND, took a huge sip. He lowered his right hand, which he'd been holding up in Cora Felton's face as if he were a cop on traffic patrol and she were an oncoming truck. "All right," he said, "what's your crazy theory?"

"I told you in the car."

"I couldn't listen in the car. You were babbling about freckles and yearbook photos and God knows what else. If I'd listened, I'd have driven off the road. Now I'm not drivin', I've got my coffee, and I'm ready to listen. I just hope you've calmed down enough to make sense."

Chief Harper and Cora Felton were having coffee at an all-night diner out on the highway, which at that time of night was the only game in town.

"I wasn't babbling," Cora said indignantly. "I was making perfect sense. You just wouldn't listen. All I was saying was the paper published Judy Vale's yearbook picture, which was ten years old, airbrushed, and black-and-white. So she's younger, they took out her freckles, and you can't see her red hair. Of course I don't recognize her."

"But now you do?"

"Sure I do. Judy Vale is the woman who stood up at the first tournament planning meeting and objected to the whole thing. Throw that in and it all makes sense."

"I'm thrilled it makes sense to you. You mind explaining it to me?"

"That's where she and Marty Haskel squared off. Not squared off, exactly, but had different views. He's fighting to keep the celebrities out, and she's fighting to close the whole thing down. At the time I thought nothing of it. Because I'm a bigot like everyone else. I wrote Marty Haskel off. I figured he works in a garage, does he really expect to compete with these puzzle whizzes? Turns out he did. Turns out he wasn't just blowing smoke, he really does have a chance to win the thing. Apparently it means a lot to him, and when he said he didn't want the celebrities in the tournament he was dead serious. And for good reason. You take the professionals out of the tournament, he wins it hands down."

"What about Judy Vale?"

"She stood up and argued against it. The tournament, I mean. Said she didn't see the point in it, and if it was just going to cause dissension, why should we bother? She was cute, spunky, and spoke pretty well."

"So?"

"So, here's another obstacle in the way of Marty Haskel winning the tournament. So Marty Haskel removes it."

"That's ridiculous."

"Is it? An hour after Marty Haskel finds out he's number two in the tournament, number one is bumped off. Now, Marty can claim it doesn't matter who's number one, but I'll bet you a gin and tonic it does to him. And you were sold enough on the idea you went to see the standings and went to question Marty. And after you did, the only thing that convinced you he couldn't have done it was the fact you couldn't connect him with Judy Vale. Well, guess what. A great big connection just got dumped in your lap."

Chief Harper frowned.

"And if it's Marty Haskel, it accounts for the body winding up at my house. If there's anyone Marty hates more than Paul Thornhill, it's me. It's my tournament. And I'm the big-time Puzzle Lady, who never even noticed him." Cora's eyes gleamed with excitement as she put all the pieces together. "So what are we gonna do now?"

Chief Harper took a sip of coffee, considered. "I know exactly what I'm gonna do."

"You gonna bust Marty Haskel?"

"No, I'm not." He took another sip of coffee, pointed his finger at Cora Felton. "You're very good when you're on my side. When you're not, you're not. That's the problem. You can make black sound like white. The town meeting's where the whole thing began? I don't think so. Not according to Ned Doowacker." Chief Harper shook his head. "That wasn't where the whole thing began at all."

37

HARVEY BEERBAUM CAME TO THE DOOR IN A BLUE SATIN ROBE with the initials *HB* monogrammed on the pocket. It was chilly for the robe, and Harvey shivered as he blinked sleepy eyes at Chief Harper and Cora Felton.

"This better be important," he griped. "I've got a tournament to run tomorrow. And *you* should be sleeping," he added insinuatingly to Cora. "You have a *big* day."

"Maybe, maybe not," Chief Harper said grimly. "Tell me, who's in first place?"

"Paul Thornhill."

"Not anymore," Chief Harper said, and pushed on by.

Harvey Beerbaum, on being told of Paul Thornhill's recent violent demise, was considerably chastened. "Good God," he said, "I had no idea. I went to sleep early. Big day tomorrow. Need to be fresh. Well, this certainly changes things. Horrible understatement. I don't know what to say. Everything seems wrong." He led them into his living room, gestured toward the couch.

Cora, who'd never been in Harvey Beerbaum's home before,

and never had a desire to, found herself repulsed by the furnishings. Crossword-puzzle art was everywhere. Framed puzzles, framed covers from puzzle books, even paintings of puzzles adorned the walls. Several trophies on the mantlepiece had Harvey's name inscribed on them.

Cora looked at the hearth, wished the fire were lit. It was cold in the room. The glass doors to the patio were uncurtained, heightening the effect.

Harvey Beerbaum sat in a leather director's chair with his back to the window. "Now then," he said. "This is a tragedy, of course, but the tournament should go on. I assume that's what you came to say."

"Actually, no," Chief Harper said. At Harvey's expression he added, "Not that I'm saying it shouldn't go on, but that's not what I came to talk about. I came about the barbecue."

Harvey Beerbaum blinked. "Excuse me? What barbecue?"

"The one you had last fall. With the players here. The crossword-puzzle people, I mean. Surely you remember."

"Yes, of course. What about it?"

"Paul Thornhill was there?"

"Yes, he was."

"What about his wife?"

"No, she wasn't with him."

"Do you remember just who *was* here?"

"Certainly. Paul Thornhill, Craig Carmichael, Zelda Zisk. Ned Doowacker, Don Hinkle, and Beverly Platt."

"What about Judy Vale? Is there any chance she was here?"

Harvey Beerbaum shook his head. "None at all."

"Do you know what she looks like?" Chief Harper said. "Aside from her picture in the paper?"

"No, that's all I've seen," Harvey Beerbaum replied. "But surely that's enough."

"I assure you it isn't," Chief Harper said glumly. "The picture is very misleading. Judy Vale was actually a young woman with green eyes, red hair, and freckles. None of which show in the picture. So

I wonder if it's possible you were mistaken about her not being at the barbecue."

"Don't be absurd," Harvey Beerbaum said. "It was my party. I know who was at it."

"The people you named are all from out of town?"

"That's right."

"Were any Bakerhaven residents at the party? Any at all?"

"No," Harvey Beerbaum said. He indicated Cora. "I invited her, of course, but she had a family function to attend."

Cora nodded dolefully, as if she still deeply regretted missing the barbecue, and wondered what particular excuse she'd invented.

"I see," Chief Harper said. "Now, this barbecue, what time did it break up?"

"It was September. It still stays light out fairly late. People began leaving around eight. I believe by nine everyone was gone."

"But some left as early as eight?"

"Yes. Some of them had to drive back to New York City. A few stayed over."

"Would you happen to recall who?"

"No, I wouldn't. It's not as if they stayed with me. Why is it important?"

"Ned Doowacker stayed in Bakerhaven. He may have met Judy Vale that night."

Harvey Beerbaum's eyes widened. "You suspect *Ned* of these crimes?"

"Not necessarily," Chief Harper replied. "But if Ned met Judy after your cookout, others may have too. Whether that makes them witnesses or suspects, I don't know. But I mean to find out."

"Well, there are only the six of them," Harvey Beerbaum said. "And only four of them came to the tournament. The other two aren't here."

"As far as we know," Chief Harper said meaningfully.

Now Beerbaum's eyes narrowed. "You suspect the people I *didn't* select to be celebrity contestants?"

"It's a thought," Chief Harper said. "I don't know if it occurred to you, but Ned Doowacker took not being picked quite personally. Others might have too."

"I assure you they didn't," Harvey Beerbaum said. "Don Hinkle only came to the barbecue because he happened to be passing through town. And Beverly Platt didn't want to do it—I actually asked her over Zelda Zisk."

"Really?" Chief Harper said, perking up. "And does Zelda know that?"

"Of course not," Harvey Beerbaum said. "You think I want to offend someone?"

"You offended Ned Doowacker."

"Anything offends Ned," Harvey Beerbaum said. "He'd have been offended even if he had been picked."

Cora Felton, who'd been looking for a spot in the conversation to weasel her way in, found it. "Tell me something, Harvey. Did you go out with your friends after your barbecue? Were you in the Rainbow Room that night?"

"Of course not," Harvey said. "It was my party. I had to clean up."

Cora could imagine that. Harvey's puzzle-encrusted living room was fastidious, with nothing out of place.

Except that the glass doors were open a crack, and the wind was whipping through. No wonder it seemed so cold. At first Cora thought she'd imagined it, but now as she watched, the door swung in an inch.

"Harvey," Cora said. "Your door's open."

Harvey frowned. "What?" He turned. "That's odd. I was sure I locked it. I always lock the doors and windows before I go to bed."

Harvey got up, went to the glass doors, and locked them.

Only they didn't lock. Harvey was turning the knob that should have shot the bolt, only it wasn't catching the other door. Puzzled, he pulled the door open wider, looked outside.

"Oh, my God!" he exclaimed.

Chief Harper was out of his chair like a shot. "What is it?"

"My door. Someone's broken the lock."

"Since you locked up tonight?"

"Must have been. The way it is now, the door won't lock, and I'm sure I locked it."

Chief Harper spun around, surveyed the living room. Aside from the glass door, there were only two exits from the room: the open entrance to the foyer, where they'd come in, and a closed door on the opposite wall.

"Where's that door lead to?" he asked.

"My office."

"Is there another door out of there?"

"No. Just a closet."

"Where's the light switch?"

"To the left. Just inside the door."

Chief Harper crossed to the door. As he went, he drew his gun.

Cora Felton was thrilled. As far as she could remember, it was the first time she'd seen him draw it. Of course, Cora had her own gun in her purse. She considered pulling it out for backup, decided against it. The chief would be angry, and Harvey would be shocked.

Chief Harper sidled up to the door, taking no chances. He turned the knob, pushed the door open. Reached his hand around, switched on the light.

Cautiously, Chief Harper peered into the room. He saw nothing, but his nostrils detected the faint odor of whiskey in the air. He flailed his arm, waving back Cora Felton, who was creeping up to look. Raising his gun, he edged his way into the room.

Harvey Beerbaum's office was small and cluttered, with one window, a writing desk, computer desk, typewriter stand, bookcases, file cabinets, and a closet. Unlike the rest of the house, the office was a mess, with books, magazines, and papers everywhere.

It was also freezing. The window was wide open, but there was a screen on it, indicating no one had gotten in or out.

Still, there was that odor of whiskey. Could someone be under the desk? No, a glance showed there was no room.

How about the closet? Could someone be hiding there?

As Chief Harper had the thought, the closet door moved slightly.

Chief Harper's heart leaped. Adrenaline raced through his veins. Good God, was he actually going to have to shoot someone?

Swiftly, he crept across the office, thinking hard. The closet door would open out. Did he want to be on the side by the knob? Then the open door would frame him, making him a target. But if he was on the other side of the door, where the hinges were, he'd have to reach all the way across to grab the knob. And what if the killer started shooting through the door?

He's a strangler, Chief Harper reminded himself. *He doesn't use a gun.*

Chief Harper flattened himself against the wall near the closet door.

The odor of whiskey was stronger.

Chief Harper reached out his hand, grabbed the knob, flung the door wide. With both hands he leveled his gun.

At nothing.

It took a second to see him. There, whimpering on the floor of the closet, curled up in a ball, and reeking of drink.

The intruder.

Craig Carmichael.

38

ROGER WINNINGTON, CRAIG CARMICHAEL'S ATTORNEY, RAN HIS
hand over his bald scalp, frowned, and pointed his finger at Cora
Felton and Harvey Beerbaum, who were sitting across from him in
Chief Harper's office. "I'm not comfortable talking in front of
them."

"I understand that," Chief Harper told him. "But seeing as how
it's four A.M., I don't really want to debate the matter. These people
are in charge of the tournament. If your client is willing to withdraw, we have no problem, and these people can go home. If he in-
sists on being allowed to play, then they'll have to hear him plead his
case."

"He's not going to plead *anything,*" Roger Winnington retorted.
"If this is a murder investigation, I'm not inclined to let my client
make a statement. On the other hand, I didn't drive up from New
York to say, 'No comment.' It so happens my client would like *very*
much to play in this tournament, if such a thing could be worked
out. For that reason, I would like to explore certain possibilities
with you. *Hypothetically,* of course."

"Of course," Chief Harper said dryly. "But I should warn you. My hypothetical threshold shuts down around two A.M. So whatever you gotta say, spit it out quickly, or I'm goin' home, and your client will spend the rest of the night in that cell back there. Then tomorrow, when the judge wakes up, you can be as hypothetical as you want."

Roger Winnington fiddled with his tie, which hung loosely around his neck. "Okay, the hypothetical is this: *Suppose* I were to concede my client was guilty of criminal trespass."

"That'd be a damn small concession on your part, considering where he was found."

"All right. Suppose the facts are these: My client knows *absolutely* nothing about any murders. Indeed, he is *shocked* and *dismayed* to learn that Mr. Thornhill is the latest victim." Roger Winnington grimaced. "Though *dismayed* might not do it—he's truly not really dismayed. And *shocked* might not do it either, because my client might have a *vague* recollection of hearing *someone* say *something* to that effect before he left the bar. Though I am not willing to *concede* the point."

"God save me," Chief Harper said. "What *are* you willing to concede?"

"I told you. Absolutely *nothing*. What I'm saying here makes *no* concessions whatsoever, it's merely *exploring* possibilities."

"Hurry up and explore 'em or I'm going home."

"All right, all right, look," Roger Winnington said. "All of this is off the record, and none of it's binding against my client. But here's the deal. Craig didn't kill anybody, he never would. All he wants to do is win the tournament. He was concerned with his position in the standings. He was third, but only a few points ahead of the fellow who was fourth. Craig couldn't bear the thought of that guy beating him. Nor could he bear the thought of losing to the guy who was second, a man who was just a rank amateur. Anyway, he kept drinking and brooding about it until he got good and drunk, and when he got drunk enough he decided to break into this guy's house to get a peek at the puzzles to give himself an advantage over his competition. Granted, a horrible, shameful thing to do.

"But there are *two* things to consider. One, it is not Craig Carmichael acting here, it is the *whiskey* talking. And, two, Craig *never* saw the puzzles—he was so drunk he couldn't find them. So there's no harm done, and no reason why he shouldn't play."

"*Attempting* to cheat doesn't count?" Chief Harper asked. "What planet are you from?"

"You'll pardon me, Chief, but I thought the legal matters were your business, and the contest was *theirs.* Mr. Beerbaum, my client is not particularly lucid, but he managed to get this across. Exposure in this matter will not just cost him the tournament, he will be ostracized from the crossword-puzzle community. He will never be able to compete again. It would be the equivalent of a life sentence."

"That's going a little far," Harvey Beerbaum protested. "It's entirely conceivable that in time he might be accepted again."

Roger Winnington made a face. "I think the key word here is *might.* Do you speak for the crossword-puzzle community?"

"Of course not."

"There you are. But if you drop him from your tournament, you will in fact be speaking for the crossword-puzzle community. You will be preempting their power and making a decision best left to *them.*"

"Nonsense," Harvey Beerbaum said. "We're running this tournament, and we must enforce the rules. It's as simple as that."

"But—"

"Whoa, time out," Chief Harper interposed. "I'm sorry to interrupt your little tangent, but I happen to have this murder here."

"Which my client had nothing to do with," Roger Winnington said. "He was drinking in the bar of a local restaurant. Perhaps you could supply me with the name?"

"The Country Kitchen?"

"Is that the one that looks like a huge log cabin?"

"Yes, it is."

"Fine. My client was drinking at the Country Kitchen most of the evening. You *should* be able to find people who saw him there."

"I saw him there," Cora Felton volunteered. "But what's it prove? He could have gone out, killed his rival, and come back. He'd still have lots of witnesses who saw him there. But you can't prove he was there all night."

The look Roger Winnington gave her was not kind. "I can raise a logical inference," he said. "Built around the fact no one will have seen him go *out*. But I thought we were just talking off the record here about what's really what. Off the record, my client didn't kill anybody. Please don't quote me on that, but it happens to be a fact. So—"

"You wanna move things along?" Chief Harper interrupted, looking at his watch.

"You think Craig did it? I don't. I think this alleged break-in is *totally* unconnected to the homicides. Unless it's your theory my client snapped, bumped off Paul Thornhill, and then decided to do this gentleman in. If so, how do you account for the other murders? I'd be *very* interested to hear."

Chief Harper scowled. "All right. What do you propose?"

"Frankly, I'd like to go to bed. As I doubt if there are any hotels nearby, that probably means driving back to New York. That's rather inconvenient if I have to show up tomorrow morning—this morning—to get my client out of jail. If at all possible, I'd like to wrap things up right now. So, what do we have here? You drop the murder counts, and you're left with the burglary. Considering nothing was stolen, that might go away. Or at least be reduced. Anyway, it's Mr. Beerbaum's house. He might not wish to press charges."

"Is that so?" Harvey Beerbaum said. "Have you ever had *your* property broken into?"

"No, I haven't, and I understand your just ire. So we have a situation here." Roger Winnington turned to Chief Harper. "I assume you're not waking up the judge to handle it now?"

"That would be a correct assumption."

"I thought so." Winnington steepled his fingers. "So, here's the way it goes, Mr. Beerbaum. Tomorrow morning you will either be in the town hall, officiating at the completion of your crossword-puzzle tournament. Or you will be in the county courthouse, pressing charges against my client. The choice is up to you."

Harvey Beerbaum frowned.

"I would imagine that would cause a *certain* backlash in the crossword-puzzle community," Winnington went on. "A juicy bit of *scandal*. And the thing about scandal is, nobody ever gets it right. Particularly people who aren't there. You know how the story will go? Craig Carmichael, ostracized from the crossword-puzzle community for *getting* the answers from Harvey Beerbaum and then getting caught. Your name will forevermore be connected with shame and scandal. Whether people believe you gave the answers to Craig Carmichael or not."

Harvey Beerbaum began to wriggle in his chair. "Now, see here. I don't want to send anybody to jail, and I don't want to ruin anybody's life. But there's no way I'm letting him compete. The possibility of him winning the tournament is totally unacceptable. No, I simply cannot allow it. He has to withdraw."

"He can't withdraw without an explanation."

"So say he got sick."

"If he were sick, he'd go home," Winnington said complacently. "Chief Harper, will you let him go home?"

"Not on your life. He's still a suspect in an ongoing murder investigation. He stays in town."

"There you are," Winnington said. "So he *can't* withdraw."

"Well, he can't play either," Beerbaum said.

"So what *can* he do?"

"He takes a dive," Cora said.

The men looked at her.

"Huh?" Winnington said.

"He makes a mistake and loses. And I don't mean in the play-off. He's not even one of the final three. He makes a mistake on the seventh puzzle tomorrow morning. I don't care what it is, just so it's

252 / PARNELL HALL

enough to knock him out of the finals. He's a smart man, he'll know what he needs to get wrong."

Cora pushed her glasses up on her nose. "If he does that, we have a deal. And we won't embarrass him by revealing any of this. Unless, of course, he's a killer, in which case all bets are off. But, barring that, we have a deal." She stuck her finger in Winnington's face. "You got that, Mr. Lawyer Man? You with your *mud-of-scandal-sticks-to-you* threats. Are we perfectly *clear*? Your client *doesn't* make the finals. Because if he *should* make the finals, Harvey and I will step in right *then* and *there* and disqualify him for *cheating*. So you make *damn* sure that he *doesn't*."

Cora leaned back in her chair and smiled at the three men, whom she had just rendered speechless.

"There," she said. "That wasn't so *hard,* now, was it?"

39

SHERRY MET CORA AT THE FRONT DOOR.

"You're still awake," Cora said. "When did the cops leave?"

"About an hour ago. They got floodlights, searched the backyard for evidence."

"Find anything?"

"I doubt it. Sam Brogan was not communicative, but I watched out the window. They bagged a few papers, but they're more likely litter than anything the killer dropped." Sherry pointed to the headlights retreating down the road. "Chief Harper drive you home?"

"Uh-huh."

"Where were you?"

"You wouldn't believe," Cora told her.

Cora brought Sherry up to date on the situation. It took a while because there was a lot to tell, what with the Judy Vale revelation, the Harvey Beerbaum barbecue, and the Craig Carmichael intrusion. By the time Cora was finished she had changed into her nightgown and climbed into bed. She yawned, stretched, said, "Whatever happened to those brownies?"

Sherry gawked at her. "Are you kidding me?"

"You mean you didn't wrap them up? They'll go stale. Even *I* know that."

"We had a murder at our house. Or have you forgotten?"

"That's no excuse. *We* didn't get killed. Life goes on."

"Cora, forget the brownies. What about Billy Pickens? Did Chief Harper ever get around to him?"

"Not unless he's out there now."

"I hope not."

"Why? I trust you and Aaron paid a call."

"Come on," Sherry said. "You think I missed your sign?"

"I'm sure you didn't. So what's his story?"

"Same as his wife's."

"Oh?"

"As of now, they seem to be on the same page. She knows he's vulnerable, knows he desperately needs an alibi. Only trouble is, they were both out last night."

"Together?"

"No."

Sherry sat on the edge of the bed and filled Cora in on the Billy and Sara Pickens situation, including them switching cars.

"Aaron knows that?" Cora asked.

"Of course."

"And he's sitting on it?"

"I'm sure he is," Sherry said.

Cora looked at her sharply. "You mean he didn't say he was?"

"Cora," Sherry said irritably. "Aaron's not publishing it. It was too late to be in this morning's paper, and it won't be in tomorrow's. I'll make sure of that, but I don't want to talk about it."

"You all right with Aaron?" Cora said.

"We're fine," Sherry said. "I'm just angry with myself 'cause I should have made this explicit, but I didn't, and it didn't occur to me till you said so. Anyway, the point is they switched cars. That implies guilty knowledge."

"You think he's the killer?"

"Or she is, and he's covering."

"And why would either of them kill Paul Thornhill?"

"Because Paul knew he or she killed Judy Vale."

Cora frowned.

"What's wrong with that?" Sherry demanded.

"Nothing, that's the problem. Everything's right with that. Because of this barbecue. Paul Thornhill might have been around just about the time Billy Pickens hooked up with Judy Vale. If Thornhill saw the two of them together, then he's a witness, and Mrs. Roth is a witness, and that's what the two of them were gabbing about on Fun Night."

"Yeah," Sherry said. "But how do they hook up at Fun Night? How does Mrs. Roth know Thornhill's a witness? Or vice versa?"

"I don't know," Cora said. "Because I don't have all the facts. But if either Billy or Sara Pickens is the killer, it just might work."

"I thought you were trying to prove Billy Pickens *wasn't* the killer."

"I am. But the facts are the facts. If he did it, I'm not going to shield him."

"You think he did?"

"Well, there's one big thing against him."

"What's that?"

"He knows where we live. Whoever killed Thornhill had to know where we live. Or at least *find* where we live. Which wouldn't be that easy when you throw in that the killer had to lure Thornhill out here. Or bring his dead body. Well, Billy Pickens not only knows where we live, he was just here. Telling us a story practically guaranteed to make us rush out and start investigating. So he not only knows where we live, *he knows we won't be home.* And he's practically the *only* person who would know that."

"That's pretty bad," Sherry said. "You passing any of this on to Chief Harper?"

"Not on your life. I don't *know* he's guilty. The man came to me for help. I'm not going to throw him to the wolves."

"So what are you gonna do?"

"I don't know." Cora considered. "Actually, I'd like to break into Marty Haskel's again, see if he's still got his crossword puzzle."

Sherry gawked at her. "You're joking!"

"When I tossed the place, I found a copy of Thornhill's puzzle in Marty's upstairs bedroom. A blank copy. Just like the one in Thornhill's mouth."

"Tossed?"

"Don't start with me. The fact is, Marty had the puzzle."

"So? If his puzzle was at home, he wasn't out planting it on a corpse."

"He could have come back and got it."

"Why didn't you ask him, then? When you were out there with Chief Harper, why didn't you ask where it was?"

"I couldn't figure out a way to slip it into the conversation. Harper's withholding the puzzle, and I couldn't admit I'd seen it."

"What about the tournament?" Sherry asked. "Is it going ahead as scheduled?"

"Yes. And I'm totally dorked, and it's all my fault." Cora shook her head in disgust. "I had the perfect out. Craig Carmichael trying to peek at the puzzles could have stopped the whole show, if I'd just played my cards right. Harvey and the chief and Craig's lawyer were so tied up in knots they were never going to agree on anything. If I'd just kept my mouth shut, they'd probably still be talking."

"Why didn't you?"

Cora grimaced. "I couldn't help myself. I think it was the sleazy shyster oozing pretentious, condescending legalese. I just wanted to stick it to him. To wipe that smug smirk off his lips. I didn't even think of the consequences. I just had to do it."

"So you *saved* the tournament?"

"Ain't that a kick in the face? Chief Harper's gonna make a brief statement, then he's gonna let 'em play. And I gotta do the commentary."

"You know what you're gonna say?"

"Not a clue." Cora looked at the clock. "And I gotta be up in three hours."

"You sure do. Better get to sleep."

"Yeah." Cora heaved herself out of bed, headed for the door.

"Hey!" Sherry said. "Where are you going?"

Cora turned back and smiled—her trademark Puzzle Lady smile. "Unless there's another corpse in the backyard, I'm going to have some brownies."

40

THE TOWN HALL WAS PACKED. ASIDE FROM THE CONTESTANTS, AN area had been roped off in the back for spectators, and it was jammed. Everyone in town had heard what had happened, and everyone was there.

The TV people were there too. The Channel 8 crew, and two other crews from New York.

Sherry Carter, standing in the back with Aaron, noted that Becky Baldwin was still hanging out with Rick Reed.

She also noted Aaron Grant's parents in the crowd. So far, they had not acknowledged Aaron's presence.

Cora Felton, bleary-eyed from lack of sleep, stood onstage with Harvey Beerbaum. The TV crews had all tried to interview her when she arrived. None had succeeded. Cora had pushed on by, ignoring the microphones thrust in her face, the shouted questions regarding the body found in her yard. Keenly aware of the cameras still trained on her, Cora was expending a great deal of energy just trying not to yawn.

Or to give Harvey Beerbaum a good swift kick in the behind.

After all, she had saved the man's bacon, bailed him out when the lawyer had him buffaloed. And yet there he stood, with the same supercilious smirk on his face, taunting her with the prospect of her commentary. He had already brought the subject up three times. Once more, and Cora would be ready to scream.

On the other side of the stage, Iris Cooper paced back and forth and glanced at her watch. It was five minutes after ten, past time for the tournament to begin. She had nudged Harvey, to no avail. He, like everyone else, was waiting on Chief Harper.

At ten-ten the chief finally came in the back door and pushed his way through the crowd. Following in his wake was the new widow, Jessica Thornhill. Fending off questions from the media, the two of them ducked under the restraining rope holding back the spectators, wove their way through the tables of contestants right up to the front of the room.

Iris Cooper descended on them instantly. "What's the story?" she demanded. "Can we get on with it?"

"That's what I want to talk about," Chief Harper told Iris. "Let me make my statement."

He stepped to the microphone. "Ladies and gentlemen. By now you are all aware of the tragedy that has struck this town. Last night there was a third murder. This time the victim was one of the contestants. In fact, a key contestant, the one who was in first place. I am referring, of course, to Paul Thornhill, whose body was discovered late last night."

A general hubbub greeted this statement.

Chief Harper raised his hands to quiet the crowd. "I know there are rumors flying around. I would like to address them now. One, that we have a suspect under arrest. This is not true. We have questioned people, and we will continue to question people. But at the present time, we have no suspect in these murders. As of right now I don't know who did it. But I assure you, I intend to find out.

"Another rumor is that the killing of Paul Thornhill took place at the home of one of the tournament cohosts. This rumor is true. To the best we can determine, at some time last night, while Miss

Cora Felton and her niece Sherry Carter were out, the killer lured Paul Thornhill to their house and murdered him in their back-yard."

The reaction from the crowd was even louder. Chief Harper waited for it to subside.

"Another rumor is that because of the killings, I intend to close this tournament down. I must say I have considered it, and it is an option. There are, however, other options. In this matter, I have been swayed by the wishes of Jessica Thornhill, Paul Thornhill's widow. She has asked to be allowed to address you. I am going to let her do so now.

"Mrs. Thornhill?"

Jessica Thornhill stepped to the microphone. She was not dressed in black, although no one could possibly hold that against her. She was up from New York, not expecting to need black. Her blue wool dress was probably the closest she had.

Her hair was pulled back from her face and fastened with a rub-ber band. Her eyes were red, her cheeks raw from tears. Her voice shook when she first spoke, then steadied with her resolve.

"My husband is dead," she began. It was here she stumbled for a moment before going on. "I want Paul's killer caught. That is more important to me than any tournament. You must see that. Surely you can understand.

"But I understand how you feel too. You came here, you paid your money, you put in your time. I could refund your entry fees, and I am willing to do that, if it would help catch Paul's killer. But I fear it would not. If you pack up and go home, what if the killer is among you? What if he is an out-of-towner who simply leaves?

"I could not bear that.

"I will not allow it.

"That must not happen.

"And you don't want that either, merely to get your money back. You want to play the game." Here again, her voice trembled. "And Paul would have wanted it too. This contest should continue for Paul's sake. In his memory. At least, that's how I feel."

Jessica Thornhill swayed slightly, clung to the microphone. "But we have a problem. The police have an investigation to pursue. If the tournament goes forward, it ends this noon, and once it ends, you go home. With the same result as if we'd called it off. It will not do."

Jessica snuffled, then braced with resolve. "So here is what I propose. We suspend the tournament—"

This announcement was greeted with howls of protest and a general swell of grumbling from the crowd.

Except from Cora Felton, whose heart leaped as if she had just gotten a death-row reprieve. Cora controlled herself, tried not to let the TV cameras catch her grinning outright.

"No, wait! Hear me out!" Jessica cried. "I didn't mean forever. We suspend it for one day, and *one day only,* completing it tomorrow at this same time."

The crowd hubbub lessened, as people digested this new wrinkle. Cora scowled.

"Now then," Jessica continued, "I know the hardships this will cause. The out-of-towners will have to stay over another day, the local people will have to miss work. That is no problem. If you are staying over, I will pay your bill. Likewise, I will compensate you for lost wages.

"And I will also sweeten the prize. In addition to the other incentives, I offer *one hundred thousand* dollars for anyone with *any* information leading to the arrest and conviction of the murderer of my husband."

Jessica Thornhill smeared a tear from her cheek. "I hope you are all willing to do that. For Paul."

Whether they were willing or not, at least there were no audible protests. The mention of one hundred thousand dollars had silenced the crowd.

With one exception.

From out of nowhere, Joey Vale staggered forward. No one had seen him coming, as he had slipped through the rope while Jessica Thornhill was speaking, and suddenly he was there, lunging to the microphone before anyone could stop him.

262 / PARNELL HALL

He was a fright, even by his recent standards. His flannel shirt was buttoned wrong—the uneven tail hung out over a pair of ripped and filthy jeans. His work boots were unlaced and clomped as he walked—indeed, the fact they stayed on his feet at all seemed nothing short of miraculous. He was unshaven, his hair was matted, and his eyes were red. For ten in the morning, he seemed quite drunk indeed.

With a snarl, he wrenched the microphone from Jessica Thornhill. "Is that right?" he demanded of the crowd. "Is that how it works? She puts up money, and you all go along? A hunnerd—hundred—thousand dollars for the killer of her husband?" Joey regrouped and bellowed, "Well, how much for the killer of my wife? Doesn't Judy's murder count for anything? Just because I haven't any money, doesn't anybody care? You don't, do you? You care about that son of a bitch, but you couldn't care less for her."

Joey Vale whirled on a trembling Jessica Thornhill. "How about it, sweetie? You care who murdered her?"

Chief Harper pushed between them, flipped a high sign to Dan Finley and Sam Brogan in the crowd. The two descended on Joey Vale and marched him away.

It took a second for Joey to realize what was happening. When he did, he began kicking and screaming. As the officers hauled him off, Becky Baldwin detached herself from Rick Reed and the camera crew, who were filming this with glee, and followed him out the door.

Up front, as Cora Felton and Harvey Beerbaum moved in to console Jessica Thornhill, Chief Harper picked up the microphone from the floor.

"Sorry for the disturbance, ladies and gentlemen," he said. "Before we were interrupted, Mrs. Thornhill was asking if you were willing to suspend the tournament for one day. Well, you'd better be, because that is now a police order. Due to an ongoing police investigation, this tournament is hereby suspended until tomorrow morning at ten o'clock."

41

AARON GRANT WOULDN'T LET SHERRY ALONE. "WHAT HAVE YOU got that you're not saying?" he persisted.

"Nothing that you can print."

"What have you got that I *can't* print?"

"Aaron, that's not fair."

"Sherry, you're talking fair? That newscaster's on the air at six o'clock. I'm in the paper tomorrow morning. And I don't have a single thing he hasn't got. That gives him a good twelve hours' head start."

"Old argument, Aaron. You've used it before."

"That makes it any less valid?"

Cora Felton came out of the town hall to find them arguing on the steps. "Ah, good, you two lovebirds are together. Aaron, can you give her a ride home?"

"Where are you going?" Sherry asked.

Cora Felton waved her hand airily. "That's on a need-to-know basis, and Aaron here doesn't need to know."

"Oh, for goodness sakes," Aaron said. "What is this, a conspiracy?"

"Of course it is," Cora replied. "I'm finding out everything I can and giving it all to Rick Reed. Boy, are you newspeople paranoid."

"Oh, is that right?" Aaron Grant said bitterly. It was the first time Cora could recall seeing him angry. "Tell me something, willya? Am I in or am I out? It was my understanding *I* was the good guy, withholding the juicy little tidbit about Billy Pickens and his wife swapping cars. Or is that how it works? Anything I happen to learn, you tell me if I can print. And anything I don't learn, you don't bother to tell me."

Before Sherry could retort, Aaron's parents came out the door. His mother smiled and started over, but his father, seeing the expression on Aaron's face, grabbed her by the arm and piloted her down the front steps.

"Gee," Sherry said, "I must have the plague."

"Oh, for God's sake!" Aaron cried, throwing up his hands. "Everything is *not* my fault."

With that he turned and stalked off.

"What was that all about?" Cora asked, watching him head in the direction of the *Gazette* offices.

"I don't know," Sherry said. "But every time we have a fight, he brings up how he can't compete with Rick Reed."

"And Becky Baldwin's still following Rick around?"

"Exactly."

Cora shook her head. "Men are so stupid. I remember my husband Henry—"

"Could we leave Henry out of this?"

"Certainly. I left him out of everything I could. So Joey Vale's back in jail again?"

"He's certainly headed in that direction."

"At least he's making work for Becky Baldwin."

"Yeah. I wonder if he can afford to pay her."

Cora sighed. "Well, looks like I'm stuck with you. You wanna hang out here or you wanna come with me? I don't have time to take you home."

"Where are you going that you couldn't tell Aaron?"

"There are people I need to see who wouldn't talk to me with a reporter hanging over my shoulder."

"Well, duh," Sherry said. "You wanna be more explicit?"

"Well, duh?" Cora said. "Sherry, for a bright, mature woman, every now and then you sound like you're back in high school."

"Are you evading the question?"

"Well, duh," Cora said. "Of course I'm evading the question. You think I wanna let you in on all my secrets?"

"What secrets?"

"Exactly," Cora said. "I *have* no secrets. And I got only twenty-four hours to crack these crimes. It's like working with a gun to my head. Worse than that, if I *can't* solve 'em in twenty-four hours, not only do I fail, but I gotta do crossword-puzzle commentary for Harvey Beerbaum."

"So who you wanna talk to?"

A jingle of earrings announced the approach of Zelda Zisk. The immense woman tripped lightly down the steps with awesome ease and dexterity. Her makeup, striking as ever, featured a heart outlined in eyebrow pencil on her left cheek. Her flamboyant topcoat was of royal purple and gold.

Cora could forgive her the excesses. When Zelda dressed that morning, she had no idea Paul Thornhill was dead.

Or did she?

Zelda was a large woman—strong enough to choke a man.

But why would she?

While Cora watched, Zelda Zisk lowered herself into a tiny blue Fiat and backed out of her space in the parking lot.

"Come on," Cora told Sherry.

"Huh?" Sherry said, but Cora was already down the steps.

Sherry hopped into the passenger seat as Cora gunned the motor, backed out, and zoomed out of the lot.

"Zelda Zisk?" Sherry asked.

"Uh-huh."

"Why Zelda Zisk? Do you think she killed Thornhill?"

"Someone did," Cora said grimly.

42

IT SEEMED FITTING THAT IN A TOWN WHERE MOST HOUSES WERE
white with black shutters, Zelda Zisk had managed to find one that
looked like a gingerbread house. Zelda's bed-and-breakfast had
more pointed peaks than structures twice its size, its facing was
stucco rather than wood, and it was painted light chocolate brown
with dark chocolate trim. The house couldn't have suited Zelda
better if she'd owned it, though Cora knew she was from New
York.

Zelda was subdued, for her. "You're here about Paul." She
sighed tragically and shook her head. The effect was like dropping
a box of silverware on the sidewalk. "Horrible business. Come on
in. They let me use the living room. We can talk there."

Cora and Sherry followed Zelda inside to a living room domi-
nated by a large marble fireplace and decorated with dolls. There
were china dolls, straw dolls, cloth dolls, plastic and rubber dolls.
They lined the mantlepiece and the windowsills, nestled on shelves
and end tables, even hung on the walls.

"I know, I know," Zelda said, as Cora and Sherry gawked at the surroundings. "It's like being on the 'It's a Small World After All' ride at Disney World." Zelda laughed deeply, then seemed to recall the solemnity of the occasion. "You get used to it after a while. Sit down and let's talk. You'll pardon me if I move things along, but I gotta make calls if I'm not gonna be back to the city till tomorrow."

"Oh?" Cora said. "If you don't mind my asking, you have a day job?"

"Of course I do." Zelda snorted. "What, you think I do puzzles for a living? I'm a stockbroker. If I'm not gonna be back till tomorrow afternoon, someone's gotta cover."

"What if they can't?"

"Then I go home. No disrespect meant, but it's just a charity tournament."

"What about the police investigation?" Cora asked.

Zelda shrugged. "I don't recall anyone instructing me to stay. If they want me, they know where to find me."

"Have the police talked to you already?"

"Why would they? Frankly, I don't understand why *you're* talking to me."

"You knew Paul Thornhill."

"Yes, I did. And I'm saddened and dismayed by his loss. But there's nothing I can do. We have to move on."

"I'd kind of like to catch his killer," Cora said.

"And I'd like to help you. But I don't know anything that would be of use."

"Maybe not. But would you mind answering a few questions?"

"Hey, I let you in. But could you make it quick? I gotta make those calls."

"Did you know Thornhill well?"

"I knew him from the games. Young up-and-comer. Bright, handsome, personable, everything going for him. And then he marries an heiress. Real rags-to-riches story. If I were a guy, I might be jealous of another guy having so much luck."

"Were you jealous anyway?"

Zelda smiled and bobbed her head, resulting in chimes. "Yes, I was. Good point. Gender doesn't enter into it. Yes, I was. Paul was just so successful in every way. So talented. And so skilled. He wasn't just a good solver, he was a good constructor too."

"Don't the two go hand in hand?"

"Not at all. *You* construct, and I've never seen *you* compete. On the other hand, I've been in the top ten for years, and I can't construct worth a damn." Zelda made a face. "That's why I did those drawings. Not that I can draw either. But Harvey asked me and I had to do something. It doesn't really hurt me to be bad at drawing—so the sketches aren't great, it doesn't matter, it's not what I do. Better that than turn in a lousy puzzle, let 'em see how poorly I construct."

"And you weren't jealous that Paul could?"

"Of course I was. He had a real flair. Sensitive, artistic, imaginative. He constructed really clever, ingenious puzzles. But I didn't kill him because of it. That would be absurd."

"I admit it seems unlikely," Cora mused. "Tell me something. You were at old Beerbaum's barbecue when this tournament was first planned last September?"

"That's right. Why?"

"Did you go out afterward?"

"No. As I recall, I went straight home to the city."

"You drove home that night?"

"I don't remember, but I must have."

"How do you know?"

"Because I didn't stay here. I booked this bed-and-breakfast for the tournament, and it's the first time I've stayed in Bakerhaven. Why do you want to know about the barbecue?"

"Whoever killed Thornhill probably knew him. Most of the people who knew him were there that day."

"You mean Craig Carmichael and Ned Doowacker? That's quite a stretch."

"Did they go out with him after the barbecue?"

"I have no idea."

"But you don't think either of them would have killed him?"

"No, I don't."

"That leaves you."

Zelda laughed, causing her jaw to ripple. "Oh ho. Clever interrogation technique. I think you've trapped me."

"Somehow I doubt it," Cora said cheerfully. "Do you have an alibi for the time of the murder?"

"Am I supposed to know the time of the murder?"

"You do if you killed him."

"Unfortunately, I didn't. Kill him, that is. Therefore I don't have an alibi for the time of the murder—whenever that was—and you got me dead to rights."

"How about yesterday evening, eight to midnight?"

"I can give you eight to ten. I was at the Country Kitchen. You saw me there. Having drinks with a young woman who happens to know my mother-in-law." Zelda made a face. "How's that for *inhibiting*? Ordinarily, I might have stayed out, let some guy buy me a drink. But under the circumstances, I was back here by ten."

"Anyone see you come in?"

"Nope. I'm the only guest. And the people who run this place were out." Zelda cocked her head, which was both musical and disconcerting. "So how about it? Is my alibi good enough?"

"I'm afraid not," Cora told her.

"That's what I figured." Zelda's eyes twinkled. "Then I guess those business calls will have to wait. There's another call I gotta make first."

Cora frowned. "Gonna call your lawyer?"

"No, my husband." Zelda giggled, and jingled. "I can't wait to hear what he says when I tell him I'm a murder suspect."

43

CHARLOTTE DRAKE WAS HOME. SHE USHERED SHERRY AND CORA into a neat but inexpensively furnished living room, said, "All right, talk. But make it quick."

Cora Felton smiled. "Make it quick? You act as if I have something to tell you."

"You mean you don't?" Charlotte said.

"Quite the contrary. I think you have something to tell me."

"Well, I don't," Charlotte said.

Cora sized her up. Charlotte was dressed today in sweater and jeans but had makeup on and her hair curled. "You just come from the town hall?" Cora asked.

"What's that got to do with you?"

Cora shrugged. "It's not a big admission. Everybody was just at the town hall. Were you there with your husband?"

"Yeah. So?"

"Where's he?"

"He and Ray went over to Chuck's to watch the football game. Chuck's got a big-screen TV."

"At eleven in the morning?"

"They like to get a head start."

"Uh-huh," Cora said. "The police been here yet?"

Charlotte paled. "What?"

"I take it they haven't. You better get ready."

"Why would the police come here?"

"Because Thornhill got bumped off last night."

"So? What's that got to do with me?"

"Ned Doowacker's a suspect. You're his alibi."

"Oh, my God!" Charlotte gasped.

"Exactly," Cora said. "Now what have you got to tell me?"

"Oh, my God!"

"That's a bit repetitious," Cora said, "but it'll do for a start. You alibiing Ned Doowacker for the whole night, say eight to twelve, or just for an hour or two?"

"This can't be happening," Charlotte said. "The police think Ned did it?"

"He's just one of many suspects. But they asked him for an alibi, and guess what he said?"

"Damn it to hell."

"Not quite. But he wasn't particularly pleased. When pressed, he named you."

"To the police?"

"That's right. You're the alibi he gave them to check."

"That son of a bitch—"

Cora nodded. "Admittedly, not the most heroic of men."

"So how will they check? The police are gonna come here?"

"Unless you head them off by going there. You could drop by the station, make a statement." Cora could almost see Charlotte's mind whirring, calculating. "Before the football game's over," she added.

"Yeah, I could do that," Charlotte said.

"I assume Ned Doowacker has a perfect alibi, otherwise you wouldn't be so eager to supply it."

"I assure you it was completely innocent," Charlotte said. "We had some drinks, shot some pool."

"How's Ned shoot?" Sherry asked.

Charlotte frowned at the interruption. "Why?"

"No reason. He just doesn't strike me as the pool type."

"Ned's very smart." Charlotte said it defensively. "You live with a man who watches football all the time, it's nice to talk to someone who's smart."

"And last night wasn't the first time you'd ever seen Ned," Cora said. "You made the date the night before. But you'd met him some time back."

"What if I did?"

"The police may not be interested, but I am. Way back in September, when you first met Ned—was that in the Rainbow Room?"

"How do you know?"

"I have his side of the story. I'd like to hear yours."

"Side of the story?"

"Bad choice of words. Viewpoint, perhaps. He remembers Judy Vale as being there. He doesn't remember her, really, but he recognized her as someone he'd seen before, and that's the only place where it could have happened. So I'm wondering if you know if she was there that night."

"Sure I do. As a matter of fact, I got a ride there with her because it was Saturday night and the boys were playing cards."

"Did you notice who else was there that night?"

"What do you mean?"

"There's been a lot of talk about Billy Pickens being the guy Judy was sweet on. Could they have been together at the Rainbow Room that night?"

Charlotte shrugged. "Maybe."

"Well, where did you get the idea those two were an item?"

"Are you kidding? I got it from Judy."

"She told you about Pickens herself?"

"Sure she did. Judy wasn't one to keep a secret."

"I see," Cora said. "And what about you? Did you tell Judy about Ned?"

"Me?" Charlotte said. "What's there to tell? It's not like we were sleeping together."

"Maybe not, but did you tell her anyway?"

"I might have."

"And did she tell you anything in return? About what went on that evening? Say, maybe on the car ride home?"

Charlotte's gaze faltered. Cora pounced.

"What is it?" she demanded. "Didn't you go home with Judy that night?"

"No," Charlotte said defensively. "But there's absolutely nothing wrong. So Ned gave me a ride home. What's the big deal?"

"Nothing," Cora said. "So you went home with Ned that night. And Judy drove herself home, and you talked about it later?"

"Oh, all right," Charlotte snapped. "She wanted to know all about Ned. And there was really nothing to tell."

"Maybe not," Cora said. "But Judy wouldn't leave it at that, would she? She wanted to know about the guy who drove you home."

"Well, sure, that was only natural, since I didn't go home with her."

"What did you tell her?"

"I told her I met a crossword-puzzle guy, brainy type, quiet and shy."

"What did she say to that?"

"For some reason that really amused her. She said, 'What a coincidence. Quiet and shy, huh?' "

"What did she mean by that?"

"I don't know. I thought she meant she met a shy guy too, but she didn't say. The next thing I know she's running around with Billy Pickens, so maybe she's talking about him. But he's not shy."

"Uh-huh. Tell me something. Were there other crossword-puzzle people at the Rainbow Room that night?"

"I didn't notice."

"What about Zelda Zisk?"

"Who?"

"The really big woman with all the jewelry. And the makeup. Surely you would have noticed her."

"Well, I didn't. I got involved talking with Ned."

"If he's so shy, how'd that happen?"

Charlotte smiled. "That's funny, really. He spilled my drink. Ned's kind of clumsy. He was sitting next to me at the bar, he reached for some peanuts, he knocked my glass over. Of course he apologized and cleaned it up and bought me another. And we got to talking."

"Interesting," Cora said. "You think he did it on purpose? Knocked your glass over?"

Charlotte frowned. "No, Ned wouldn't do that," she said, but she was clearly considering it.

"Now, last night, when you were talking with Ned, did he mention that first night you met?"

"Why do you want to know that?"

"Humor me. Did Ned talk about it?"

"Well, of course he did. He laughed about it. Spilling my drink and all. He asked if I wanted him to spill another."

"Witty guy," Cora said. "And of course he must have talked about the tournament, and how he was doing, and how he felt about it."

"I'll say," Charlotte said. "That's one topic he wasn't shy about. Good Lord, you would have thought it was the end of the world, being fourth."

"Did he talk about the guy who was third?"

"Did he ever. Now, there's a guy he could have killed, if he was going to kill someone." Charlotte put up her hand. "I shouldn't say that. I'm only kidding. The fact is, Ned didn't resent Paul Thornhill half as much as he did the other guy. The number-three guy."

"Craig Carmichael?"

"That's the one. Boy, did I get an earful about Craig. Craig and his four points. Not that I knew who Ned was talking about. Not that I've ever seen the guy. Come to think of it, that made me laugh. And you know how Ned described him?" Charlotte grinned. "'Quiet and real shy.' I had to cover my mouth to keep from laughing out loud. Ned Doowacker calling someone quiet and shy."

"So you've never seen Craig Carmichael?"

"No, I haven't. From what Ned says, he doesn't exactly stand out."

"No, he doesn't," Cora agreed. "So going back to the night you and Ned first met—the night he spilled your drink—if Carmichael was in the bar at the time, you probably wouldn't have even noticed."

Charlotte frowned. "That's funny."

"What?"

"When you put it that way, with what Ned said last night. Well, I'm not sure." Charlotte crinkled up her nose, trying to remember. "But I think he said he was."

44

"My lawyer said I shouldn't talk to you."

Cora Felton put her foot in the door to keep Craig Carmichael from slamming it. "Yes, I know," she said. "Your lawyer's quite a fellow. I was there when he made his statements. I must say they were *most* impressive."

"Then go away."

"Craig, are you acquainted with my niece, Sherry? You should be. Why don't you invite us in to chat?"

"I said go away."

"I know you did. And I'm quite impressed with the way you're standing up for your rights. When I see your lawyer again, I will give you high marks. But here's the situation. It is absolutely true that you don't have to talk to me. But if I want to talk to you—well, you can't shut me up. So, the question is, do you want me to talk out here in the hall, or would you like to invite me in?"

Craig Carmichael scowled. His room was on the second floor of a bed-and-breakfast. The other three rooms on the floor were rented to crossword-puzzle contestants, and the door to one of them was open a crack, with an eye peering out.

"All right, come in," Craig said.

He stepped back, and Cora and Sherry entered the room. It was your typical bed-and-breakfast room, with a double bed covered with a colorful quilt, a bureau, and two overstuffed chairs of dubious vintage. Cora flopped down in one, offered the other to Sherry, and pointed Craig to the bed. He ignored the suggestion, stood facing them.

"All right. What is it you have to say?"

"Well," Cora said. "Let's start off with what *you* have to say. Which is nothing, because your lawyer told you not to talk. And I sure have to admire the way he blackmailed Harvey Beerbaum into dropping the charges against you."

Cora fished her cigarettes out of her purse, lit up, and took a drag. Sherry frowned but said nothing. "Well, I got bad news for you, Craig," Cora continued. "I don't give a rat's fanny what anybody says about me. And I don't care much what they say about Harvey either—he happens to be one of the few men in North America I haven't managed to marry, so it's no skin off my nose."

Cora cocked her head, flicked her cigarette. Ash tumbled to the floor. "You following all this, Craig? I'm getting to the payoff, and I'd really like you to have the setup. It's pretty simple, really. Harvey won't tell anyone you tried to steal the answers last night. But I *will*. If you don't cooperate and tell me what I want to know, I'll blab to every Tom, Dick, and Mabel I know. I'll ruin you in the crossword-puzzle community. I will make you a laughingstock, I will make you living poison, I will make you the crossword contestants' kiss of death. Am I gettin' through to you, Craig? I'll embarrass you to hell and back, and your clever lawyer won't be able to do a damn thing about it. Except sue me for slander, and he won't do that, and you know why? Because truth is a defense for slander, and I got the witnesses to prove it. Do you really want that to happen?"

Craig Carmichael looked ill. He sank down on the bed, rubbed his temples.

"So," Cora said brightly. "What do you say we have a friendly little chat?"

Craig sighed. "What do you want to know?"

"That's more like it," Cora said. "And the good news is, I don't want to know about last night. I wanna ask you about that barbecue at Harvey's house. When the idea for the tournament first came up. You were at the barbecue."

"Yes, of course."

"After the barbecue, some of the guests went out for drinks at the Rainbow Room. Did you go along?"

Craig Carmichael pulled a handkerchief from his pants pocket, became absorbed in weaving it back and forth through his fingers. "Yes, I did."

"Who else went?"

Craig's eyes followed the path of the handkerchief. "Ned Doowacker and Paul Thornhill."

"Paul Thornhill was there?"

"That's right."

"Fascinating. When you went to the Rainbow Room for drinks, did you happen to see a pretty young woman by the name of Judy Vale?"

"I don't know any Judy Vale."

"She's the woman who was killed last Tuesday night."

"I know that, but I don't know her."

"Okay. Let's go at this another way. Did you see Neddie Doowacker talking to some woman in the bar?"

"Yes," Craig Carmichael said. He stopped pulling the handkerchief through his fingers, looked up. "Is that her?"

"Did you see the woman she came in with?"

Craig resumed weaving. "I didn't see her come in."

"Did you see her talking with another woman?"

"No, I only saw her talking with Ned."

"I wish I had a picture of Judy Vale," Cora mused. "I'd really hate to drag you down to the morgue."

"The morgue?" Craig Carmichael trembled.

"Judy Vale was very pretty. She had curly red hair and freckles."

"You mean the one who spoke up in the meeting?"

Cora could only marvel at that. Craig Carmichael had seemed almost comatose at the first tournament planning meeting. "That's right. The one who spoke at the meeting. Was that woman in the bar that night?"

"Well, she was talking to Paul, but then he went off to play pool."

"Was she talking with anyone else?"

"Yes, but I didn't know his name."

"Young man, good-looking, athletic, and strong?"

"Strong, yeah, but not that young. Not that good-looking either."

"So you don't know this man?"

"I didn't know him then. I know him now."

"Oh? And who is that?"

Craig Carmichael went on weaving, never missed a stitch.

"The local guy who's number two. Haskel."

45

MARTY HASKEL, DRESSED IN JEANS AND A GREASY WHITE T-SHIRT, was in the service station, taking the transmission out of a truck. He barely glanced up when Cora and Sherry came in. "Car break down?" he grunted.

"No," Cora said.

"Then go away. I ain't open."

"You could have fooled me," Cora retorted. "I suppose you aren't working on that truck either."

"I'm workin' on the truck. It's due tomorrow afternoon. Rich bitch says, Don't worry, if you miss work, I'll pay. Well, that don't get Charlie his truck back. Bitch can give out all the dough she wants, but I bet she can't fix a transmission."

"You bitter about that, Marty?"

Marty Haskel snorted. He looked up at her with eyes dark with malice. "Sheesh, lady, you got some nerve. You hassle me from the word go. You bring the cops to my house to question me like a suspect. My schedule's thrown all out of whack because the wife of a pretty boy happens to have money. And you ask me if I'm bitter about that. Why would I be? Me, I'm tickled pink. I'm just as happy as could be. I'm working on my day off, I'm wastin' a nice Sunday afternoon. I'm not winning no puzzle contest. So why don't you get out of my garage and let me work."

"You didn't like Paul Thornhill much," Cora Felton observed.

"Lady, we been all over that. I hated his guts, and that's a fact. I told you that the last time."

"Yeah, but you didn't tell me you knew him before."

Marty Haskel's eyes flicked up. "Huh?"

"Rainbow Room. Early this fall. You met Paul Thornhill then."

"Oh, you figure so?" Marty Haskel sneered. "Lot you know. You think a big star like him would notice a guy like me? Well, think again. I never said boo to Thornhill in the Rainbow Room, and he never said boo to me."

"But you knew he was there."

Marty Haskel scowled. "That's the stupidest thing I ever heard. What do you mean, *knew* he was there?"

"I mean you knew who he was. When Paul Thornhill was shooting pool in the Rainbow Room, you knew he was a celebrity crossword-puzzle contestant."

"No, I didn't. I just figured he was some dorky tourist."

"So you *did* meet him in the Rainbow Room," Cora said triumphantly.

"We may have shot pool. Trust me, I didn't kill him because he beat me at pool."

"So he won?" Cora Felton asked.

Marty Haskel made a face. "Now you're gonna make a big deal about that? This was barroom eight ball on a small, crowded table. It's as much luck as skill."

"I'm sure it is," Cora agreed. "So Judy Vale saw you lose to Paul Thornhill."

Marty Haskel's face hardened under the grease. "Say, what are you trying to pull?"

"I'm trying to get some straight answers," Cora replied. "You have to admit, you haven't been too forthcoming. You never mentioned Paul Thornhill before. You never mentioned meeting him with Judy Vale."

"Judy Vale," Marty Haskel said. "Who said anything about her?"

"Wasn't she there that night?"

"How the hell should I know? I never even thought about this till you brought it up."

"Well, think about it now. Last September, in the bar, you're playing pool with Paul Thornhill. Was Judy Vale there?"

Marty Haskel choked back his enraged reply, instead furrowed his brow in thought. "As a matter of fact, I think she was," he said.

"And did she speak to Thornhill?"

"I think maybe she did. I can't be sure, though."

"And you say you didn't know who he was when you shot pool with him. Did you know who he was *before* he left?"

"Someone may have mentioned something."

"Oh, is that right?" Cora Felton said. "And could that someone have been Judy Vale?"

"It might have been," Marty Haskel said grudgingly.

"So," Cora said, "in that first planning meeting for the tournament, when Judy Vale stood up and spoke against the tournament, and Paul Thornhill stood up and was introduced, it all came back. That night in the Rainbow Room, Paul Thornhill beating you at pool, Judy watching, telling you he was a celebrity—it all clicked, didn't it? The pretty girl who laughs, who sees you lose. Then runs off with someone else. Was Billy Pickens there that night?"

Marty Haskel, primed for an angry retort, tripped instead on the change of subject. "Billy Pickens? What are you talking about, Pickens? Who said anything about Pickens?"

"Wasn't he there?" Cora asked serenely.

"If he was, it's the first I knew of it." Marty Haskel shook his head. "I can't follow what you're talking about, lady. You're scatterbrained."

Before Cora could defend her logic, there came the sound of a car approaching fast. Brakes squealed, and Chief Harper's police cruiser fishtailed into the service station and rocked to a stop. The chief jumped out, strode over to the garage, and slammed open the door. If possible, he looked less pleased to see Cora than Marty Haskel had.

"Miss Felton, I'd like a word with you."

"That would be fine, Chief," Cora said meekly. "I'm just having a word with Marty here. And he's telling me some fascinating things about meeting Paul Thornhill last fall. In the Rainbow Room after Harvey's little cookout."

"I'm sure he is," Chief Harper said sourly. "Marty, I'm sorry if you've been bothered. I should point out that just because Miss Felton came along with me last night, she's not making her own independent investigation, and you have no need to answer her questions." He stared Cora Felton down. "As I'm sure she is aware."

"Oh, absolutely, Chief," Cora said blithely. "And I'm certainly glad you're here in your *official* capacity. Seeing as how Marty has already admitted to meeting Thornhill last fall, losing to him at pool, and being informed who he was by Judy Vale, who happened to be looking on that night, I'd suggest you try some questions of your own. In particular, I'd ask Marty where his crossword puzzle is."

Chief Harper glowered at her.

"Because," Cora went on, unabashed, "he admittedly had a thing against Paul Thornhill, so he might have kept a copy of his puzzle, if only to mock it."

Chief Harper turned from Cora to Marty Haskel. "You got that puzzle, Marty?"

Marty Haskel shivered. "You wanna shut that door?"

"Sorry," Chief Harper said. He stepped inside, closed the garage door. "You got that puzzle?" he repeated.

"What if I do?"

"Frankly, Marty, I'm just trying to judge how batty Miss Felton's ideas are. You keep that puzzle 'cause you hated Thornhill?"

"I didn't say I kept the puzzle."

"No, but you did, didn't you? Marty, I wanna help you, so humor me. Did you take a copy of Paul Thornhill's puzzle home?"

"Yeah, I did."

"Did you do it? Did you fill it in?"

"No, I didn't."

"Why not?"

"I looked at it, saw it was simple. No challenge, not worth my time."

"Couldn't you tell that before you brought it home?"

"Yeah. So?"

"So why'd you bring it home?"

"You're missing the point, Chief," Cora intervened. "That's *why* he brought it home. To gloat over Paul Thornhill's simple, stupid puzzle."

Chief Harper frowned. "Marty, you're telling me you've got a copy of Paul Thornhill's puzzle, unfilled-in, at home?"

"Yeah. So?"

"I want it."

Marty blinked. "Huh?"

"I need that puzzle. Let's go get it."

"You gotta be kidding."

"I'm not. Come on, Marty. Let's go."

"In the middle of a transmission job?" Marty Haskel held out his hands. "I mean, look at me."

"Go wash up, Marty. I'll wait for you. I'm sorry, but we're going now."

Marty Haskel stared at Chief Harper in disbelief. Then he turned and stomped off to the sink in the back of the garage.

Cora Felton pulled Chief Harper outside. Sherry followed, closing the garage door.

"All right, what's the story?" Cora hissed, with a quick glance to make sure Marty Haskel was out of earshot. "What are you doing here?"

"What am I doing here? That's a laugh. As if you didn't send Judy Vale's neighbor to the police station to see me."

"Oh, she went?"

"You're so surprised? Charlotte Drake says you practically drove her there yourself. Though, the way I understand it, you wouldn't have had time to give her the ride. You've been pretty busy."

"I happen to be chasing down a very good lead. You hear what I just said about the Rainbow Room?"

"Yes, I did, and I got your broad hints too, and I will be checking out whether Marty Haskel still has his puzzle." Chief Harper squinted at her suspiciously. "What made you think he had a puzzle in the first place?"

"Just a lucky guess," Cora said. "After all, the guy's obsessed with Thornhill. Anyway, if he can't find his puzzle, it'll be extremely incriminating."

"Sure," Chief Harper said. "I'll suspect him of being a total moron if he had a puzzle, left it on Paul Thornhill's body, and then admitted having it in the first place. You mind telling me how that makes any sense?"

"He was stunned by the question about the puzzle. He didn't expect it. He wouldn't be the first perp to blurt out something wrong."

"I'll check it out," Chief Harper said. "But I don't think it matters."

"Why not?" Sherry cut in. "Come on, Chief. This is the way you two always talk at cross-purposes, when you're holding something back. Why don't you like Marty Haskel for it? What new evidence have you got?"

Chief Harper looked at Sherry, shrugged. "Okay, you got me. I'm not keen on Marty as a killer because other people look better."

"What other people?" Sherry asked.

"I don't know, because I haven't sorted it out yet, but I got a lot of new faces. Sara Pickens kills Judy Vale for stealing her husband. Sara kills the other two to cover it up. Jessica Thornhill kills Judy Vale for stealing *her* husband. She strangles Mrs. Roth to cover that up, then kills Thornhill in a fit of rage. Or Charlotte Drake, insanely jealous of Judy Vale, does her in. Does in Mrs. Roth to cover it up, then bumps off Paul Thornhill to help her boyfriend Doowacker."

"My," Cora said placidly. "The only thing I can agree with is your comment about not having thought it out yet, Chief. With so much illogic flying around, it's hard to pick any one thing, but hadn't you decided your killer couldn't be a woman because Thornhill was too strong for a woman to kill?"

"Not anymore." Chief Harper grimaced. "But I don't want this in the paper." He leveled his finger at Sherry. "If I tell you, you promise not to tell Aaron?"

"Don't worry," Cora said. "They're barely speaking." Before Sherry could retort, Cora said, "Spill it, Chief. What have you got?"

Chief Harper lowered his voice. "Autopsy report came in. Thornhill was strangled, like we thought. Only there was a contributing injury. Blow to the back of the head. He was knocked out, *then* strangled."

"Knocked out first," Cora mused. "That's very interesting."

"It puts a whole new spin on the crime and means even the women could have done it. So suddenly the suspects have doubled. Which is all I need."

"Tell me something, Chief. These crazy scenarios you just gave me. For Jessica, Charlotte, and Sara Pickens. You got anything to back them up?"

"Actually, I do. And I like it because it's the opposite of what you think."

"What do you mean?"

"About the crossword puzzle found on the body. You're obsessing about Marty Haskel. And whether he still has his puzzle. Well, guess what? Paul Thornhill's car was left parked just up the road from your house. It was unlocked. And there was a briefcase on the front seat full of crossword puzzles. Just like the one on the body. So if Jessica Thornhill, say, wants to leave a puzzle, it's right there in the car."

Cora frowned. "And why does she leave the puzzle?"

"Why does anyone leave the puzzle?"

"I don't know. But if you figure the killer left all three puzzles, that would tend to indicate someone local. Not Jessica Thornhill."

"Right," Chief Harper said. "So what local person do you like for these crimes? Besides Marty Haskel, I mean. You gonna accuse the neighbor, Charlotte Drake? You've certainly done enough already to mess up her life."

"No way!" Cora protested. "I helped her out. I sent her to the cops before they came looking for her."

"Yeah, well, then you didn't think it through," Chief Harper said. "Not with news crews all over town. She walks out of the police station and there's Rick Reed shovin' a microphone in her face and askin' her what she's doin' there. All she said was no comment, but I'll bet you tongues will wag when *that* appears on the evening news. So I wouldn't count on bein' in the young lady's good graces."

"Oh, hell," Cora said. She heaved a sigh, thought a moment. "Okay, you were saying about the crossword puzzles found in Thornhill's car. I want one."

"Why?"

"I think we're missing a bet. The crossword puzzle on the body might be a clue."

"But there was nothing written on the crossword puzzle."

"So maybe the clue's the crossword puzzle itself. After all, Paul Thornhill wrote it."

Chief Harper looked at her incredulously. "Now you're telling me Paul Thornhill left behind a crossword puzzle, telling you who killed him? That's the stupidest thing I ever heard."

"Maybe so, Chief. But I want a copy of that puzzle."

"Okay. Hang on a minute."

Chief Harper fetched a puzzle from his cruiser, handed it over.

"You got 'em in your car?" Cora said. "Better make sure Marty Haskel doesn't get his hands on one on the way to his house."

"He'll be taking his truck. So I don't have to drive him back. Anyway, there's your puzzle. You wanna look at it and tell me who killed Paul Thornhill?"

"Not right now, Chief. But thanks all the same."

"You mean you can't tell me anything from this puzzle?" Chief Harper said ironically.

"Maybe not, Chief," Cora said. "But let me know if Marty Haskel has one."

46

"WHAT ARE YOU UP TO?" SHERRY ASKED AS CORA PULLED OUT OF the service station.

"Can you do that crossword puzzle for me?"

"Of course I can. Why?"

"I wanna study it for a clue."

"Cora."

"Or at least I wanna *claim* that's what I'm doing."

"You wanna bluff someone?"

"Yes, I do."

"And who would that be?"

"Everyone."

"Cora."

"Well, everyone but you."

"I'm going to strangle you. Which is the wrong thing to say, under the circumstances, come to think of it. Cora, stop being enigmatic and tell me what's up."

Cora piloted the car around an S curve in the road. "I feel terrible for Charlotte. I was stupid, I didn't think, I really messed things up for her. I gotta try to make it right. Maybe I can, maybe I can't. Still, I gotta give it a shot."

"Cora. The woman is no saint. She was running around on her husband. It's not the end of the world if she gets caught."

"It is if it's my fault. I gave her advice. She acted on it. It was bad advice, and now she's in the soup. She's dorked because of me. If I couldn't give her good advice, I should have kept my mouth shut."

"Cora, have you lost sight of the fact there's a killer at large?"

"Not at all. It's all tied up together." Cora grinned, gunned the motor. "I feel like the hero in some sci-fi movie. I've got till tomorrow to save the world, trap the killer, clear Billy Pickens of three homicide charges, save Charlotte Drake from the media, and wriggle out of Harvey Beerbaum's insidious little puzzle-commentary trap. Hell, maybe I can patch up you and Aaron too while I'm at it."

"Aunt Cora."

"Sorry, I shouldn't joke about that. He's a rotten, no-good scum. You're just lucky you found out before you married him. I always found out after."

"Cora, that's not funny."

"It isn't when your husband's Melvin, that's for sure. You know he wanted alimony from me? Can you imagine that—a property settlement where your fourth husband winds up paying money to your fifth? Or was it my third husband?" Cora frowned.

"Where are we going?" Sherry said, trying to change the subject.

"Downtown. We need to check in with the media."

"Are you kidding?"

"I thought I'd have a little talk with Mr. Channel 8."

"Rick Reed? How come?"

"Because I don't want him running that footage of Charlotte."

"Think you could talk him out of it?"

"Not a prayer."

"Planning on bribing him?"

"I can't bribe him. I got nothing he wants."

Sherry's eyes widened. "No! I'm not!"

"You're not what?"

"I'm not having dinner with Rick Reed."

"I never said you were."

"No, but that's your scheme. The jerk's always had the hots for me. I make a play for him, and he kills the footage. Ordinarily I'd never do it, but you figure I'm fighting with Aaron on the one hand and I'd love to ace Becky Baldwin out on the other. Is that how you see it?"

"Not at all. But it's certainly an idea. I wonder how you came up with it."

"Oh, you do, do you? You wanna look me in the eye and tell me you weren't planning on my help?"

"If I did I might drive off the road," Cora replied. "Besides, I *do* need your help. I need you to fill in Thornhill's puzzle for me."

"Right," Sherry said. "And what are you going to do with that?"

"I'm going to trap a killer."

47

"That's right," Cora Felton said. "I've uncovered the clue that cracks the case."

Rick Reed was at his insinuating best. "And yet you won't tell us who it is?"

"I'm sorry. I can't."

"Because you promised Chief Harper?"

"Actually, I haven't spoken to Chief Harper."

"Miss Felton, are you telling me you know who the killer is, but you *haven't* told the police?"

"I have no proof. It would be unfair to accuse someone when I have no proof."

"In other words, you *don't* know who the killer is."

"Oh, but I do. And I expect to get proof. It's just a matter of time. Unfortunately, there *is* no time, on account of the tournament. After the tournament tomorrow, the witnesses will all be scattered to the four winds, and it will become impossible to prove who committed these crimes. Tomorrow morning at ten A.M. the seventh puzzle will be given out. It is a forty-minute puzzle. After that, the scores will be tallied and the three finalists will be chosen. Then they'll compete in solving the last puzzle in front of everyone, working on three giant grids.

"But before that happens, while the scores are still being tallied, I will take the microphone and tell everyone who the killer is."

"I thought you had no proof."

"I don't."

"Then why are you making this announcement?"

"As a warning to the killer. That if the killer shows up tomorrow morning, he or she will be caught."

"Why do you say *he or she*? I thought you said you knew who the killer was."

"I *do*. I don't want *you* to know." Cora Felton looked directly into the camera. Her benign face filled the screen. "Last warning. I know who you are. I know what you did. Tomorrow I'm going to get you."

"There you have it," Rick Reed told the camera. "The Puzzle Lady, Cora Felton, issuing a challenge, daring a killer to show up. Does she have the goods, or is she just blowing smoke? We'll find out tomorrow morning, at town hall, at the conclusion of the seventh puzzle. You can bet most of Bakerhaven will be there, and Channel 8 will be there to bring it to you live. From Bakerhaven, this is Rick Reed, Channel 8 News."

Cora Felton scooped up the remote control from the coffee table and put the TV on mute. "Well," she said. "What do you think?"

"Not bad," Sherry said. "I can hardly tell you're bluffing. And I happen to *know* you haven't got a thing."

"Think we'll get some action?" Cora said.

"You can bet on it," Sherry said. "It's nights like this I wish Aaron had his own place so I didn't have to stay here."

"Oh, sure. Like you'd really run out on me. Nights like this are not why you wish he had his own place."

"Don't start with me," Sherry said.

"You're the one who brought up the subject."

"The subject was getting the hell out of here," Sherry pointed out. "I'd say we should check into a motel, if they weren't all booked solid."

"That would defeat the whole purpose."

"What whole purpose? Don't bluff me, Cora. You only gave that interview so they wouldn't run the footage of Charlotte coming out of the police station."

"You don't think I'm trying to trap a killer?"

"Oh, sure. But not because you know who it is. Because you haven't the *faintest idea* who it is, and you're desperate."

"Thanks for your support," Cora said dryly.

The phone rang. Sherry got up, padded into the kitchen, answered it. "Hello?"

"Get her on the phone!" Chief Harper's roar was so loud Cora could hear him in the living room. "Get her on the phone! Now!"

Cora came through the kitchen door, took the phone from Sherry. "Hi, Chief. How's it hangin'?"

"Are you crazy? Are you nuts?" Chief Harper bellowed. "Go on television, say you know who did it! I can't believe you did that!"

"Why not?"

"Why not? I'll tell you *why not.* Because it's either the truth or it's a colossal lie. If it's a lie, you got no business sayin' it, and if it's the truth, you should have brought it to me."

"Weren't you listening, Chief? I was quite candid. I admitted right off that I have no proof."

"Of course you have no proof. You have no proof because you haven't got a clue. You don't know who killed those people any more than I do."

"Maybe not, Chief, but I *do* have a clue. That crossword puzzle you gave me."

"What about it? Did you solve it?"

"A child of four could solve that puzzle, Chief. It's not particularly hard."

"And it told you who the killer is?" Harper sounded bewildered.

"That wasn't what I meant, Chief. The puzzle's important because, aside from us, the killer's the only one who knows it was found on the body. Or at least was *left* on the body."

"What do you mean by that?"

"Well, since we haven't told anybody we found it, the killer doesn't know for sure we did. As far as the killer knows, someone else came along before we got there and took that puzzle."

"What the hell are you talking about?"

"Maybe someone swiped it. Maybe a gust of wind blew it away, for all the killer knows. Anyway, you withheld the fact we found it, and that's really good, because we can use that to our advantage."

"Oh, yeah? Well, I got news for you. The crossword puzzle doesn't mean a damn thing. In the first place, Marty Haskel had his, so there's that theory out the window. And I got the report back from the handwriting expert. Guess what? Mrs. Roth solved her own puzzle, and the doodle was doodled by Judy Vale. The killer didn't leave either of them."

"Then the whole thing makes no sense."

"No kidding. So where do you get off going on television saying you know who did it?"

"Sorry, Chief, but I figured it was our best shot. Like I say, the killer doesn't know what we know. The killer doesn't know if I'm bluffing. For all the killer knows, it might be true. Unfortunately, we don't know what the killer knows, so we just have to wait."

"For what?"

"To see who tries to kill me."

48

"A CAR'S STOPPING IN THE ROAD," SHERRY REPORTED.

"I see it," Cora said, peering out the crack in the curtains.

"I don't like it. We should have let Harper come over."

"Oh, sure," Cora scoffed. "People are really going to come calling, with a police cruiser out front."

"He could have had someone drop him off."

"You like sitting in the dark with a cop all night?"

"I wouldn't mind now. Someone's certainly stopped on the road."

"Yeah. Can you see him?"

"Now it's a him?"

"Or a her. I just can't say *him or her* all night, no matter how PC it might be."

"Cora—"

"I have a gun. We're in our house. I don't think anybody's gonna break in and strangle me before I can pop them."

"I'm glad you're so cocky. We're like the nitwits in some horror movie. Hiding in a dark house when there's a demented killer lurking out there."

"In that case, we got nothing to worry about," Cora said serenely.

"How is that?"

"You're the ingenue, and I'm the comic relief, and they always survive."

"This isn't a movie," Sherry said.

The front doorknob clicked.

Cora and Sherry looked at each other.

"Didn't you lock the front door?" Sherry hissed.

"Of course not. If I locked the front door, how could anyone break in?"

Cora fished the gun out of her purse.

The front door swung open.

A shadow filled the doorway.

Cora aimed the gun.

A voice said, "Hey, where are you?"

"Aaron?" Sherry said.

"Oh, there you are," Aaron said. He closed the door, crept in, and joined them in the living room.

"You realize you almost got shot?" Sherry said irritably.

"Don't be silly," Aaron answered. "Cora wouldn't shoot me."

"Oh?" Sherry said. In the dim light she could see her aunt put away her gun and take out her cigarettes. "She happens to be rather excited about her little trap."

"I don't blame her. That was a damn good interview, Cora. If I were the killer, I'd want to do you in."

"Well, thank you for saying so." Cora smiled and lit her cigarette. "What a polite young man. And just how would you go about doing that?"

"I'd leave my car on the road and sneak up on the house. Which isn't that hard to do. I just tried it. Did you see me coming?"

"We saw you stop and park your car. We didn't see you after that."

"No good," Aaron said. "It means all the killer has to do is park another hundred yards down the road, and you're dead."

"The killer's not coming at all, with your car parked down there."

"Why not? He parks down the road, cuts through the woods, doesn't even see my car."

"Nice try, but it's no go," Cora said. "I can't have you screwing this up. You came to see Sherry, say what you gotta say to Sherry, then go home. My plan's got little enough chance of workin' without you messin' it up."

Aaron, put on the spot, could think of nothing to say.

Sherry didn't help him. "You've embarrassed him, Cora. He didn't come to see me. He came for the story."

"Don't be foolish," Aaron said. "The paper's gone to press."

"So what did you come to say?"

"I didn't come to say anything," Aaron replied. "I just came to see you. I didn't count on getting thrown out."

"I don't mean to be a killjoy," Cora told Sherry. "If you wanna go with him, that's fine."

"I'm not leaving you alone," Sherry said.

"Then I'm a killjoy. Aaron, beat it. You can talk to Sherry tomorrow. Right now, get your car off the road." Cora put her arm around Aaron's shoulders. "Come on, let's go."

Cora literally pushed him out the front door.

"Hey," Aaron protested. "What are you doing?"

"Sorry," Cora said. "But she's not going with you, and you guys won't talk in front of me, so you gotta go."

Cora slammed the door, gestured toward the road. "Come on, I'll walk you down to your car."

Aaron heaved a huge sigh and set off down the drive.

Cora kept pace, peeped up at him. "I don't know what you did to honk her off, and it's none of my business, but if there's any way you could fix it up, it's probably worth the effort."

Aaron shook his head. "I'm not entirely sure myself."

"Well, could you give me a hint?"

"It's stupid, but when she met my parents, I made the mistake of introducing her as your niece instead of my girlfriend."

"Oh."

"I know that was wrong, but her reaction was way out of proportion. I've apologized, but nothing seems to make it right."

"I see."

"I don't. What's going on?"

Cora stopped, looked up at Aaron. He was a nice young man. Maybe a little too young. Young, unspoiled, and idealistic. And naive enough to see things in black and white, with no shades of gray. Still, a nice young man.

As men went.

Sherry could do worse.

Cora put her hand on Aaron's shoulder. "Let me tell you something. Sherry's ex-husband, Dennis, was an abusive jerk."

"I know."

"Did you know they eloped? Her sophomore year. Ran off and got married. Just like that."

"So?"

"She never met his parents until after the wedding. They were angry with Dennis. They disapproved."

"So?"

"That was the first time he got drunk and hit her."

Aaron gawked at Cora, his mouth open.

"Now get out of here. I got a killer to catch."

Cora left Aaron standing there, went back inside.

"You took a long time," Sherry said.

"He didn't want to go."

The phone rang, saving Cora from further explanation. She plodded into the kitchen, picked it up.

"Miss Felton?"

"Oh, hi, Harvey." For once, Cora was glad to hear his voice. "What's up?"

"I just saw you on TV. Have you lost your mind?"

"No, but it's nice of you to ask." Cora hit speakerphone so Sherry could hear.

"This is no laughing matter," Harvey snapped peevishly. "I turn on the eleven o'clock news and there you are, pulling some crazy stunt. In the middle of my crossword-puzzle tournament."

"I thought it was *our* crossword-puzzle tournament."

"You know what I mean. You're supposed to be doing color commentary on the finals, not pulling some grandstand play to undercut everything I've done."

"You *don't* want me to name the killer? I'm going to have trouble explaining that to the police."

"But you don't know who the killer is."

"Wanna bet?"

"I beg your pardon?"

"I'll make you a bet. If I nail the killer, you do the commentary."

"You don't want to do the commentary?"

"I don't want to steal your thunder. If I'm gonna hog the spotlight discussing the murders, I wanna give you equal time."

"Miss Felton. It seems to me you are going to great lengths to avoid talking about crossword puzzles."

Cora's heart skipped. "You want my bet or not?"

"And what do I get if I win? In the event you *can't* name the killer?"

"What do you want?"

There was an icy tone of malicious triumph in Harvey's voice. "*We* do the commentary. You *and* I. *Together.* At the *same time.* We *each* have a microphone. We can ask each other questions. Discuss strategies. *Challenge each other's expertise.*"

Cora was too stunned to speak.

"So?" Harvey said insinuatingly. "Are you game? Do you still want to wager?"

"You're on," Cora said, and clicked off the phone. She grimaced at Sherry. "Don't you just hate it when somebody calls your bluff?"

"You are in serious trouble."

"Tell me about it."

"Doing the commentary alone was going to be iffy. *This* you may not survive."

"Can you help me?"

Sherry shook her head. "We could try a few rehearsals with me playing Beerbaum, but what's the point? I'd either have to take it so easy on you it wouldn't be useful, or I'd crush you like a bug."

"That's not very nice."

"Wait'll you hear Harvey. If I were you I'd call him back, say you want to call off the bet."

"I can't do that. It would be like admitting I don't know anything."

"You *don't* know anything."

"My point exactly." Cora exhaled loudly. "I need a drink." At Sherry's look she put up her hand. "But I'm not going to have one. I'm gonna keep a cool head and catch a killer. Because that's my only way out of this mess."

Cora flung open a cupboard door, took out a box of chocolate chip cookies. "Come on. Let's have a snack and see who wants to kill me."

Cora and Sherry went back in the living room and took turns watching at the window.

An hour passed.

They finished the cookies.

This time they didn't see a car. The doorknob simply turned.

Sherry, at the window, felt a sudden chill. She whirled in astonishment to discover her aunt snoring on the couch. Sherry rushed to her, shook her. "He's here!"

"Mumph," Cora mumbled, batting her arms away.

The front door swung open.

Cora's floppy drawstring purse was on the coffee table. Sherry grabbed it, groped inside.

A figure appeared, silhouetted in the doorway.

Sherry's fumbling fingers found the gun. She gripped the handle, yanked it from the purse. Good Lord, could she be doing this?

Maybe not. Her finger wasn't even on the trigger. Where *was* the trigger? And what about the safety? Where the hell was that?

Her heart thumping madly, Sherry raised the gun.

"That's far enough!" she cried. "Stop or I'll shoot!"

The intruder gasped and stepped back.

Leveling the gun, Sherry crept cautiously forward, found the floor light, and clicked it on, lighting the face of the intruder.

Billy Pickens.

49

"YOU WERE REALLY GOING TO PLUG HIM?" CORA ASKED SHERRY.

"I wasn't going to shoot him, but I wasn't going to let him strangle me either."

"Admirable sentiment," Cora said. "I quite agree. Okay, Billy. Let's have it, and it better be good. Why shouldn't I turn you over to Chief Harper right now?"

"He's probably not awake," Billy said.

Cora cocked her head. "A sense of humor? Billy, are you surprising me with a sense of humor? Or should I take that as the bravado of a beaten man?"

"Take it any way you want," Billy said. "But give it to me straight. Did you mean what you said on the air?"

"You know, everybody asks me that," Cora said. "You wanna know if I peg you as the killer?"

"No, I wanna know if you know who the killer is. If so, maybe we could cut a deal."

"A deal? Are you saying you *are* the killer?"

"Nah. But if you're going to do what you said—make some dramatic announcement tomorrow morning in town hall, explain the facts of the case, and tell who the killer is—well, can you leave me out of it?"

"Or you'll kill me?" Cora asked. "Come sneaking up to my house to try to bump me off?"

"I just came to talk."

"So you left your car way down the road and came creeping up to my house in the dark."

"I didn't want my car parked in your driveway in case the police came by."

"This time of night? You really think that's gonna happen?"

"Well, after what you said on TV . . . Did you mean it? Do you really know who did it?"

Cora Felton rubbed her forehead. "We're going around in circles, Billy, and it's gettin' me dizzy. We're not talkin' about me, we're talkin' about you. Why shouldn't I call the police, tell 'em you came sneakin' up on my house?"

"Come on, look at me. I'm not even armed."

Cora shook her head. "The killer's a strangler, Billy. You bring your hands with you?"

"Why would I want to harm you?"

"If I knew you were the killer, Billy, you might have no choice."

"Yeah, fine. But I happen to know I'm not the killer, so I know that's not possible. So who is the killer?"

"Why do you want to know?"

"What?"

"What do you care, as long as it's not you? Isn't that enough?"

Billy exhaled in frustration, set his jaw.

In the silence that followed, Sherry said, "Why'd you move your car, Billy?"

The guilty reaction was almost comical. Billy Pickens looked like he'd been caught with his hand in the cookie jar. "Who told you that?"

"No one told me. I saw you do it. When we left your house, Aaron and I drove two blocks, stopped, and waited. Sure enough, right away you and your wife came out and swapped cars. Now, is she covering for you, or are you covering for her?"

Billy turned to Cora, his face the picture of alarm. "Is that it? Is that who you think it is? Do you think it's Sara?"

"Hmm," Cora said judiciously. "Very interesting. You give an excellent impression of a man concerned for his wife. Or a killer, trying to make himself *appear* like a man concerned for his wife."

Billy started to retort, then considered. "If you know who the killer is, you know which. Stop playing games and tell me. Is it her?"

"Why'd you move the car, Billy?"

Billy glared at Cora for a moment, then snorted in frustration. "You know why I moved the car." He jerked his thumb at Sherry. "She pointed out that the position of the cars in the driveway made it look like I must have gone out. We swapped them around so the question wouldn't come up."

"It's come up now, Billy," Cora said. "Sherry, run it by me again, what you saw with the cars."

"Billy went out for pizza in the Nissan. After he came back his wife went out shopping in the mall. But when we came to see him, the station wagon was parked in the driveway and the Nissan was in the garage. The fact the cars swapped position would indicate both of them went out."

"Exactly," Cora said. "Your wife went out and so did you. Now, where did you go that night at approximately the same time Thornhill was killed?"

Billy started to protest, realized it was futile. "I went looking for Sara."

"Why?"

"She'd been gone too long. I was concerned."

"Did it occur to you she might be involved in the killings?"

"No. Not the mother of my little girls. I know she couldn't be. Still . . ."

"Still, you weren't sure."

"It sounds terrible when you say it like that. Let's just say I was confused."

"Let's just say you *are* confused," Cora corrected. "You see my problem here? If you're not the killer, there's no way you could have known Paul Thornhill was gonna die. So when you say, I was concerned where my wife was, it *seems* like it should make sense, because you're concerned where she was when a man was killed. But if you didn't know he was going to be killed, there was *no* reason to go out."

Billy Pickens glowered.

"Thought up another lie yet?" Cora asked sweetly.

Billy sulked.

"I think payback is fair game," Cora said, "and that's what you were thinking. You had your fun with poor Judy Vale, and now you're wondering if your wife's playin' around."

"Now, look—"

"No, you look," Cora interrupted. "I'm not interested in your marital problems. I've had enough marital problems in my day, and frankly, they bore the stuffing out of me. It's late, I'm tired, you've worn out your welcome. What is it you want?"

"I told you. Tomorrow, if you make an announcement, can you leave me out of it?"

Cora Felton shook her head. "Billy, I can downplay it, soft-pedal it, temporize it, and call it alleged. But if you think I can tell the story of Judy Vale's murder without mentioning you, you can forget about it. You had an affair with her. Your wife knows it, Judy's husband knows it, the neighbors know it, and half of Bakerhaven knows it. Look on the bright side: Those two little girls you keep dangling in my face are too young to know it. If it's a small part of the story, it's gonna fade away. And if you or your wife is the killer, it's gonna be pretty insignificant by comparison.

"So, do me a favor, willya? Sneak back down the road, get in your car, and go home to your wife and kids. I'm waitin' for someone to try to kill me. If it isn't you, get the devil out of here and give someone else a chance."

50

"WAKE UP, YOU'RE ALIVE."

Cora Felton opened her eyes to find her niece standing over her. Cora was on the couch in the living room. She yawned, stretched. "And no one tried to kill me?" she asked.

"I'm afraid not. And you're due at the town hall in an hour with the solution to three murders. Otherwise, you have to play microphone tag with Harvey Beerbaum."

Cora moaned. She sat up. "Aw, gee, Sherry. Did I really say that? That I knew who the killer was? What a stupid thing to say."

"Yes. That seems to be Chief Harper's opinion too."

"Yeah, I remember. I don't suppose *he* solved the murders last night?"

"You can call him and ask, but I wouldn't count on it."

"No, I guess not." Cora groaned, rubbed her head. Her hair looked like a rat's nest. She fished a cigarette out of her purse, lit it, and took a drag. "Sherry. The puzzle. Thornhill's puzzle. Did you do it for me?"

"Yeah, I did it."

"And?"

Sherry grimaced. "And it's not gonna help. Paul Thornhill didn't even write it."

Cora's head shot up. "You're kidding! Who did?"

"No one."

Cora scowled. "What?"

"It's an AutoFill."

Cora winced and put up her hand. "Sherry, I have a headache. Could you try to talk in words that make sense?"

"Sorry. Sometimes I forget you know nothing about crosswords. Well, Thornhill did this one on the computer. He used a program like Crossword Compiler, and he created his grid. Then he filled in his long answers that were going to be the theme of his puzzle.

"Then he hit AutoFill. And the computer whizzed through the thousands of words in its memory and filled in the rest of the puzzle. It's a pretty neat program. The only problem is the computer can't differentiate, so it's apt to use words no one ever heard of. For instance, here it throws in the word *Nahuatls,* which is out of place in such a simple puzzle."

Cora gawked at Sherry. "You're saying the computer wrote the puzzle?"

"That's right."

"I don't understand. I thought Paul Thornhill was supposed to be this young hotshot constructor."

"Well, you wouldn't know it from this. The clues aren't very good. And his theme doesn't even work. Here, take a look."

APOLOGIES
by Paul Thornhill

ACROSS

1 "Maybe _____" (Buddy Holly hit)
5 Juniors' juniors (Abbr.)
10 Alack's partner
14 Regulation
15 Coffee additive
16 Country bumpkin
17 Mine entrance
18 Greeting
19 Grad

DOWN

1 Confederate general
2 Video's partner
3 "I was too _____" (Brenda Lee's apology)
4 So far
5 Stupid bore (Var.)
6 Greek mountain nymph
7 Booty
8 Angel's wear
9 With finesse

20 Type of rummy
21 Beginning of Elvis's apology
23 Divinity
25 Mai _____
26 Tint
27 Uto-Aztecan languages
32 Packs away
34 Was able
35 "At the _____" (Danny and the Juniors hit)
36 British bottom
37 "I'm _____" (theme of this puzzle)
38 Cub's dad
39 Misery
40 _____ cum laude
41 Amusingly risque
42 Climbing plant
44 Wife of Zeus
45 Street guide
46 Tot's farewells
49 End of Elvis's apology
54 Head cover
55 Arab prince
56 Movie segment
57 Bear or Berra
58 Vocalize
59 "Exorcist" actress Burstyn
60 Prayer ending
61 Eye problem (Var.)
62 Burrito condiment
63 Brew

10 Ali Baba's land
11 "To Sir With Love" singer
12 Border on
13 Trucking rig
21 Charged particles
22 Praise
24 British Revolutionary War general
27 "_____ Rae" (Sally Field Oscar winner)
28 Distinctive atmosphere
29 "I ran all _____" (Impalas' apology)
30 Heavy burden
31 Nimble
32 Sayings
33 Believe (archaic)
34 Arrive
37 Assumes
38 Pointed remark
40 Remain
41 Suds
43 Come out
44 Nocturnal scavenger (Var.)
46 Cofounder of Czechoslovakia
47 Champing at the bit
48 Reek
49 Not so much
50 Leave out
51 Ivy-covered
52 Bruins' school
53 "Farmer in the _____"
57 Bark shrilly

"The theme of the puzzle is *sorry*. His long answers are song snippets. One of his quotes comes from the lyric, *I ran all the way home, just to say I'm sorry.* Another comes from, *I'm sorry, so sorry, please accept my apology. Love is blind, and I was too blind to see.* Which only fits if you know the whole damn verse, and the answer doesn't give you that.

"And Elvis's apology, *I'm a fool, but I love you, dear, until the day I die,* has nothing in it about being sorry, no matter how long you string out the verse. Worse than that, it's wrong. The actual quote is, *I'm a fool, but* I'll *love you, dear, until the day I die.* He didn't even get that right."

"Sherry, I don't know what you just said except the puzzle isn't good."

"That's the gist of it."

"Then I don't understand. Zelda Zisk said Paul Thornhill was a whiz."

"Yeah, well, maybe he figured it's a freebie for a charity event, why should he bother? At any rate, this thing's electronic. It's not gonna help you. Unless you wanna argue someone killed him for writing a lousy puzzle."

"Damn."

"I'm sorry."

Cora looked up at Sherry pleadingly through a haze of cigarette smoke. "You're sure about this? It's an electronic puzzle, he didn't even write it?"

"I'm sure."

Cora looked like a child who's just been told there's no such thing as the Easter Bunny. She inhaled, shuddered, let out a wrenching, smoky sigh.

"Then Harvey wins."

51

CORA FELTON WAS TRAPPED. SHE SAT ON THE STAGE OF THE TOWN hall like a prisoner in a cell. A prisoner with no chance to escape.

On one side of her sat Harvey Beerbaum, a smug and gloating Harvey Beerbaum, who was practically drooling at the prospect of watching her fail. Harvey had spent several minutes with a sound technician, gleefully testing the second microphone with which he planned on demonstrating just how much better a cruciverbalist he was than the much-vaunted Puzzle Lady.

Cora wondered if Harvey had any idea just how completely he would succeed.

On the other side of her stood three giant puzzle grids on upright stands. The three grids on which the finals would be played. The three grids on which she would be called upon to comment. So far, the only comment that came to mind was, "Gee, not many black squares." Which was certainly true. As Sherry had warned her, this was a *hard* puzzle, a fifteen-by-fifteen of the type found in the Friday or Saturday *New York Times.*

A *killer* puzzle.

In front of her, the one hundred or so contestants worked feverishly at their tables on the seventh puzzle. Some were finished, but none had left the room. Not this time. They couldn't have if they wanted to. They couldn't have got out the door.

In the back of the room, cordoned off by a rope, stood the spectators. Due to Cora's promise that she would publicly unmask the killer, the crowd today was a solid wall of flesh that spilled out the town-hall doors and down the front steps.

Which was why Cora Felton was sitting miserably next to Harvey Beerbaum, instead of slipping out for a smoke. Even if she could have made it through the crowd, the people out there would all have questions she wouldn't want to answer. Chief Harper, for instance, would want to know what she intended to say. And she would be hard-pressed to tell him since she didn't know herself.

Since she didn't have a clue.

And so Cora Felton sat in the front of the room like a condemned prisoner, watching the giant clock tick down the minutes to her execution.

Cora began to sweat. God, she needed a smoke. Her eyes flicked around the room, looking for a way to escape, but there was none. Directly in front of her was the Thornhills' table, eerily empty now, its blue cardboard divider dividing no one.

Behind it, at various tables, were contestants Marty Haskel, Ned Doowacker, and Zelda Zisk—all finished, of course—and former contestant Craig Carmichael, also finished after supposedly taking a dive. Cora wondered vaguely if he had.

In the crowd she saw Sherry and Aaron, and Becky Baldwin and Rick Reed. Judy Vale's neighbors, Charlotte Drake and the horsey-faced Betty Felson, and their respective husbands, were there too. So were Billy and Sara Pickens, who must have gotten a baby-sitter for the little girls. There was also a couple who looked vaguely familiar; it took a few moments for Cora to place them as Aaron Grant's parents.

Also in the crowd were Jessica Thornhill, no longer competing of course, and Joey Vale, who seemed uncharacteristically sober, either due to the solemnity of the occasion or the fact it was too early in the morning to be drunk. Both would be there seeking vengeance for their dead spouses. Both would expect answers.

Answers she did not have.

The craving for nicotine was very strong. Cora remembered a pack of Nicorettes she'd purchased ages ago, in one of her unsuccessful attempts to kick the habit. Could it still be in her bag?

Cora picked up her drawstring purse, rummaged through.

Wow. She'd brought her gun. The thought tickled her. Maybe she could shoot her way out. Yeah. Fat chance. Like Butch and Sundance at the end of the picture.

Where was that Nicorette?

Cora held the purse on her lap, pulled the top open, peered in.

A piece of paper caught her eye. Thornhill's puzzle. She'd stuck it in her purse and never looked at it. Well, what did that matter now? The computer did it anyway.

Harvey Beerbaum nudged her.

Cora Felton started, saw Harvey pointing and smirking, and looked at the clock. Uh-oh. Cora struggled to her feet, plodded to the microphone, said, "Five minutes," for the benefit of the ten or twelve people still working.

Five minutes.

With a feeling of icy doom, Cora marched back to her chair.

Dead woman walking.

Cora sat down again, tried to gather her thoughts. She had a paper in her hand. What was it? Ah, yes. Paul Thornhill's crossword puzzle.

Like the one the killer had left on his body.

The fact the police had withheld.

The thing nobody knew.

Except the killer, of course.

But no one else.

Cora felt a faint spark of hope. Could that do it? Could she nail the killer with that one simple fact?

What if she revealed the puzzle?

Chief Harper would go ballistic. It would be a major breach of trust. He would never again take her into his confidence.

And it wouldn't accomplish anything. The puzzle proved nothing. The killer would not be caught. The solution would not be revealed.

She would just look like a fool.

Even before Harvey got his shot at her.

Cora, watching the minutes ticking by, knew there was no possible hope, no possible way to save face. Even producing all three puzzles wouldn't help her. They didn't prove anything. What could she possibly say about them?

Cora had the other puzzles in her bag. She jerked them out, added Craig Carmichael's *Curious Canines* and Judy Vale's doodle to Paul Thornhill's *Apologies*. She flipped through the three puzzles, read the solutions over.

Paul Thornhill's only depressed her further. The puzzle was, as Sherry'd said, bad. Boring. A hell of an epitaph.

Epitaph.

In defeat, Cora glanced at the big clock, relentlessly ticking down the seconds till her execution.

52

"TIMES UP!" HARVEY BEERBAUM ANNOUNCED. "EVERYONE STOP working. If you still have a paper, hold it up and our volunteers will be around to collect it."

Cora sat, clutching Judy Vale's doodle. She had an impish impulse to hold it up, let a volunteer come around and collect it. She smiled slightly, then stuffed the puzzles back in her purse.

"All right. This is it," Harvey Beerbaum said gleefully. "This is the moment you've been waiting for. The judges will tally up the answers, and the three top finishers will meet in a one-puzzle play-off, right before your very eyes on these giant grids. Are all the puzzles collected? Very well. Then would the volunteers please take down the restraining ropes and let the spectators in?"

Harvey Beerbaum had seriously underestimated the will of the people. Before the volunteers could make a move, the crowd had surged forward, ducking under and climbing over the ropes before simply sweeping them away. Within seconds, everyone from outside had shoved in, filling the town hall to capacity.

Ordinarily, Harvey would have been nettled at having his authority ignored. Today he was merely pleased so many people were on hand to witness his triumph over the Puzzle Lady. Harvey's introduction of Cora was smug. "And now, before we get to the final event, my colleague, Miss Cora Felton, has an extremely *special* announcement. Miss Felton?"

Cora rose from her chair, stepped up to the mike. "Thank you very much, Harvey," she said sweetly. She grabbed the mike stand, said crisply with complete confidence, "It is time to unmask a killer. I'll try to be brief, because I know you're all eager to see the play-off. But first we have the little matter of these murders to solve.

"We are here today largely thanks to Jessica Thornhill, who made this extra day of the tournament financially possible. I see Jessica in the crowd with Chief Harper. If she could come up here with me . . . Here, Jessica. Take my seat."

All eyes were on the young widow as she made her way to the front and sat down.

"Also in the crowd I see Joey Vale. As Joey pointed out to all of us, he is every bit as interested in this matter as Mrs. Thornhill. Just because he does not have her vast resources, the death of his spouse is no less tragic, and the solution to the crime every bit as crucial. I am going to ask Joey Vale to come up here too."

Joey Vale stood up. Though his flannel shirt was unbuttoned and his eyes were bloodshot red, he had at least shaved and combed his hair, a vast improvement from his previous appearance. His demeanor was also better. He made his way to the front of the room, allowed himself to be offered a chair on the other side of Harvey Beerbaum.

"Good," Cora Felton said. "So, there we have the two interested parties in the case. The third victim, Felicity Roth, alas, had no close living relatives. Her murder is nonetheless heinous, and her killer must be found.

"And how can we do that? Only by reviewing the evidence. The evidence and the suspects.

"Here is what we know.

"Judy Vale died first. Her death was shocking, brutal, tragic.

"And yet . . .

"When it happened, no one was surprised. Because everyone knew who killed her. Her husband, Joey Vale. He had a history of violence, she had a history of infidelity. A familiar pattern. He'd beat her up, she'd pay him back by sleeping around. Furious, he would beat her up again. And so on. It had been going on for ages. No one was surprised when Joey finally went too far."

"Hey," Joey Vale protested. "You got me up here for *this*?"

"Please," Cora said. "I have to lay out all the facts and theories. That doesn't mean they're true."

Cora turned back to face her rapt audience. "To continue, the case against Joey Vale looked rather bad. However, he had an alibi. At the time of the murder, he was at the Rainbow Room shooting pool. Was his alibi any good?" Cora waggled her hand. "Yes and no. It would have been possible for him to have left the Rainbow Room just long enough to commit the crime. Not likely, but possible. So Joey Vale's alibi was not enough to rule him out.

"Which brings us to the murder of Mrs. Roth. Which clarifies things greatly."

Cora pointed at Joey. "The murder of Mrs. Roth exonerated Joey Vale. He has a perfect alibi for it. Not like his alibi for the murder of his wife, an alibi that *appears* perfect. For the murder of Felicity Roth he has an alibi that *is* perfect. On the night Mrs. Roth was killed, Joey Vale was in jail. During the entire time that the murder could possibly have been committed. No tricks, no illusions, no ifs, ands, or buts. The facts are unequivocal. Joey Vale simply couldn't have done it. He is not the killer.

"So who is?

"At this point, more suspects begin to appear. Mrs. Roth was seen at Fun Night talking to several people, including Paul Thornhill, Marty Haskel, and Billy Pickens. Which is very significant when you consider the location of her house and when you consider she was subsequently murdered. In all likelihood, Felicity Roth saw Judy Vale's killer.

"So who was that killer?

"At this point, we don't know.

"Now we must flash ahead to the murder of Paul Thornhill. Mrs. Roth talked to him at Fun Night. A significant fact. We knew it, but we ignored it. So, in a way, we are to blame. For it's now obvious Felicity Roth spoke to Paul Thornhill because he knew something about Judy Vale's death."

Cora Felton spread her arms. "How is that possible? Judy Vale was killed a good three days before Paul Thornhill even came to town. What is it he could have known?

"And what of Marty Haskel? Felicity Roth spoke to him too. Does that mean *he* knew something of Judy Vale's death? And, if so, why isn't he dead?

"Or Billy Pickens, for that matter?"

Cora smiled. "To get at the truth, I decided to work backwards. I said to myself, never mind who wanted to kill Judy Vale, let's see who wanted to kill Paul Thornhill.

"A surprising number of people had motives."

Cora pointed to the TV cameras in the back of the room. "Thanks to Harvey Beerbaum, the winner of this tournament will be profiled on television.

"Would a person kill for fifteen minutes of fame?

"You bet.

"People have killed for a lot less.

"So who profits from Paul Thornhill's demise? All the contestants who thought they couldn't beat him in the finals. Or who were afraid they wouldn't *get into* the finals.

"These include Ned Doowacker, Craig Carmichael, and Marty Haskel.

"Of the three, Marty Haskel would seem the best bet. Mrs. Roth talked to him at Fun Night. He hated Paul Thornhill. And he's local. The other two weren't even in town when Judy Vale was killed.

"And yet . . .

"Last September Harvey Beerbaum threw a barbecue. The celebrity contestants were all there. That night, some of them, including Paul Thornhill, Craig Carmichael, and Ned Doowacker, went out to the Rainbow Room.

"And met Judy Vale.

"Does that make them more suspicious than Marty Haskel?

"It might, except he was there too. And actually lost a game of pool to Paul Thornhill.

"With Judy Vale looking on.

"Reason enough for murder? Maybe not. But flash forward to the tournament planning meeting, when Harvey Beerbaum introduces his celebrity contestants. Paul Thornhill stands up and takes a bow. Marty Haskel is immediately on his feet, objecting to professionals competing in the tournament. And no sooner has he had his say but who should stand up and start shooting the tournament down but Judy Vale. The same attractive young woman who saw him lose to Paul in the Rainbow Room. And now she's bad-mouthing the tournament. Suggesting it be shut down.

"Well, think how that sounds to Marty Haskel. He doesn't want the professionals there, but if they are, he's gonna do his best to beat 'em. But by God, he wants the chance. He doesn't want some silly girl who has no personal interest in the tournament mucking things up on a whim. And in the normal course of events, she wouldn't be a problem.

"Except something happens. Women picket the town hall, protesting the tournament. Marty Haskel is sure Judy Vale is behind it. She isn't, it's merely a coincidence, but Marty doesn't know that. He's furious, and he strikes."

Marty Haskel, to his credit, heeding Cora's earlier admonition to Joey Vale, glowered in silence.

"Which explains Mrs. Roth. She knows Marty's the killer and confronts him at Fun Night.

"Bad move. Instead of dancing to her tune, Marty does her in.

"And why does he kill Paul Thornhill? He actually has two motives. Paul Thornhill is the only celebrity contestant he can't beat. He is in second place. By killing Paul Thornhill, he becomes number one.

"Or—and this is the theory I like—Paul Thornhill knew something about the first murder. And that is why he had to be eliminated."

Cora smiled. "Case closed? Not yet. There are other suspects.

Ned Doowacker was in fourth place, just missing the play-off. With Paul Thornhill dead, he is third. And he was jealous of the celebrity contestants, because he wasn't chosen as one. He was also in the Rainbow Room and met Judy Vale.

"So did Craig Carmichael, who was in third place, but by a thin margin.

"Is there anyone else? Ah, yes. Zelda Zisk. She was not in the Rainbow Room that night, never met Judy Vale, and apparently had no connection with her whatsoever. In a mystery novel, this would make her the chief suspect."

Cora took a breath.

"There is one more suspect.

"One more person who must be considered.

"The person who is always the first suspect when a married man is murdered.

"The spouse.

"The wife.

"Jessica Thornhill."

Jessica Thornhill sprang from her seat. It occurred to Cora that if she was acting she was very good. The tears in her eyes were genuine. "Stop!" she cried, rushing to the microphone. "How can you do this to me?"

Cora caught her by the wrists, held her firm, pulled her up tight. "I have to," she said. "Don't you understand? If you want your husband's killer caught, I have to lay out the facts."

Jessica sobbed, backed away, and subsided into her seat.

Cora clapped her hands. "Enough with the theories. It is time to name the killer. But first I want to show you the evidence that told me who the killer was."

Cora reached into her drawstring purse, pulled out three sheets of paper. "Do you see these? They were found at the crime scenes. The police have been withholding them, hoping to trip the killer up with details of the murders only the killer would know. This is no longer necessary, since I know who the killer is."

At the table Mrs. Thornhill had vacated earlier, Chief Harper looked ready to have a stroke. His face was bright red, and he was sputtering, as if having a hard time catching his breath.

"So what are these papers and why were they left? Well, if you were at Fun Night, you'll be familiar with two of them." Cora held one up. "Craig Carmichael's puzzle, *Curious Canines,* was found on the body of Mrs. Roth.

"Paul Thornhill's own puzzle, *Apologies,* was found on his body." Cora held up the puzzle. Out of deference to Jessica, she didn't add that it had been rolled up and stuck in his mouth.

Cora held up the third paper. "The puzzle found with Judy Vale is somewhat different. Here, take a look. It's just some words that she doodled on a piece of paper. The key word is *lover.* The intersecting words are *Joey jealous, lights out,* and *or else.*

"You can see why this message immediately directed the police's attention to two people, Judy Vale's husband and her lover.

"Her husband was rather quickly cleared.

"Her lover was another question. Could he be guilty? If not, *what did the puzzle mean?*

"And here we have a problem. Judy Vale scribbled her puzzle herself. Mrs. Roth solved her puzzle herself. And who solved Paul Thornhill's puzzle?"

Cora held it up, pointed to it.

"No one. This copy is solved, but the one on Paul Thornhill's body wasn't. It was a blank copy.

"But he did write it. It was his own puzzle. The one he composed for Fun Night. The question is, did the killer leave it for me, or did Paul Thornhill leave it for me, to tell me who killed him?"

Cora smiled. "I know. That's a very stupid concept. But in point of fact, these puzzles are quite revealing. And one of them tells us who committed the crimes.

"How can we tell which one?" Cora beamed. "Fortunately, we have an expert in our midst. A linguistic genius. A man well-versed in every sort of puzzle. Harvey, would you step up here please?"

Harvey Beerbaum, completely taken aback, gawked at Cora with his mouth open. "I beg your pardon," he sputtered. "What sort of nonsense is this?"

"Oh, come on, Harvey," Cora said. "Don't be so modest. Don't hide your expertise." Cora put her hand to the side of her mouth, in the gesture of one sharing a confidence, and said into the microphone: "Harvey and I have a little friendly wager going. He bet I couldn't name the killer. If I can, he's gonna do the commentary for the finals. If I can't, we both are. Come on up here, Harvey."

Harvey Beerbaum reluctantly and suspiciously got to his feet. "What's the big idea?"

"Just what I said," Cora told him. "Here's the three puzzles. Or the two puzzles and the doodle, if you will. Here, take a look.

"First, we have the doodle by Judy Vale.

"And Craig Carmichael's puzzle, solved by Felicity Roth.

"And Paul Thornhill's puzzle, which had not been solved."

P	A	T	H	S	■	O	G	L	E	S	■	C	D	E
A	P	R	I	L	■	M	O	O	R	E	■	H	A	D
S	H	A	D	O	W	B	O	X	E	R	■	O	L	E
T	I	M	E	C	A	R	D	■	■	E	R	W	I	N
E	S	P	O	U	S	E	■	D	I	N	A	H	■	■
■	■	U	M	P	■	B	A	R	E	F	O	O	T	■
G	E	N	T	■	A	R	R	A	S	■	U	K	E	■
A	D	O	■	T	I	D	I	E	S	T	■	N	R	A
L	I	P	■	A	R	A	B	S	■	E	D	A	M	■
S	T	O	P	P	A	G	E	■	G	A	P	■	■	■
■	I	R	E	N	E	■	C	O	S	I	E	S	T	■
J	A	N	E	S	■	K	E	E	P	S	A	K	E	■
A	R	T	■	T	R	E	N	D	S	E	T	T	E	R
D	I	E	■	R	A	N	E	E	■	C	L	E	W	S
E	A	R	■	Y	E	S	E	S	■	T	E	N	S	E

CURIOUS CANINES
by Craig Carmichael

ACROSS

1 Ways
6 Leers at
11 B–F connection
14 Eliot's cruelest month
15 "Arthur" star
16 Possessed
17 Sparring dog?
19 Bullfight cheer
20 Work record
21 German field marshal Rommel

DOWN

1 Fake jewelry
2 Genus of plant lice
3 Chaplin persona
4 Robbers' roost
5 Congressman and Union army officer Henry Warner
6 17th century card game
7 Not bad
8 Bagels and _____
9 Before (Arch.)

23 Marry
24 Shore of TV fame
26 Arbiter
27 Shoeless
30 Fancy dude
33 Handwoven wall hanging
34 Tiny Tim's instrument
35 Fuss
36 Most kempt
38 Gun club
39 Sass
40 Desert people
41 Cheese
42 Work obstruction
44 Clothing chain
46 "Goodnight, _____"
47 Most comfy (Var.)
51 Dames
53 Memento
54 Oil paintings
55 Fashionable dog?
58 Expire
59 Hindu princess
60 Detective's finds (Var.)
61 Corn unit
62 Affirmatives
63 Present, for instance

10 Most peaceful
11 Hungry dog?
12 Surrealist Salvador
13 Paradise
18 Stinging insect
22 English flyboys
24 Risks
25 Retirement funds
27 Payoff
28 Edible pod
29 Mets or Yankees
30 Fellas cohorts
31 Change text
32 Scoreless dog?
33 Saying
36 Carole King album
37 Persia, now
41 Letter
43 Before, in prefixes
44 Leaves
45 Feature
47 Gives up
48 Consumed
49 Angles
50 Curt
51 Green gemstone
52 Operatic solo
53 Leg joint
56 Actress _____ Dawn Chong
57 Printers' measures

B¹	A²	B³	Y⁴	■	S⁵	O⁶	P⁷	H⁸	S⁹	■	A¹⁰	L¹¹	A¹²	S¹³
R¹⁴	U	L	E	■	C¹⁵	R	E	A	M	■	R¹⁶	U	B	E
A¹⁷	D	I	T	■	H¹⁸	E	L	L	O	■	A¹⁹	L	U	M
G²⁰	I	N	■	I²¹	M	A	F	O	O	L²²	B	U	T	I
G²³	O	D²⁴	H	O	O	D	■	■	T²⁵	A	I	■	■	■
■	■	T²⁶	O	N	E	■	N²⁷	A²⁸	H	U	A	T²⁹	L³⁰	S³¹
S³²	T³³	O	W	S	■	C³⁴	O	U	L	D	■	H³⁵	O	P
A³⁶	R	S	E	■	S³⁷	O	R	R	Y	■	B³⁸	E	A	R
W³⁹	O	E	■	S⁴⁰	U	M	M	A	■	B⁴¹	A	W	D	Y
S⁴²	W	E	E⁴³	T	P	E	A	■	H⁴⁴	E	R	A	■	■
■	■	M⁴⁵	A	P	■	■	B⁴⁶	Y	E	B	Y	E	S⁴⁷	S⁴⁸
L⁴⁹	O⁵⁰	V⁵¹	E	Y	O	U⁵²	D⁵³	E	A	R	■	H⁵⁴	A	T
E⁵⁵	M	I	R	■	S⁵⁶	C	E	N	E	■	Y⁵⁷	O	G	I
S⁵⁸	I	N	G	■	E⁵⁹	L	L	E	N	■	A⁶⁰	M	E	N
S⁶¹	T	Y	E	■	S⁶²	A	L	S	A	■	P⁶³	E	R	K

APOLOGIES
by Paul Thornhill

ACROSS

1 "Maybe _____" (Buddy Holly hit)
5 Juniors' juniors (Abbr.)
10 Alack's partner
14 Regulation
15 Coffee additive
16 Country bumpkin
17 Mine entrance
18 Greeting
19 Grad

DOWN

1 Confederate general
2 Video's partner
3 "I was too _____" (Brenda Lee's apology)
4 So far
5 Stupid bore (Var.)
6 Greek mountain nymph
7 Booty
8 Angel's wear
9 With finesse

20 Type of rummy
21 Beginning of Elvis's apology
23 Divinity
25 Mai ____
26 Tint
27 Uto-Aztecan languages
32 Packs away
34 Was able
35 "At the ____" (Danny and the Juniors hit)
36 British bottom
37 "I'm ____" (theme of this puzzle)
38 Cub's dad
39 Misery
40 ____ cum laude
41 Amusingly risque
42 Climbing plant
44 Wife of Zeus
45 Street guide
46 Tot's farewells
49 End of Elvis's apology
54 Head cover
55 Arab prince
56 Movie segment
57 Bear or Berra
58 Vocalize
59 "Exorcist" actress Burstyn
60 Prayer ending
61 Eye problem (Var.)
62 Burrito condiment
63 Brew

10 Ali Baba's land
11 "To Sir With Love" singer
12 Border on
13 Trucking rig
21 Charged particles
22 Praise
24 British Revolutionary War general
27 "____ Rae" (Sally Field Oscar winner)
28 Distinctive atmosphere
29 "I ran all ____" (Impalas' apology)
30 Heavy burden
31 Nimble
32 Sayings
33 Believe (archaic)
34 Arrive
37 Assumes
38 Pointed remark
40 Remain
41 Suds
43 Come out
44 Nocturnal scavenger (Var.)
46 Cofounder of Czechoslovakia
47 Champing at the bit
48 Reek
49 Not so much
50 Leave out
51 Ivy-covered
52 Bruins' school
53 "Farmer in the ____"
57 Bark shrilly

As Harvey Beerbaum examined the puzzles, the frown on his face deepened into a scowl.

Cora Felton watched with glee.

Harvey looked up at her in utter frustration.

"So, Harvey, have you figured it out? Which of these puzzles fingers a killer? Can you tell?"

"Certainly not," Harvey said indignantly. "And you can't either. This is just a bluff. Quit stalling."

"Oh, I'm not stalling. *I* know the answer. I just wanted to give *you* a chance." Cora took the puzzles out of Harvey's hand. She reached up, patted him on the cheek. "It's all right, Harvey. I'll take it from here."

Cora stood watching with an almost maternal look on her face until Harvey was forced to slink back to his seat.

"So," Cora said brightly. "As I was saying, one of these puzzles names a killer. Which one could it be?"

Cora held up *Apologies*. "Strangely enough, Paul Thornhill's crossword puzzle tells me who killed him. As promised, it is time to unmask the killer."

Cora turned, looked directly at Jessica Thornhill. "And the killer is . . ."

Cora paused, raised her finger.

Then she spun around a hundred and eighty degrees and pointed. "Joey Vale!"

53

THERE WAS A STUNNED SILENCE IN THE ROOM. SHERRY CARTER sucked in her breath. She gawked at Cora Felton, unable to believe her ears. Clearly her aunt must have lost her mind. What could she be thinking? To arbitrarily accuse Joey Vale, the one person everyone in town hall knew for a fact could not be the killer. She had even said so herself.

Harvey Beerbaum grinned broadly, his suspicions confirmed. Cora had been bluffing after all, and her machinations with the three puzzles had been just a trick. "Excuse me, Miss Felton," he said brightly, eyes twinkling. "Did you say *Joey Vale*?"

This sally was greeted by laughter from the crowd. Even Joey joined in. He shrugged his shoulders to the assembly at large, inviting them to share his bafflement at the lunatic ravings of this addled old woman.

Cora Felton, for her part, was doing nothing to dispel that impression. She tittered slightly, as if having just come to the embarrassing realization she was using the wrong salad fork at a formal dinner. "I'm sorry. Did I say Joey Vale? I don't know what came over me. I didn't mean to say that. Pretend you didn't hear that. Let me try again."

Cora cleared her throat. "I have told you many things that might have happened. Now I am going to tell you what actually did. After Harvey Beerbaum's barbecue last fall, Paul Thornhill, Ned Doowacker, and Craig Carmichael all went drinking at the Rainbow Room. I wondered about that—why they chose the Rainbow Room over some more-upscale establishment like the Country Kitchen."

Cora turned, pointed. "The answer is Jessica Thornhill. Paul Thornhill's wife wasn't in town, and it was his night to howl. But at the barbecue he'd agreed to take part in the charity tournament. Jessica would be along for that. Naturally, he didn't want to go pick up women any place he'd later visit with his wife. The Rainbow Room was perfect. It was the type of place Jessica would never go.

"So what happens? He gets to the Rainbow Room, meets and flirts with Judy Vale. He shoots pool with Marty Haskel and beats him. Since he's won, he has to play another game. He loses that one, then looks around for Judy.

"And where is she? By all accounts, she's gone home with Billy Pickens. This is the story I got from all the witnesses I interviewed. It was so widely attested to, I took it at face value.

"And yet . . .

"On closer examination, no one *saw* her leave with Billy Pickens. Everyone *assumes* she did. Just as everyone *assumes* Billy Pickens is the man with whom she had the affair. It was simply common knowledge.

"And it simply wasn't true.

"Thornhill went looking for Judy, and there she was outside. Just where she told him she'd be. He found her there, and he drove her home in his car. To an out-of-the way bungalow on the other side of the railroad tracks on the far side of town. On a night her husband was out playing cards. What a perfect setup for Paul Thornhill: a quick assignation before driving home to New York. With a woman he's unlikely to ever see again.

"Oh, yeah? Bad luck for Paul Thornhill. The first tournament planning meeting, there she is. He avoids her like the plague, counting on her to be equally discreet.

"Bad luck again. Discretion was never one of poor Judy's virtues. During the discussion, she stands up and donates her views. While she appears to be talking about the tournament, Paul Thornhill knows she is talking to *him*. He realizes that she is the type of woman who will not keep quiet, will not be discreet, and will not go away.

"Paul Thornhill is trapped. He is coming back to Bakerhaven with his wife. His rich, jealous, possessive wife, who is devoted to her trophy husband, but who will cut him off without a cent if she catches him playing around. Judy Vale is a nightmare. She can't be warned off, she can't be bought off, she can't be scared off. And she can't be reasoned with.

"She has to go.

"On the night in question, Paul Thornhill tells his wife he's going out to the movies. Instead, he drives to Bakerhaven, leaves his car out on the road, and comes sneaking up Judy's front path. Joey's car is gone. The coast is clear. He knocks on the front door. Judy's surprised to see him but invites him in. She offers him a drink and leads him into the kitchen, where he promptly strangles her and then drives back to New York just in time to get home from the show. He's seen the movie the day before, just in case Jessica happens to ask him about the plot, even though she's unlikely to give a damn.

"And there it is. A perfect crime.

"Except for one thing.

"The witness.

"Felicity Roth. Who was looking out her window the night of the murder and saw him go inside. Which answers the one question that's bothered me all along. Why was Felicity Roth talking to Paul Thornhill at Fun Night? She had no interest in crossword puzzles. No, she's talking to him because she saw him at Judy Vale's. Only she's lied to the police about it, and she's the only one who knows.

"Except for one other person who's figured it out. Figured it out while he sat in jail while Mrs. Roth was being killed. Figured it out and plotted his revenge.

"So, as soon as he got out of jail he checked his facts, confirmed his theories, laid his plans, and—"

Cora Felton's denouement was cut off by a savage, almost inhuman cry as, with a snarl of rage, Jessica Thornhill sprang from her chair and, clawing and scratching, hurled herself on her husband's killer, Joey Vale.

54

CORA FELTON SAT ON THE FRONT STEPS OF THE TOWN HALL, smoking a cigarette. She sat alone—everyone else was inside watching the three finalists, Marty Haskel, Ned Doowacker, and Zelda Zisk, compete to solve the last puzzle. Through the closed door Cora could faintly hear the voice of Harvey Beerbaum doing the commentary over the loudspeaker. Cora smiled slightly, took a drag on her cigarette, blew out the smoke. It was cold on the steps, and Cora tugged her wool coat around her.

The door opened and Sherry Carter slipped out and sat on the steps next to her aunt.

"How you doing?" she asked.

"Okay. How's it going in there?"

"Nip and tuck," Sherry said. "They're pretty evenly matched. Marty Haskel's working the upper left corner, Zelda the lower right. Doowacker's sort of all over the place."

"How's Harvey doing?"

"He's rather dry and boring. You'd have been more fun."

"Yeah, well, you can't have everything." Cora took a drag, blew out the smoke. "If it isn't over, why are you out here?"

"I figure you got five or six minutes before Rick Reed aims a camera at you. I wonder what you're gonna say."

"I already said most of it."

"Yes, but they're gonna ask you about Thornhill's crossword puzzle. Are you gonna tell them that it was meaningless, just part of your bluff?"

Cora grinned. "No, that's the icing on the cake."

"What do you mean?"

Cora dug in her purse, fished out the puzzle. "You know how you told me he created this puzzle with AutoFill, and that's why it's got bad words like *Nahuatls* in it? And the Presley quote is wrong? Well, that gave me the clue. Because Thornhill was supposed to be some hotshot constructor. So, why would he make a mistake like that? And why would he turn in an electronic puzzle? Because he was too distracted to do it himself. His mind was overloaded with the mechanics of a murder. The only part of the puzzle he did was the three long clues and the word *sorry*. Which was revealing too. From Paul Thornhill's point of view, he's just pulling phrases out of a bunch of fifties love songs to create a theme, but subconsciously he's confessing. Not to the murder, but the infidelity. Which in his mind is worse and is uppermost in his thoughts. In the puzzle he's confessing to Jessica. I mean, look at the song lyrics he pulled his quotes from. *I ran all the way home, just to say I'm sorry. I'm sorry, so sorry, please accept my apology. Love is blind, and I was too blind to see.* And *I'm a fool, but I love you, dear, until the day I die.* Kinda says it all."

Cora blew a smoke ring. "And that's the payoff. By the time I'm done explaining all that on TV, Mr. Smarty-Pants Beerbaum, who couldn't tell *anything* from the puzzles, is going to have a hard time faulting me on my expertise."

"I'll be damned." Sherry chuckled at the thought, then frowned. "There's one thing I don't understand. Why does Joey Vale leave the puzzle on the body? Has *he* figured out it means Thornhill's Judy's killer?"

"Not at all. He's not that smart. But he's not that dumb either. He realizes he has an airtight alibi for the Roth killing. So if he can kill Thornhill and tie it to the other murders, he will have committed the perfect crime. The problem is Thornhill's not local, so there's no connection. The connection, of course, is Judy, but Joey can't advance that theory without exposing his motive for murder.

"So how does he tie the one killing to the others? First, he makes it a strangling. Second he kills him at our house to imply local knowledge. Third, he shoves that crossword puzzle in his mouth. I bet he enjoyed doing it."

"Why do you say that?"

Cora sighed. "Because Joey really loved his wife. I know you won't understand. You were in an abusive relationship, you wanted out of it, you got out as quick as you could. And rightfully so. But Joey and Judy's relationship was something else. Everyone *says* he beat her up. But everyone says that *after* her murder. I saw her body in the morgue, and there's not a bruise on it. No, I think Joey and Judy were a couple who lived for histrionics. She'd have an affair, then he'd find out and fly into a rage, then she'd cry and say she was sorry, then he'd forgive her. And this would happen again and again, but, basically, they really loved each other. So when Thornhill killed Judy, Joey had to strike back."

"And how'd he know Thornhill was the killer?"

"He didn't. He thought it was Billy Pickens. Just like everyone else did."

"Cora—"

"I mean at first. Joey gets out of jail and starts following Billy, looking for a chance to do him in. Only Billy comes to our house to ask for help. That doesn't jibe with Joey's theory of the crime—why would a guilty man do that? So Joey figures it must be Thornhill after all. He drops Billy, hightails it over to Thornhill's bed-and-breakfast. I don't know what pretext he would have used to get Thornhill outside—faked a phone call from the tournament committee, most likely—but he doesn't have to. Joey no sooner gets there than Thornhill goes out for booze. Joey follows him to the liquor store, accosts him in the parking lot. Thornhill is terrified. He killed the guy's wife. And Joey *knows*.

"Of course, Thornhill denies it. Tries to stonewall. To his surprise, Joey doesn't hit him. Instead, he tells Thornhill to follow him to our house. To let *me* hear his story.

"That seems plausible to Thornhill. He knows I've been helping with Chief Harper's investigation. He buys it. He drives to our house, trying to think of what to say.

"Of course, we're not there. Not after Billy Pickens lit a fire under us. We're out investigating. As Joey Vale figured.

"So Joey and Paul Thornhill drive up our driveway. Thornhill, lulled into a sense of false security, climbs out of his car, and Joey promptly hits him on the head. He strangles him, drags him out in the backyard, and sits him at the picnic table. He wants this murder tied to the other two, for which he has a perfect alibi. He figures the combination of strangling him and killing him at our house will do it.

"He drives Thornhill's car down the driveway and parks it on the road, so it will be longer before anyone finds the body. On the front seat of the car is a briefcase full of crossword puzzles. This is too good to pass up. The other murders came with crossword-puzzle clues. So why not this one? He takes the puzzle, shoves it in the mouth of his wife's lover."

"And how did he know Thornhill was her lover?"

"She told him."

"You're kidding."

"How do you think Joey always knew who she was sleeping with? You think the neighbors told him? No way. He'd accuse her of having a lover, get her to admit it and tell him who it was. He knew about Thornhill, same as he knew about Billy Pickens."

"You gonna tell Rick Reed about Billy Pickens?"

"Hell, no. I'm just telling you. I can leave him out of the story just fine."

"I still don't understand about the crossword puzzle. You say

Joey left it on Thornhill because there were crossword puzzles found on the other bodies. Well, maybe Joey found his wife's doodle. But if he didn't kill Mrs. Roth, how could he know about the puzzle found with her?"

"I kind of hate to tell you."

Sherry frowned. Then her eyes widened. "Oh, no!"

Cora shrugged. "Sorry. You told Aaron. He may have promised not to print it, but he's a newsman, and facts are bargaining chips. And you know he wanted to ace Rick Reed out on Becky Baldwin's story."

"So Aaron told Becky, and she told Joey," Sherry said in disgust. "That's how Joey knew."

Cora nodded. "Only way it fits."

From inside came cheers and the thunder of applause.

"Guess someone won," Sherry said. "I better go check who."

"No need," Cora said. "From the sound of the cheer, it's a home-town boy."

Becky Baldwin came crashing out the door, a huge smile on her face. "He won, can you believe it? Marty won!" She swooped down on Cora. "Rick's just shooting a question or two with Marty, then he'll be out to interview you."

"You still Joey Vale's attorney?"

"Yeah. Why?"

"You seem rather pleased with the turn of events. Of course, I suppose it means work."

Becky gave her a look of reproach. *Please.* The thought never crossed my mind."

"And yet you're out here lining me up for an interview to accuse your client of murder. Interesting." Cora furrowed her brow. "Oh, of course. You figure his crime's sympathetic, and you want to taint the jury pool."

"Heaven forbid," Becky said.

Marty Haskel came out, holding the first-place trophy. If winning it pleased him any, Cora wouldn't have known it. He looked cranky as ever.

Marty spotted Cora sitting on the step. He wandered over to her,